20 Miles

to

Justified

a Novel
by

Arley Owens, Jr.

20 Miles to Justified
Copyright © 2014 Arley Owens, Jr.

This is a work of fiction. Any resemblance to any
person, living or dead—any organization, enterprise,
place, or event—is coincidental. The characters and
settings are either imaginary or used fictitiously.

Bible quotations from the
Authorized King James Version

Why Do Fools Fall In Love
(Levy Morris and Frankie Lymon)

Cover Art (Rights secured by Author):
Front: B.S. Smith
Back: CL Owens

Editor: Pitman Sanders

First Printing July 2014
Printed in the U.S.A.

Soft Cover Edition
ISBN: 978-0-9896273-0-6

SHORTY MAE PRODUCTIONS
P.O. BOX 81102
MIDLAND, TEXAS 79708

To the Unheralded
Warriors, who
keep the faith
in this age
of apostasy

Be not forgetful to entertain strangers: for thereby some have entertained angels unawares.
- Hebrews 13:2

ONE

SOMETHING WAS UP with Clyde: he'd left a voicemail on her cell phone at five a.m. instead of notifying Thornton he wouldn't be coming in today. Wyoming Carter yawned while unlocking the glass door of Kelly's Rentals, stepped inside, and entered her numerical code to keep the alarm from going off in thirty seconds. Yawning again, she went behind the pay counter, dropped her purse in front of a computer crammed between stacks of manuals on a narrow desk, turned on the registers, retrieved a bank bag from the floor safe, filled the cash drawers, made coffee, and toggled the open sign switch.

Kelly's shut down at six Monday through Saturday, and noon on Sundays. She normally worked open to close weekdays, with an hour off for lunch. For morale purposes she'd told the two cashiers scheduled to start this Friday morning to sleep in because she would be bailing on them two hours early. They'd be arriving at ten instead of the usual eight-thirty. All the employees except her and Clyde Burns, the accountant, had to stagger their two days off each week—including the mechanics, who reported for work an hour before the store opened at eight. It had taken awhile to be accepted by the rest of the upfront crew after she'd informed Thornton Kelly if she couldn't have every weekend off like Clyde, he'd have to find someone else to manage his store. Some of them had threatened to quit if he didn't make an exception in their case too, but Thornton hadn't budged an inch and they'd all backed down.

Being a pretty blonde with big boobs definitely had its advantages.

Thornton's pickup flashed past the glass façade. A couple of minutes later he stormed through the door.

She rested her forearms on the pay counter and merged her fingers, pretending not to notice his pissed off scowl.

"Burns better have hitched a ride with you, Wyoming, because I didn't see his car in the parking lot."

"He woke up before dawn with a stomach virus."

"Virus my ass . . .!" Thornton angrily gripped his waist. "He called me last night and asked for the day off, and I didn't give it to him. His butt is mine come Monday morning."

Thornton's fowl mood didn't deter him from ogling her breasts. He'd never hit on her, but she knew he wanted to. Fear of being slapped with a sexual harassment suit kept him at bay. Too bad he had a wife and kids, the guy was sexy and loaded. He finally stopped undressing her with his eyes, and went out back to check on the mechanics like he did every morning, making sure they had all the heavy equipment operating properly. The oil patch and construction accounted for ninety percent of Thornton's income, and renting a faulty machine practically guaranteed a company would take its business elsewhere.

At four o'clock she'd be leaving Kelly's Rentals and Odessa, Texas behind until Sunday night. She had mixed emotions about the weekend ahead.

LEAVENWOOD POP. 2155

Clyde grinned with elation when he finally saw that particular city limits sign—he only had twenty more miles to go. His ass was numb from driving so long. Easing his foot off the accelerator to obey the speed limit, which had dropped to forty, he passed two gas stations and a convenience store on a two-lane void of traffic before entering the small town. It was Friday afternoon and not a holiday, yet they were closed. If they'd gone out of business it happened recently, all three looked carefully maintained. He found more of the same while cruising down *Main Street*, according to the road signs.

Leavenwood looked like a well kept ghost town.

On the other side of the creepy municipality, he passed a place called Roy's Automotive. A raised bay door indicated at least one resident had to work for a living. He soon reached the outskirts and the speed limit returned to seventy. When he tried to speed up the engine of his new Chevy Malibu sputtered in protest. A backfire blasted his eardrums and the damn thing died. He coasted to the shoulder and repeatedly cranked the motor, but only managed to run the battery down.

"Shit . . .!" he popped the hood and climbed out of the car, figuring the master fan belt must have broke. Finding it intact, he locked the Malibu and started walking back to Leavenwood, grateful the one enterprise that hadn't shut down for the day was a mechanic's garage.

Spring had freshly arrived, but the southeast Texas breeze carried a chill that made him wish he'd worn a jacket. Clyde paced briskly along the highway's edge, rubbing his hands for warmth, still puzzled over the absence of traffic. He hoped whatever repairs the Malibu required wouldn't take long because his new lady friend was expecting him at six o'clock. According to the directions she'd emailed, five miles after driving through Leavenwood he'd come to a four-way stop. A left turn would put him on a fifteen mile stretch of road that led to Justified.

When you get to Justified, her instructions read, *turn left at the first traffic light and keep going until you come to a stop sign. Make another left there. I live four blocks down that road.*

They'd met on the internet two months ago and this would be his first time to see Lee Milan in person. She'd only put Texas next to her profile picture, leaving the city she resided in blank. He'd never been in this part of the state, and didn't know Leavenwood or Justified existed until she'd emailed her address and explained how to get there. The two towns weren't on the state map, at least not on the one he'd bought. They weren't listed on the internet either. He couldn't think of a reason they wouldn't be in this day and time, but as long as Lee hadn't screwed up the directions, that didn't matter.

Undoubtedly she'd posted her most flattering photographs on the adults only social site as had he, but hopefully they were reasonably true depictions of her pretty face and shapely body. She'd confessed to putting on a few pounds since the latest ones were taken, and that made him a little nervous. He also hoped she hadn't lied about her age. Having a fat middle-aged wreck open the door instead of the svelte thirty-year-old he'd been lusting after would be a nightmare. He'd listed his age honestly at thirty-nine when filling out his personal information, but the latest photos of him were almost four years old, a fact he hadn't mentioned to Lee, so he felt uneasy about that too.

A rush of lustful excitement had raged through him when he'd received a notification that a Lee Milan wanted to be friends. Her profile picture depicted a gorgeous young white woman with lush shoulder-length dark hair, and big brown eyes that made his mouth water. The photograph stopped just short of showing the nipples on a pair of bountiful breasts. He'd drooled over Lee's entire gallery, most of which showed off her incredible figure scantily clad. Unable to get the bombshell out of his mind since, he'd begged her to get a web cam when she wouldn't give him a phone number so they could interact beyond their keyboards, but she'd refused. Then, early last night, she'd totally blown his mind with an email, asking if he'd like to spend the weekend with her, concluding the invitation with a detailed route to her place.

Lee had informed him she lived about an eight hour drive from Odessa, so he'd asked his boss for Friday off to keep from having to wait until Saturday to make the trip, as he couldn't get to Justified before midnight if he worked his normal eight to five shift. The heartless bastard wouldn't hear of it, prompting him to fake being sick that morning. He'd notified Lee to expect him by six, but had planned to surprise her by arriving an hour earlier.

That plan went down the drain when his engine stalled.

He stepped into the open bay of Roy's Automotive at twenty to five. A tall, muscular black man had his arms raised to the oil pan of a pickup perched in the air on a hydraulic lift, tightening the plug with a socket wrench.

"Hi there," said Clyde. "My car broke down right outside of town, and hope you can fit me in as soon as possible. I'm supposed to be at Justified by six, so I'll gladly pay extra."

The mechanic took him in with a sulk for several seconds, almost looking pissed off, then aimed the wrench at a door about twenty feet to Clyde's right. "Talk to the boss about it, he's in the office."

No one answered his knock. Clyde grabbed the knob and found it locked. When he turned back towards the bay, his breath left him in a frightful gasp that so emptied his lungs he feared for a moment they'd collapsed. The black man and pickup were gone, and the lift had been lowered to the floor without making a sound.

He heard the office door open behind him and spun around.

A short, fat, bald man with a thick unlit cigar jutting through blubbery lips barked out, "What the hell are you doing in my garage, motherfucker? We're closed."

Terrified, and reeling with confusion, he pointed at the hydraulic lift. "There was a black man working on a pickup right there just a second ago. He told me to talk to his boss because he was busy. My car broke down a short ways out of town and I asked if he could help me."

"They ain't no niggers working here, motherfucker."

He inhaled an anxious breath. "Stop calling me that. My name is Clyde Burns and I need help."

"You're trespassing on my premises, so I'll call you whatever the fuck I want. Now get out of here before I put a boot up your ass."

Try it, you fat son-of-a-bitch, and I'll make you eat it! he wanted to say. Instead he turned up his palms like a beggar. "Please, it's very important that I get to Justified by six. I'll pay double whatever you normally charge."

"Take your fucking problem some place else, we're closed."

"All right, I'll pay you triple!" he cried to the fat man's back before the hateful prick could make it inside his office.

Two stubby legs stopped moving, and the uncouth lard ass slowly turned around. A civil expression had replaced anger on his jowly face. "What seems to be the problem?"

"I don't know. The engine backfired and died, and I couldn't get it to start again. It's practically brand new, so I can't imagine what's wrong."

"What make is it?"

"Chevy Malibu."

The fat man bobbled his cigar up and down several times, apparently pondering whether it would be worth messing with even at triple rates. Looking as if he'd finally reached a decision, he yanked the stogie from his mouth and pressed the knuckles of the flabby hand holding it against his waist, grossly indenting a massive roll of cellulite. "Why is it so important for you to get to Justified by six?"

He explained the special occasion, and the fat man

actually grinned.

"Need relief from a case of blue balls, huh?" He jabbed the cigar between his yellow teeth. "All right, come with me to the tow truck."

Clyde followed him out of the bay and to a corner of the building. The obese proprietor turned right, but when he did likewise all he saw was a tow truck parked next to a red Honda Accord. He turned all the way around, but still couldn't locate the fat man.

Skin crawling with ghoulish apprehension, he went back into the bay, telling himself the mechanic and owner had to be playing tricks on him. It did nothing to settle his nerves because he couldn't imagine how either had pulled off their disappearing acts. He opened the office door and glanced inside. No one was in there.

"Whoa!" he shouted as someone tapped him on the back. Almost tripping himself from spinning around so fast, Clyde settled his feet and gawked at the black mechanic, still holding the ratchet he'd used to tighten the oil plug of the pickup, that once again rested atop the raised hydraulic lift.

"The boss told me to fetch your car and tow it back here. Come on with me and we'll go get it."

He gaped incredulously at the mechanic, fright washing over him like a torrential rain as cold fear cramped his bowels with a blast of nausea.

"Come on let's go, I ain't got all day."

Choking back a wad of bile his quivering stomach had launched to the back of his throat, he cleared it with a cough and wiped a dribble of snot off his upper lip. "The owner said I was mistaken about a black man working here. He was going to tow my car but he . . . he . . . ."

The mechanic tossed him an impatient frown, tapping his foot as though his intelligence had been insulted.

"This is just a j-joke, right? You and your boss are just pulling my leg. Right?"

"I don't know what the hell you're talking about, man. You want my help, then come on and let's go. Otherwise I'll get back to my oil change. Now are we going or not?"

Nerves stretched as taut as a fishing line with a marlin on the hook, macabre perplexity pounding his brain, he timidly nodded.

"Some people," muttered the black man while exiting the garage.

Expecting another vanishing act, it surprised him to reach the tow truck without incident. Still worried something weird was bound to happen, he climbed into the cab and shut the door. The mechanic started the engine, pulled to the street, and asked which direction.

"That way," he pointed, relaxing a little.

They soon reached the Malibu.

"Is there anything I can do to help?" Clyde asked as the tow truck came to a stop behind his car.

"Yeah, try to start it one more time. If it runs, drive it to the shop and save yourself a tow charge."

Amazed the strange guy was actually being considerate, he told him he'd ran the battery down.

"If you didn't drain it totally it'll have rebounded enough for at least a couple of tries by now."

Clyde got behind the wheel and gave it a try. The engine fired right up, purring like a sated kitten, indicating the fuel injectors must have encountered some contaminated gasoline before. He hoped that was the problem because it wouldn't take long to have the tank drained and replenished with clean fuel. Foot on the brake, he checked the rearview mirror to make sure no cars were coming before making the u-turn, but his jaw dropped as another gasp of fear blasted from his lungs.

The tow truck was nowhere in sight.

Overwhelmed by terror, he headed for the four-way stop— praying another stream of bad gas wouldn't cause the engine to stall. If it did, he'd walk all the way to Justified if he couldn't hitch a ride. He wasn't *ever* going back to that eerie town.

Something was grossly out of whack in Leavenwood, Texas.

⟡

The tick-tock chimed. Larue smiled . . . the pleasant sound soothed him. His eyes were glued to the swinging silver stick. Its proper name eluded him at the moment, but he remembered it made the tick-tock work.

⟡

"Would you stop it!" Wyoming laughingly shouted, fending off her boyfriend's groping hands.

"Come on, blondie, give me some shoogah."

"Fly the plane, Robby!"

"It's on auto-pilot, nothing to worry about. Now come on, give Robby boy a little smoochie poo."

They were flying to Louisiana in Robby Gorgan's Cessna to spend the weekend at his father's *fishing cabin*, as Robby called it—a gross misnomer for a beautiful two-storey lake house. Wyoming knew she was little more than just another pretty face to the spoiled rich boy, but deep pockets meant big fun. They'd met last year at The Oil Show in the Ector County Coliseum and he'd asked her out. Having a boyfriend at the time, she'd turned him down. Three months ago the guy proposed so she'd ended the relationship, let Robby know she was available, and they'd been dating since.

Born with a silver spoon in his mouth, he couldn't relate to her working class world. Robby liked his sex far too rough to suit her, but she'd keep pretending otherwise for now, due to him being such a big spender. Raised by white trash parents in a dysfunctional household, she'd given up the idea of ever getting married back in her teens because the concept of family had become synonymous with bitterness, resentfulness, and bondage. Now twenty-seven, her resolve to shun the altar hadn't weakened at all.

When a guy got too serious about her, she always broke it off. This millionaire's son didn't figure to ever pose such a problem, but she'd be leaving him soon because of his sexual attitude. Robby seemed to shed his lovable personality along with his clothes, and an overly aggressive, almost beastly persona took over until he climaxed. If she spoke to him about it he might try to change, but that would make it an even more unpleasant experience for her—knowing he wasn't being himself when they made love.

She finally yielded to his kiss, and Robby grabbed her right breast. Mistaking the moan that rose in her throat as a reaction to pleasure, he squeezed harder, causing more pain.

Though he hadn't been able to surprise Lee by showing up an hour early as intended, the Malibu hadn't acted up again so he'd still be arriving before six. Clyde passed the city limits sign of Justified, drove up a steep hill, and saw the traffic light while coasting down the other side. He turned left per her instructions—soon arrived at the stop sign, turned left again, traversed the four blocks, and slid his key from the ignition at five thirty-five. She lived in a handsome blonde-brick house with evergreens lining the sidewalk. One on either side of a protruding entryway, situated behind a curved concrete porch, book-ended the front door.

It opened almost immediately after he pushed the doorbell, and there stood the vision he'd hoped to see. Lee Milan looked scrumptious in a sleeveless yellow shirt and matching shorts. Both fit her so tight the shape of her fantastic bulges and curves wouldn't be more discernable if she was naked, for her perky nipples showed her to be braless. She had gorgeous legs and lovely feet, visible because she wore flip flops, also yellow. A sexy smile indicated her eyes were pleased as well.

"So glad you could make it, Clyde. Please come in."

His gonads tingled with anticipation as he savored Lee's butt while following her into the living room. The weight she'd mentioned gaining had only enhanced her charms. Either that or cameras failed to capture the true splendor of her face and body. "You look more beautiful than your pictures, Lee. I didn't think you possibly could."

"I hope you're not just saying that. Have a seat on the couch and I'll get you a beer. Bought a case of Bud Light just for you."

He grinned. They'd shared their favorite foods and beverages online. "How thoughtful of you, thanks. And no, I wasn't being polite—you really do surpass those pictures, and they're all incredible."

"Well thank you. I must say you look a bit older in person."

"Yeah um—" he nervously cleared his throat "—I was thirty-five when those pictures were taken."

"Don't worry, I like it. Your hair's much darker than it is in all your pics."

Unable to tell if that was good or bad, he shrugged. "It was almost white until I turned twenty. Then it started getting darker for whatever reason. But at least it's turning brown and not gray."

As if sensing his insecurity, she broadened her smile. "Looks good on you. Accentuates your blue eyes."

She really seemed to mean it, which considerably relieved him. "At least my height hasn't changed. I'm still five eleven."

"And I'm still five four. Do I look fat to you in person?"

"Oh lord no, you look great."

"I hope you're not just saying that, Clyde. I've gained five pounds since my thirtieth birthday and can't seem to get it off. Well make yourself comfortable and I'll get your beer."

He set down and a minute later had a cold bottle of Bud in his hand. "What's that you're drinking?"

"Water." Still standing in front of him, she held up her glass and gazed at it, wistfully. "Alcohol is off limits to me until I get back to my correct weight." Her eyes sought his, and she smiled again. "Did you have any trouble following the directions I sent?"

"No, but I had a trippy experience in Leavenwood. That is one *strange* town. I was going to surprise you by getting here an hour early, so it was only four-thirty when I drove through, yet all the businesses were closed except for a place called Roy's Automotive. The reason I didn't get here by five is because my car died and I had to walk back to town. It was the spookiest thing . . ." he told her about the freakish experience. Not a word of it fazed her. She didn't seem sympathetic or skeptical. If he'd merely been speaking about the weather, she couldn't have appeared less impressed. "I'm not exaggerating anything, Lee. It all happened just the way I said."

She took a sip of water.

"You don't believe me, do you."

"Is your beer cold enough? My refrigerator's been acting up the last couple of days. I've had to turn up the thermostat twice."

Frowning, he nodded and took a nip. "Why are you

dodging what I just told you about the fat man and mechanic?"

"Maybe because we're standing right behind you."

A lightning bolt of fear paralyzed him—he couldn't make himself look back.

The voice belonged to the black mechanic.

TWO

THE HAIRS ON the back of his neck were bristling. Lee should have been terrified, yet her face was stoic. Clyde inhaled a deep breath, rose from the couch, and warily turned to confront the two strange men.

There was nothing behind him but a few feet of carpet that ended below a closed window.

"What's wrong?" asked Lee.

Entrails churning with fear, he whirled around to face her. "What are you people?"

She merely stood there, looking confused.

"Answer me!"

"Why, whatever do you mean, Clyde?"

"What do I mean?! You know exactly what I mean."

Her frown lines appeared. "I ask if you had any trouble getting here and you say you're glad I brought it up like you want to tell me something, but you just sit there saying nothing for several minutes instead. So I ask if your beer's cold enough and you get this petrified look on your face, stand up and turn around, then you look at me and ask 'What are you people?' You're freaking me out, Clyde."

A surge of nausea assaulted his stomach and he turned instantly feverish. "You didn't hear me telling you about Roy's Automotive?"

She shook her head, eyes blazing with extreme concern.

"Oh boy . . ." feeling the strength leave his legs, he dropped back on the couch. "I don't know what to say."

"You really thought you said something about a Roy's Automotive?"

He nodded, fighting an urge to vomit.

"Well you didn't."

"I guess not since you say so, but I could have sworn I did, and got worried that you didn't believe me, then . . . ."

"Then what?"

"Never mind." He turned up the bottle and guzzled a mouthful of beer to settle his stomach. It only half worked. *Maybe all that shit in Leavenwood didn't really happen either. Maybe the Malibu never broke down. Nah, dammit I know it did, just like I know I told her about Roy's!*

"I'm not interested in pursuing a relationship with a man suffering from delusions."

"I'm not delusional, Lee. At least I wasn't before I got to Leavenwood."

"I want to believe that, but the way you're acting, I'm not so sure."

The distrustful look on her face devastated him. If she'd really heard him convey his experience at that disturbing auto repair she'd have thought him mad, so he'd caught a big break, though a very disturbing one. Totally baffled as to why she hadn't heard him relay it, he drummed up a lie— knowing it was the only chance he had of winding up in bed with her. "Turnpike trance, that must have been what happened. I'd been driving over seven hours when I got to Leavenwood. I must have slipped into a daydream. I didn't get much sleep last night over being so excited to finally meet you in person, so I must have sort of dozed off again with my eyes open and thought I was telling you about Roy's Automotive, while actually I was only daydreaming it."

In truth he'd slept like a baby after beating off while fantasizing about her.

Lee sighed with apparent relief and said, "That's happened to me before. I drove for a long stretch one time and seemed to wake up when I pulled into my drive. I couldn't recall anything about the last fifty miles or so. What was it you thought happened in Leavenwood?"

"Oh it was just a crazy daydream, let's talk about something else." He said it light heartedly as if certain nothing really occurred in that creepy town, but he knew full well it had. At least his mind refused to believe otherwise.

"No, I want to hear it," she persisted.

Seeing she wouldn't relent, he took a big swig of beer and laid it all out.

An alarmed expression testified she heard it this time. "Wow . . . that's really frightening, Clyde."

"Yeah, it sure was. I guess the delusion must have started when my car died. I must have dozed off and dreamed the whole thing, then woke up when I got it started again." If the mechanic hadn't spoken to him in her living room he could almost believe that to be true, the tale sounded so ludicrous. He still had bubbles in his blood over her not hearing his first recount. Why hadn't she?

The doorbell rang.

"That's dinner. Hope you meant it when you said you like Chinese."

"I did," he assured, grateful it wasn't the mechanic or fat man come to call.

"Would you like to freshen up?"

"Um, sure." His face felt grimy from the long drive, and he needed to take a leak.

She aimed a pretty finger at a door directly past the hall opening. "There's the bathroom. I'll get our food and set the table. The kitchen's at the open end of the hallway—join me when you're done."

Robby was grappling her breasts from behind, pinning

her to his lap in a seat behind the cockpit. Wyoming felt more fearful of a midair collision than turned on. "Shouldn't you at least be looking out the window? We might get hit by another plane."

"No chance. The pilot would see us."

"Not if he's doing the same thing you are."

"Stop worrying, Wyoming, we're flying through clear skies with zero wind turbulence. We could take a twenty minute nap if we wanted to."

During the meal they discussed how their jobs were going. Lee was a graphic designer and obviously made a good living since she owned her home and had very nice furniture. He'd lied and claimed to be an accounting consultant. In reality he kept the books at a heavy equipment rental company, and helped work the counter when Wyoming Carter and the cashiers got swamped by customers, which happened a lot these days. The spoken-for blonde had starred in most of his fantasies since joining the company eighteen months ago. Now Lee had replaced her as the number one mental box office attraction.

"Why wouldn't you give me your phone number?" He relinquished his chop sticks while asking.

Lee swallowed a bite of steak tips and rice, chased it with water, and smiled. "Because I wanted to coax you up here."

"All you had to do was ask, us talking on the phone wouldn't have deterred me."

"It's been my experience that when people meet on the phone before seeing each other face to face, things usually don't work out in the end. I wanted to see your real personality, not what you wanted me to perceive through mere talk."

That puzzled him. "Okay, so why the refusal to use a web cam? You'd have been able to see me then."

"Only in two dimensions, which could have given me a false read as well. Plus I wouldn't have been able to sense your aura or smell you."

"So how are my aura and body odor rating?" he quipped with a grin.

A slow smile came to her. "Very high. How about mine?"

"Blowing the top off the rating thermometer."

Instead of the response he expected, she turned somber. "I lied to you about the phone and web cam. The real reason I resisted is because my voice can't be transmitted by telephone, and my image wouldn't have shown up on your monitor."

"So you're a ghost, huh?" He appreciated dark humor. It appeared they had a lot in common.

"No, but I'm not a typical human. I'm quite *atypical* actually."

"Ah, so you're a vampire, I get it now."

"Stop teasing, I'm being serious."

"Sure you are," he ribbed. "How do you explain your pictures if you can't be seen by a web cam?"

"Those are photographs of self portraits painted by me, computer enhanced to make them look like snapshots. I lied about the weight gain in case you noticed subtle differences when you saw me in person. I'm an exceptional artist but no one can paint a perfect representation."

If Lee wanted to extend the mind game it was fine with him, so long as they wound up in bed together. "Okay, so how come I can see and hear you in person?"

"Because I have the power to will you to, face to face."

"Oh-Kay."

The tick-tock's silver stick swayed back and forth, almost hypnotizing him. In lucid moments he could actually tell time, but now the numbers were meaningless. Roman numerals, seemed like they were called, but he couldn't be sure. Other symbols danced in his brain, forming equations sent to him from a source he'd never been able to figure out. His thought processes didn't operate through words, and when he tried to think like normal people the symbols stopped arranging their intricate patterns. The tick-tock was his friend, it never accused him of being a genius.

That word again. What did it mean? It was Mother, wasn't it? Yes, Mother first called him that. Why? Larue couldn't remember, but would never forget being taken to that place he'd finally mustered the courage to escape from after twenty years.

Dink Dank? No, that wasn't what everybody called it. The title evaded him at the moment so he quit worrying about it. What did twenty mean anyway? He couldn't remember that either.

"I see you need convincing, Clyde. Come with me."

Lee led him to the hall bathroom and his reflection peered back at him from a large mirror. Yet even though she stood right beside him, hers didn't. He slammed his eyes closed, so seized by fright the floor seemed to be spinning beneath his feet.

"I have the power to make you see and hear me, Clyde, but the mirror can't be manipulated to take in the illusion because it has no mind. Neither do telephones or web cams."

He slowly raised his lids and turned towards her. "What are you?"

"I once was what you'd call an angel."

"Was?"

"Mm hmm."

"So you're not really a woman?"

"Oh I'm a real woman all right. Those of my kind have no gender per se, but all of us are either receptive—which can best be described in mortal terms as feminine—or proactive. Were I the latter I'd have acquired the attributes of a man rather than a woman when my likeness was altered to human form after being cast to Earth for doubting God. Being bound to this world until judgment day is my punishment."

For several moments he stood there gaping at her with his jaw dangling, then it dawned on him she had to be putting him on. "That's a trick mirror, right? You don't seriously expect me to believe you were cast out of heaven like a demon, do you?"

She exhaled a tired sigh. "I'm not a demon, Clyde, but I am a spirit locked inside a woman's body until Christ returns to earth. After that I'll be liberated to once again abide in God's presence. Until then, other than being immune to any form of illness, I must suffer all the problems, frailties, and needs of a human female. One of which is the yearning for a man, which is why I lured you here."

A severe coughing fit forced him to hack a load of phlegm into the lavatory to keep from suffocating. When his lungs finally relaxed, he rinsed his mouth and splashed cold water on his face.

Lee handed him a towel. "I thought about waiting to tell you—even toyed with the idea of deceiving you indefinitely—but it wouldn't be fair. I must say you're taking it better than I thought you would."

The engines started sputtering. Robby hurried to the pilot's seat and began manipulating the controls. Wyoming jumped into the copilot's chair and fastened her bra. "What's wrong?"

"I don't know, but buckle up—we're gonna have to land this bird."

Eardrums thumping with the beat of her racing heart, she put her blouse back on and started buttoning it while peering ahead at the highway they were descending to. The lights of a town loomed in the near distance. "Thank God there's not any traffic."

"Yeah, we really caught a break—this'll be a piece of cake."

"Are we in Louisiana?"

"Mm mm, southeast Texas."

Lee brought him a fresh beer. They were back in the living room and he'd finally calmed down enough to think clearly. Clyde turned up the bottle and swallowed two gulps before lowering it. "How long have you been alive?"

"For thirty years as Lee Milan, but God brought my kind into existence long before one of His highest ranking archangels rebelled against Him. That's when time began. Before that there was no passing of seconds, minutes, or hours. God and the unfallen angels still dwell beyond time, but those that sided with the archangel were cast out of heaven when he became Satan and they were transformed to demons. That cataclysmic event triggered what astronomers call The Big Bang. I didn't rebel against the Lord, but I doubted His wisdom in creating man, as did others of my kind. Now we're forced to live out mankind's history as one of them until it runs its course.

"I've been born and have died more times than I can remember. When this body expires my essence will be inserted into another ovary, and without fail that egg will be impregnated with an x chromosome and I shall once again come into the world as a female infant. I'll grow up as a girl who won't know what she truly is until puberty. That's when the enlightenment will come in its full scope."

A disturbing thought crossed his mind that maybe he'd had an accident before reaching Leavenwood and was lying in a hospital somewhere in a coma—the mechanic, fat man, and Lee being nothing but figments of his imagination. It dissipated the moment he began finding the idea preferable to this strange twist of reality. "Um, won't you know you're different as a little child when you can't see yourself in a mirror?"

Lee shook her head. "I can see my reflection."

"But what about your next set of parents? They won't be able to, so they'll know something's different about you."

"Clyde, those like me are all born to parents condemned to the same fate. All of us are told what we are at a very early age, but the memory of once being in the presence of God doesn't fully manifest until puberty. The body I presently inhabit is infertile, but if I were to have children they'd have once been angels too. We were all cast down here at the same time and automatically took on the form of adult humans initially, ranging in age from eighteen to ninety. As the old died off they returned as babies borne by the younger members, and it's continued that way ever since. Several times I've unknowingly lain dormant in an ovary for years after a previous death until conception takes place, not realizing it until my memory fully returns at puberty and I can compare my last demise with the date of my latest birth."

Wyoming gazed at the Cessna 421 B Golden Eagle, thinking how odd it looked sitting in an open field. Robby had made a hard right after coasting away the landing speed on the highway, leaving the tail section pointing towards the shoulder where they'd been standing for the last ten minutes, hoping to catch a ride.

But no one had driven by.

They waited a while longer, then gave up and headed for the town on foot.

"Tick-tock," said Larue in synch with the silver stick. Back and forth it went, easing the sadness welling within him. "Tick-tock, tick-tock, tick-tock . . . ."

Lee had excused herself to use the bathroom thirty minutes ago. Despite his anxiety over all she'd told him, Clyde began to grow amorous, thinking she must be readying herself for a trip to the bedroom. But another sensation also emanated from his loins at the moment. Afraid she might get upset if he went searching for a john besides the one in the hall that she was using, he knocked on the door. "Um, I hate to disturb you but nature's calling."

She didn't answer. He tried the knob and found it unlocked. "Lee, I'm coming in—just want to make sure you're all right."

The bathroom was empty.

He drained his bladder and went looking for her, baffled as to how she'd managed to leave without being seen. The door was clearly visible through the hallway opening. From his vantage point on the couch he'd been idly gazing that direction since she'd closed it.

Clyde searched the entire house, even checking the closets, but couldn't find her.

One room, accessed directly from the living room, mystified him. It looked like a giant bathroom with its tiled walls and floor, but had no toilet, lavatory, or shower—only a faucet with a short water hose attached, and a floor drain beneath four steel rings. Two were attached to the wall about five feet above the drain, the other pair hung three or four feet below them. They looked very strong and conjured images of a dungeon.

Figuring she must have gone outside, he went to the backdoor, located in her kitchen. He'd never seen one connected to the hallway like a bedroom before. There was a building near the alley gate in her backyard. Light streamed through a single window and an open door. He crossed the lawn and entered a spacious room with a bare concrete floor—upon which stood a dozen easels supporting large canvases, all except one depicting Lee in a different sexy pose he'd seen before on his monitor back in Odessa.

Once again having to hold back vomit, Clyde gawked at a portrait of the fat man of Leavenwood.

THREE

"TOLD YOU THAT'S how I did it."

Clyde jerked his head to the left. Lee had appeared.

"Where were you?" His voice came out raspy—fear had dried his throat upon seeing the fat man's depiction among Lee's self portraits.

She strolled across the room, stopped at a portrait identical to her profile picture, and struck the same pose. "I'm embarrassed to say I'm not immune to constipation. I was sitting on the toilet when you barged in so I temporarily quit allowing you to see me. When I do that, you can't hear me either, so I couldn't tell you. Seeing you intended to pee, I got off the commode until you finished. Come on, let's go back in the house."

"Why did you paint him, what's he to you . . .?" he pointed at the representation of the fat man, not bothering to look at it.

Lee frowned. "Him? What are you talking about?"

"That fat man. He's the guy that owns Roy's Automotive."

"Fat man! You're freaking me out again, Clyde—that's a painting of me you're pointing at."

"Huh . . .?" he cut his eyes to the canvas and saw her beautiful face captured in oils. "B-But it was a portrait of the fat man, Lee—I swear!"

Eyes angrily narrowed, she gripped her waist and heaved a sigh. "I'm sorry but this just isn't going to work out. It's time for you to leave, and don't ever come back."

⊘

"Tick-tock, tick-tock, tick-tock, tick-tock, tick-tock, tick-tock . . . ."

⊘

They'd combed the small town but hadn't spotted a soul. All the businesses were closed, and though lights blazed in most of the houses, nobody answered their doorbells. After awhile they'd started pounding on the doors and repeatedly pushing the buttons, but no one would respond. Wyoming stepped away from the locked office of the only motel they could find, and wearily set down on a concrete step. "Where is everybody?"

"I don't know," Robby grimly replied. "It's only nine-twenty, yet we haven't seen a single person or any traffic."

A frightening and very likely explanation came to her. "This place must have been evacuated. I hope it wasn't some sort of plague that caused everyone to leave or we could be in serious trouble."

"Nah," Robby ran a hand through his wavy blonde hair, "there're too many cars parked in driveways for everyone to have driven away after being notified of a contagious disease, and they'd have turned off the lights before leaving, at least in their houses if they'd been given advanced warning. Something apparently caused everybody to hide or sneak out of town on foot, and whatever, or whoever, scared them into doing that must have moved on."

"Let's hope you're right and we just haven't seen whatever scared them yet. I've never heard of Leavenwood before, have you?"

"Nope."

"What are we going to do? I'm getting hungry."

Robby shrugged. "We can sleep in the plane but as for supper, I guess we'd better start looking for a vending machine. Most motels have at least one with snacks."

They found two, fully stocked, but neither worked, nor did the coke machine. She hoped they wouldn't have to resort to vandalism for something to eat.

Clyde couldn't believe it—Justified was nothing but a bigger version of Leavenwood. Having encountered the first traffic light immediately, he hadn't driven downtown before Lee kicked him out because her instructions had called for a left turn there.

To keep from going anywhere near Roy's Automotive, he'd decided to spend the night at a motel and leave Justified tomorrow morning opposite the direction he'd entered it. He'd found four but they were closed like everything else. He hadn't seen a single car, pickup, truck, or motorcycle while driving all over the weird town, looking for a place to crash.

His nerves were rigid with frustration, disappointment, and fear. The first two emotions were fueled by the fact he'd fallen for Lee despite her not being a normal woman, only to be rejected as a lunatic because of that fucking fat man. But what the hell was going on with these two strange towns?

Their cell phones couldn't pick up any signals and none of the payphones had dial tones. Wyoming wanted to smash the window of a bakery they were walking past so she could steal some of the pastries on display. She could tell by the hungry glaze in Robby's eyes he felt the same temptation.

As they continued on she spied something in a diner that shouldn't have been there since the place was closed. "Look there, at that first table on the right!"

Robby stopped and turned towards the door that punctuated a wall of glass like Kelly's Rentals.

"See it?"

"Yeah, somebody's gotta be in there!"

A platter loaded with two hamburgers and a mountain of fries sat atop the table, next to a steaming cup of coffee. Robby started banging on the door, shouting to be let in.

Noticing it move slightly with each blow, she pushed and the door swung open. "Just as I thought, it's not locked."

They hurried inside.

The burgers smelled so wonderful it took all her willpower to resist reaching for one. She hungrily gazed at them as Robby hollered, "Hey, you've got two customers out here!"

"We're closed, motherfucker," a masculine voice rang out. It came from an opening where servers could pick up food orders without having to enter the kitchen, but she couldn't see the angry man who'd shouted.

Robby stuffed some fries in his mouth, grabbed the hamburgers, motioned his head for her to follow, and made for the door. She started that way, but a hand seized her shoulder from behind.

"Bring back my grub, motherfucker, or I'll break this bitch's neck!"

A horrid fat man with yellow teeth clenching an unlit cigar gripped her tight.

Her knees buckled and she swooned.

Every apparent exit road curved back towards town at some point. Clyde hadn't been able to find any way out of Justified except for the highway he'd driven down from Leavenwood. He felt sick about going through that bizarre place again, but it was the only way back home. The two routes at the four-way stop that didn't connect the two towns merely formed a long loop.

While driving, he kept pondering Lee's explanation about what happened in the bathroom—how she'd turned invisible when he'd *barged in*. The term bugged him because he'd done nothing of the sort. He carefully rehashed the scenario and it just didn't add up.

I told her I was coming in to make sure she was all right, why didn't she say something before I opened the door? Maybe there's another way in and out of that bathroom. Yeah, that would explain it . . . and if that's the case I'm not the fucking lunatic, she is—thinking she's an angel stuck in a woman's body. But how did she pull off that mirror trick?

At length he concluded she'd told him the truth. None of it made sense otherwise. That meant the two weirdos at Roy's Automotive must be condemned angels too, since they could disappear like her. But dammit, that didn't explain what happened to the pickup and hydraulic lift, or how that painting of the fat man suddenly turned into a portrait of Lee.

Wyoming opened her eyes to find Robby helping her off the floor. She'd inherited an odd quirk from her alcoholic mother: fainting when something drastically startled her. It happened at Kelly's Rentals once when a hamster jumped out of the cash drawer. No one would confess putting it there but she suspected Clyde Burns was the culprit because he'd gotten a big laugh out of it.

"Are you all right, Wyoming?"

She noticed the hamburgers were back on the platter with the fries. "Yeah. Where's that man?"

"I don't know." Robby looked terrified and his voice reflected it. "He caught you when you fell, and laid you down real gently. I put the burgers back like he demanded— he cussed me out for ruining his supper by touching it— then bolted out the door. I ran outside, hollering I'd give him fifty bucks for the meal, but he was gone. Wyoming . . . it was like he just vanished."

That fanned the flames of her already blazing fear, adding full scale panic and an overwhelming sense of helplessness to the ominous perplexity tormenting her. Nonetheless, she couldn't pry her eyes off the food because of her aching stomach. "I'm *so* hungry. Let's eat that and leave some money on the table."

⟳✦⟲

Clyde sped past Roy's Automotive doing seventy with no intention of slowing down, but he hit the brakes and pulled to the curb after driving by a cafe named Tyner's Diner. The place had a glass front, and not only had he actually seen two people sitting inside, one of them looked like Wyoming Carter. If that blonde was really her, she could explain the mystery of Leavenwood. She wouldn't be dining in an establishment with a CLOSED sign on the door without being in the know.

He turned around but quickly stopped again—shifted to park, and got out of his car, leaving the Malibu idling in the street. The girl was Wyoming all right. She and the man had left the diner and were running towards him.

Gawking at him as if eyeing an alien from outer space, she shouted, "What are you doing here, Clyde?!"

"I was heading home from Justified and saw you while passing by. Tell me about this fucked up town."

She took a moment to catch her breath. "I don't know anything about it, other than I want to get out of here. Thank God you saw us—we need a ride back to Odessa."

"How did you get here?"

"We were flying to Louisiana in Robby's Cessna but engine trouble forced him to land on the highway. The plane's in a field about two miles down this road."

He winced. "That's the same way I got acquainted with Leavenwood, my car broke down . . . ."

Wyoming's pretty face didn't have a modicum of color left in it by the time he finished relaying everything that had happened since, including all the mysterious details about Lee Milan.

"Must be the same fat man we saw because he disappeared on us too," her date warily reported. "We just finished eating the guy's supper. Let's make tracks for Odessa."

"No way."

"What do you mean no way!" Wyoming ejaculated.

"I'm taking you guys to see Lee first, so y'all can prove to her I'm not lying about the fat man. I'm crazy about that woman but she thinks I'm just crazy period."

Lee believed him now because of his two witnesses, but Clyde wished he'd only brought one. The sultry brunette had eyes for Robby Gorgan, and the rich playboy hadn't taken his off her since relaying his interactions with the fat man. Wyoming didn't seem to care. Apparently the only thing on her mind was getting back on the road.

"Um, I think the fat man and mechanic must be like you, Lee." Clyde said it more to get her attention than really wanting to discuss it.

"What makes you say that?"

"Their ability to become invisible."

"How many of you are there?" Robby asked with a charming smile that made him want to puke.

"About ten thousand."

Clyde frowned. The combined populations of Leavenwood and Justified came close to that amount. "Why are you all in southeast Texas?"

Lee raised her brows. "Very astute of you, Clyde, I'm impressed. Yes, we're all here. This is where we were cast when we were cursed to take on human form. Justified and Leavenwood are bustling with activity around the clock, but the vehicles we drive can't be seen when they're moving unless we will them to be. No normal human can perceive the doors opening and closing as we come and go from our various businesses and shops.

"I have another confession to make. I lied about not hearing you relay your experience at Roy's Automotive, and being constipated. That trip to the bathroom was only a ruse to make you start looking for me and wind up in my studio. I knew you were telling the truth about seeing the fat man on my easel because I put that painting there. I was also aware of the mechanic speaking to you in my living room. He's the one who swapped the paintings while you were looking at me. He quit allowing you to see him or his pickup after telling you to talk to his boss, and as a result you couldn't hear him lower the lift before you turned around. When you came back all fidgety after the fat man disappeared, he raised it again while you were opening the office door, and once again enabled you to see him and his vehicle. He did the same with the tow truck when you started your car.

"The three of us are allies. They saw to it your car stalled, and also made Robby's plane engines start malfunctioning so he'd have to land near Leavenwood. The fat man, as you call him, baited Robby and Wyoming inside the diner so you'd see them when you drove by, and bring them here to convince me you were telling the truth."

Seething with angry confusion, he abandoned the couch and started pacing. "What was the point of flipping me out at Roy's Automotive? I don't get it."

"So you'd tell me about it, laying the groundwork for giving me a reason to think you were crazy and kick you out at the correct time. This whole affair was carefully synchronized so you'd arrive in Leavenwood while Robby and Wyoming were sitting in the diner. It was all designed to get the three of you to my place." A peculiar, almost frightening expression rose on her face, and she turned to Robby. "Do you hear the voices of hell calling out to you, Mister Gorgan? They're crying welcome . . . welcome . . . welcome."

"Tick-tock, tick-tock, tick-tock, tick-tock, tick-tock, tick-tock—" Larue stopped for a moment. A muddiness in his already foggy perception startled him. He fought the urge to weep. How long, how long would it be this time before, before . . . couldn't think it right, had to continue, must continue: "Tick-tock, tock-tock, tick-tock, tick-tock . . . ."

Whatever they were doing to Robby in the next room involved inflicting excruciating pain. The horrendous sounds of him being tortured made her tremble with terror. He'd started screaming soon after they closed the door and hadn't stopped since. Wyoming pressed her palms harder but still couldn't prevent his cries of agony from reaching her ears.

A big black man had materialized like a ghost the moment Lee asked Robby if he could hear the voices of hell. In a flash he'd cuffed Robby's hands behind his back and dragged him away with Lee following. They were powerless to help him—the fat man held a pistol in each hand, promising a bullet between the eyes should she or Clyde rise from the couch.

These evil people couldn't have once been angels—Lee had clearly lied about that. Shame mingled with fear as she prayed Robby's torment would satisfy the monstrous fiends so she wouldn't be a victim too. If she and Clyde weren't going to be spared she'd beg to be taken next—she couldn't bear another round of this mounting terror. It'd be far better to know her fate right away than to suffer the horror of wondering what awaited her as Clyde screamed his lungs out.

FOUR

ROBBY FINALLY QUIT wailing and Wyoming knew they'd killed him.

The fat man ordered Clyde to fetch a roll of plastic from a closet, then made him unroll it from the bathroom in the hallway to the room Robby had been forced into.

"Now open the door, motherfucker."

Clyde did so and the fat man told him to sit back down.

Out walked Lee and the black man—both naked and clutching gore-coated knives, upper bodies smeared with blood that slowly ran down their legs. They opened their bloody mouths and removed dentures composed of steel teeth shaped like a shark's. Raw meat and slivers of human skin were wedged between every tooth.

"My god, you're cannibals!"

"No, Wyoming," said the female man-butcher, real teeth getting blood stained from the movement of her lips. "Though we do sometimes hack away human flesh from living bone, we're not cannibals. Every piece of Robby's carcass will be put aboard his plane along with his bones. They'll be turned to ashes when my cohort parachutes out after setting it on fire. We didn't eat anything. Robby's vice required us to bite him."

"What are you really?!" shouted Clyde, glaring at Lee—anger as much as fear resonating in his voice.

"Spirits trapped in human form as I said. There's a tad more to the story than I told you, that's all. While we're on the earth it's required of us to execute certain criminals whose appetites are so voracious, and methods so cunning, they'd never be captured otherwise. Robby Gorgan was a sadistic pedophile, using innocent children to satisfy a perverseness growing within him like a cancer. He's killed eight kids in the same manner he died. Shrewdly, he always picked victims no one could connect him to, and never visited the same city twice in search of one. He never would have gotten caught, so we've prevented numerous other children from dying at his hands."

Clyde grimaced and palmed his temples. His extended fingers looked like trembling antlers sprouting from his head. "Why did you have to involve me? I've never seen Robby Gorgan before tonight."

The fat man laughed while lowering his guns. "Because she likes you."

A blush rose on Lee's blood-splattered face, the pink hue between the crimson droplets sickening to behold. "I'm not allowed to be intimate with a normal man until he knows precisely what I am. I had to introduce you to the truth in stages, so I devised this means to do it. I lied when I told you I'd thought about deceiving you indefinitely—the idea never even crossed my mind."

The black man aimed an inquiring frown at Lee and loudly cleared his throat.

She nodded. "Yes, go ahead and bag the remains and clean the room. I'll shower and give our visitors a tour. We'll take Clyde's car. I don't want to frighten them any further by instantaneous travel."

"I'll be sitting in your back seat with my guns, motherfucker," said the fat man to Clyde. "You won't see me unless you get out of line, but I'll be watching you both the whole time."

Clyde couldn't think straight. Seeing human blood on Lee's beautiful bare breasts had so screwed with his head he feared he might lose his mind. How could he know if she'd told the truth about Robby being a child killer? Lies she'd confessed to kept piling up, so she could be lying about that too. He hoped joining that social network hadn't been the worst mistake of his life.

At Lee's instruction he'd driven to the courthouse. They got out of his car and she led the way. Wyoming walked beside him as they followed her into a judge's chambers.

"Make yourselves comfortable," Lee instructed while pushing a button on an apparatus sitting atop an impressive desk.

A section of bookshelves whirled around to reveal a large monitor.

"What you're about to see is gruesome, but it will convince you that Robby's death was justified. You're going to witness his last murder exactly the way it happened." She handed each of them a paper bag.

He squinted at her. "What's this for?"

"Just in case."

If he'd ever had any doubts about the death penalty, Robby Gorgan permanently removed them. The carnage playing on the screen so revolted him he'd have taken a knife to the cruel bastard himself. After raping a cute little girl who couldn't have been more than six years old, he put some false teeth in his mouth that had razor tips, and repeatedly bit her face while mutilating her body with a knife. The cold-blooded monster didn't even have enough mercy to kill her beforehand. She'd been butchered alive.

"God I've seen enough, turn that damn thing off!"

Wyoming had lunged forward and vomited into her bag at the beginning of Robby's atrocity.

It took all his resolve not to do likewise now.

Lee wiped a tear from her cheek and pushed a button.

The screen went blank and the books reappeared.

His alarm clock woke him.

⟊

"Tick-tock, tick-tock, tick-tock, tick—"

"All right, Larue, enough of that. It's time to put you to bed. You stayed up all night staring at that damn grandfather's clock again."

⟊

Clyde stared at the luminous dial, amazed at how incredibly lifelike everything had been. At the beginning of the nightmare he'd left Wyoming a voicemail saying he'd woke up sick, like he'd been tempted to do after Thornton refused to give him the day off. He snickered while easing out of bed: only an idiot would fake being ill under those circumstances. That alone should have alerted him it was only a bad dream.

⟊

Wyoming readied the cash registers, made coffee, and flipped the neon sign switch. Kelly's Rentals was open for Friday business. Her nerves were fried. She'd been startled awake by a terrifying nightmare, and hadn't been able to shed the memory of it.

She heard a car approaching and glanced towards the

front as Clyde's Malibu passed by. The coffee maker quit gurgling so she filled two cups and held one out to him when he walked in.

"What's the matter?" he asked while accepting it. "One of the mechanics try to hit on you again?"

"It shows, huh?"

"Yeah. Who was it? I'll have a talk with him."

"Nobody, that's not what's bothering me, Clyde. I had an awful nightmare last night and you were in the worst parts of it. I dreamed my boyfriend got hacked to death by two angels bound to earth in human form."

Clyde dropped the cup and didn't bother looking down when it splattered on the floor.

FIVE

CLYDE WAS SO stunned it took him a minute to find his voice. "Shit, Wyoming, that's exactly what I dreamed last night!"

She fainted.

He grabbed her armpits to keep her from falling, and shook her until she came to—accidentally copping a feel of the sides of her breasts in the process. Once she could stand on her own he started cleaning up the mess he'd made. Wyoming was fully alert by the time he finished, and they exchanged nightmares.

She hadn't dreamed about his first encounter with Leavenwood or Lee, and her plane flight hadn't appeared in his, but the parts they were both in so uncannily matched they were finishing each other's sentences. Eerier still, she'd woke up at the same point in her dream as he had his.

"This is crazy . . ." he vigorously rubbed his forehead and drug his hand down his face. "You don't suppose it really happened."

"No. It couldn't have, Clyde, or we'd remember driving home."

He gave that some serious thought but it didn't satisfy him. "Call Robby and make sure he's alive. If he is, then you're right."

Before she could make the call Thornton walked in looking super pissed—glaring at him like he'd just called his wife a slut. "Burns, a Lee Milan sent me an email and wanted me to thank you for a pleasant visit. What the hell's up with that? You've got no business giving people my email address."

Clyde swallowed hard to keep from puking his fear-frozen guts out, then sucked in a deep breath and held it until his queasy stomach quit threatening to expel his breakfast. "I didn't give it to her, Thornton, I swear."

"Then how'd she get it?"

"I don't know but she didn't get it from me."

"He's not lying," defended Wyoming.

"How would you know?"

She wilted, unable to explain for obvious reasons.

Thornton lightened up, apparently thinking his challenging question had spawned the mortified look on her face. "Who is she, Burns?"

"Someone I met on a social site."

"Well she must have hacked your contact list or she couldn't have gotten my email address since you didn't give it to her. I'd cut ties with her if I was you." He went out back to check on the mechanics.

Clyde set down at the cashiers' computer and called up his email account. Paychecks were doled out at Kelly's Rentals the old fashion way instead of by direct deposit. Thornton wouldn't allow him to get a modem so he could access the internet from the one in his office even at his own expense, but Wyoming had sweet talked him into buying one for the computer she and the rest of the upfront crew used. Until then only the mechanic foreman's had internet capabilities, in order to get parts at the cheapest price.

She peered over his shoulder. "What are you doing?"

"Emailing Lee to find out how she got Thornton's address and why the hell she sent that fucking message."

He completed the task and waited until Thornton came back through the front and left for the day before checking for Lee's reply. His nerves tensed when he saw she'd responded.

Hi Clyde,

I emailed your boss so you'd know you were really here, though to you and Wyoming it now seems as if the two of you merely dreamed it. Impossible to explain how this sort of thing happens in a way you'd understand. I was given this method to verify that I told you the truth about what I am. As for how I got your boss's email address, well you wouldn't understand that either. I would much rather have emailed you and listed enough details to convince you directly, but I'm not allowed to do that because of being personally interested in you (there're all sorts of rules I must follow when becoming involved with a man). You'll receive further verification soon if you haven't already.

Have a good day!

Lee

"Listen to this, Wyoming!" He read it aloud. Her faded complexion worried him, so he hurried to the counter but she waved him off.

"I'm not going to pass out, Clyde. I'm trying to keep from throwing up."

"Yeah . . . I know what you mean." He stepped to the computer and logged out.

The phone rang.

"Kelly's Rentals." Wyoming's voice sounded cheerfully professional, belying the aghast facade she'd been wearing since hearing Lee's reply. "Well hello, Mister Gorgan, what a nice surprise to hear from you. What's up?"

Once again he had to hold a deep breath to keep his oatmeal down. She hadn't called Robby yet and he feared the further verification Lee mentioned had just arrived. A moment later Wyoming confirmed it when she broke into tears.

"That was R-Robby's father," she sobbed while cradling the phone. "Robby's plane exploded in midair near a small town in southeast Texas. They found the wreckage at dawn.

Oh, Clyde . . .!"

Wyoming threw herself into his arms, leaving him no choice but to hold her as she bawled on his shoulder. The putrid sensations pulverizing him nullified the thrill he'd have felt being in this position under normal circumstances. He'd fantasized this scenario many times—her crying his name with elevated emotions while pressing her voluptuous body against him. But not like this. Lust hadn't evoked the cry and carnal desire could hardly describe her motivation. He owed this moment, along with the trepidation that stole the pleasure of it, to Lee Milan. She and the black man really had butchered Robby Gorgan and made his death look like an accident.

Wyoming finally pulled away. She dug a handkerchief from her purse and daubed the corners of her eyes while weepingly gawking at him. "I can't believe this, Clyde."

"Me either, but it really happened. Somehow while we were asleep in our beds we were also several hours into the future interacting with Lee and her two cronies . . . and went back in time when we woke up."

"But not Robby," she sniffled. "He died there."

The bastard damn well deserved it, he thought, not about to say it out loud. Another possibility entered his mind that caused a different type of fear to ripple through him. What if Lee had deceived them, and Robby hadn't been a merciless child killer after all?

After bawling it all out with only Clyde in the store, Wyoming had managed to keep her emotions in check from the time the first customer came in until four o'clock. She could have worked till close since the special occasion that had prompted her to make arrangements to leave early this Friday no longer existed, but the hurricane of fear and remorse whirling inside her demanded release, and she dared not let it out at Kelly's Rentals. Her coworkers would insist on knowing what troubled her, and no one but Clyde could possibly understand. They'd think she'd gone mad.

She cried like a grieving widow and cursed like a drunken sailor all the way home.

Clyde had told her the name of the social site where he'd met the strange woman. She called it up on her computer, joined under a fake name, and typed Lee Milan in the search bar. Her beautiful face soon appeared and the profile read:

Lee Milan
Location: Texas
Occupation: Graphic Designer
Sex: Female
Age: 30
Hair: Brown
Eyes: Brown
Height: 5'4"
Body Type: Curvy
Smokes: No
Drinks: Yes
Hobbies: Painting
Orientation: Straight
Marital Status: Single
Seeks: Single White Male 30 – 40
Must be: Attractive non smoker that's fun to be with
Fetishes: None
Tattoos: None
Body Piercing(s): Ear Lobes
Web Cam: No
Cunnilingus: Yes
Fellatio: Yes

Anal: No
Group Sex: No

Wyoming clicked through Lee's pictures and immediately understood why Clyde had been so excited to spend the weekend with her. She checked the photos of her friends and found they all looked like normal people. The fat man and black man weren't on there. She canceled her membership and tried to find Leavenwood and Justified, but neither showed up in the state of Texas.

The look on Lee Milan's face when she'd stepped into the living room after butchering Robby really worried her. The black man's features never wavered from inscrutable indifference, but Lee's expression had appeared sort of lustful rather than the solemn façade of someone bringing a killer to justice. It might have stemmed from savoring the fact a child killer had been forced to taste his own medicine, but how could she be sure? And how could she know whether or not the mysterious recording they'd been shown hadn't been a fake? Normal people could manipulate videos into appearing to be an actual event, so it would be easy for that weird woman to have done so.

"He's coming around," Larue heard Mother say. "His eyes are starting to focus."

"Mm hmm," said Ethel.

He'd gone to that other place again, where coherent thought became abstract blurs. The scientists didn't know why his mind couldn't persistently stay in the rational world, and had never bothered trying to find out. They were only interested in picking his brain in its normal state.

"Larue, I called Callaway's. Paul and J.T. are on their way to get you."

"Mother, no! I won't go back there, I won't!"

Ethel glowered at him. "We can't take care of you, Larue. Stop being so selfish."

Tears dribbled down his cheeks. "Mother, please don't do this to me."

"I'm sorry, but your sister's right—we can't take care of you. I wish you were normal, but you're not. You're a genius who's a helpless baby even though you're twenty-five years old. It was too hard getting through these last ninety days without the extra income from Callaway's. Your sister and I don't earn enough to feed and clothe three people after paying the mortgage and all the other monthly bills. I'd have to apply for food stamps and that's something I'll never do—it's too much like being on welfare. If you could hold a job it would be different, but you can't."

He folded his arms over his belly, lowered his head, and pouted. "You're not really my mother and she's not my sister."

"I may not have given birth to you as I did her but I'm still your mother. You were a wandering four-year-old with no home and no hope. If I hadn't taken you in I doubt you'd be alive today."

"But you gave me away only a year later and let scientists raise me."

"Now that's not fair, Larue . . ." she grabbed his chin and made him face her. "You get to spend a weekend with us each month, three holidays, and thirty days every summer. I nurtured you as any mother would her child as you grew up, and spanked you when you needed it."

The phone woke him. He angrily reached for the receiver and barked, "This had better be an emergency whoever you are, calling me so early on a Saturday."

"Clyde, it's Wyoming. Sorry to bother you but we need to find out what's really going on with Lee Milan and those two strange men."

Their last word on the matter yesterday before the cashiers arrived had been to let their emotions settle over the weekend so they could think clearly. "I thought we agreed to wait until Monday to hash this out."

"We did, but I just can't. And we need to tell the police what happened. They'll never believe me without you corroborating everything."

"Shit, Wyoming, they wouldn't believe you if you had a dozen witnesses."

A long pause indicated she was thinking that over. *"You're probably right, so that leaves us only one option. We have to go back there and get some type of proof."*

༼ঌ

"I can't believe I let you talk me into this." Clyde gripped the steering wheel as if choking it to death, probably wishing his fingers were wrapped around her throat instead.

Wyoming understood his reluctance but they simply had no other choice.

When they finally reached the first of their two destinations she almost threw up a vending machine cupcake imbibed at a gas station a few miles back. There were vehicles on the road, people on the sidewalks, customers coming and going from the businesses lining Main Street.

"The city limits sign did say Leavenwood, didn't it?" Clyde

muttered in an awestruck tone.

"I was too surprised by the traffic to even think about looking at it, but this is definitely the same town we were in last night." She raised her digital camera and snapped two quick shots of the diner as they cruised past.

"The police won't find Robby's fingerprints, Wyoming. That table's been wiped clean at least a dozen times by now, and the cup and platter have made at least one trip to the dishwasher."

"You're right about that, but if the door hasn't been washed there might still be some on it. He slapped it repeatedly with both hands while hollering to be let in."

Clyde pulled into the parking lot of Roy's Automotive and gave her a sarcastic smirk. "Okay, Wyoming, let's go see the fat man."

They entered through an open bay. Two mechanics were putting new tires on a van. Both were young and white.

"Never saw either of them," whispered Clyde while making for a door.

It opened before they reached it and a lean man at least twenty years older than the tire changers stepped out, carrying a small waste basket. The guy had appealing features she figured had probably been pretty arresting in his youth.

"What can I do for you folks?" he asked with a friendly grin while emptying the container into a big rubber trash can.

Clyde glanced around as if reassuring himself they'd come to the right place. "Where's Roy?"

"You're looking at him."

"You're the owner?"

"Mm hmm."

A confused frown leapt on Clyde's face. "I'm looking for a bald, fat man who smokes cigars. He told me this shop belonged to him."

"You must be looking for a Roy's Automotive in some other town. I don't know anybody fitting that description."

"Does a black mechanic work here?"

"No, just me and those two gentlemen over there . . ." he pointed at the mechanics.

"Were the three of you here yesterday?"

"Yeah," the owner answered with a trace of annoyance in his voice. "Why are you asking?"

Seeing the situation required a more tactful approach, Wyoming smiled and said, "Was yesterday a local holiday or something? The whole town seemed to be closed down when we passed through."

"Nope, just another regular Friday. No offense, but I'm getting a little uneasy about all these odd questions, so unless you need something fixed I'll get back to my paperwork."

"Um no," Clyde awkwardly responded, "we'll be on our way . . . ."

They drove to Justified and found its commerce district as active as Leavenwood's. Clyde combed the neighborhoods. Kids were biking down sidewalks, teenagers were playing basketball in driveways, lawns were being prepared for summer's arrival, a young couple was washing their car, and some little girls were trying to master the hula hoop in their front yard. He maneuvered back to the main drag—headed the direction of Leavenwood, cut a right at the last traffic light in town, turned left at a stop sign, traveled a few blocks, and parked at the curb in front of Lee Milan's house.

She followed Clyde down the walk, and a busty redhead answered the doorbell.

"Hi, I'm Clyde Burns, a friend of Lee's."

"Who?" said the woman.

"Lee Milan."

"I'm sorry but you've got the wrong address."

"But this is where she lives," Clyde insisted, "I was here

last night."

"Excuse me? This is my house. I don't know anyone named Lee Milan, and I'd have seen you if you came here last night because I was home all evening."

Clyde turned pale with shock. His lips were moving as if to speak, but no words came forth.

"Ma'am, my name is Wyoming Carter and I came to this house with Clyde last night, or at least one just like it. May I ask your name?"

"Blinda Love."

"Nice to meet you, Blinda. How long have you lived in Justified?"

"Justified? Never heard of it."

"B-But that's the name of this town."

Blinda Love's apple-green eyes narrowed as she tilted her head a few degrees. "Listen, lady, I don't know where you think you are, but this is Turnaton and has never been called anything else to the best of my knowledge."

Clyde Burns and Wyoming Carter seemed like two normal people who'd had an elaborate prank pulled on them. Blinda could sympathize, having been the butt of some fiendishly clever practical jokes orchestrated by her ex husband. "Where are you two from?"

"Odessa," said Clyde.

"Who told you Turnaton was called Justified?"

He nervously cleared his throat. "Lee Milan, and it's the name on the city limits sign as you enter town from Leavenwood."

"Leavenwood? Never heard of it either. You're apparently the victim of a hoax. She must have had a phony sign made and somehow fastened it to the real one."

"There you go, Larue."

He detested the way J.T. Glade said it. The scientist acted is if he'd just accomplished some monumental task, when all he'd done was adjust his seatbelt to make it more comfortable. They wouldn't allow him to unfasten the lockable straps and increase the length himself for fear he might try to bail out of the van. If it had been at rest instead of moving seventy miles an hour their concerns would have been warranted. The vehicle had been equipped to retrieve homesick geniuses who had difficulty settling into the new surroundings their parents condemned them to. No one but he saw it that way though—the stupid kids felt as privileged to be admitted to Callaway's as their ignorant moms and dads.

"I've sure missed you these last three months," said Roger Benz, the other scientist in charge of him. "I see you've put on a few pounds from eating your mama's good home cooking."

"She's a good cook but she's not my real mother."

"I know that, Larue."

"My weight will fluctuate back to normal in two-point-three weeks—three hundred forty-four hours—or twenty thousand, six hundred, and forty minutes if you'd prefer to measure it that way."

Roger laughed. "I'll take your word for it, Larue."

"Not me," snickered J.T. "I want it in seconds."

"Very well. I'll be trim again in one-point-two-three-eight-four-zero-zero million seconds according to my current metabolic rate. By the way, Roger, you're veering a quarter inch too far left of the highway's center. I hope you don't cause us to have an accident."

Clyde pulled to the side of the road and carefully checked the city limits sign. Wyoming stood beside him, her face revealing she experienced the same creepy bewilderment that tortured his mind. Unmarred paint on the bolts fastening it to the pole proved they hadn't been loosened, yet it read *Turnaton.*

"It said Justified when we passed it coming into town, I'm sure of it."

Wyoming signaled her agreement with a weak nod.

"Let's ask Blinda Love if she'll let us come inside to see if the interior of her house is the same as Lee's." He didn't know if Wyoming liked the idea or not, she merely shrugged while heading for his Malibu, treading somberly as if leaving the graveside after a beloved family member's funeral.

Callaway's Research Complex looked more like a group of condominiums with the same stone facades than a scientific conglomerate colloquially referred to as a Think Tank. Child geniuses were the only students admitted to the academic section. A Callaway's degree carried more prestige than any tech-oriented university, but he hadn't been admitted for that purpose: the knucklehead scientists studied him. Larue closed his eyes when they neared the gates, and thought back to the day Mother found him near the spot she'd taken her girl scout troop camping.

The first occurrence of the spells that rendered him practically mindless had seized him, and he'd come out of it to find he'd wandered miles away from home. When coherency finally returned he'd been informed that his recollection of the town's name had somehow been corrupted because no such city existed. He knew that wasn't true but couldn't prove it because no road map, atlas, or any site on the internet had it listed. The authorities hadn't been able to find his real mom, so Mother had been granted the legal right to keep him as a foster son. Soon thereafter she'd acquired power of attorney and legal guardianship over him for life.

Blinda Love opened the door wearing a deep frown. "You two again?"

"Yeah, um, Wyoming and I would like to see if the interior of your house matches Lee Milan's as uncannily as the outside does."

"I think you'd better go before I call the police."

"Wait!" he cried as she started to shut the door. "Lee's house has a building in the backyard she uses as an art studio, and her kitchen's in an unusual spot—it's at the end of the hallway where you'd usually expect to find a bedroom."

She paused and gawked at him as if he'd just read her mind. "So does mine."

"May we please check it out?"

Her big expressive eyes, that had narrowed with firm intent to rid herself of two lunatics, were now wide with intrigue. As if yielding to an impulse contrary to common sense, she pulled the door fully open while stepping backwards, and motioned for them to come inside . . . .

The room where Robby Gorgan had been butchered was a comfortable den with no plumbing of any kind, but the dimensions were identical. The other rooms matched Lee's as well. Only the furniture and carpeting differed from hers. Clyde started scratching the back of his neck and cleared his throat. "I don't know how to explain what happened last night, but thanks again for letting us have a look around."

"No problem," Blinda assured with a bemused smile. "This is the most bizarre thing I've ever heard of."

They hadn't mentioned Robby to Blinda Love but his picture was on her coffee table. His death had made the front page of the local paper. *Millionaire's Son In Fatal Plane Crash Near Turnaton*, the headline read. Justified and Turnaton mirrored each other, occupied the same geographical location, but existed in different dimensions— at least that was the only answer to this crazy mystery he could come up with. Of course he dared not tell Blinda Love that. "How long have you lived in Turnaton?"

"Three years. I moved here from Amarillo after a messy divorce. That's where I'm from originally."

"Is that when you bought this house?"

"Mm hmm. Could I persuade you to stay for supper? I'd like to help you figure out this fascinating coincidence."

"Thanks," he said without conferring with Wyoming, "we'd love to."

⟡

The commissary food didn't taste as good as Mother's, and the sterile atmosphere always made him miss her cozy kitchen. He selected wiener schnitzel, mashed potatoes, green beans, and lime sherbet for dinner.

Tabitha Gershwin unloaded her tray, stacked it on top of his, and cast him a smile as she sat down. A greasy whitehead, bulging between her nose and mouth, begged to be popped. "Good to have you back, Larue."

"I hate this place."

"I know and I'll never understand why. I love it here."

"Yeah, well you're not being analyzed like a guinea pig— they're educating you—but that's still all you are to them."

She giggled and brushed a lock of brown hair from her pimply forehead. "You should feel grateful to be special. If I didn't have brains look where I'd be with this homely face."

"You're not homely, Tabitha, just ill-complected." He refrained from telling the seventeen-year-old she had nice tits and would have a lovely figure if she'd drop the twenty pounds and seven-point-two-six ounces her frame wasn't built to carry. If only he'd had the same discretion at four he might not have wound up here.

Mother couldn't believe such a young boy could not only read, but had the innate talent to cipher numbers like a computer, measure distance with his eyes as accurately as any instrument, and determine the exact weight of people and objects by merely looking at them. She'd thought there'd be some sort of prize money if she could get him listed in Guinness World Records. To her delight she soon wound up receiving hefty checks on a monthly basis from Callaway's Research Complex instead, when the chief administrator got wind of his abilities.

The sympathetic, hospitable, and very hot redhead waved goodbye from her front porch as they drove away.

Discovering her to be a very open minded woman, he'd shared his theory of Justified and Turnaton existing in separate dimensions. She'd agreed that would adequately explain everything, but didn't appear to believe it.

Wyoming did though.

Clyde found himself wishing it'd been Blinda Love rather than Lee Milan that had invited him down for the weekend. If Lee wasn't such a strange woman he might have felt differently, but couldn't be entirely sure about that.

The city limits sign still read *Turnaton* when they motored past it.

Wyoming yawned, and it dawned on him they'd visited with Blinda far too long. "It's almost nine o'clock and we've got an eight hour drive ahead of us. We'd better turn around and get a couple of motel rooms."

"There's a motel in Leavenwood. Assuming the town's still normal, we can sleep there."

He shuddered at the possibility it wouldn't be. "We shouldn't chance it, let's go back to Turnaton . . . ."

SIX

ONLY A SKELETON crew stayed at Callaway's on Sundays and none of them were scientists. Pretending to be aimlessly wandering around the compound, Larue calculated his escape. This time he knew better than to go to Mother's. He loathed thieves but his survival depended on him being one. Three debit cards rested in his hip pocket—each had a different name, and less than fifteen minutes ago inhabited the wallets of a trio of janitors. It had been an effortless maneuver, calculating the exact trajectory required to extract the billfolds in a manner they wouldn't feel them being removed and reinserted into their trousers.

Having never had a bank account, he'd known very little about ATM machines. Tabitha had told him how they operated, and that only a certain amount of cash could be pulsed at one time. Once he got to the city he'd hit all of them quickly as possible and hide out in some town small enough that he could walk to all the stores. The janitors would rightfully claim they hadn't withdrawn the funds and wind up having their accounts reimbursed.

In exactly fifty-point-seven-two seconds the gates would open for an approaching laundry truck that came and went seven mornings a week. Unbeknownst to the driver, he'd be leaving with a passenger in back.

Clyde had changed his mind about spending the night in

Turnaton, not wanting to run the risk of waking up in Justified. He'd seen a sign on the east side of town that said *CONROE 40 Miles*, so he'd driven there and stopped at a motel on the outskirts of the city.

Wyoming had prompted his concern by speculating on something he hadn't thought of. They'd been discussing the oddity of him not being able to leave Justified without taking the highway to Leavenwood, which led to him seeing her and Robby at the diner.

"If you'd really driven there," she'd said, "I wonder if we wouldn't have had the same problem leaving Leavenwood. Maybe there's not a physical way to get out of that dimension, and that's why Lee pulled us into it through a dream."

"But Robby's plane was really destroyed," he'd pointed out.

"Yes, Robby really flew to Leavenwood all right, but he was the only one who wound up there in his physical body. Lee made him think you and I were as real as he was. Of course we thought so too at the time. We both know that city limits sign said Justified when we first passed it today, but do you recall seeing any traffic before we did?"

"No," he'd answered. "Now that you mention it, I don't remember seeing anything at all until we came over the hill."

"Do you see where I'm going with this, Clyde?"

"Yeah, Justified turned into Turnaton right after we drove past the city limits sign, and that's bound to be what happened in Leavenwood."

"Mm hmm. And when we drove out of whatever town Leavenwood had turned into, it must have changed back before we passed the sign on the other side of town."

They'd made a point of checking it after leaving Roy's Automotive, and the sign had read *Leavenwood.*

He'd never been to Conroe before, but having heard of it all his life as had Wyoming, they'd chosen to spend the night there. He knocked on the door of her room and it soon opened. "Ready for breakfast?"

"Sounds good," she said with a sleepy smile.

They settled at a table in a restaurant next to the motel. Wyoming studied the roadmap while waiting for her order.

"Turnaton's on here, Clyde."

"Look northwest of it and see if there's a town where Leavenwood is."

A few seconds passed and she nodded. "It's called Piler Creek."

His plan failed. Larue had only managed to pulse nine hundred dollars instead of several thousand like he'd intended. He'd discovered going to another pulse machine made no difference. Each card had been declined when he'd tried to withdraw the maximum three hundred a second time, and would remain ineffective for twenty-four hours. He thought about buying some clothes and luggage with the cards but soon discarded the idea. A rubber devil's mask Tabitha had given him hid his face from the ATM cameras, but he couldn't wear it in a store, the clerks would think he'd come to rob them.

If the janitors hadn't already learned their debit cards were missing they soon would, so the purloined pieces of plastic were useless to him now. He paid cash for a pocket knife and cut them into tiny shards, then did the same with the mask.

While chewing a mouthful of bacon and egg it occurred to him Robby Gorgan's tragic death had made Wyoming available. Of course now wouldn't be a good time to ask her out. Besides, she'd probably be put off by their age difference. She didn't go long between boyfriends. They'd met the day she started working at Kelly's Rentals, and since then she'd had three before Robby, breaking up with each one when they'd proposed to her. He'd gotten to know her well enough by the time she dumped the third one to ask why such a romantic act prompted her to end the relationship.

She'd answered with, "I'll never get married, Clyde, and once a guy gets the notion of putting a ring on my finger I know it's time to bail because he'll keep trying no matter how many times I turn him down."

Not the marrying kind himself, he'd started working up the nerve to ask her out, but an additional statement had shut him down cold. "There's this rich guy I met at the Oil Show that's been begging me to go out with him, and now that I'm free again his wish shall be granted. He's a terminal playboy so I don't think I'll have to worry about him ever proposing."

Ironically, Robby Gorgan had indeed been *terminal*.

ॐ

Tabitha whizzed around the compound in her go kart, thinking about Larue. She hoped he wouldn't get hurt. His mindless spells were unpredictable and he lacked any sense of self preservation while going through one. He might wander into traffic and get run over. She'd promised to keep his escape plans to herself, and would certainly do so, yet she knew the sooner he got caught the better off he'd be, for his own good. If he hadn't needed her devil's mask and information about ATM's he wouldn't have told her anything.

His brain far outshone all of those at Callaway's combined, including the scientists. All he had to do was look at something, or someone, and he could rattle off every pertinent structural attribute about that thing or person to the minutest detail. And his mathematical skills were unheard of through the annals of history. He'd yet to be given a complex equation he couldn't instantly solve in his head. Paul and J.T. were constantly trying to come up with one to thwart him so as to ascertain his ceiling, but had yet to even cause him to hesitate before spouting out the answer. Larue found it all boring, and wanted to lead a normal life. The poor genius didn't have a prayer of doing so, but simply couldn't come to grips with that fact.

She'd known him since the day of her admittance nine years ago. He'd been sixteen at the time and already resented being at Callaway's, having lived there longer than she'd been alive. The three months he'd spent at his foster mom's when he escaped the first time had seemed like a lifetime to her, so she prayed he'd get caught soon and come back in one piece.

"No, Mom," Blinda answered, "still not seeing anyone."

"Since when did you become so independent?"

"I haven't. The men I've met so far just don't ring my bell, or command my respect. Well, except for this handsome guy that dropped by yesterday. He has that certain something that draws me to him the same way Elvis Presley did, even though he doesn't look like him."

"Did he ask you out?"

"No, and odds are I'll never see him again, he lives in Odessa. He came to my house by mistake, but I don't want to go into all that." She couldn't, her mother would think she'd flipped. "When Daddy wakes up from his nap, tell him he owes me a phone call."

"I'll do 'er."

"How's the weather up there?"

"It's Amarillo, hon, you know better than to ask that."

She laughed. "It's a beautiful day here in Turnaton. Well, I'll let you go . . . ."

⚬⚬⚬

"Watch out for that drunk up ahead, Clyde, he's liable to wander onto the road—and don't you dare stop if he tries to hitch a ride."

Already eyeballing the dude staggering along the bar ditch, Wyoming's warning was unnecessary. When they drew closer he noticed the guy seemed awfully well groomed for a wino, and his gait indicated a problem unrelated to inebriation.

"What are you doing?!" Wyoming screeched with alarm when he pulled over.

"He's not drunk, he's retarded. We can't leave him out here in the middle of nowhere."

Clyde parked and got out of his car. "Hey there, where are you headed?"

A pair of blank eyes looked his way. "N-No can . . . think . . . have to . . . wait till . . . till . . . L-Larue, Larue think again."

"Larue? Is that your name?"

The poor soul wrestled with the question for several seconds before nodding.

"Come on, Larue, get in my car. You're not safe out here."

The guy was taller and heavier than Clyde, so he hoped it wouldn't be necessary to manhandle him. A sigh of relief vacated his lungs when Larue started for the Malibu.

He buckled him up in the backseat on the driver's side and got behind the wheel.

Wyoming relaxed upon seeing he'd picked up a mentally handicapped person who'd gotten lost, rather than a soused vagabond hoping to bum a ride.

"Larue, my name is Clyde and this is Wyoming. Wyoming, say hello to Larue."

A warm smile accompanied her greeting.

Larue merely stared ahead, evidently unable to process the gesture.

They cruised along in silence for the next twenty minutes. He planned to stop at College Station, the first normal town on the Odessa side of Leavenwood—or Piler Creek as the case might be—and drop Larue off at the police station. They wouldn't be finding out if the town was Leavenwood or Piler Creek because he'd be driving to College Station from Turnaton, unless the city limits sign read Justified instead. If it did he'd backtrack and leave Larue in the hands of the Conroe police department, then plot a different course for home. The sign announcing the way to College Station read the same in Justified as it did in Turnaton, but except for the road to Leavenwood every highway he'd taken to leave Justified had circled back to that weird town.

Thunderheads loomed in the near distance, dark and menacing. "Shit, we're heading into a storm—looks like a mean sucker too. If I wind up with hail dents on my new car I'm holding you responsible, Wyoming. This trip was all your idea."

A strong wind gust rocked the Malibu and a nerve-jarring thunderclap set his teeth on edge. Before long dense sheets of rain made it hard to see very far ahead, so he slowed to forty. Several drivers pulled over to wait out the storm.

"You're not properly centered in your lane," said an articulate voice from behind him. "Need to veer right five thirty-seconds of an inch."

Clyde quickly adjusted the rearview mirror so he could see his passenger's face. Larue's big brown eyes were now clear and bright.

"I apologize for my previous incoherency. It's an odd sporadic affliction that almost completely nullifies my thought processes—sometimes just a few minutes, sometimes for as long as twenty-four hours. It also renders me quite lugubrious, but when I have some object to focus on, such as a grandfather's clock, my melancholia becomes bearable. If nothing draws my attention I just take off walking to keep my cerebration from being further destabilized by gloomy sentiment. I can go days or only hours between spells. I vaguely recall you introducing yourself but can't remember your name."

The abrupt change in Larue totally boggled his mind. The guy who couldn't even form a complete sentence when he'd picked him up, now spoke like a college professor. *Talk about your Jekyll and Hyde.* "I'm Clyde Burns and this is Wyoming Carter."

"Nice to meet you. May I ask where you're taking me, Clyde?"

"We're heading for Odessa. I'd planned to have the police in College Station find out where you belong and get you there—but since you can tell me that now, I'll take you. Where do you live?"

"I wandered away from my home when I was four in the same condition you found me in, and haven't been able to go back because nobody can locate the town. It doesn't appear to exist, but I know it does."

Wyoming turned towards the backseat. "What's the name of the town?"

"Justified."

He nearly swerved off the road, and Wyoming fainted.

"What's wrong?!" gasped Larue.

"Uh . . . are you sure that's the name of the town you're from?"

"Yes. Why did Wyoming pass out?"

"It's a long story but she'll be fine. Where do you live now?"

"Nowhere!"

The panicked response worried him, so he proceeded cautiously. "Funny, you don't look like a homeless guy. How old are you?"

"Twenty-five."

"You said that calmly. Why are you lying about where you live? Did you escape from an asylum or something? You can tell me. I promise I won't take you anywhere you don't want to go."

"No . . . not an asylum, a think tank outside Conroe. Scientists have been studying me for twenty years. My foster mother has power of attorney over me and won't let me leave there because they pay her for the right to analyze some peculiar abilities I was born with."

He reached over and grabbed Wyoming's shoulder—gently shook her until she opened her eyes, readjusted the rearview mirror to its correct position, and placed his right hand back on the steering wheel. "What sort of abilities, Larue?"

"I can solve extremely complex mathematical problems in my head as quickly as a computer, and instantly calculate distances. With a glance I can determine the dimensional proportions, weight, stress factors, etcetera of anything. To give you an example, you'll pass that vehicle on the right side of the road in precisely five-point-two seconds. It weighs thirty-one hundred, ninety-nine pounds, and eleven-point-six ounces."

Clyde didn't know if Larue had estimated the exact time, but about five seconds ticked by before he passed a red sports car. Apparently too scared to drive during the storm, the driver had chosen a bad place to park. Only the upper half of a beautiful set of mags were visible above the mud. Someone must have offered a ride because he didn't see anybody walking.

Now fully alert, Wyoming asked what was going on, and he explained Larue's example.

"Did he get it right?"

"Far as I know. If he didn't he came real close."

She looked down the road, then at her watch. "Larue, how long will it take us to reach that roadside park sign up ahead?"

"Eight-point-one-three seconds."

"Wow, that's incredible!" she exclaimed as he drove by it.

"Your watch tells time in micro seconds?"

"No, Clyde, but I counted exactly eight seconds from the time Larue said it until we passed the sign."

"Why did you faint?" asked Larue.

Wyoming sighed and gazed through the blurry windshield. "Because Clyde and I had a frightening experience in Justified."

"You've been there?! You've really been there?!"

He snickered at Larue's childlike exuberance. "Oh yeah. We got acquainted with Justified day before yesterday, but haven't been able to find it again—only a town called Turnaton. Have you ever heard of Leavenwood?"

Larue whistled and clapped his hands as if applauding a rock band who'd just played one of his favorite songs. "Yes, I've heard of it—oh what a happy day! Ever since I wandered away from home I've been trying to convince somebody that Justified and Leavenwood are real but nobody believes me. Now today I meet two people who know they are. My uncle lives there, at least he used to. He had an auto repair shop."

Sharp tingles pulsated across Clyde's scalp and down his back. "We was a mechanic?"

"Yeah. He let me play with his timing light once when he tuned up my mother's car in our garage—she wouldn't go to his shop for some reason, or visit him at his house. That device fascinated me. I always wondered what the inside of his house and shop looked like."

"So you've never actually been to Leavenwood?"

"Oh sure I have, Clyde, but my mother wouldn't stop at my uncle's house or his shop, and wouldn't tell me why. She finally drove by his house once when I kept begging to see where he lived. I saw his shop every time we went to Leavenwood because it was on the road we drove into town on."

Clyde cut his eyes to Wyoming, knowing she had to be wondering the same thing—could Larue be talking about the fat man? While he didn't know the obese asshole's exact age, he had to be at least fifty. "Your uncle wouldn't happen to be a bald overweight guy named Roy, would he?"

"Well his name's Roy all right—Roy Milan—but he was a slim, handsome man with a full head of brown hair. Of course that was a long time ago, so no telling what he looks like now. My father died a few weeks after I was born, and it was just me and my mom, so I relished every minute I got to spend with him."

Bound to be related to Lee, thought Clyde. *Or maybe all those weird angels go by Milan. Very unlikely he's the fat man. I don't think that guy could ever have been called handsome no matter how slim he may have been in his younger days.*

"There was something odd about his relationship with my mother," Larue continued. "I could sense it even though I was only a little boy. Every visit was the same—he'd spend about two hours playing with me, then my mother would make me go to bed. My uncle always gave her this peculiar smile when she'd say, 'It's your bedtime, Larue.' He'd have breakfast with us the next morning and be on his way. When I was taught about sex I suspected that's what she and my Uncle Roy were doing. Ever since then I've doubted he was really my uncle."

Clyde doubted it too after hearing that. He was also having doubts about something else—Lee's kind having to will a normal human to see them. Since Larue was from Justified he had to be like her and the other inhabitants of those two weird towns, so why had he been visible while stumbling down the side of the road in such a pathetic mental state he had to concentrate to remember his own name? And why did his reflection show up in the rearview mirror?

Another lie could be chalked up on Lee's account.

Wyoming peered at Larue. "What's your last name?"

"Milan."

"What's your mother's name?"

"Lee."

"Lee Milan?" Clyde almost screamed it.

"Yes."

"Is she a pretty brunette with brown eyes?"

"Well she had those features, and was *very* pretty when I last saw her, but that was twenty-one years ago. She was thirty when she had me, so she's fifty-five now."

A torrent of bitter confusion whirled inside his head. What had prompted Lee to lie about being infertile and living numerous lives? Why not admit she'd looked exactly the same since taking on human form? That had to be the case since she still looked thirty, the age Larue thought she'd been when he was born, and the age she still claimed to be. None of it made sense. How could an angel in human form be a pathological liar?

Now hold on a minute, he scolded himself, *Lee's given a valid reason for every lie she's confessed to so far. I'm sure she can explain the rest . . . if I ever see her again.*

If Lee had always looked like she does now, then so had the fat man, which meant he definitely couldn't be Roy Milan. He decided to find out how much Larue knew. "Aren't you curious why I asked if your mother was a pretty brunette?"

"No. You obviously met one named Lee Milan when you were in Justified."

"Yes I did, and she told me an interesting tale. She thinks she was once an angel."

Larue gasped and slapped the back of the headrest. "Then you actually met my mother, Clyde! That has to be her—it has to be! I guess she'll never get over that stupid delusion, but I'm glad to hear she hasn't lost her looks."

More proof Lee has always been in the same body, he thought. None of those angels had died since being turned into men and women, therefore not one of them had ever been born and learned what they really were at puberty. But obviously they could reproduce. What sort of creatures did they spawn? Were all of them gifted with special abilities like Larue? He probed further. "Um, I'm inclined to believe her and so is Wyoming."

"Well you shouldn't, that's silly."

"So you don't think you were once an angel?"

A sarcastic laugh flew out. "Of course not."

"Lee told me all her kind become aware of being cast out of heaven and remember all their past lives by the time they become adolescents. Why didn't you?"

"Because I've never been an angel and neither has my mother."

He glanced at Wyoming and saw she was frowning too. "What about your uncle, doesn't he think he was once an angel?"

"Mm mm."

"Did your mom tell you if your dad thought he'd once

been one?"

"I never knew my dad and was never told anything about him. I don't even know his name. My mother wasn't married to him, that's why my last name's Milan like hers."

They cleared the storm and he kicked the speed back up to seventy. Not long thereafter he could read the Turnaton city limits sign.

A few seconds later Larue squealed with joy and shouted, "I'm home at last—I'm home at last!"

Shock made Clyde yank his foot off the accelerator—all the traffic had vanished. He groaned as they entered a suddenly vacant town. Turnaton had turned into Justified. "Well, Wyoming, you wanted proof and here we are. Exactly what do you suggest we take with us to verify our wild tale? Pictures won't do a damn thing. Of course it probably doesn't matter since we may never get out of here."

She gazed at the empty main drag of Justified they were gliding down, moving steadily slower as he still had his foot off the pedal. He didn't bother stopping at any red lights.

"What *should* we do, Clyde?" They were only going twenty by the time she finally answered.

"Haul ass for Odessa . . . if we can."

"Let's take Larue with us. Maybe somebody will listen with three people swearing Justified and Leavenwood exist."

"No, this is where I belong . . .!" the back door flew open and Larue jumped out of the car. The momentum caused him to fall and roll on the pavement, but he quickly got to his feet and took off running.

Clyde braked to a stop and watched him disappear around the corner of a barber shop. "We should go after him. He can't help us convince anybody—they'll only think he's crazy too—but I don't feel right about leaving him in this fucked up town."

A flash of light assaulted his eyes, and Clyde found himself reentering the city limits behind a blue van he'd been tailing before the town uncannily changed.

"My god," Wyoming fearfully muttered, "we're back in Turnaton."

The van made it through the first intersection before the light turned red and he had to stop. "So much for taking Larue back with us, he's in another dimension now. What say we get the hell out of here and forget all about Justified and Leavenwood and the creepy people who live there?"

She grimaced. "What about Robby? He didn't die from a plane crash, he was murdered."

"No. If we weren't lied to, he was justifiably executed."

"How will we ever know if we don't get to the bottom of this?"

"Maybe it's better that we never do . . . ."

Larue kept running until his burning lungs and rubbery legs forced him to stop in a residential area. He wondered where all the people were. With no traffic he'd easily be able to spot Clyde's Malibu before being seen by him or Wyoming, but the empty streets made him very uneasy. By the time his heart quit pounding and he could breathe normally again, adrenaline no longer buffered a burning pain in his left elbow. The pavement had scraped it pretty severely when he'd fallen after making his escape.

Knowing only one way to get to his mother's house, he had to go back to the road where he'd bailed from Clyde's car. If need be, he'd use the buildings for cover and sneak across town behind them. Hopefully Clyde had driven on instead of trying to find him.

A dizzying blur clouded his eyes and when it ceased, vivid memories of his childhood before he'd wandered off flooded his brain: recollections that had lain dormant since he'd left here. This town had but one resident, his mother, and other than Uncle Roy, only two people ever came to visit her—a fat bald man and a hulking negro.

Why hadn't he remembered it before jumping out of Clyde's car? His mother really had once been an angel suffering God's judgment. He'd wandered off during one of his spells all right, but she'd told him he would. She'd been forced to cast him into the real world. The strange awakening assured those sleeping memories had been revived because he'd reentered Justified. He started sobbing through gritted teeth as the horrid recollection of losing his mother painfully crystallized, along with the brutal realities of his situation.

"I'm so sorry, Larue," the woman who'd given him life had spoken with a sorrow-filled voice. "This is the time I've been telling you about—the time I must send you away forever. Those of my kind can't make babies amongst themselves . . . your father was a normal human, that's why you can't live here anymore. I love you too much, son—I shouldn't have kept you here this long. Because I did, the part of me that's in you will make you different than the people you'll be with from now on—you'll be much smarter than most of them. Unfortunately something else is about to happen. You'll feel like you're having a bad dream in which you can hardly think or speak. It will pass and you'll be normal again, but it'll be a reoccurring problem the rest of your life."

At that moment she'd picked him up and hugged him tight, repeatedly kissing his cheek while doing so, then lowered him to his feet as tears poured down her pretty face. "You're about to see a bright light that will soon go away. When it does, you'll be in a different world and won't be able to recall a lot of things that you know now. You'll remember me and your Uncle Roy but no one else you've ever met here, and you'll scoff at the notion of my having ever been an angel. Someone else will finish raising you but you'll never forget that I'm your real mother. I love you, son. God be with you always."

Immediately after she'd bidden him farewell a blinding flash of light had forced his eyes closed. He'd opened them to find himself walking down what appeared to be the same hill she'd taken him to, but his mother was gone, and the first of his many spells had seized him.

Motivated by sheer terror, he started running again. If he didn't get out of Justified very soon his heart would implode. A regular human could dwell in this place as safely as the angels cast down from heaven, but not an offspring of the two after reaching a certain age. Eighteen hundred days after such a baby's birth, the angelic heart fibers started separating from their human counterparts, and the organ would be completely disintegrated within two hours.

That's why he'd been sent away.

Larue glanced at his watch as he ran. "Oh cursed fate, I've already wasted fifteen minutes!"

SEVEN

PILER CREEK POP. 2155, the sign read as they rolled past. Roy's Automotive apparently closed on Sundays, but not the diner where Wyoming had encountered the fat man. It appeared quite busy. Clyde winked at her and said, "Wanna stop for a snack?"

"Sure."

"Not on your life, I was only teasing."

"So was I. The sooner we get out of here the better."

He heaved a big sigh of relief when they motored by the other city limits sign.

⟡

Larue hadn't made it to the edge of town before feeling the effects of his deconstructing heart. He had to take quick shallow breaths to keep from coughing. His lungs refused to work at full capacity and violently rejected any attempt to inhale more than a mouthful of air. Feeling the circulation dwindling in his limbs, he could now barely walk, much less run. A road sign twenty-point-two feet ahead beckoned him. Down that road was a stop sign, and four blocks after turning left there, he'd reach his mother's house.

If she hadn't moved to another one.

That thought clouded his already weakened vision with tears. Justified was patterned exactly like a town occupying the same location in the real world, reflecting even the minutest structural change, and would do so indefinitely. If that town built a new school, one just like it automatically appeared in its ghostly twin. But there were no teachers or students or any other people in Justified besides his mother. Therefore every house or any other building was hers for the taking.

Another cognition had been awakened from dormancy as well. The fat man and negro were the only residents of Leavenwood. That's why his mother had never stopped at Roy Milan's house or auto repair shop—they were mere duplicates of his residence and place of business in the real world, ergo he had to be human, and Larue couldn't help suspecting that Uncle Roy was really his father.

He couldn't quit stewing over that guy and the beautiful blonde. At the time their queries had aggravated him, but he'd woke up this morning with a burning question he wished he'd asked: why had they expected to find their Roy in his place of business?

"What's got you so preoccupied?" asked Matilda, refilling his coffee cup.

"Aw, just wondering about something. A couple dropped by my shop yesterday looking for the owner. When I said that was me, the guy said he thought a fat bald man owned it. Practically accused me of lying to him."

She giggled. "About being the owner, Roy, or bald and fat?"

"You're a laugh a minute, girl. Anyway, then the woman asked me if last Friday was a local holiday because the whole town seemed to be closed down when they drove through."

That put a frown on her face. "Well why in the world would she think that?"

"Don't know."

"Humph, last Friday was no different than any other."

"No, Matilda, it sure wasn't, and that's why her question keeps nagging at me. You didn't shut the diner down for a spell for some reason did you?"

"Mm mm. We opened at six a.m. and closed at ten p.m. same as always. I can't imagine why she'd think everything was closed."

"Me either."

"Well, like they say—it takes all kinds of people to make a world."

He couldn't tell Matilda why the blonde's question bothered him so much. Twenty-one years ago the only woman he'd ever loved had kissed him goodbye after telling him they must forever part. She'd also said certain elements of their time together would vanish from his mind the moment he drove out of . . . whatever the name of that town was that *always* appeared to be closed down.

It lay only twenty miles away, but Turnaton never transformed into it anymore as it had every Friday during those all too few wonderful years, changing back when he went home. She'd taken his surname when she got pregnant, but wouldn't marry him. If she'd ever told him why, he couldn't remember it now—anymore than he could recall her first name, or anything about their son.

His life had been relatively uneventful until the year he turned twenty-five. An announcement came in the mail saying his name had been drawn from a box containing ten thousand others randomly selected across the state. He'd won five hundred dollars, but had to collect it in person at an address in the town whose name he could no longer recollect. The instructions had puzzled him because the route led straight to Turnaton. It wound up being a hoax, but a magnificent one, because *she* had sent the phony prize announcement in order to lure him to her house. The first time he saw her, the doubts he'd developed about ever falling in love and been demolished.

He could vividly remember she'd given him a legitimate reason for not being able to contact him directly, but hadn't retained a single word she'd said about it. He'd spent every weekend at her house and gone home each Monday, letting his help handle things at the shop until he arrived, sometimes well past noon. After their son's first birthday she'd insisted he go home on Saturday mornings. From the night they met until she broke it off, not a single Friday night passed without them making love, yet he couldn't remember any details about their sex life.

Rapidly losing all coordination, Larue stumbled across the front yard, and barely managed to ring the doorbell before collapsing on the porch. He heard the door open and a woman shriek, but couldn't open his eyes to verify it came from his mother . . . .

Clyde's concern over what she'd thought to be a drunken bum staggering along the bar ditch had surprised her. He'd even been willing to drive Larue home without knowing how inconvenient or expensive the offer might turn out to be. Wyoming couldn't help admiring him for it. Like every man who didn't prefer boys, he'd made goo-goo eyes at her from the start. Flirty, a bit conceited, far too complimentary, insincerely attentive, she'd pegged him as a shallow womanizer.

He'd been lost in thought since they left Piler Creek, and probably assumed the same thing occupied her mind—the fate of Larue. While she certainly hoped he'd be okay, and Lee would accept him, she'd been analyzing Clyde while gazing at the road ahead. Men were easy creatures to read, and she'd never failed to correctly assess any guy's true nature early on, but something told her she might have finally misjudged one.

Larue could hear his mother weepingly shout instructions to someone, but still couldn't open his eyes to see who. It was as if his numb lids had been sewn together, as well as his unfeeling lips.

"We've got to get him out of here—it may already be too late!"

He felt motion . . . someone had draped him over their shoulder and was carrying him.

"Oh, son," his mother cried from behind him, "you shouldn't have come back. I realize you couldn't remember while on the other side, but you shouldn't have come back. If you survive this, whatever you do don't go anywhere near Turnaton or Piler Creek ever again. Your presence will cause them to transform into Justified and Leavenwood. It's going to be very difficult for you to remember this warning when you get back to the other side, so keep repeating it in your mind over and over and over, and don't stop."

Don't go near Turnaton or Piler Creek, he told himself at her command. *Don't go near Turnaton or Piler Creek. Don't go near Turnaton or Piler Creek . . . .*

"Hang on, son, don't give up! If we can get you back on

the other side in time, your heart will be normal again!" A deep sob escaped her. "Hold on, Larue, please hold on . . . !"

EIGHT

CLYDE PULLED INTO a restaurant parking lot in Brownwood at a quarter till two. They were halfway home and more than ready for lunch. Stopping to pick up Larue and having to slow down during the thunderstorm had impeded their progress. He'd planned to make it this far by one at the latest.

A smiling waitress said, "Seat yourselves," and followed them as they selected a table. He ordered a cheeseburger, fries, and coffee. Wyoming requested a chicken salad sandwich and iced tea.

"Pretty remarkable coincidence we ran across Lee's son, don't you think?" he asked.

Wyoming nodded. "Maybe Lee arranged it."

"Maybe so. No telling what she and her allies can do. I wonder why she lied to me about living so many lives?"

"Who knows?"

"And about being infertile."

"No telling . . ." a glint of fear rose in Wyoming's big blue eyes. "I just hope she didn't lie about Robby being a child killer, because if she did—"

"Then she's a devil not an angel."

"Exactly, Clyde."

Roy tossed his golf clubs in the back of his pickup and started for Turnaton. The golf course only had nine holes, but that beat the hell out of Piler Creek's driving range. When he passed his shop, the guy and blonde invaded his thoughts again. They'd had an investigative air about them, and he wouldn't be surprised if whoever they were looking for was selling drugs or contraband. What gave them the idea they might find the guy in his garage he'd never know, but the bigger question was why they'd thought Piler Creek had shut down last Friday.

He'd never get over that woman who lived in another world, yet he couldn't even remember her first name. She'd seen to that—had to have—but why? Her beautiful brown eyes and gorgeous face were as vivid in his memory now as the last time he'd seen them. So was her fantastic body, and yet he couldn't recall anything about the texture of her breasts, even though his hands had been on them countless times. What had it felt like when he'd made love to her? Why hadn't she let him retain those memories, or at least let him remember what it had been like to kiss those pretty lips?

"Did you grow up in Odessa?"

"Mm hmm."

Wyoming already knew he had, having overheard one of the cashier's mention it. She wanted to know more about Clyde without appearing too curious, so she'd started with that innocent question. He seemed far more interested in his food than why she'd asked, so she forged ahead. "Have you always been single?"

"Yeah."

"Never met the right girl, huh?"

He laughed. "There's no such thing for me. I'm definitely not looking to start a family. I've got five nieces and three nephews that satisfy my hankering for kids. I get to spoil them and hand them off. My brother and two sisters hate me for it—not to mention their spouses."

That hit a nerve. She only saw her siblings' children at Christmas, and had never gotten close to any of them. Her parents insisted on having all the family together then, and the routine never varied. Christmas morning everyone had a good time—opening presents, catching up on each other's activities, and watching the kids play with their toys. The yuletide cheer lasted until after the noon feast, at which time her mother would start drinking. By mid afternoon she'd be blitzed and start in on her father. Their arguing would escalate into an obscene verbal brawl and her siblings would join in, choosing sides, and she always left crying at that point—swearing she'd never go back to that ancient doublewide with its nicotine-stained walls.

Roy hit the brakes and skidded to a stop on a horizontal stretch of pavement that formed a ledge between the steep upper and lower inclines of the Turnaton side of the hill leading into town. A cattle truck had rammed a Ford sedan. It lay on its side across the middle of the road with the drive wheel still spinning. He got out of his pickup and trotted to the car, where the truck driver stood, sadly shaking his head while lowering a cell phone.

The airbags hadn't deployed, but a seatbelt had kept a dazzling unconscious redhead from falling to the passenger door. There weren't any cuts or abrasions on her pretty face, and he could tell she was breathing normally by the rhythmic movement of her large breasts. She'd evidently rolled her window down before the crash because he didn't see any broken glass. The windshield and other windows were still intact. He reached inside and killed the engine.

A square jawed Mexican with a Kirk Douglas dimple on his chin, and a dazed look on his face, the truck driver explained what happened: "She veered right like she was pulling off the road, then suddenly tried to make a u-turn. I don't know why she didn't see me. If I hadn't been trudging uphill with a full load there's no telling how bad this would have been. I almost managed to stop in time—just a few more feet and I would have. As you can see, I hardly dented the side of her car, but it popped over on its side anyway. I called the police. Help should get here any second."

As if being cued, sirens announced an approaching ambulance, followed by a squad car.

"How old are you, Clyde?"

"Thirty-nine. Why do you ask?"

Disappointment replaced her curiosity. "Just wondering."

He pulled out his wallet and left a five dollar tip, two thirds the price of his meal. She felt that was far too much and tried to leave fifty cents for her end, but Clyde said, "Keep it. I'm picking up the tab and tipping for both of us . . . ."

When they got back in the car she opened her purse, fished out a hairbrush under the pretext of intending to comb her hair, and purposely dropped it next to Clyde. "Whoops, how clumsy of me."

He seemed oblivious as to why she'd leaned over to pick it up with her right hand instead of logically retrieving it with her left. Studying his profile as he turned the ignition, she inhaled an exhilarating whiff of his musk. It turned her on again, as it had at Kelly's when he'd held her after she'd broken down over Robby. Nonetheless, she couldn't get over him being thirty-nine. She'd thought he couldn't be any older than thirty-five, perhaps even as young as thirty-three. Older guys didn't put her off, she'd dated plenty of them, but the idea of going out with one on the verge of turning forty repulsed her.

❧

The redhead woke up before a policeman and the medical team got out of their vehicles. She glanced around with a confused glaze in her eyes that evaporated once she'd assessed the situation. Then she swung her right leg as gracefully as a ballerina, planted her foot on the passenger door, and unbuckled her seatbelt.

"You shouldn't move, lady," the truck driver cautioned.

"I'm not injured, I just fainted." She proceeded to climb out the window.

Roy helped her down and thoroughly enjoyed doing it. The woman had a great body.

The cop walked up. "Are you all right, ma'am?"

"Yeah, I'm fine."

"Good. Tell me what happened."

"A car seemed to just suddenly appear right in front of me. I didn't dare try to pass because somebody could have been coming over the hill in the other lane, so I hit the brakes and cut right to keep from rear-ending it, but the driver did the same thing, so I had no choice but to make a hard left or I'd have driven through the guardrail—" she pointed towards a deep ravine running alongside the lane she'd been driving down. "Then I saw the truck and passed out because I thought I was about to die."

The truck driver verified her actions but never saw the car.

"How about you, sir? Did you see the vehicle she's talking about?"

Roy shook his head.

"We'll get back to this in a minute. Right now we need to clear the road. I'll need every man here to help me."

The medical team helped them push the Ford back onto its wheels, and left while the cop drove it off the highway, having to crawl across the seat from the passenger's side because the driver's door wouldn't open. He came back holding his ticket book. "What's your name, ma'am?"

"Blinda Love."

"Well, Belinda, I'm citing you for negligent collision. I'll need your license, registration, and insurance card."

"It's Blinda, not Belinda. I'll have to get my purse . . . ."

Roy felt bad for the lady, but there couldn't have been another car or he and the truck driver would have seen it.

When the cop drove off and the truck driver continued his journey, Roy handed her a business card. "I can get those dents out of your car at a reasonable price, ma'am. My name's Roy Milan, I own Roy's Automotive in Piler Creek. We do body work as well as engine repair."

She accepted it with a smile. "Thanks, Roy. If my insurance company allows me to pick my own repairman I'll certainly consider it."

"They can't tell you where to take your car."

"Oh? I didn't know. I've never been involved in an accident before."

You're damn lucky to have survived your first one, he thought. "I'll beat the cheapest rate you can find by five percent. Well I'll be on my way. Drive safely, ma'am."

When he reached his pickup she hollered, "Hey, please wait a minute!"

He turned around.

"Would you mind following me home? It's not far—I live right here in Turnaton. I'll make you a nice dinner for your trouble."

He'd like nothing more than to oblige her, but she was worrying needlessly. "Your car will make it just fine, ma'am, the crash didn't affect the engine or drive train."

"That's not the reason I'm asking," she nervously relayed. "I'm afraid to be alone right now because I know I didn't imagine that car."

She looked more confused than scared. He didn't know what to say.

"Look, I'm not crazy—that car just suddenly appeared right in front of me, and since you didn't see it, it had to have disappeared." She made a sour face and wearily shook her head. "You must think I'm a loon."

"I think your eyes were playing tricks on you, that's all." He meant it.

"No, that car was really there. Something very odd is going on because a man and woman came to my house yesterday, thinking they'd been there the night before, but it wasn't my home they went to. They'd gone to one just like it—same address and everything—only it wasn't in Turnaton. They found it in a town named Justified that they . . . ."

"That they what, ma'am?"

"Swear occupies the exact same ground as Turnaton."

His adrenal glands had started working the second she'd asked if he'd follow her home, but that statement kicked them into high gear.

"Dammit, what's taking Hoyt so long?" Larue heard his mother say. "He's bound to have gotten the message by now."

"You might as well chill," said the man who'd carried him here. "Anxiousness won't help the situation."

"Larue *would* have to show up on a Sunday."

"Yeah, tough break. And Hoyt *would* decide to head home fifteen minutes before he did."

He'd been lowered onto his back on a soft patch of earth. Though his will to live kept steadily ebbing, more memories of being sent away as a child were rapidly returning. He suddenly recalled the negro and fat man had been standing behind his mother when she'd told him goodbye. It took the concentration of all three of them to open the gateway to the other side. While that part of his mind continued delving into the past, he kept repeating *Don't go near Turnaton or Piler Creek.*

More memories returned: the fat man's name was Hoyt and the negro went by Earl. His mother could have summoned them with her mind and they'd have instantly appeared, had this been any day of the week but Sunday. When the sun rose on that day, they were as mortal as normal humans until Monday dawned. She'd left an urgent message on Hoyt's answering machine to meet her and Earl at the golf course. The gateway lay on the summit of a hill just north of it. In their world none of them could climb that hill without the other two accompanying them—an invisible barrier prevented it. Only landline telephones worked in this world, cell phones were useless, so if Hoyt hadn't listened to that message on his machine at least twenty minutes ago, Larue knew he was done for.

Severe pain radiated from the center of his chest, and he could barely breathe at all. He wished he could tell his mother goodbye, but couldn't even open his eyes, much less speak.

She once again reminded him to keep repeating the warning.

Larue did so, despite knowing his heart would give out any second. It wouldn't do to face God with the sin of disobeying his mother freshly recorded as his last earthly act.

Blinda hoped Roy Milan didn't think she'd been coming on to him. A glance at the rearview mirror revealed he wore a smile on his face. The light turned green before she reached the intersection. She slowed down, coasted left around the corner, and another quick look to the rear verified he hadn't changed his mind about following her home.

Clyde Burns had told her he thought Justified lay in a different dimension but otherwise mirrored Turnaton to the letter. She'd politely agreed that explanation made as much sense as any, while inwardly rejecting the notion. But the moment that car appeared from out of nowhere, she knew Clyde's hypothesis to be a fact. The driver must have slipped back to his proper domain immediately after she'd been forced to turn left, since neither the truck driver nor Roy had seen the vehicle.

"We've got a motherfucker of a problem, guys."

"Hoyt! Thank God you're here! Hurry, we've got to get my son to the gateway right now!"

Larue once again felt himself being heaved across a shoulder. He figured out it was Earl when Hoyt spoke again from several feet away.

"Something got fucked up on my way home—for a few seconds I was on the other side and a lady saw me. She nearly rammed my trunk we were so close. Damn this motherfucking pathway is steep! Anyway, what the fuck do you think happened?"

"I don't know," said his mother. "Do you suppose we're nearing the end of our sentence at last and the barrier's weakening because of it?"

"Nah, we couldn't be that fucking lucky. What do you think, Earl?"

"Maybe Lee's extreme anxiety over Larue, and my frustration that you'd picked a real bad time to go home caused some sort of rip in the dimensional fabric."

"Maybe so," his mother agreed.

Or maybe, thought Larue, wishing he could voice it, *my coming back caused the rip. Don't go near Turnaton or Piler Creek. Don't go near Turnaton or Piler Creek. Don't go near Turnaton or Piler Creek* . . . .

Survival instinct drove him to keep repeating the warning, but he could feel his life slipping away.

"I'm glad you finally decided to get your tubes tied, Lee— we don't need this kind of shit. I'll bet that surgeon is still mad over finding out he was brought here to cut you open instead of rolling in the hay with you. Good thing he didn't know I was only bluffing when I threatened to blow his head off if he didn't. Earl made a damn good nurse, didn't he? Wonder how your daughter's faring on the other side. Let's hope she doesn't wind up here someday too, unlikely as that would be."

I've got a sister?! Larue wished Hoyt would continue and give some details about her, but the next words he heard came from his mother.

"That would be a nightmare but thankfully, very unlikely to happen as you say. I don't ever want to go through this again. Keep repeating the warning, son, we're almost there."

Soon after she said that, Earl gently laid him on the ground.

"All glory to God, we got here just in time!"

N-No, Mother . . . I'm afraid you d-didn't. Larue could no longer breathe—his lungs had stopped functioning.

"Goodbye again, son. Make sure this is the last one, and God be with you always . . . ."

☙❈❧

Wyoming's personal questions had gotten his hopes up, but she hadn't wanted to know anything else about him after asking his age. Her lack of interest could only mean one thing. On the bright side, at least he'd learned their age difference negated any possibility of her saying yes to a date before he'd gotten the nerve to make his move. They'd reach San Angelo soon, and less than three hours from there he'd be dropping her off, never to be alone with the stacked blonde again.

Maybe I'll give Blinda Love a call. We could meet up at Fort Worth and have a big ball in Cow Town, or maybe she'd even be willing to come to Odessa if I've sparked her interest. I'm damn sure not going back to Turnaton.

Lee Milan would never be anything more than an online friend from now on. At least he prayed that'd be the case, because he couldn't prevent her from spiriting him to Justified again through a dream if she chose to. He'd still love to bone the gorgeous brunette, but feared pursuing her might cost him his sanity.

☙❈❧

Blinda waited on the porch as Roy parked and got out of his pickup. He must have been a handsome devil before succumbing to middle age, she thought. If not for the wrinkles surrounding his care-worn eyes, and a bit of turkey skin softening his strong chin, he still would be. His brown hair didn't appear to be thinning, and a touch of gray on the sides enhanced his confident, yet humble manner. "I hope I haven't detained you from something important."

"Nah," he said, making his way up the walk, "I was just heading for the other side of town to wile away the afternoon on the golf course."

She unlocked her front door and welcomed him inside. "Would you like some lemonade?"

"Sure."

"It's a lovely day, we'll drink it on the patio."

They were sitting at a lawn table in Blinda Love's backyard. A pitcher of cold lemonade and a plate of oatmeal cookies adorned the center.

"I know you must find my tale very hard to believe, Roy."

"No I don't . . ." he took a sip from his glass and braced himself for her reaction. "I've been to the town that couple spoke of, many times."

Her eyes practically doubled in size. "You have?"

"Yeah. There really is an invisible town that looks just like Turnaton, sitting right where Turnaton does. You're the only person I've ever told. I can't remember its name because the woman that enabled me to enter that world did something to my memory when she broke up with me. I can't remember her name, what her house looks like, or even what part of town it's in. Twenty-one years have gone by since I last saw her."

Blinda leaned forward and rested her chin on her hands, fascination riveted to her face. "How did you get there?"

"I just drove to Turnaton every Friday evening and that town would be there instead. No matter how often I made the trip any other time, I always wound up in Turnaton." He told her about the phony grand prize that had brought him there initially.

"And you can't remember anything about her?"

"Oh I'll never forget what she looked like . . . the smell of her perfume . . . how happy I was."

"Sounds like you were in love with her."

He nodded and downed some more lemonade.

"That couple I told you about mentioned another town I'd never heard of called Leavenwood."

"That makes two of us."

"It apparently coexists with Piler Creek . . ." she bit into a cookie.

Hearing that, made it all click. "That couple—the woman's a good looking blonde, isn't she."

Blinda stopped chewing and narrowed her eyes. "Why yes she is. How did you know?"

"That explains why the guy thought I was fudging about being the owner."

"Excuse me?"

"Sorry, sort of talking to myself there. A guy and a blonde came in my shop yesterday, asking some peculiar questions. Now I think I know why. They're bound to be the same couple that came to see you."

"Ah, home at last." Clyde turned right from the interstate

exit road. Ten minutes later they were at Wyoming's apartment.

She unbuckled the seatbelt and stretched her arms. "I've got a leftover pizza in the fridge with only two pieces missing if you're interested."

"Sounds good if we're not talking store bought."

"Mm mm, restaurant made."

"Then by all means, lead the way."

He'd never been in her apartment before—she'd been outside waiting for him when he picked her up yesterday. Knowing what every employee earned, since he cut every paycheck Thornton Kelly signed, it surprised him to see she lived in an efficiency. Wyoming made an excessive amount for such a rather easily staffed position.

"Not what you expected is it, Clyde."

"Um, to be honest, not even close."

She let out a short laugh. "This may surprise you, but I'm no spendthrift. I bank every dollar I can because I've only got me to depend on the rest of my life."

"Smart girl." He started rubbing his belly. "Now then, about that pizza."

"Have a seat at the table and I'll nuke it."

"Got any beer?"

"Yeah, Robby always keeps a case in the—" her face dropped and she started crying. "Oh, Clyde!"

Once again she flung herself into his arms, crushing her breasts against him as tears dribbled onto his shoulder. The wild sensation of her midsection merging with his, gave him a hard on. Wyoming had to feel his crotch bulging, but instead of backing off as he expected, she pressed harder. Unable to resist the temptation when she did that, he grabbed her butt with both hands and pulled.

She reared her head back, gave him a hot teary-eyed stare, then assaulted his mouth with a passionate kiss, that he ravenously returned.

❦

"Next stop, Callaway's Research Complex."

"No, I won't go back there! No! No! No!" His eyes popped open. "I-I'm breathing . . . I'm breathing . . . *I'M BREATHING!*"

"Hey, mister, are you all right?"

Larue raised his head to see a little boy walking towards him. He glanced around and saw he lay on a hill. It took him a moment to recall he'd been suffering one of his spells and had come out of it while sleeping, to find himself locked in a nightmare. He'd been the only passenger on a train, and the conductor had been instructed to drop him off at the cursed think tank.

He clearly remembered that before losing coherency his lungs had completely shut down and the icy fingers of death were wrapped around his heart, squeezing it into a useless pulp. Thank God that had only been a bad dream too.

NINE

HE PULLED HIS lips from Wyoming's and freed himself from her embrace. "I can't do this."

"W-Why?" she stammered, confusion blazing in her shocked eyes.

"Because you're too vulnerable right now. Gawd I can't believe I'm saying this—if you only knew how many times I've dreamed of this happening, you couldn't imagine it either—but I just can't go through with it. I'd be taking unfair advantage of a tragic situation."

She stood there gaping at him, aroused features dripping with disbelief, breasts heaving as she panted for air. "But I want you to."

"Goodnight, Wyoming." He hurried for the door, knowing he couldn't keep from ravishing her if she said those words again.

"Clyde!"

He closed it behind him and took a deep breath. *Have I lost my fucking mind? No, get the hell out of here, that's what I've gotta do.*

Wyoming came outside as he started the car. She waved for him to come back, but he hit the gas and sped away.

Lee Milan's name came off the marquee. Once again Wyoming assumed the starring role of his fantasies, and he'd never be able to fall asleep tonight without masturbating over what might have been. He knew he'd blown his only chance to share her bed, but that didn't bother him as much as the thought of seeing the disgust on her face in the morning if they had screwed. Everything that motivated her now would be long gone by then, and she'd be asking herself if she'd lost *her* fucking mind.

༄

Roy enjoyed two helpings of Blinda Love's shrimp gumbo before finally calling it quits. He wondered why she hadn't just called a friend to keep from being alone, instead of practically begging a total stranger to follow her home.

"Would you like some dessert?"

"Sure," he answered without thinking.

"You have two choices, pineapple upside down cake or lemon pie."

"Uh, on second thought I'd better pass. Didn't leave enough room."

She cleared the table, poured them each a cup of coffee, and retook her seat. "Forgive me for not thinking to ask long before now, but do you smoke?"

"No."

"Me either, but I was going to fetch an ashtray if you did. I'm not one of those pompous people who refuse to allow smoking in their homes."

That made him smile. "Neither am I. My dad always has a cigarette in his hand."

"Sounds like my mother. So your father lives with you?"

"No, I live alone but he visits a lot."

She sighed. "My daddy hasn't visited me since I moved here from Amarillo. He can't handle the long drive and won't get on a plane, so my mom always has to come by herself."

"Is that where your parents live?"

"Mm hmm. I drive up there every Thanksgiving and stay through Christmas. I wonder if they celebrate holidays in that invisible town?"

He shrugged and raised his cup.

"It's a shame you can't remember more about it, Roy. I find this whole thing so fascinating. How many people do you suppose know about it?"

"Couldn't say, but I doubt very many. Reckon that couple will ever come see you again?"

"Clyde and Wyoming? Probably not."

"Well if they ever do, please call me. I'd like to talk to them."

"Oh you can call *them* if you want, Roy. They live in Odessa and I know their last names."

"I spent twelve-fifty plus tax on this pocketknife but that's the rest of it." Larue handed the stolen cash to J.T. Glade, along with the implement he'd used to chop up the debit cards.

Following a hunch they'd find him here, Mother had taken the scientist to the hill where she'd first laid eyes on him twenty-one years ago. He had no recollection of coming to this location. The last thing he remembered clearly besides the two nightmares was riding in the back seat of Clyde's Malibu. He'd started downhill with the little boy, and J.T. had spotted him. Shame had compelled him to confess his pickpocket caper immediately.

"Don't worry, Larue, you won't be prosecuted."

He resented the smugness on J.T.'s face. "Of course not. You can't probe my brain if they put me in jail, can you."

"You watch your mouth, boy!" shouted Mother. "One more impudent remark out of you and I'll wash it out with soap."

J.T. donned a concerned frown. "How'd you hurt your elbow, Larue? That's a nasty looking scrape."

"Don't know. It must have happened during my mindless spell. I'd had another one a few hours before, and came out of it in the backseat of a Malibu with a man and woman in front. Their names are Clyde Burns and Wyoming Carter. They live in Odessa and you need to call them because there's got to be a way to get me back home. They've been to Justified." Something stabbed at the back of his brain when he said that—a sensation so strong it made him dizzy.

And afraid.

Wyoming sat staring at a slice of pepperoni pizza she was holding in front of her face with both hands. She'd only taken one bite and several minutes had passed since. Thoughts of Clyde held her spellbound.

Once the initial sensation of being grossed out over his age passed, she'd realized something about him made her feel safe and secure. When his musk filled her nose as she'd cried on his shoulder Friday morning, a peculiar sensation had come over her, for it possessed an aphrodisiacal quality. That smell had extremely aroused her while titillating her nostrils in her kitchen, but it was the way he'd returned her kiss that kept her idly gazing at the pizza.

Only a very special man could have pulled away, when he'd so obviously yearned to keep his lips melded to hers. She knew he'd wanted to rip her clothes off and make love to her right there on the kitchen floor—and he'd known she'd been his for the taking—yet for her sake, Clyde had chivalrously forced himself not to take advantage, displaying the most remarkable strength of character she'd ever witnessed.

Savoring a close-up view of Blinda's bosom as she refilled his cup, Roy asked where she'd intended to go before the accident.

"Piler Creek. Those cookies we ate on the patio came from that bakery on Main Street. I was going there to pick up some biscuit dough."

"Oh, I figured you made those cookies."

"I wish." She set down and took a quick sip of coffee. "That cake and pie I offered you for dessert came from there as well. I love their biscuits. All I have to do is preheat the oven to four-fifty, place the preformed dough on an un-greased cookie sheet, slide it in, set the timer for thirteen minutes, and I'm set for the work week. There're ten to a batch, and I eat two with honey for breakfast every weekday morning. They keep so well, twenty seconds in the microwave makes them taste oven fresh. I've never bought anything from there that wasn't exceptional. I don't know why they don't open Saturdays and close Sundays instead."

He grinned. "It's owned by a Jewish family, very devout."

"Ah, that explains it. I've never seen that pretty teenager who works there without a Star of David necklace around her neck, but I thought it was merely ornamental because she wears so many others with it."

The pretty girl she mentioned was the youngest of four children born to Ezra and Liat Gold. They'd successfully raised three upstanding sons and their daughter Shayna would be graduating with honors soon. She went with his lead mechanic Hal Turner's younger brother, and he'd overheard Hal giving the boy advice on the correct procedure for pleasuring a girl through oral sex. It had really ruffled his feathers because he'd known those kids all their lives, and couldn't picture them doing anything more serious than kissing. "So you drop by there every Sunday?"

"Mm hmm. Last Friday I had to deliver a notice to a farmer who lives halfway between Piler Creek and College Station, so I picked up the pie and cake for a weekend splurge when I drove back through. I bought the cookies when I picked up last week's biscuit dough."

"What do you do?"

"I'm a process server."

"What's that?"

"Someone who personally delivers a procedural notice requiring a signature. Most times it's for a collection agency who fails to get payment for an overdue credit card debt. It can really get unpleasant at times—especially when I've been given the wrong address. I hate having to put my foot down when someone refuses to sign, but I won't back off until they do. Thankfully that doesn't happen very often. I enjoy driving, and usually the people I serve are polite about it."

He couldn't imagine this nice lady acting like a bitch for the sake of a collection agency, but could easily envision her being a hot one in the sack. "When did you move here from Amarillo?"

"Three years ago after a nasty divorce. My ex-husband tried to screw me out of everything, but my attorney saved the day and I walked out of that marriage with enough money to pay cash for this house and stash a tidy sum in a savings account."

"What brought you to Turnaton?"

"Would you believe a dart?" she answered with an embarrassed grin.

"A dart?"

"Yeah. I wanted a brand new start far away from my ex in

a town I'd never been to before, but it had to be in Texas. So I pinned a state map to the wall, took five steps backwards, and threw a dart—aiming at the lower east side because I'd been all over Texas except that one area."

"And it landed on Turnaton."

"Nope, Houston. But there was no way I wanted to live there—it's far too big a city for me. So I threw the dart again."

"Ah, then it hit Turnaton."

"Uh-uh, Piler Creek, dead center on the dot representing it. I drove down, got a motel room, and looked around town. I didn't see any FOR SALE signs, so I decided to call a realtor. There weren't any listed in Piler Creek so I called one in Turnaton. There were only three houses available and I didn't like any of them, so she showed me a brochure of what Turnaton had to offer. The moment I saw the picture of this house I told her I wanted to check it out, and it was love at first sight. That's how I wound up in Turnaton."

He swallowed a sip of coffee and smiled. "Well, sounds like it all worked out for you."

"Oh yes. I love it here, only . . . ."

"Only what?"

"I've made friends with several ladies, but haven't met a guy I feel close to. Oh I've been on several dates since I moved here, but haven't gone out with the same man twice, even though they all keep asking me to. Vibes weren't right, know what I mean?"

"Mm hmm."

"Anyway, enough about me. Tell me about you, Roy?"

He shrugged. "You already know the highlights. Not much to tell beyond that."

"When did you move to Piler Creek?"

"Grew up there, and have never lived anywhere else."

She daubed the corners of her sexy mouth with the tip of her right middle finger, somehow not scratching her face with the pointed red nail. "What about the other women in your life, besides the one you told me about?"

"I sometimes take in a movie or go bowling with the gal who runs Tyner's Diner on Main Street."

"What's her name?"

"Matilda Tyner. She was born and raised in Piler Creek too. Neither of us had a steady during high school, so we'd go to all the dances together and I'd take her home, but we pretty much went our separate ways in between, dancing with whoever we wanted."

"Is it a serious relationship now?"

He chuckled. Matilda would have too if she'd been there. "No. We have an unspoken agreement to use each other that started way back then and has continued since."

"So you sleep with her?"

"Mm hmm, but don't get the wrong idea—we're not lovers. We only use each other to let off steam when we both happen to have a head full of it at the same time. I called a hiatus during my time with the woman I told you about. Matilda was a good sport and never asked me her name or where she lived, so I never broke the promise I made to the woman not to tell anybody. Of course there's no danger of my doing that now, since I can't remember.

"When I got past the horrible early stages of a broken heart, I called Matilda and asked if she'd like a party partner—that's the term we sometimes use to see if the other's in the mood—and we picked up where we left off. It would've surprised me if she'd said no because it had been a five year drought for her. You see, she's never had sex with anyone else, and other than the woman who devastated me, neither have I."

Blinda gasped. "My god, that poor woman must be madly in love with you, Roy. Shame on you for using her like that."

Her indignation made him laugh. "No, no. Matilda *is* madly in love but not with me. There was a boy our age who stole her heart when we were sophomores, and she's never gotten over him, and won't until she's pushing up daisies. When we um, do it, she never cries out my name, only his. You see, she pretends it's him she's with."

"Well that's just sick." Her shocked expression revealed any sympathy she'd felt for Matilda had turned to revulsion.

"Yeah, from your perspective it sure must seem so. But it helps Matilda deal with the pain and . . . one other thing too of course. And it helps me deal with that other thing. Matilda started the ball rolling and asked if I'd pretend to be him. You see, we'd always confided everything to one another—I never told any of my male friends half the stuff I'd freely spout out to her, and still do except about the woman I fell in love with. Same with her. None of her girlfriends know a fraction of the things she's told me. We've always been close that way. Matilda was one of the prettiest girls in school and thought I was cute, but for some reason there're no sparks between us. Other than when we, you know.

"Anyway, the first time was a rough experience for both of us, but we tried it again a few weeks later, and before long it became a routine part of our lives. Along the way we learned how to please each other real well. When it's over, it's like we've done nothing more intimate than play a game of checkers."

That seemed to mollify her. She took a sip of coffee and leaned forward, still holding the cup. "What happened between her and the guy she's so crazy about? She didn't strike his fancy or what?"

"Far from it." His insides twitched with remorse as that life changing event resurfaced full force. "She asked me to tell him I suspected she liked him. You see, he was real shy and Matilda hoped that might encourage him to call her. She was too scared to approach him herself because she knew if he rejected her she'd be scarred for life. Anyway, I just flat out told him Matilda thought he'd hung the moon. The guy got so excited he left a bruise on my back from pounding it in gratitude for me telling him. He called her right away and asked her to the movies, but he and another boy in our school got killed in a dune buggy accident before he could keep that date."

Blinda's eyes turned misty. She set the cup down, leaned back in her chair, and folded her arms beneath her bulging breasts, that had been tempting him since he'd first laid eyes on her. "That's one of the saddest stories I've ever heard. If you're so sexually compatible, how have the two of you kept from falling in love?"

"The magic just isn't there for us, and we both know it never will be. We're best friends, but neither of us feel those vibes you spoke of."

She gazed at him for a thoughtful moment and said, "Am I to assume you'd stop having sex with her if you had feelings for someone else, like you did while seeing that woman in the invisible town?"

He nodded. "Matilda knows that too. Believe it or not she's rooting for me to find someone special again—we both want the best for each other. But twenty-six years have rolled by since I fell in love with that woman in the invisible town, and I haven't fallen for anyone since, so I'm not really expecting another visit from cupid. What drove you and your ex apart?"

⌘

Clyde had been sitting at his computer since wolfing down a pressed ham sandwich right after he got home. He'd read Lee's email again—the one she'd sent Friday morning saying he'd receive further verification soon—and then started searching for Blinda Love. She wasn't on any social network or the adults only site where he'd met Lee. The White Pages had her listed as S. Blinda Love and showed her age range in parenthesis. She was somewhere between thirty-six and forty.

⌒∽✦∾⌒

Blinda didn't want to dodge Roy's question, but decided to put it in a nutshell to keep from boring him. "We just fell out of love."

He gave her a sad smile. "I didn't know that could happen. I always figured once you fell for somebody you loved them for life."

"Well, for all I know that may be true. I'm not sure now that I wasn't merely infatuated with him. He's handsome, witty, charming, and *very* well off, but he's a real prankster—loves to pull off unique practical jokes, and doesn't know where to draw the line. I got tired of never knowing if he was serious or not, and that marked the beginning of the end for me. We started arguing over the silliest things and went to bed angry so often we hardly ever made love anymore.

"He wouldn't let me get a job and it got to where I dreaded him coming home from work. And by then I'd gotten bored being a mere housewife. He started finding fault with everything I did, and before long the beautiful house he bought for us to live in as a present for me our first Christmas together became a war zone. Neither of us wanted kids. When I got to know the real him, I discovered that was about the only thing we'd ever actually had in common."

CRAWO

Larue left the infirmary with his banged up elbow neatly bandaged. Tabitha greeted him in the hall. He frowned at her. "Were you aware no ATM would permit a second maximum withdrawal for twenty-four hours?"

She grinned and nodded.

"Why didn't you tell me?"

"Would it have made any difference?"

"Yeah, I'd have made the proper plans for such a contingency. You wanted me to get caught, didn't you."

The smile turned into an incensed smirk. "Larue, if I'd wanted you to get caught I'd have told somebody what you were up to. I'll admit I don't want you to leave, but I would never rat you out, silly. Where's my mask?"

"I cut it all to pieces."

"Dammit, Larue, you had no right to do that!"

"How can you say that?" he smugly retaliated. "If you weren't expecting me to get caught as you claim, then you'd have never seen it again anyway."

"I never said I didn't expect you to get caught, because I did. You owe me twenty-four dollars, that's what I paid for it."

CRAWO

"It's nearly ten," said Roy, looking at his watch. "Suppose I should head home."

After she'd told him about her marital breakdown, they'd chatted for almost two hours, and Blinda didn't want him to leave until he absolutely had to. "Do you have to go so soon?"

"No, but tomorrow's a work day so I figured you might be ready to call it a night."

"Mm mm, I'm a night owl, so unless you're tired, please stay a while longer, Roy. It's so nice to enjoy the company of a man again."

A charming grin crossed his face. "In that case, could I have a piece of that pineapple upside down cake? I'm getting a little hungry."

"Of course," she giddily replied. "Think I'll have some as well. I've developed a case of the munchies too."

"Oh yes, Clyde, fuck me! Oh god keep fucking me! Faster! Faster!" Hand moving ninety miles an hour, he pumped his load onto his stomach and sighed as Wyoming finally vanished from his mind's eye.

He reached for the tissue box on his nightstand, wiped away the jism, tossed the soiled paper on the floor to be picked up in the morning, and went to sleep.

TEN

SHAYNA DIDN'T WANT to go to school. She'd drank a bottle of cough syrup before going to bed, and the codeine had produced the most wonderful dreams—all of them in brilliant color and extremely vivid—but she'd woke up groggy from the aftereffects. She wearily swung her legs off the bed and sat there for awhile, holding her cloudy head in her hands, thinking how she thoroughly hated Monday mornings. When she finally got her bearings, she ignited some incense to hide the smell of hashish, loaded her one-hitter, and lit up. She wanted to smoke a whole pipe, but wouldn't have been able to maintain. If Papa ever found out she got high, he'd beat her with his belt like a redheaded stepchild, with Mama screaming at her in Yiddish until his arm gave out. Then she'd get her spanking paddle out of the closet and take over, while Papa bellowed his lecture.

Feeling a bit less sluggish, Shayna washed her face and brushed her teeth. Blessed with an unblemished swarthy complexion, she had no need for makeup. Her long eyelashes were so thick and dark, mascara or eyeliner only cheapened the beauty of her large hazel-blue eyes. She dabbed a little gloss on her lips to make them shine, then combed her long, straight golden-brown hair—the color a mix of Papa's blonde curls and Mama's dark tresses. Her features pleased her, for they drew admiring glances from everybody, regardless of age or gender—but she hated her height and tiny boobs. Mama had a beautiful full figure and a statuesque altitude of sixty-seven inches, but she'd stopped growing at five-one and an A Cup. Now almost eighteen, there was no hope of growing taller or her tits getting any bigger unless, God forbid, she should get fat. A boob job was out of the question—she'd have nothing artificial beneath her skin. She felt women with breast implants might as well have LOSER tattooed on their foreheads, except for those needing reconstructive surgery.

Chastisement for doing drugs couldn't begin to compare to what her parents would do if they knew what she'd done yesterday. Her boyfriend Jeb Turner had taken her parking in the late afternoon, and she'd left her virginity at the bottom of a hill north of the Turnaton Golf Course. She'd been too stoned to feel anything, but Jeb had gotten off almost immediately. He'd been eating her for almost a year, but she would *never* put her mouth on a penis—*ever.* Just the thought made her want to puke. She'd almost done that very thing yesterday when the wildest hallucination occurred: a beautiful lady and two men—one of them a tall African American carrying a guy on his back—suddenly appeared, and hastily made their way up the hill, then disappeared a few seconds later. Jeb had been outside the car taking a leak at the time, or she'd have made him look to verify it was only the psilocybin mushrooms working their magic.

Wyoming handed him a cup of coffee when he entered Kelly's Rentals, and surprised him with a quick peck on the cheek. He grinned while taking the cup. "What's that for?"

"Being such a gentleman last night."

"Oh I was no gentleman, believe me. If I hadn't known you'd hate yourself this morning, wild horses couldn't have dragged me away."

She gave him a warm smile. "Well I don't know that I would've hated myself if you'd gone through with it, but I certainly wouldn't have the tremendous respect for you I do now, Clyde. You're quite a guy, Mister Burns."

"Well in that case I'm glad I fled the scene." He took a sip of coffee and grinned again.

"I'd like to show my appreciation by inviting myself over to your house this Friday and fixing whatever your little heart desires for supper. My tiny apartment is no place to entertain a gentleman such as yourself."

It looked like walking away from a sure thing last night might have been the smartest thing he'd ever done. If he wound up getting laid by Wyoming on a regular basis, it definitely was. "Are you serious?"

"Mm hmm. What's your favorite food?"

"Chinese is my favorite takeout, but as for home cooked it's a tossup between stuffed cabbage and enchiladas."

She made a sour face and put her hands on her hips. "You would pick two things I've never made before."

He laughed. "Well just tell me what you're used to cooking, and I'll tell you which dish I like best."

"Okay. I make a terrific meatloaf and have never gotten any complaints about my spaghetti. Your other options are baked chicken, pot roast, shepherd's pie—"

"Say no more! I love shepherd's pie."

Larue resisted the urge to reach across the table and pop a huge ripe pimple bulging on Tabitha's left cheek, moving like a lily pad on a wind troubled pond as she chewed a mouthful of scrambled egg. To his right sat a boy genius from Dallas who'd been kidnapped last year. The kid didn't see it that way of course. Being a gullible nine-year-old, he considered it an honor to be here.

Poor sap.

Roy eased onto a stool at the counter. Matilda set a cup in front of him and filled it with coffee. Her faded blue eyes looked more fatigued than usual. She worked like a dog but nobody could convince her to take a day off. The fresh bleach job on her once naturally blonde hair made her look a bit cheap. It would mellow in about a week and not appear so blatantly artificial. When she didn't give him his usual morning greeting and bright smile, he knew she must be in need of a party partner. It had been a few weeks since he'd requested one, and they hadn't been together since.

"What can I get you for breakfast, Roy?"

"Looks like you could use something for breakfast."

A rapid nod verified it.

"I'll just have this one cup of coffee, then open the shop and get my guys lined out."

"Good. Meet you upstairs in half an hour."

She lived above the diner. Thirty minutes from now they'd be in her bed and she'd be calling him by another name.

Blinda smeared honey over a piece of toast. She'd have to do without her usual biscuits this morning, but didn't mind. If her trip to the bakery hadn't gotten deterred, she wouldn't have met Roy Milan. He'd stayed until eleven last night, and she hoped he didn't have a sleepy blue Monday ahead of him. It had been great spending the evening with such a pleasant, unassuming, and apparently honest man. If he'd had the nerve to ask her out, she'd have accepted immediately. He'd obviously wanted to, that unmistakable look on his face had given him away.

Maybe he will today when I bring my car in, she thought with a smile. There'd be no five percent discount deducted from another price estimate because she wouldn't dream of having anyone else repair it. Something dawned on her and she frowned. *He'll never ask me out if he fears I think he's too old for me. I should have flashed on that last night and let him know my ex-husband was forty-eight when we got married.*

She took a bite of toast and smiled again while chewing. *Well I'll just have to casually mention that today then, won't I.*

Larue entered Roger Benz' office without knocking, and presumptuously seated himself.

The scientist looked up with a frown. "I'm quite busy at the moment, Larue."

"I don't care. Stop whatever you're doing and listen to me—I've come to a firm decision. You might be able to make me stay here because of Mother, but guess what? From this moment on Callaway's will be rooming, boarding, and doling out their fifty dollar weekly allowance to a useless moocher."

Roger grinned. "Refusing to cooperate, eh? Vell ve haf vays to make you cooperate, mein friend."

He hated being unable to keep from laughing. Roger knew he could always strike his funny bone by talking like a tyrannical kraut. "Go ahead, keep it up, but all you're going to get out of me is a giggle. I've jumped through my last hoop for you and J.T."

"Larue, we're not using you for entertainment, we're trying to figure out what makes that marvelous brain of yours operate the way it does. And if we ever do, imagine the good you'll have done for all mankind."

"Yeah . . . soldiers will be able to kill more efficiently, and frequently, and mercilessly. No thanks."

Roger sadly shook his head. "We're not involved with the military, Larue, though I'll admit what you say is true: every branch of the armed services would greatly benefit from your skills. Knowing the exact weight, trajectory, and precisely how long it will take for any land vehicle, ship, or plane to get from point A to point B would make them rather easy to take out without wasting ammunition. But think of the constructive benefits. With just one look you can tell the maximum amount of stress anything can tolerate. If we discover that can be taught, a structural engineer could specify the exact safety margins of an aging bridge, the precise amount of metal fatigue of a passenger jet, or the life expectancy of an ocean liner by sight."

He groaned. "It obviously can't be taught, Roger, or someone would have already discovered how. I've been stuck in this place for twenty years! Ten more than you as a matter of fact."

"Say you're right . . ." Roger rose to his feet and stretched. "What makes you think we might not discover it can be genetically reproduced? It obviously was in your case."

"No, I was born with it, I didn't get it from a serum."

"You know what I mean, Larue."

"Dammit, look at it from my perspective. You get to go home to your wife and kids every weekday at five o'clock, and can do whatever you want on weekends. I'm stuck here all the time except for a total of fifty-seven days a year—a mere fifteen-point-six-one-six percent of a regular solar year, fifteen-point-five-seven-four percent of a leap year. Either way over eighty-four percent of my time is spent behind these prison walls."

Roger looked befuddled. "I'd consider myself the luckiest person on earth if I had your gifts, Larue, even if I could never leave here. So would any scientist. Your name will go down in history, my friend. Somewhere down the road a Nobel Prize is waiting for you, along with numerous other accolades."

He groaned again. "The only prize I want is my fucking freedom!"

☙❧

A shared parking lot separated Tyner's Diner from a hardware store. Blinda had never been inside either. She touched up her lipstick, scooted across the seat, and got out of her car. She'd served two people that morning without having to take any grief, and decided to eat lunch before turning her dented Ford over to Roy. Her boss had granted her the afternoon off so she could tend to the matter.

It didn't take long to spot Matilda. The other two women wearing aprons were still in their twenties, perhaps even their late teens. Other than being a tad too wide in the hips she had a nice figure. It pleased her to see Matilda required a bra two sizes smaller than what she wore. Unfortunately she had striking facial features that time had only begun to erode. However, Matilda obviously owed her hair color to a beauty salon like she did, so they were even on that, leaving her one up on the competition in the hips and bust. During the last days of her short stormy marriage, she'd dyed her brown hair to irritate her ex, who hated redheads because they made him think of his overbearing stepmother. Discovering it gave her a sexier look, she'd continued doing it since.

Laminated menus and napkin-enfolded silverware lay in front of each chair encircling the few empty tables. She set down at the nearest one and perused the lunch items.

"Hi there."

She looked up to see Matilda waiting to take her order. "Hello."

"We're running a special today on barbecue sandwiches— two for the price of one."

"Think I'll just go with a tuna melt sandwich and coffee."

"Very good. I've never seen you in here before. New in town, or here to grab some goodies at Gold's Bakery?"

"Neither, I live in Turnaton. I had an accident yesterday and am here to get my car repaired at Roy's Automotive."

The business smile she'd been wearing turned warm and friendly. "Why for heaven sake, you must be Blinda Love! Roy told me about meeting you yesterday."

Wow, I guess he really does *tell her everything.* She returned the smile. "Yeah, that's me."

"Well it's nice to meet you, Blinda, I'm—"

"Matilda Tyner?"

"Well now how did you know that?"

"Roy told me about you too."

Matilda chortled a hearty laugh and gave her a wink. "Well you guys must have *really* talked last night over dinner. He told me you make a mean ass shrimp gumbo."

"It's my mother's recipe. I'll jot it down for you if you'd like."

"Thanks, honey, but I can't touch the stuff. I'm allergic to seafood."

It was getting difficult to view Matilda as a competitor.

She couldn't help liking her.

"Hey, Blinda!"

She turned to find Roy stepping away from the door, which closed behind him automatically. His cheeks were smooth and ruddy from a recent shave, and lined with a broad grin. He'd had a heavy five o'clock shadow yesterday. "Hi there. I was going to hand my car off to you after eating a bite."

"Ah . . ." he took the chair across from her. "So what price am I beating?"

"None. I didn't bother shopping around since it's bound to cost more than my deductible, and my insurance company will be footing the rest of the bill whatever it comes to. Is there any place to rent a car here?"

"Nah, but don't worry, I've got a dandy Honda I use as a loaner. You can drive it till you get your car back."

"Great, you've saved me a bundle already."

Matilda winked at him. "Your new friend and I just got acquainted."

"So I see. What's the Monday special this week?"

"Barbecue sandwiches. Two for the price of one."

"Sounds like a winner. Bring me two, and a glass of tea."

When the competition got out of earshot, she leaned forward and quietly said, "Matilda's quite attractive. I'm amazed there're no sparks between you two."

"Yeah well," he leaned back in his chair and sighed, "that's a mystery that'll never be solved."

"Here you go . . ." she handed the banker a bag of bagels.

"Thank you, Shayna. I'm surprised to see you working here on a Monday."

"Papa gave Terry and Jean the day off."

"Oh. Well have a nice day."

"You too, Mister Gray."

School let out an hour ago and she'd be stuck in the bakery until it closed at eight. She normally only helped out from noon to five on Sundays, the day Papa's two gentile employees had off for their day of worship, but both of them had been granted a long weekend in lieu of overtime for having to work a double shift last Friday so her parents could attend a friend's funeral in Galveston. They hadn't gotten home until after midnight Saturday, as Papa refused to travel on Shabbat, and she'd made big plans with Jeb while having the house all to herself. Alas, a peculiar incident had occurred early Friday night that'd fouled everything up.

She'd pulled off her panties and leaned back against the front door, holding her skirt up while Jeb ate her. They were pretending her parents would arrive any second, so he had to make her come before they did. The sense of danger enhanced the thrill. Just when he'd started making her feel *really* good the doorbell rang. She'd pushed him away and quickly turned to look through the peephole, but hadn't seen anyone. Deciding it must have been one of the neighborhood kids pulling pranks, she'd lifted her skirt so Jeb could resume, but at that precise moment someone started banging on the door. She'd dropped the hem and immediately opened the door to again find nobody on the other side. They'd smoked a jumbo earlier, and snorted some coke, but neither were hallucinogenic, so they couldn't explain it.

The oddity had pulled her out of the mood, and she'd put her panties back on. Pissed over her unwillingness to continue, Jeb had gone home. His childishness warranted punishment so she'd refused to talk to him on Saturday. Yesterday he'd called her at the bakery, humbly apologized, and said he'd scored some quality mushrooms. They'd driven to Turnaton after she got off work, and along the way she'd finally given him permission to take their relationship to the ultimate level like she'd intended to do in her bedroom last Friday night.

༄

Roy estimated it wouldn't take more than three days, five tops, to get the Ford whipped back into shape. He delegated the job to Hal Turner, and walked Blinda to the side of the shop where the loaner was parked.

"Well here she is: your wheels for the next few days." He handed her the Honda keys.

She smiled while admiring the red two door Accord.

"Almost matches the color of your hair. She runs like a top, rebuilt the engine myself." The hair comparison seemed to bother her. He hoped she hadn't taken it as an insult.

"It looks like a new car," she finally said after a lengthy silence.

"I have Hal to thank for that, and he'll do the same with yours. He does great body work and paint jobs."

"Um, there's something I meant to tell you last night, Roy, but failed to get around to it."

"Yeah? What's that?"

"I'm not really a redhead."

When she hadn't dropped any hints after asking him to stay a while longer, he'd concluded she liked him as a friend but hadn't felt those *right vibes,* most likely because of his age. Apparently she already saw him as a trusted one or she wouldn't have confessed that. He grinned and shoved his hands in his pockets. "Well you sure fooled me. What's your real hair color?"

"A little darker shade of brown than yours. And uh, I forgot to mention that my ex husband was . . ." her cheeks blossomed with a genuine shade of red. "Oh pooie, I'm not gonna beat around the bush. Just so you know, if you were to ask me for a date, I wouldn't turn you down."

A sensual giddiness surged through him. Until she'd asked him to follow her home yesterday, he'd figured this bodacious woman wouldn't give a man his age a second look. Then by the time he'd left her house, the wild hope she'd made the request with romance in mind had been totally wiped out. "So you'd actually go out with an old codger like me?"

She laughed and slapped him on the shoulder. "You're not an old codger, Roy. Well?"

"Well what?"

Her features twisted into a give-me-a-break frown.

"Oh! Uh, yeah, I'd love to take you on a date."

"Good. How about tonight?"

"Um, sure. What time, and where would you like to go?"

The minute she got home, Wyoming stripped and ran a bubble bath. They'd been swamped with customers all day, and right now she wouldn't trade soaking in hot water, surrounded by nothing but peace and quiet, for a million dollars. During his lunch break Clyde had read an email from Lee Milan on the store computer. She didn't know what it said, but the pale look on his face when he'd whispered, "Give me your email address so I can forward it to you," had alarmed her, and she'd been jittery since. They couldn't take a chance on being overheard in the store, and she hadn't been able to leave the counter so he could tell her in his office.

She wasn't about to read the email until after luxuriating in bubbly suds for half an hour, because she had a feeling those were probably going to be her last relaxing moments of the day.

It turned out to be a forty minute bath instead.

Hair wrapped in a towel, she stepped into a pair of bunny house shoes and tied her bathrobe sash while making for the refrigerator. She poured a trickle of Jack Daniels into an eight ounce glass, filled it with Mountain Dew, and went to her computer desk, bracing herself for bad news.

Hi Clyde,

I'm crying as I write this. Before I tell you why I'm upset, there are several things I need to clear up. First off, I've never been anyone since being cast to earth but the woman you met. And though I am indeed infertile now, thanks to a doctor I baited here some time ago, I wasn't always so. As to why I deceived you about being endlessly reincarnated—well, I'm ashamed to say that I'm a shallow woman in one respect. More about that later.

Twenty-six years ago I lured a man here named Roy Milan. He's the real owner of Roy's Automotive, but not the one you went to. Leavenwood is the invisible twin of a town named Piler Creek. The town I live in is the phantom replica of a town in your world called Turnaton. The fat man and black man are condemned to live in Leavenwood, while my place of imprisonment is Justified.

We can visit each other whenever we want, but must always sleep in our own homes. There really are about ten thousand of us, but we're scattered across the face of the globe, and no more than five are gathered at any particular urban site. Turnaton has a population of over sixty-five hundred people but only one person lives in Justified—me. Hoyt, whom you call the fat man, brought the Chinese food to my door when we had dinner.

Rarely do I ever let a man know that I'm the sole citizen because it's more comforting for most to think I live in a normal city that just happens to be in a different dimension. Plus I avoid a barrage of questions such as how can I get food and clothing from stores with no one stocking the shelves or clothing racks, how can I fill up my car, get things repaired, and so on.

When I end a relationship and the man crosses the barrier for the final time, he remembers my essence but not his interactions with me, nor my name, or the town's—though he retains the memory that it lies where Turnaton does.

Anyway, Roy Milan and I were lovers. I got pregnant by him and had a son. Through all the centuries it had never happened before, despite the countless normal human males I'd slept with, and I didn't learn the reason why until I got the tubal ligation I mentioned. I did that after a daughter came along, despite my extreme diligence to avoid being impregnated again. (By the way, none of my kind can mate with each other, nor do any of us desire to. In your world it would be deemed more disgusting than incest.)

I took Roy's last name but we were never married, nor could we have ever really wed. My son's name is Larue Milan and I'm writing this a mere hour after saving his life a second time, but the internet won't send it until tomorrow because it can't detect my emails on Sundays.

He came to Turnaton and it immediately transformed into Justified, just as it always will if he enters the city limits. If he were to go to Piler Creek it would likewise turn into Leavenwood. Clyde, Larue can't live in my world—no child spawned by my kind can after turning five Hebrew years or they'll die. I love my son and I live in fear he'll somehow wind up back here. I'd have lost him if he hadn't remembered how to find my house, and we barely got him out in time.

Roy recalls that I bore him a son but can't remember anything about him, not even that Larue thought he was his uncle (more about that later). He also knows that I took his surname, but my first name was erased from his memory when he left for the last time.

I selfishly kept Larue until two weeks before he would have turned Hebrew five, which is eighteen hundred days. As a result, he'll always suffer a mental affliction that will come and go the rest of his life. I passed my daughter through the gateway right after weaning her. I did it for her sake, and wish with all my heart I'd done the same with Larue. She can live without fear of entering Turnaton or Piler Creek because they won't transform for her, and she'll never have the periods of mental deterioration that'll always plague Larue. However, he has one thing going for him she doesn't, due to his prolonged stay with me. It made him a genius on the other side, while my daughter is like any normal human female, despite being borne by a woman who was once an angel. Incidentally, all offspring of my kind can be seen by anyone, heard on the telephone, their reflections show up in mirrors, etc.

I've only recently been able to access the internet. Before then I didn't have a means to lure a man here except one living within a fifty mile radius of Justified. On Sundays I'm as human as you are with one exception—my voice still can't be heard on a telephone, nor will my face show up on a web cam in your world, only mine. Seven Sundays a year we're allowed to cross to the other side for a few hours, but must stay within the radius I spoke of. It was during such a time that I first saw Roy Milan in the very diner where Hoyt set the trap for Robby Gorgan. Of course I was in the one in Piler Creek at the time.

We don't have the power to make ourselves visible when we're on the other side, and no one can hear us. So I wrote him a letter and dropped it in a mailbox before we returned to our world. That's how I inveigled him to my house. Had he lived beyond the radius, my letter would have vanished when the vehicle transporting it crossed the invisible line.

There are certain restrictions I'm unable to override while having a relationship. The man can only cross the barrier on a Friday between dawn and midnight, Turnaton won't transform into Justified for him any other time. He can leave whenever he chooses but must do so before sunset the following Monday, and once he does the barrier becomes impenetrable to him until the next Friday. You were brought here under special circumstances (Robby Gorgan's execution) and couldn't leave my world until I sent you back.

Now back to what I learned when I got my tubes tied. I had never been in love until I met Roy, and that emotion eradicated something in my reproductive system that had prevented pregnancy until then. Impossible to explain how I became aware of it, but the moment that surgeon finished manipulating my fallopian tubes, I did.

I'd have stayed with Roy as long as he lived had I been permitted to. Unfortunately, when one of my kind has a child, they must part with the mortal parent a week before the child is released to the other side. If Larue hadn't been Roy's son I wouldn't have been so selfish, or love Larue the way I do. My feelings for my daughter are merely a vague maternal fondness in comparison.

I kept Roy in the dark about all the above. When our son turned one, I made sure Roy was never alone with Larue, and insisted he go home on Saturday mornings. I'd started explaining everything to Larue at that time and feared he'd slip up, despite me telling him not to say a word about it to Uncle Roy. A child born to one of my kind suddenly knows how to talk, walk, and think like a seven-year-old the day they turn ten months if they're still in our world at the time. Before then, they're as limited as any human baby. I didn't want Larue to have to bear the pain of knowing he'd have to leave mommy AND daddy behind, so I told him his father died shortly after he was born.

Now I'll explain my shallowness. I never know how long I'll fancy a particular man so I pretend that I'm doomed to live many normal lifespans in different bodies to keep him from being afraid to commit to me. Most of my previous relationships didn't last long enough to compel me to confess the lie, which obviously I'm forced to do when a man sees I'm not aging like he is. So, you may be asking yourself, why is she confessing this to me?

Clyde, it's because I'm begging you for a favor!!!!

Wyoming wept while reading the requested favor and some additional information about Lee and her world. She no longer doubted the woman's integrity, and could only imagine the pain that poor condemned angel had to deal with.

ELEVEN

LIAT GOLD HAD been using the sweet old woman as an alibi for years. Terry and Jean thought she was doing nothing more than delivering a chocolate cake to the crippled Jewish lady in Turnaton, like she did every Friday. Not once had they, or her husband Ezra, suspected her adultery. After she dropped off the gift and visited a few minutes, she'd be heading for a motel to meet her lover. She'd hated having to miss the rendezvous with Peter last week, but never could have forgiven herself for not bidding a final farewell to her dear friend Saul, God rest his soul. Ezra, too, had wept unashamedly through the entire funeral.

Thank God for Ezra's faithfulness. She and Shayna only attended the Saturday service but he started each Sabbath at the synagogue—a tiny structure on the south side of Piler Creek, used by the few Jewish families living in the area—arriving by Friday's sunset to observe Rabbi Beckermann lighting the candles before reciting Kiddush. They always left together, and the rabbi had never been known to return home after Shabbat evening services before eleven. That gave her plenty of time to make love with Peter and beat her husband to bed.

She loved Ezra and cherished her Hebrew heritage, but she had needs he'd long quit satisfying. He was sixty-two and she'd soon be sixty, yet her cravings were still as strong as they'd been in her youth. Ezra wouldn't hear of going to a doctor for help like most men his age did these days, and hadn't even considered it twenty years ago when he'd mysteriously become impotent practically overnight. She suspected he'd just lost interest in sex, for reasons God only knew. Nonetheless, he unquestionably still loved her.

Guilt had besieged her over being unable to dismiss lustful thoughts about a beautiful boy of eighteen Ezra had hired. He always selected four kids who'd just graduated to help out when Terry and Jean went on vacation, and that fateful July Peter had been one of them. Then still in her prime, she'd been very much aware of his exploring eyes. Peter helped her close the bakery one Sunday night when Ezra had gone home early, and confessed he'd fallen in love with her. Having already slept with him in her mind at least a dozen times by then, she'd taken him into a back room and said, "I'm in love with my husband, Peter, but if you're willing in spite of that—have protection and promise to be discrete—I'll be intimate with you here and now, but never again. Understood?"

He'd eagerly nodded, and they'd soon united loins on an illicit bed of aprons spread across a baking table.

Peter was thirty-eight now, married, and living in Conroe. She knew he'd leave his wife for her if she asked him to, but despite her inability to resist him after promising herself she'd only cheat on her husband that one time, Ezra still owned her heart.

A few days ago Shayna had gotten a hard slap in the face when she'd asked, "Do you and Papa still have sex?"

Tears had poured from her eyes as she'd watched her beautiful daughter run to her room crying. She'd immediately loaded a bowl with ice cream and carried it to her, apologizing. "You caught me by surprise, Shayna, and I overreacted. I'm very sorry I slapped you, but Papa's and my love life is none of your business. Understood?"

Shayna had accepted the bowl but not her apology. "You and Papa have always said I could come to you with anything."

"And you can," she'd replied.

"That's not true or you wouldn't have slapped me."

"I explained that and said I was sorry, but you should have known better. Oy, my mother would have clotted me with a closed fist if I'd made such an inquiry. That's an inappropriate question for any child to ask a parent."

That had satisfied Shayna, but she'd felt horribly guilty, knowing she wouldn't have reacted that way if only the answer could have been an honest yes.

Remorse gnawed at her as she crossed the hill into Turnaton. At this point she always thought about driving straight home after delivering the cake, but she knew lust would prevail same as always and she'd start for the motel upon leaving Edna's house. "All mighty God, forgive the weakness of this foolish woman."

He took one last bite of shepherd's pie and leaned back in his chair, patting his stomach. "I didn't like it one damn bit."

Wyoming laughed. "Yeah, I can see that, Clyde. You only forced down a third of the pan."

"You're a good cook."

"Thank you. So what are you planning to do about Lee's favor?"

He'd been asking himself the same question all week. "I called the Conroe chamber of commerce and the lady I talked to didn't know anything about a think tank outside of town, but suggested Callaway's Research Complex might be what I was looking for. So I called and the guy that answered said what goes on there is highly confidential. I said, 'Well, can you at least tell me if a man named Larue Milan is staying there?' and he gave me a firm, 'I'm not allowed to answer questions of that nature,' and hung up."

"Well how rude."

"Yeah . . ." he took a swig of tea. "I promised Lee I'd do it if I could find him, and asked if she could help me out with that. She emailed back that she couldn't. You'd think with those condemned angels being able to know exactly when Robby was going to be flying over their area, and set up that complicated scenario with the three of us, they'd easily be able to locate Larue, but *NO!* they can't do that."

Wyoming picked up her fork and started toying with the leftovers on her plate. "It's awfully odd they can't. When I read the part where she asked you to tell Larue he has a sister I started crying. We've got to find him, Clyde, we've just got to."

"We? Lee didn't lay that on you."

"She might as well have. Did that chamber of commerce lady have any further suggestions?"

"Nope."

"Then Larue must be at that research complex."

"That's what I figure too, unless he hasn't gotten caught yet. With his mental problem it'll only be a matter of time before he does."

Wyoming flattened a pyramid she'd formed after fashioning an almost perfect rectangle the girth of a deck of cards with the same ground beef infused mashed potatoes. "Well at least you can take care of her other favor. It's so strange you can't just do it by phone or mail."

"Yeah . . . finding Roy Milan is no problem, but I sure hate to go back there."

"Why? You know we can trust Lee to get us out if it should turn into Leavenwood."

"*Us* out?"

"I'm going with you, Clyde . . . ."

Roy had taken Blinda out every night this week—to a movie on their first date, a fancy restaurant at College Station the next, bowling Wednesday, roller skating Thursday, and tonight she'd insisted on taking him for a ride in her newly repaired Ford. Hal had put the finishing touches on it yesterday, leaving it to sit twenty-four hours for the paint to dry. Matilda had treated them to supper at the diner, and they'd visited with her a couple of hours afterwards. They'd left about ten minutes ago. He was in his pickup, following Blinda to Turnaton. If all went well tonight, he'd make his move for that all important first kiss.

Liat Gold passed him, heading the other way. That Ezra was a *lucky* man. In her younger years his wife had what Roy had always considered to be the perfect body, and a very sexy face. Time had somewhat diminished the quality of both—adding a touch of gray at the temples of her thick dark hair, that still hung to the middle of her back after all these years—but Liat was still extremely lustworthy. Not only had Ezra been lucky at love, fortune had also smiled on him. People came from miles around to buy his wares, and he now owned Piler Creek Storage Units, the car wash, practically every vending machine in town, and Hats & Boots, managed by his youngest son Joseph. Ezra had recently approved the blueprints for another Hats & Boots to be built in Turnaton.

The Gold's moved to Piler Creek from New York his junior year. Several months prior, Ezra had bought the old doughnut shop nobody had been able to keep open for long—expanded it—and dubbed the place Gold's Bakery. It became a hit in Piler Creek right away, and when word spread throughout the region, it really started generating cash. Liat had been working the front when he'd paid his first visit to the new establishment. She was twenty-four at the time and still nursing her second son. He'd gone there with a buddy, and their gawking appreciation of her feminine glory had been so obvious, she'd giggled and said, "Take a picture, boys, it'll last longer."

After he got to know her they'd become good friends and still often laughed about the incident. She'd had her third son at twenty-six, and he'd always suspected Shayna to be an accident because she hadn't come along until a whopping sixteen years later. His conscience bugged him for not saying anything to Liat about the conversation he'd overheard concerning her daughter, but he prided himself on being a feller who minded his own business. Besides, Shayna and Jeb were bound to get married.

Larue lay on his bed gazing at the ceiling. His quarters were comfortable, and had a nice bathroom, but still felt like a prison cell. Various escape plans formulated in his mind of their own accord, but he didn't entertain any of them. A third attempt would be useless—he'd only wind up being brought back here. Mother had granted him the three months he'd begged for after he'd broken out the first time, but he hadn't been able to sway her before the deadline. He'd regularly carried out the trash, swept and mopped the kitchen floor, scrubbed the tubs and lavatories in both bathrooms, and vacuumed all the carpeting on his own initiative to convince her to let him stay by then. The last of several mental lapses he'd suffered during that time had prevented him from waxing her car like he'd intended to as a final coat of icing on the cake.

But it wouldn't have made any difference even if he'd been able to complete the task. She'd bought the house soon after committing him to Callaway's as a child—counting on them to foot the bill for a thirty year mortgage and monthly installments on a new car. She'd bought several automobiles since then, and the one she currently drove was paid off, but having to make three house payments without that income had driven away any possibility of allowing him to stay with her.

Roger and J.T. refused to discuss Clyde and Wyoming, or call them to verify his tale. But Clyde and Wyoming knew— *they knew* Justified and Leavenwood existed, because they'd been there.

A sudden panging bounced around inside his head, making him inexplicably fearful again.

The gratifying sensation of feeling protected had enveloped Wyoming all evening. She'd basked in Clyde's presence because of it. Occasional whiffs of his musk had made it all the sweeter. If he wasn't an admitted hound, she might even consider the possibility of spending the rest of her life with this guy she so respected—without marrying him of course. She didn't cheat on boyfriends and expected total fidelity from them as well. Clyde would never quit being a skirt chaser, he'd said as much.

"What are you in such deep thought about?"

"Larue," she lied.

"Yeah . . . keeps bugging me too. Don't you want another drink? You've only made one from that hooch you brought over."

"I'm not in a partying mood tonight."

"Guess I'd better hold off on the idea of another brewski myself, since I'll have to drive you home soon." He said it while gazing at an empty bottle in his hand.

She went to the kitchen, returned to his living room with

a full one, and swapped it for the empty.

He squinted at her. "Why'd you do that?"

"I don't want to go home tonight, Clyde."

His eyes bolted wide. "You mean—"

"No, I don't mean that. I'll sleep on the couch. Something about this house is very soothing, and I know I'll be tossing and turning all night in my apartment. Now we can discuss what we're going to do about Larue without you having to worry about drinking too much beer."

All he'd hoped for at this stage was a goodnight kiss, but Blinda's greedy tongue strongly indicated she wanted far more than that. They were standing outside her door. She opened it and pulled him back inside, keeping her hungry lips glued to his. Roy kicked it closed and grabbed her left breast. A moan gushed into his mouth from hers, hot and urgent, then she started feverishly massaging his groin. Taking that as a full green light, he unbuttoned her blouse, slid his hands inside, unhooked her bra, and wrestled the garments off with her assistance, letting both fall to the floor. Heatedly excited to see her large breasts uncovered, he ended the passionate kiss and stepped away from her.

The mouthwatering mounds of pink-tipped flesh were maddening to behold. Jayne Mansfield size with Marilyn Monroe areoles, they protruded from her chest firm and proud at slight angles, sagging just enough to confirm no surgeon had tampered with this magnificent display of God's handiwork. His unblinking stare made her blush, but an embarrassed smile revealed his fervent admiration delighted her. She allowed him to drink in her busty beauty for about half a minute, then went to work on his shirt. It soon joined her blouse on the carpet.

Hormones raging, he grappled the tantalizing globes greedily, savoring their smooth, exquisite texture as his impatient fingers squeezed the silky flesh and his pleasured palms caressed her lust-stiffened nipples. Soft sighs flowed from Blinda's parted lips as he continued exploring her mammary treasures, and grew much louder when he lowered his head—nursing each perky summit as eagerly as a baby extracting milk.

He kept it up for several minutes, then sought her mouth as his hands returned to her chest. Their tongues were like two warring serpents engaged in a battle neither wanted to end. The lustful sounds emerging from Blinda's throat as he turned her luscious boobs every which way but loose, drove him wild.

When he came up for air, Blinda kicked off her shiny black heels. He knelt to the floor and yanked her spandex slacks to her ankles in one fluid motion. She pulled her feet out of them while he slithered her panties down her shapely smooth legs. Feasting his eyes on the wedge of thick brown hair between her thighs, he threw the silky garment behind him, and attacked.

"Oh god!" she cried when his lips engulfed her swollen clit. She clawed at his hair while he explored her vulva with his tongue, and moaned ecstatically when he started plunging it in and out of her tight, dripping canal. He gave her love button a final nibble, stood up, and took off his jeans.

Blinda hit her knees, and started sucking like a newborn calf.

"Fuckin' A . . .!" he dropped his hands onto her bobbing head as her hot, vacuuming mouth flooded him with pleasure.

All of a sudden she stopped and looked up at him with a sultry smile. "Wow, you get hard as fast as a teenager, don't you."

Before he could say anything, she had her lips wrapped around his dick again.

"Oh fuck yeah . . . suck it . . . suck it!"

Experience had taught Matilda when to let up before he lost control. Blinda seemed to think he could last indefinitely, the way she kept increasing the pace. Nearing the brink, he grabbed her head and pulled out of her mouth, letting her know with his eyes what he wanted to do next.

She rose to her feet, wiped the moisture off her friction swollen lips, and huskily said, "Let's go to my bedroom."

Clutching his stiff shaft like a lifeline, she towed him to her boudoir. Still holding it, she lay down on her bed, pulled him on top of her, ran the head up and down her creamy slit a few times, and finally turned loose.

A loud gasp launched from her throat when he shoved it in. "I hope you're ready, Blinda, because I'm gonna fuck the living shit out of you."

"Oh yes . . . do it!" she cried when he started pumping. "F-Fuck the living shit out of me . . . !"

Each thrust forced a lusty groan from her mouth.

"You fuck as good as you look, Blinda, but by the time I'm through with you, you'll be lucky if you can fucking walk!"

She suddenly detonated beneath him. He forced himself to hold back—determined to make her come a second time so she'd never dream of giving him up. "I fucking warned you, didn't I. Get ready, because I'm gonna take you to the stars again."

Before long she cried out and again thrashed her hips in orgasmic frenzy. This time he threw his head back and joined her. "Take that, you hot bitch!"

When her cries of pleasure finally began to wane, he silenced them with a deep kiss.

"Oh my god," she panted as he slid his face beside hers and rested his full body weight on her. "Matilda must have gone crazy having to go without this for such a long time."

"So you liked it?"

A throaty laugh filled the air. "Liked it? Hell, nobody's ever made me feel that good, Roy. You're amazing."

"So are you. I've wanted to do this from the moment I saw your head dangling after that truck hit you. I stood there thinking, 'Man she's pretty, and what a fantastic rack.' I thought I must have been hearing things at first when you asked me to follow you home. I almost pinched myself to make sure I wasn't dreaming."

She giggled and started stroking his hair. "You didn't feel me up while I was out, did you?"

"Don't think it didn't cross my mind," he teased. "If that truck driver hadn't been there, who knows."

"Have you always been this good?"

The question hurled him into the past. What had the mother of his son thought of his sexual prowess? She must have told him but he couldn't remember now, or anything else about making love with her—only that she'd made him the happiest he'd ever been. He rolled over on his back and sighed. "Nah, you have Matilda to thank for that. Practice makes perfect, as they say."

"So she's an expert lover too?"

"Yeah, if there is such a thing. I guess Matilda and I sharpened each other up pretty good through the years."

She turned onto her side. "Funny, I would have been offended by your obscenity if you weren't so gentlemanly otherwise. The sudden shift in your personality had the opposite effect—it really turned me on. Especially when you said you were going to F the you-know-what out of me. Feeling you inside me while you said it, made me so hot I couldn't keep from answering back as lewdly. I've never talked like that before."

A shudder ran through him. He'd been an idiot to let it all hang out like that without knowing how she'd react. Instinct had taken over, and could have gotten him barred from her awesome body. "I'm sorry, I should have kept my mouth shut. Matilda and I learned a long time ago that sleazy bedroom talk makes for a hotter time in the sack for us. Thank God you weren't offended."

"Oh I'm so glad you didn't hold back, Roy. It took sex to a new level for me—a very thrilling level."

He couldn't help but laugh. "And to think I was going to drive home tonight feeling lucky if I came away with a goodnight kiss."

"You're kidding!" she laughingly exclaimed. "You must have known I wanted you by the way I so aggressively coaxed you into asking me out."

"No. For all I knew you just wanted to hang out with me because of how much you enjoyed my visit the night before."

She ran her fingers through his chest hair and teased his nipples by tracing circles around them with the edge of her long thumbnail, going from one to the other every few seconds. "Yes, I really like hanging out with you . . . and now that I know you're a great guy all the way around, you'll never get rid of me."

"Hope not."

"Um listen, Roy, about Matilda. I really like her. Do you think you could possibly take care of us both without wrecking your health?"

Blinda hadn't turned on the lights so he couldn't read her face, but nothing in her tone indicated she wasn't serious. "Are you saying you don't mind if I keep sleeping with her?"

"You're still in love with the woman in that invisible town, aren't you?"

"Yeah . . . reckon I always will be."

"Well, since I know I can never really have you totally to myself anyway, what's the harm?"

"None for me. Matilda and I only use each other two or three times a month these days, so there's no danger of me spreading myself too thin. But what about you? I'm not about to share you with another man."

A languid sigh emerged. "I've had enough boyfriends and candy-flower romances to last a lifetime—and I've been married, so I know what that's like. I knew if we were sexually compatible I'd be completely satisfied because you make me so happy otherwise. And now I know we're *really* good in bed. I don't want to hear about you taking care of Matilda, but as long as it doesn't interfere with our relationship in any way, I'm okay with it. And I know she needs it."

"But what if you wind up falling in love with me?"

She rolled over on her stomach and sighed again. "I think I already have."

TWELVE

SHAYNA KISSED HER parents, set down, and bowed her head as Papa thanked God in Yiddish for His many blessings, and petitioned Him to bless the food they were about to partake for breakfast this Sabbath morning. Religious to a fault on Friday nights, he relaxed after coming home from temple, and enjoyed the one day he took off from the bakery each week.

"... on dank, ohmain."

Mama picked up a platter of scrambled eggs, scraped a large portion onto a plate, garnished the eggs with several strips of kosher beef bacon, and set it in front of Papa, who was busy buttering his toast. She then put a third the amount of each on two plates, and handed her one.

"What did you and Jeb do for entertainment last night, sweetheart?"

"The usual, Papa. Just hung out with the gang." For about fifteen minutes. Afterwards Jeb made her come twice with his mouth in the backseat of his car, before sheathing his penis with a condom and quickly satisfying himself inside her. They'd been peaking on coke at the time.

"Did Edna enjoy her cake?" he asked Mama.

"Oh yes, I enjoyed a piece myself."

"I wish the bakery hadn't taken away my sweet tooth. I don't know how you've kept yours through the years, dear."

An I-told-you-so frown sprang to Mama's face. "Ezra, I didn't insist on sampling every fresh batch of every item the way you did when we started out. If you'd trusted the recipes like you do now, you could still enjoy an occasional slice of cake or piece of pie the way I do."

Papa sighed. "This is probably true. So, Shayna, I understand we're expecting a guest after three stars this Shabbat."

"Mm hmm. She's a sweet girl, you'll love her."

"She's the daughter of the new track coach, Ezra," said Mama.

"The Oscar Booth I've been hearing about?"

"Yes, Papa," Shayna answered for her. She'd met Priscilla last month when the Booths moved here from Dallas. They shared the same English class, and had hit it off immediately, despite her envy. Priscilla had gorgeous dark brown hair and beautiful brown eyes, which she admired—it was her large breasts and height that aroused her covetousness: she stood as tall as Mama and almost matched her bust size. During their first conversation Priscilla had proudly claimed to be anti-drugs, and asked if she used any. She'd silently lied with a shake of her head. No one except Jeb knew she got high, just as nobody else knew she'd lost her virginity. Being a popular girl, she had a reputation to protect.

They got to Piler Creek at five-thirty. A sign showed Roy's Automotive closed at two on Saturdays. He'd never bothered to read it before.

Clyde turned left from the parking lot and headed towards the center of town. He'd fantasized about Wyoming last night—imagining he'd walked into the living room naked, jerked the covers off her to discover she'd anticipated the move and had shed the t-shirt he'd given her to wear for pajamas. While looking up at him with a wicked smile, she'd kicked her left leg over the back of his couch, dropped her right foot to the floor, and begged him to ram his dick in her. He'd popped the moment he mentally granted her request.

They'd discussed what to do before turning in, and had decided to make the trip next Friday after work, crash for a few hours at the lone motel in Piler Creek, and hopefully find Roy Milan at his shop Saturday morning. A lot of auto repair dealerships shut down at noon on Saturdays, and they'd had no reason to suppose Roy's Automotive wasn't one of them. But he'd woken up much earlier than expected and found his overnight guest sitting in the kitchen drinking coffee. Antsy to get it over with, he'd packed a change of clothes, driven Wyoming to her apartment so she could do likewise, and they'd hit the road before ten, breakfasting on burritos purchased at the same place he'd gassed up the Malibu.

There were several Milan's in Piler Creek but no Roy's, and none with the initial R listed in The White Pages. Roy Milan either went by his middle name, a nickname, or had an unlisted phone number. Wyoming had rightfully pointed out that it was such a small town anybody they ran across could probably tell them where he lived if they failed to locate him at his shop.

Knowing they'd have many such opportunities at the diner, he stopped there.

A crew of teenagers were carousing at a big circular booth. Most of the tables were occupied—the majority by coffee drinking, cigarette smoking adults. They set down at an empty one and a middle-aged blonde came over.

"Hi there. Menus are on the table. What can I get you to drink?"

He gave her a polite smile. "We'll both have iced tea. Can you tell me where Roy Milan lives?"

"Sure," she answered with a curious grin. "Thought I knew all his friends and relatives, but don't recall ever seeing you before."

"We met last week at his shop and a mutual friend asked me to pass on a message."

"Oh yeah? Who's the mutual friend?"

"Lee Milan."

The blonde frowned and studied him a moment. "Don't know her either. How is she a friend if she's a relative?"

"They just happen to have the same last names," interjected Wyoming. "It's very important that we talk to Roy."

"Well speak of the devil." The waitress pointed at the door while saying it.

Clyde turned to see Blinda Love of all people, walking in with the very man they were looking for.

She spotted them and grinned. "Well hello there!"

Roy Milan tailed Blinda to their table, an incredulous gawp plastered to his face. He obviously recognized them.

"Remember me . . .?" Clyde got up and extended his hand.

Lee's former paramour shook it as Wyoming invited them to sit down.

⤳✵↶

Shayna eyed the stranger while chewing a bite of banana split. He looked like an older, sexier version of Jeb—eyes a pretty shade of blue that really stood out, light complexion with blondish brown hair. He introduced himself to Roy Milan as Clyde Burns. The stunning blonde he'd walked in with identified herself as Wyoming Carter. She noticed Priscilla seemed to be admiring him as well. She'd seen the redheaded lady many times. Hardly a Sunday went by that she didn't pop in the bakery for biscuit dough.

Both women had intimidating busts like Mama and Priscilla, making her feel *oh* so inferior. Being much shorter than all four didn't help. She couldn't understand why God hadn't seen fit to give her big tits and had decreed she be diminutive in stature. Sometimes she got downright angry about it.

Wyoming opened her purse while Clyde explained to Roy Milan they'd come to Piler Creek to fulfill a favor. She pulled out the picture he'd printed on photo paper from his computer, and slid it across the table to Clyde, facedown.

He pushed it in front of Roy, turned the glossy page over, and said, "Remember her?"

Tears glistened in Roy's eyes as he speechlessly gawked at it, sitting stone still as if paralyzed.

Blinda quickly vacated her chair, stepped behind him, and leaned over to have a look. "That's a *pretty* lady. Who is she, Roy?"

"The woman I told you about," he muttered without shifting his watery gaze.

"That woman who lives in the invisible town?!"

Wyoming cringed. Everybody in the place was looking their way. "Um, is there some place we can go? This matter needs to be discussed in private."

"We can go to my house," said Roy, still gazing at Lee's profile picture.

Shayna kept her eyes fastened to Clyde Burns until he, Roy, and the two ladies walked away from her viewpoint.

"I'm really looking forward to meeting your parents."

She turned to Priscilla and smiled. "They're eager to meet you as well."

"Let's hit the rink," said Jeb.

They'd decided to join the gang for a bout of roller skating, as she and Jeb had been accused of no longer wanting to hang out. Since they wouldn't be able to get high or have sex anyway, she'd asked Priscilla to spend the night with her.

"Wonder what that lady meant by invisible town?" queried Tony Popp, the sleek leader of their eight-member pack, comprised of the most popular kids in school—all but she and Jeb straight laced, filled with the Piler Creek Pirates spirit, and republican like their parents. She felt certain Priscilla would soon make it nine, she fit in so well.

Tony's question went unanswered.

Lee's former lover lived five blocks north of his shop in a nice house veneered with blue stucco. Blinda went nosing around like she'd never been there before as Roy led Wyoming and him to the kitchen. It smelled of bacon and friend lunchmeats like his did.

"Have a seat at the table and I'll get some coffee going. I'm telling you, I've never had anyone shock me like you did, Clyde. When you showed me that picture I thought I had to be dreaming. I'll never forget her face, but she fixed it so I can't remember her first name. Do you know what it is?"

"Lee . . ." he slid onto a chair.

"Damn, doesn't jog my memory at all. I can't remember ever calling her that. Does she still go by Milan?"

"Yeah, and I figure she always will."

Wyoming put her purse on the table and seated herself. "I agree with Clyde."

"Why does she live in a different world than ours? She must have told me but I lost the memory when I left it for the last time."

There had to be a shit load of questions the poor guy wanted answers to, but at the moment a major one bugged him: was Blinda dating this middle-aged man? He hoped they were only friends because it appeared Wyoming would never see him as anything but one. "Lee's an angel who thought God might have goofed creating Adam and Eve. As a result, she got cast to earth and is forced to live as a thirty-year-old woman for the duration of mankind's existence. She'll turn back into what she once was at the end of time. You must have really gotten to her. She told me in an email you're the only man she's ever fallen in love with."

Roy dropped the scoop he'd just filled from a canister. It hit the counter sideways, hurling a trail of coffee grounds from his coffee maker to the rim of the sink. He took a step back from the cabinet and glared at him—eyes angry and brimming with tears, bottom lip quivering as he clenched his teeth. "Then why'd she break it off, Clyde . . . why, goddammit, *WHY?!*"

He'd expected Roy's emotions to run high, but this outburst took him by surprise. "Chill out, man. That's what she sent me to explain."

Blinda rushed in and threw her arms around Roy's neck. "What's wrong, baby?"

Baby? Shit, this is a fucking fine development! "Um, I could sure use a beer before I explain everything," Clyde said tiredly. "Mind if I make a quick run to the store first?"

"You're right, to hell with coffee . . ." Roy pulled away from the bosomy redhead. "I'll do it. I need a cold one or ten right now myself. Do you want something to drink, Blinda?"

Pretty face still knotted with concern, she put her hands

on her hips and sighed. "I need something a little stronger than beer. Bring me some tequila and orange juice."

"How about you, Wyoming?"

She pulled a billfold from her purse, took out a fifty, and held it up. "I'd like a small bottle of Jack Daniels and a liter of Mountain Dew please."

"I'm springing for everybody's. What kind of suds do you swill, Clyde?"

"Budweiser. Light if you don't mind."

"I'll get us a case . . . ."

Blinda figured Roy needed a few minutes to himself, but the main reason she hadn't gone with him was so she could pump Clyde and Wyoming for information. "Is that woman trying to get Roy back?"

"No," said Clyde. "She'd love to but she can't."

"Why?"

"It's complicated and *very* weird. I'd rather not have to recount it twice if you don't mind. You'll know all we do when Roy returns with the hooch. Believe it or not she's Lee Milan, the woman who lives in your house in that other dimension."

That really poured salt in the wound.

"How long have you and Roy been seeing each other?"

She wound up talking about the accident and their week-long courtship instead of learning anything new about the shaky ground she found herself standing on because of that gorgeous bitch in the invisible town. Hearing Lee Milan couldn't reconcile with him hadn't eased her mind, and wouldn't until she learned the reason why. But there'd been one bright spot—Clyde seemed quite disappointed over her seeing Roy. That gave her wounded ego a badly needed boost. She'd asked about his and Wyoming's relationship the night they'd had dinner with her. Since they were merely friends, Clyde must have been planning to give her a tumble somewhere down the line.

Maybe she'd call him sometime. Roy would never be able to fall in love with her, and she couldn't help wondering about the titillating possibility that a secret lover might enhance the profound appreciation for sex he'd awakened in her. Providing, of course, Clyde could thrill her like Roy. She dug her cell from her purse and called up her contact list. "What are your phone numbers?"

Clyde looked at her funny while relaying his. Knowing he might be suspecting her plan made her clitoris twitch. Whatever wound up happening with Roy, she'd always be grateful to him for igniting a fire inside that would only grow hotter with time. Who knew, he might even have turned a woman who'd always had a typically normal sex drive into a nymphomaniac.

When she'd been on her knees going down on him, his lewd vocalizations had birthed something within her she'd have never thought herself capable of: a burning desire to receive and administer carnal pleasure purely for the sake of lustful gratification. Then, in her bed, that craving had been satisfied twice—both wonderfully intense orgasms casting her into a sensual heaven where no one existed but herself and her imaginary lover.

She'd known at that point her sex life would never be the same.

None of it would have happened if he hadn't told her about his strange relationship with Matilda. Roy would never know it wasn't him she'd answered when he'd asked, *What if you fall in love with me?* She'd had to bite her lip to keep from saying the man's name at the end of the sentence. If she had, Roy would have heard, *I think I already have, Elvis.*

That's what had truly motivated her to insist he keep satisfying Matilda's sexual needs—she'd have been a despicable hypocrite otherwise. She'd heard Elvis Presley saying "Suck it!" while she'd been giving Roy head, and when the king of rock and roll had said "I'm gonna fuck the living shit out of you, Blinda!" the thrill had been so maddening, she'd almost blurted out: "Oh yes, Elvis, do it!" It had been hard leaving his name out when the plea involuntarily escaped her.

***

He'd kill anyone that tried to take the picture away from him, yet Roy almost wished he hadn't seen it. Lee's beautiful face would never leave his memory, but seeing her image with his physical eyes after all these years had been devastating. Blinda met him at the door and took the liquor sacks from him. He trailed her to the kitchen, toting the beer . . . .

***

Clyde opened the bottle he'd been handed, and took a big swallow as Roy set down with his. Wyoming and Blinda were at the cabinet fixing their drinks. He waited until they planted their shapely asses, then began. "Okay, Roy, guess I should start from the beginning. I met Lee Milan on the internet . . ." when he reached the point just after Wyoming got the call that confirmed Robby's death, he stopped to let all that sink in.

His strange ordeal with the fat man and black mechanic

had astonished Roy and Blinda, but they really freaked out upon hearing Lee had pulled them into her world through a dream.

The dumbstruck mechanic emptied his bottle, fetched another from the fridge, and guzzled a quarter of it before sitting down. "How'd she do it?"

He took a pull from his before answering. "I don't know, but somehow we were in Lee's world and asleep in our beds at the same time. Now I'll get to the favor I agreed to do for her—but before I do, save your breath about asking me why she's able to defy physics in one area, yet can't do several relatively mundane things in comparison. Lee told me it's impossible for her to explain in a way that I can understand.

"Your son's name is Larue Milan. Lee asked me to find him and explain that he can't ever set foot in Turnaton or Piler Creek or they'll turn into their invisible twins, and Larue will die of heart failure. Ironically I'm responsible for him returning to Justified the day after Wyoming and I came to your shop. Lee barely got him out of her world in time. I didn't have a clue who he was. Wyoming and I were driving back to Odessa and saw him on the side of the road miles from any town, so I picked him up. When we passed the city limits sign, Turnaton turned into Justified and Larue jumped out of the car. A minute later Justified turned back into Turnaton, and there was nothing we could do but drive on.

"Lee wants you two to meet, of course it can't be here. Larue knew you as his Uncle Roy when you and her were together. She wants him to know you're really his father. Wyoming has a letter in her purse, it's a printout of an email meant for you. Lee's forbidden to ever directly contact you again by any means. It's the same for any man she breaks up with. None of her former lovers can find her on that social network I told you about—her site won't show up for them, just like it won't for you."

He chugged another swallow of Bud Light and continued. "She had to limit what she wanted to say to three hundred words because of the special nature of that particular email, and she had to waste some of them to explain something she's not allowed to pass on through me. You can't read the letter or something very bad will happen to her. She didn't say what, but I know she wasn't exaggerating because she still loves you, so you'd have heard from her a long time ago if the penalty for disobeying that restriction wasn't as severe as she claims.

"I can't even read it a second time without putting Lee in danger, and you have to hear it in person. If you were to learn what it says by any other means, it would be just as devastating to Lee as if I'd reread it. Wyoming's as much in the dark as you are right now about what it says. After she reads it to you, I'm going to burn it so nobody can read that letter a second time, because if anybody does, it'll be as bad for Lee as if she'd sent it directly to you. So listen closely. Wyoming?"

She took out the letter, unfolded it, and began.

"My dearest Roy. Since you're hearing someone read this, I know Clyde has told you all that I asked him to. Now you know what I am, as you once did, but could no longer remember after I was forced to say goodbye. Not a minute goes by that I don't think of you, darling. Our time together will always be the happiest period of my life as a woman. I state that unequivocally because I'd lived centuries before we met, and however many years lay ahead before Christ returns, I'll never love another the way I love you. Because your son reentered the world of his nativity and miraculously made it out alive, I'm allowed to impart these words to you, but will never be able to do so again, so I pray you'll remember all that I've so vehemently desired to tell you in person for so long now.

"I'll always cherish the sweet memories of making love

with you, and just being with you. Your smile, your laugh, your smell, your touch will live in my heart forever. You and you alone made me feel the indescribable joys of falling in love, and since our parting, the endless heartache that comes over losing the one you're in love with. I'd give anything to be a mere human so I could live out the rest of my life with you, Roy. Never forget that, darling. It would have been so wonderful if we could have raised our son together—and perhaps a few more children as well—like a normal family.

"Alas, I'm nearing the end of my allotted space and must close. Just know that though we will never be physically united as one again, we'll always be one in my broken heart. All my love always. Lee."

Roy started bawling as Clyde figured he would. He took the letter from Wyoming and went to the sink to burn it.

"No wait!" cried Blinda, wiping tears from her eyes. "Dammit, I've never read it before, so at least let Roy hear it again through me before you destroy it."

Wyoming grabbed it from his hand. "She's right, Clyde."

"Don't give it to me yet . . ." Blinda opened her purse and pulled out a cell phone. "Roy, I'm gonna call Matilda and tell her to get over here as soon as possible. She can read it to you after I do."

Roy shook his head. "She'll think we're nuts. You wouldn't believe any of this yourself if that car hadn't miraculously appeared. All she knows is that I fell in love with a woman who lives somewhere in southeast Texas—that's all I ever told her."

Blinda puckered her lips and whistled a harried breath through them. "You're right . . . I'm so sorry, Roy." She dropped the phone in her purse, snapped it closed, and held out her hand.

Wyoming gave her the letter.

THIRTEEN

THE GANG PARTED at nine. Jeb made the drag a few times, then took her home. Her parents were vegging out in the living room when she walked in with Priscilla.

Papa straightened his recliner as Mama put her knitting down and rose from the couch. Both were smiling.

"Folks, may I present to you Priscilla Booth . . ." Shayna bowed as if introducing a star on stage after a play.

Lee's letter had been flushed down the toilet. Her last message to the man she loved was now nothing but ashes mingling with other waste products in the Piler Creek sewer system. Clyde speculated that Lee must have been allowed that one message for the purpose of instructing Roy to find their son, warn him of the consequences of entering her world again, and explain how to avoid it. That's why she'd begged for the favor—so he'd do it, leaving her free to send her love to Roy instead.

He relayed the rest of what he knew about Lee, and caught Blinda giving him an unmistakably wanton look. The expression so contradicted the concern for Roy she'd been displaying, it made her come off like a deceitful slut. It turned him on nonetheless.

Roy opened his fifth beer and set the cap on the table like he'd done four times previously. "When did Lee have her daughter?"

"Seven and a half years after Larue was born." He turned up his fourth.

"Who's the father?"

"No idea, Lee didn't say anything about him."

"What's her name and what does she look like?"

"Don't know. Neither does Lee. She passed her to the other side when she was only six months old."

"And she wants you to find her, huh." Roy took another swig and burped into his left palm. "Well lots of luck. I don't see any way you can do that without knowing what she looks like, since you don't have a name to go on."

"She has a distinctive birthmark," said Wyoming. "We're hoping an ad in all the major papers in southeast Texas will do the trick. Lee knows she lives somewhere in this area."

Blinda tossed her a skeptical frown. "Why can't she tell you where to find her then if she knows that?"

"Because that's all she knows," Clyde explained. "Lee can sense her children's presence if they're within a hundred miles of Turnaton in any direction, but she can't determine where they are, or how close. A few weeks ago, she became aware that her daughter, who'd been taken from the area only weeks after passing through the gateway, had returned to this section of Texas."

Roy started fiddling with the bottle caps—scooping them up and dropping them on the table like jacks. "How does she figure her daughter can help Larue?"

"Lee's hoping her adopted family might take him in." Irritated by the noise, Clyde got up and held out his hand for the tops. He'd thrown his in the garbage each time he'd opened a beer. "Assuming she has one of course."

"Thanks . . ." Roy dropped them in his palm.

He disposed of the litter and sat back down. "Larue can't provide for himself because of those spells, and he obviously can't live with you unless you move to another town. I think he's at a place outside Conroe called Callaway's Research Complex. He told me he'd escaped from a think tank when we ran across him. Lee said he was in such a weak condition when he made it to her house he couldn't speak, so she wasn't able to get any information from him. When I answered her email and passed on everything Larue told us, she really got worried about him.

"A girl scout troop was camped near the gateway when she sent him through as a child. She knew the scout mother would see right away he had a mental problem. Passing through the portal so close to turning eighteen hundred days triggered the first spell I told you about. She'd hoped he'd wind up being adopted by a nice couple. If she had released him before he turned ten months he'd be completely normal like her daughter, and wouldn't cause Turnaton or Piler Creek to swap places with her dimension. Every day older a child of Lee's kind gets after that, the stronger that mental condition will be when they pass through the gateway, and yet the smarter they'll be in their lucid states."

Blinda got up to make another drink, and said from the cabinet, "Lee must have named her daughter. Why didn't she leave some form of identification with her?"

"It hurt Lee so badly to give up Larue, she knew better than to get too attached to her daughter, so she didn't give her a name." Clyde admired Blinda's ass while saying it. The black slacks fit so tight they formed a shallow valley down her crack. "But it wouldn't have done any good if she had. Nothing in Lee's world can pass through to ours except the offspring borne by her kind. An identification bracelet or a name tag—even the ink if Lee had written the name on the child's forehead—would have disappeared. When she saved Larue's life, he came back to our side wearing the clothes he had on when he jumped out of my car, because they came from our world. But whoever found him the first time saw a naked four year old boy who was able to identify himself when his mental spell passed. Lee's daughter was just a baby and hadn't learned to talk yet."

The buxom redhead came back to the table wielding her third tequila screwdriver. His eyes locked onto her breasts, seriously stretching the fabric of a clingy white blouse, and she caught him looking before he could force them away. A faint smile on her face aroused him, since his ogling had put it there.

Roy muffled another burp while lowering his beer. "Lucky thing whoever found Larue didn't live in Turnaton or Piler Creek."

"It wouldn't have mattered at that time," said Wyoming. "Lee told Clyde that Larue could have lived in either place until he reached puberty, they wouldn't have transformed till then, so she knows he was living in some other town when he did. But she's never failed to sense his presence six days out of every week that's passed since she released him, so he never went beyond the limits of her spiritual radar. She had no idea he'd come back to Justified until she saw him passed out on her front porch, because it was a Sunday, the one day of the week her built in child detector becomes dormant. If either of her kids were to stumble into her dimension Monday through Saturday, she'd not only immediately be aware of it, she'd know exactly where to find them."

Larue couldn't get anyone to play chess with him. Being impossible to beat by amateurs, even the scientists wouldn't take him on anymore. Tabitha feared competition so badly she wouldn't play anything but solitaire or video games. But he hadn't come here for sport anyway. Nobody but the inmates hung out in the game room on Saturday nights. He'd brought several legal books with him from the library, and didn't want any of the staff to notice him studying them. He couldn't chance any curious eyes seeing him carry the tomes to his room either. They might tell J.T. or Paul, and either of them would soon ascertain what he was up to. After his first escape, they'd instructed the operators who handled all communications to and from Callaway's not to let him place any more outgoing calls (a cab had awaited him half a mile from the main gate when he'd snuck away during a group hike through the woods behind the compound). They'd restrict him from the library if they even suspected, and he couldn't risk that.

He'd never be free of this place until he found a way to get Mother's power of attorney revoked.

"You're not too short," said Priscilla while admiring her china doll collection.

They were in Shayna's bedroom trading opinions of themselves, and she'd confessed her displeasure with her height. "You wouldn't think that if you were me. I can't believe you don't like your figure."

"If my waist was an inch narrower, and I had shapely hips like you instead of this box butt, I'd be pretty happy with it."

Shayna couldn't believe her ears. "You don't have a box butt, your hips are fine. I'd kill to have your big boobs."

"That's the one part of my anatomy I'm not insecure about, I must admit." Priscilla turned to face her, wearing a prideful smile. "But yours are the perfect size for your petite figure, girl. Any bigger and they'd ruin your graceful symmetry."

"Oy, graceful symmetry my ass. Whatever gave you the idea you have a box butt?"

"My brother. That's what he calls me."

"My brothers call me pipsqueak. They're all very tall like my father. I don't know how I wound up so short. Mama's five-seven."

Priscilla sat down beside her on the bed and sighed. "I don't want anyone to know this so keep it to yourself, but I've never seen my real parents because I'm adopted. So is my brother, but we're not blood kin. Mom and Dad couldn't have kids of their own. They talked a young woman out of having an abortion, and adopted my brother when he was born. I was abandoned at six months. They found me in a state foster home two years after they adopted him."

Liat smiled while knitting a pink sweater for Shayna. Ezra lay stretched out on the recliner snoring. The guttural sounds emanating from his gaping mouth had spurred a very special memory: the night of their daughter's conception.

Roy finally made coffee like he'd intended to when they'd left the diner. Blinda had insisted Clyde and Wyoming spend the night at her house instead of the motel, and needed a few cups to sober up, as did Clyde. Neither were drunk, just a little too buzzed to get behind the wheel at the moment.

Hearing Lee's message a second time had been wonderful, but completely unnecessary to help him remember it. Every word Blinda read had already been engraved on the walls of his brain the moment each left Wyoming's lips. He'd never forget a single syllable.

His conscience bothered him over Blinda. She only thought she'd already fallen in love with him, catching her giving Clyde the eye proved that. But if he didn't break it off with her she might wind up falling for real, and that'd be a travesty. He'd never be able to love anyone but Lee, just as Matilda would never love anyone but her dead sophomore. They had each other to use for sex, and it would always be that way. Blinda needed a man who could really return her love.

He'd break it off tomorrow after Clyde and Wyoming left for Odessa, and never entertain the thought of dating a woman again. Knowing he'd always have Lee's love would carry him on a cloud of happiness through the rest of his life. Only her physical presence could make the journey any more joyful.

They were on their way to Turnaton. Blinda obviously hadn't developed any serious feelings for Roy yet, so Clyde was liable to wind up in her bed tonight. When they got to her house Wyoming intended to ask for his car keys and get a room at a motel. She didn't want to risk overhearing them make love. The very thought of it sickened her.

"Did you notice that cute guy at the diner?"

"If you're talking about Clyde Burns I did," Shayna answered with a giggle.

"Yeah, I think that's what he said his name was." Priscilla put a piece of a cow's ear on the jigsaw puzzle they were putting together on her bedroom floor.

"That man he was talking to is Roy Milan. Jeb's brother works for him. I don't know why Clyde caught my eye the way he did, being such an old dude."

Priscilla grinned. "He just has a sexy air about him."

"Yeah . . . so what are the boys like in Dallas?"

"Same as anywhere I guess."

"Did you go steady with anyone?"

"Uh-uh, just played the field. How long have you been going with Jeb?"

"Since tenth grade . . ." she pressed a complicated cutout into the cow's protruding tongue. "Haven't dated anyone else since."

"Wow, that's a long time. You guys must be pretty serious about each other."

"Mm hmm, we're in love."

"What's it like?"

"Getting hit by a hurricane, that's what being in love's like. Peaceful while the eye passes over, stormy as all get out when the winds come again. Jeb and I are both prideful and stubborn, so when we have a fight, *we have a fight* now."

Priscilla found the piece that fit next to the one she'd put on the tongue. "I thought I was in love once, with my chemistry teacher."

"Really? What's his name?"

"Katherine Link."

She dropped her jaw, along with a clover-shaped piece of cardboard she'd just picked up. "You're a lesbian, Priscilla?"

"No," she replied nonchalantly, "just wanted to see how

you'd react."

"Well you nearly gave me a heart attack, that's how I reacted. Why would you do such a thing?"

"It's a mean streak I have . . ." she leaned back on her hands and sighed. "I like to shock people. Have you let Jeb go all the way yet?"

"Uh-uh."

"Wow, I figured for sure you already had. Then how do you know you're really in love?"

"You just know."

"I've gone all the way before."

"You have?"

"Mm hmm. With Katherine Link."

Shayna laughed. "Seriously, have you ever screwed anybody?"

"Nope, and I won't until my wedding night. I promised my parents I'd save myself for my husband and I never break a promise."

She'd been longing for a confidant. Having a reputation to protect, she hadn't dared risk letting her hair down with any of the girls she'd grown up with. Priscilla obviously trusted her or she wouldn't have said anything about being adopted. A confided secret that wouldn't wreck her image should Priscilla prove untrustworthy would determine whether her new friend could become her best friend. If it didn't get back to her in a few days she'd know her instincts were right. Any gossip worthy tidbit spread through Piler Creek like wildfire within minutes after the talebearer heard it, and there were very few people in this gossipy town that didn't bear that title.

Hmm . . . what secret shall I reveal?

Blinda stood on the porch awaiting her overnight guests. Clyde got out of his car, but his passenger scooted behind the wheel and drove off. "Where's Wyoming going?"

"To a motel," said Clyde, strolling up the walk. "She said she's exhausted and just wants to crash with no chance of being disturbed."

A hot twinge spiraled between her legs. *Welcome back to Graceland, Elvis!*

⸎

Liat kissed her husband on the forehead and tickled his ears. "Ezra, wake up. It's time for bed."

He yawned, stretched his arms, up-righted the recliner, and slowly got up.

Again her thoughts drifted to the night of Shayna's conception.

Like tonight, Ezra had fallen asleep in his recliner. They hadn't made love since she'd first cheated on him with Peter, as his peculiar inability to attain an erection had afflicted him soon after. Having three sons, they hadn't been concerned about not being able to bring another child into the world, but Ezra had begged her to leave him and find a new husband who could keep her happy.

"No one but you can *make* me happy," she'd said, "so how could anyone else keep me that way?"

"Oy vey . . . I can't ask you to give up sex, dear. I don't believe in divorce but this case I know God will forgive. It's not your fault I can't be a total man anymore."

She'd put her hands on her hips and cast him her meanest look. "If I ever hear you talk like that again, Ezra, God will have to forgive me for murder, because I'll strangle you in your sleep. Understood?"

He'd tried not to laugh but hadn't been able to refrain. "I am truly blessed with the best woman in the world for a wife."

"Yes you are, and never forget that. I'd be miserable without you, Ezra. If I have to use my fingers or get a vibrator, that's what I'll do, but I'll never leave you." She'd told him that to keep him from getting suspicious of Peter. Ezra was no fool, he knew she'd go crazy without an outlet for her strong sex drive, and he couldn't even bring himself to kiss her erotically for shame over his inability to follow through, much less satisfy her by any means other than his penis.

That discussion had taken place the night before Passover. About six months after a second Seder went by, she woke him on his recliner, told him to go to bed, and took a hot bath. When she came out of their bathroom naked after drying off, an amazing sight awaited her. Ezra had kicked the covers off in his sleep and lay on his back. His penis jutted through the slit in his briefs, standing as rigid as on their wedding night.

A bomb could explode beside Ezra and not wake him before he'd slept at least five hours. Until that night she'd known only way to fully rouse him during such a state— tickle his ears. Careful not to put her hands anywhere near them, she'd lowered herself onto his shaft, fearing it would turn soft if he woke up. Before long she'd enjoyed the most wonderful climax of her life: thrilling because it had felt so good, soul wrenching because she had thought she'd never have her beloved husband's manhood inside her again, and stupendously romantic because Ezra had awakened just before ejaculating. The biggest smile he'd ever worn had stretched across his face, and he'd grabbed her breasts as they came together.

Apparently for the last time, as it hadn't happened since.

Six weeks later she'd woken up with morning sickness on

the fourth day of Hanukkah, and when July gave way to August at midnight, a beautiful baby girl came out of her womb. Shayna would never know how special she was to them. They had a living reminder of one blissful downpour in the twenty year sexual drought of their forty-two year marriage.

⚮

She couldn't get Clyde all the way up no matter how hard she sucked. Blinda finally relaxed her mouth, raised her head, and sat up beside him on the couch. She'd pulled his semi-erect dick through his trousers while enjoying their first kiss. His hands had been all over her blouse, but he hadn't bothered with a single button. Something else disappointed her too. Not once did he say "Suck it!" or anything else.

"Sorry, Blinda, guess I just drank one too many beers, on top of being drained from telling Roy everything I know about Lee—seeing his reaction and all that. You really turn me on, though, don't think for a minute you don't."

She tousled his hair and smiled. "Don't worry, I understand, Clyde."

He stood up—stuffed his limp weenie inside his shorts, zipped his pants, and blew out a sigh while sitting back down. "This is embarrassing as hell."

"Has it ever happened before?"

"Uh-uh, never. But then I've never had to deliver a message to a man from a woman who lives in a separate dimension before either, so I'm really not all that surprised. Plus I feel guilty for Roy's sake, since you two are seeing each other."

Roy hadn't asked her not to say anything about his

peculiar relationship with Matilda, so she thought providing Clyde with a little information might ease his conscience and put him back in the mood. "Roy and I have an understanding. He sleeps with a woman in Piler Creek on a regular basis. There's no love or even romance, they just satisfy each other sexually. But even if he didn't have another woman in our world, I know things will never be the same between us because of his emotional response to Lee Milan's message."

The clerk started to hand her a key card but a bright light flashed, and Wyoming found herself standing alone in the motel lobby. She looked towards the highway. Not a car could be seen. "Oh shit, I'm in Justified!"

"Yeah, missy, you sure are."

She turned to see the fat man had replaced the clerk.

"Lee wants to talk to you."

FOURTEEN

THE FAT MAN took her by the arm and they were suddenly standing in Lee's living room. Wyoming had scarcely discerned that before he disappeared.

"Good to see you again," said Lee, stepping in from the hall. "I hope Hoyt didn't frighten you too much."

Holding a hand over her palpitating heart, she gave herself a mental pat on the back for not fainting. "So that's what you meant by instantaneous travel when you had Clyde drive us to the courthouse."

Lee nodded. "A number of sensors were put in place when we were cast out of heaven, and nothing can block their power no matter what gets constructed at their sites. That motel lobby you entered happens to stand over one of several in Turnaton. The rest are located where Piler Creek now stands. If you'd never been to our world before we wouldn't have become aware of your presence. I'll take you back there after we visit awhile, and no one that saw you will have a clue you ever left. Please sit down."

Recalling the horrified screams that had terrorized her when she'd last sat on the couch, she chose a chair. "Clyde delivered your message to Roy."

The condemned angel glanced at the ceiling, mouthed *Thank you Lord*, and looked at her with rapidly moistening eyes. "How did Roy take it?"

"He bawled like a baby but was extremely grateful. The man loves you very much."

She covered her face and started weeping. "I miss him so badly ...."

Wyoming wanted to console the sorrow stricken ex-angel, but couldn't speak without crying too. She took a deep breath. Trying to vent the sympathetic emotions engulfing her, she let it out slowly. Another followed, and she started to venture a comforting remark, but Lee spoke first.

"P-Please tell Clyde I can never thank him enough."

"I'll tell him."

"What about Larue?"

"We haven't found him yet, but we're pretty confident the place he escaped from is a technical conglomerate outside Conroe, and we figure he wound up back there, or will eventually."

Lee dropped her hands and gave her a tearful smile. "Even if he didn't, they'll have information on him."

"We have a problem there, I'm afraid. Clyde called and they wouldn't tell him anything."

"What's the name of the place?"

"Callaway's Research Complex. Clyde mapped the driving directions on his computer. It's located six miles east of town."

The smile turned brighter. "That's within fifty miles of here, so Hoyt and Earl will be able to nose around the next time we get to visit the other side. Oh, sorry, I'm speaking as though I were talking to Clyde. We sometimes get to cross over to your world but can't go—"

"Beyond a fifty mile radius, I know. Clyde forwarded me your email. Hope you don't mind."

"Not at all. Now I don't have to bother telling you all that information as I'd planned."

"When will you be able to cross over again?"

"In two weeks. Since you know all I've told Clyde, I don't have to explain that Hoyt, Earl, and I will be as human as you are when we do. The good news is no one at that research center will know they're snooping around, since they'll be invisible. The bad news is I can't risk seeing Larue, so I won't be able to help them."

She frowned. "What will happen if you see Larue?"

"If I were to see him or Roy they'd sense my presence and go hopelessly insane. That's the price of falling in love for my kind. Since I wasn't in love with the man who sired my daughter, it wouldn't do either of them any harm if they were to cross my field of vision while I'm in your world—my emotions wouldn't be strong enough to penetrate their psyches. Whenever Roy happens to be in the vicinity of any of those sensors I told you about, I immediately will myself to that location to get a glimpse of him. He can't sense my presence while he's in his world and I'm in mine. Unfortunately I'll never lay eyes on my son again—at least I pray I won't—because there aren't any sensors outside Turnaton or Piler Creek. Roy would lose his mind if I were to bring him here, as would any of my former lovers—that's why I'm forbidden to contact them—but Larue would lose his life because his heart would immediately revert back to the condition it had deteriorated to before we managed to get him to the other side."

An idea came to her. "It's wonderful that you can at least see Roy on occasion. I hate that he can't ever see you, but I think I know a way for you two lovebirds to communicate."

"You do?!" Lee's eyes glistened with hope for a moment, then turned sad. "I don't see how. I could slap Roy in the face and he'd never know it. We can't manipulate anything in your world except during our visits there. The only exception is when we receive special empowerment to deal with criminals such as Robby Gorgan, and even then we can only perform the operations necessary to reel them in from the physical realm and set up the scenes to make their deaths appear accidental."

Hearing that perverted bastard's name again almost made her puke. She wanted to expunge it from her memory and forget everything about him. The heartrending sincerity of Lee's favor-seeking email, and the obvious truthfulness of the restrictions placed upon the earth bound angels, had been enough to convince her that horrendous video hadn't been manipulated in any way. Clyde agreed they'd been shown the actual murder of a precious little girl, and it devastated her to know she'd been intimate with a sadistic monster. She forced her thoughts past that ugly reality and got back to her idea. "If Roy was to go to that motel lobby and leave a postcard with the message side turned up, you'd be able to read what it says, wouldn't you?"

Lee gasped and slapped her cheeks, forcing her lips to pucker like a perch's. A self deprecating laugh shot through them as she released her face. "I'm a fool. I should have thought of that when I composed my letter to Roy. Thank you so much, Wyoming—you're brilliant!"

"Yeah, well I'd agree if I could figure out how he could read a message from you. It's so sad he can't."

"Terribly sad. I can't even respond to him through you or Clyde, it'd be as severe a violation as if I communicated with him personally." Her expression turned thoughtful as something seemed to occur to her. "Wyoming, I can't ask you to tell him what I'm about to say, but there's no harm in you knowing it. I'll never fail to read his messages, and they don't have to be limited to a postcard, he can write letters— as many pages as he wants—and doesn't have to bring them in the lobby. I'll know he's there when he gets within two hundred feet of it."

She sighed with relief. "I'm glad to hear that because it solves the one flaw in my idea I couldn't figure a way around—the clerks getting suspicious of him repeatedly showing up without renting a room. Am I correct in assuming there's no harm if I were to mention what you just told me to Roy?"

Lee nodded with a knowing smile.

"You weren't allowed to tell me that I could, were you."

Still grinning, she excitedly shook her head.

"Ah, I see what you're up to. I'm all ears."

"If he were to stand anywhere within that vicinity and read the letter to himself—with arms extended so I could see the words clearly—I'd be reading along too. And it would be great if he read them aloud when nobody's watching. Anytime he might decide to do such a thing I'd instantly be there, regardless of the time of day except for Sundays. All the sensors are useless to me then. It would never bore me— I'd be thrilled if he were to do it a hundred times a week or more."

❦

Shayna grinned as Priscilla inserted the last piece, completing a humorous picture of a cartoon heifer sticking out her tongue. "You're good at this."

"I've had a lot of practice. I couldn't believe it when you said you liked jigsaw puzzles. None of my friends in Dallas would ever put one together with me, and not many of them would have paid much attention to that guy at the diner because of his age. We seem to have a lot in common, don't we."

"We sure do—I don't break promises either. Give me your word you won't tell anyone, and I'll share a secret with you."

Priscilla's face lit up. "Oh, cross my heart and hope to die. What is it . . .?"

❦

Wyoming said goodbye and almost instantaneously

accepted the key card from the clerk, feeling like she'd just beamed down from the Enterprise. No time at all had passed in Turnaton, yet she'd had a lengthy conversation with Lee over tea and pecan pie after they'd finished discussing how Roy could communicate with her.

She'd learned that Lee, Hoyt, and Earl required sustenance, secreted bodily wastes, had to sleep, and were sensitive to cold and heat like any normal human. Whatever items the supermarkets, clothing stores, gas stations, or any other businesses had in stock in Turnaton or Piler Creek, were available to them in Justified and Leavenwood free of charge. Anything those two towns didn't have, the three angels imprisoned in human form couldn't obtain. The special equipment at the courthouse was heaven sent.

Whatever they consumed didn't diminish the supply of their counterparts on the other side. Lee had vanished, then returned a few seconds later with the pecan pie. She'd then explained that one just like it still occupied its space in Piler Creek, despite being taken from the bakery in Leavenwood, leaving a vacant spot. The pie had tasted wonderful—the best she'd ever eaten—and Lee advised her to pick one up before going back to Odessa. She planned to do just that.

Lying in a comfortable bed in one of Blinda's spare bedrooms, Clyde worried he might be developing a conscience over women. She'd tried desperately to convince him not to feel guilty, but for the first time in his life a good looking woman, hot for his body, couldn't make him horny enough to seal the deal. Something weird was happening to him, something he couldn't quite get a handle on. Maybe it stemmed solely from the hopeless love between Lee and Roy, but he feared that was only the catalyst to a rude awakening that his brother had been right. His parents and sisters wrote him off as a lost cause, morally, so long ago he couldn't remember the last time any of them had badgered him about being a wolf—but his brother still swore the licentious life would one day lose its appeal.

Could that actually be happening? He couldn't deny feeling grateful for failing to score with Lee, but that was only because of Roy—he'd love to screw Blinda's eyes out. *Nah,* he thought, *there's nothing to worry about—nothing's changed—this was just a weird night, that's all. Nothing to worry about at all . . . .*

According to Blinda, Roy and a woman he'd grown up with used each other for sex without any emotional attachments, and had done so since high school, refraining from the arrangement during the years he'd been intimate with Lee. After falling in love with Roy, Lee apparently did the same with the men she coaxed into her domain. Those two belonged together and he wished there was some way to make that happen.

He'd lied to Blinda about why Wyoming chose to stay at a motel. The real reason was because she didn't want to hear any moans and sighs if he wound up in her bed. He supposed she found the idea disgusting due to seeing it as Blinda betraying Roy. But it turned out that wouldn't have quite been the case. Blinda had given him a rain check to try again some other time, and he definitely planned on cashing it in. If his dick would've responded like his ego, he'd be in her bed right now. She'd made his head swell, but the damn thing had refused to do the same beyond a pitifully useless point.

Oh sure, now you come around, you fucking traitor! he mentally yelled at his fickle penis, swiftly rising as he recalled what happened after Wyoming left:

When they entered the living room Blinda locked the

door and turned to him with a sexy smile. "Did anyone ever tell you that you have an Elvis-like charisma about you, Clyde?"

A sarcastic laugh shot out of his mouth. "Give me a break, I don't look anything like him."

"No, you don't, but the same magnetism he exuded radiates from you like sunbeams. Please, come sit with me on the couch, I want to tell you something else."

Confused, yet enormously flattered over the compliment, he set down and she snuggled beside him. "I've never moved this fast before, Clyde, but I really like you and don't want to waste any time. How about a kiss?"

Sucking face with the hot redhead thrilled him even more than he'd thought it would. Her soft lips and hungry tongue were electrically stimulating, passionately titillating, awesomely arousing, and he couldn't believe his luck when she started unfastening his jeans. He ran his hands all over her big tits, exulting in the feel of them beneath blouse and bra, looking forward to watching her take them off at his request—his modus operandi with any hot chick.

She fished his dick out with eager fingers and lowered her mouth over it. The sensual thrill sent him straight to the clouds, but ecstasy turned to embarrassment when it became obvious his half-hard wasn't going to advance any further. Blinda sucked faster but his rebellious rod stubbornly refused to rise to the occasion.

Now the memory he'd just relived had turned it to steel.

"Blinda! Get in here right now, I'm hard as a rock! I'd come to you but don't want to chance losing any steam! Hurry before I start thinking again and lose it! Blinda?!"

Several minutes went by without her responding.

Shit, she's fallen asleep!

The doorbell woke her. Blinda rolled out of bed and angrily put her robe on. She'd hoped to have Clyde all to herself long enough to finish what they'd started last night. Being totally sober and having hours of sleep behind him to weaken any sense of guilt over Roy would surely have eradicated his psychologically induced impotence. When she got to the living room and saw him let Wyoming in, she immediately started making plans for next weekend. She'd drive all the way to Odessa if she had to.

"Good morning," she cheerfully greeted the intruding blonde while mentally cussing her out.

"Good morning, Blinda."

There seemed to be a trace of animosity in Wyoming's gaze. She ignored it and turned to Clyde. "Did you sleep well?"

"Like a baby." He looked at Wyoming. "How was your motel bed?"

"Pretty comfortable when I finally got in it."

Blinda frowned at her. "Clyde told me you were beat. What happened?"

"It took me a while to finally get to my room. I don't want to go into it now, I'm anxious to get the long drive behind me. I'll tell Clyde all about it on the way home and he'll fill you in. I'm sure you two will be keeping in touch."

Wyoming's tone indicated jealousy and that worried her. If this sexy young thing wanted Clyde there were few women that could compete, and age put her at a disadvantage, having only a few weeks left before saying goodbye to her thirties. "Well at least stay long enough for breakfast."

"I had breakfast at the motel, and it's almost lunchtime. Put your shoes on, Clyde, and let's go home. You can grab something to eat along the way . . . ."

⸺⸙⸺

Liat liked Priscilla Booth and Ezra did too. Shayna had said she was sweet but hadn't mentioned her being such an angel. Not only had she insisted on rinsing the breakfast dishes, she wouldn't even let her or Shayna help put them in the dishwasher. Then she'd asked Ezra for a part time job working with Shayna on Sundays, starting today. He'd agreed and said he'd pay her trainee wages at first and give her a raise once she learned the ropes.

"Oh I don't deserve to get paid until I'm earning it, Mister Gold," she'd politely replied. "I could hardly consider myself productive while I'm merely learning what to do."

⸺⸙⸺

Clyde eased off the gas to keep from speeding as he navigated the Malibu down the steep hill on the western edge of Turnaton. "Okay, so what took you so long to get to your room last night?"

"Inter-dimensional travel."

"What?"

Wyoming grinned. "I paid for the room and the clerk started to hand me a key card, but a bright light flashed, like it did after Larue jumped out of your car, and Hoyt was standing there instead."

"The fat man?"

"Yeah, and the next thing I knew I was in Lee's living room . . . ."

By the time she finished telling him all that happened afterwards, they were in Piler Creek. He stopped at Gold's Bakery per her request. Wyoming wanted to get a pecan pie like Lee had shared with her last night.

He walked in behind her, the pleasant sound of chimes announcing their arrival. Mouth watering confections in glass display cases were the first things he noticed before finding it hard not to stare at a teenage girl being shown how to operate the cash register by another one. Both were very pretty, but the trainee looked a whole lot like Lee— same eye shape and color, same shade of dark brown hair, same breast size. If she was a few inches shorter and a decade older he'd have thought the girl *was* Lee at first sight.

A remarkably attractive middle-aged woman came out from the back, wiping her hands on a towel. "May I help you?"

"Yes," said Wyoming, "I'd like a pecan pie please."

The lady emitted a robust laugh. "I just helped my husband put a dozen in the oven. The leader of a Baptist youth group bought all we had for a picnic. Can I offer you something else instead?"

"How long till they're done?"

"About forty minutes."

Wyoming winked at him. "Well worth the wait, believe me."

***

Shayna had been showing Priscilla how to install the cash register tape when Clyde Burns walked in. She'd never expected to see him again, but now wondered if he and that blonde had moved here. Mama had come to the front to wait on them, depriving her of the opportunity. Busy removing the roll of register paper so she could try her hand at loading it without assistance, Priscilla hadn't noticed him yet. She would soon enough because Clyde kept cutting his eyes to her.

Because of her big tits, no doubt.

Liat invited the waiting customers to join her for coffee in the office, leaving Shayna to watch the front and allow Priscilla to get her feet wet—practically soundproof, the chimes couldn't be heard from here. She poured them each a cup and bade them to sit with her at a small table used for meal and coffee breaks.

She had introduced herself to the instantly likeable couple, and learned they were Clyde Burns and Wyoming Carter from Odessa. Wyoming had gotten a taste of their pecan pie last night while visiting a friend in Turnaton. They'd discussed all that out front. She'd decided not to leave them waiting there because of Shayna and Priscilla. The silly twits couldn't keep their eyes off Clyde. When their staring became painfully obvious, she'd chosen not to embarrass them by demanding they stop it, and removed him from their sight instead.

Ezra stepped in to join her for a well earned break. His puzzled frown made her giggle.

"Not to worry, Ezra, they're only here to rob us."

"Oh, is that all?" He grinned at Clyde. "Well then by all means, please take her too."

"You won't get rid of me that easy. Clyde, Wyoming, this is my hubby . . . ."

Ezra and Liat were talking to them like old friends, so Clyde asked the names of the girls in front, planning to inquire further about the one who looked so much like Lee.

"Our daughter Shayna and her friend Priscilla Booth," informed Ezra.

"Which is the taller one?"

Liat eyed him rather suspiciously. "Priscilla. Why are you so curious about her, Clyde?"

"She bears a striking resemblance to a friend of ours, and I wonder if they could be related."

"Well talk to her and find out."

He blew out a sigh. "What I need to know is too sensitive for a stranger to ask. Our friend hasn't seen her daughter since she was a baby, and has reason to believe she's somewhere in southeast Texas. I think Priscilla might be her."

The bakers' brows rose in unison. Liat lowered hers and said, "What do you need to know to find out?"

"If she was adopted and has a birthmark . . . ."

Larue walked out of the commissary with Tabitha. During lunch she'd pestered him about why he'd been reading legal books in the game room last night. He'd told her it was none of her business and swore never to speak to her again if she breathed a word of it to any of the scientists. Her exceptional aptitude for algebra, geometry, and calculus apparently left little room in her brain for common sense logic, or she'd have known without asking. Maybe if he was an orphan like her the people at Callaway's might feel like family to him too. But he wasn't—he had a real mother and a real home in Justified.

He grabbed his head as that crazy sensation seized him again. Why did that name frighten him so?

"What's wrong?"

"I don't know, Tabitha. I've developed some sort of quirk. Whenever I say the name of the town I'm from, or even think it, I get an almost painful sensation of fear."

"Maybe you were abused as a child and ran away from home rather than just wandering off during one of your spells like you've always thought, and your subconscious is trying to reveal it to your conscious mind."

He didn't know until the kid spoke that the nine-year-old from Dallas was following them. Larue turned around and glared at him. "Who told you about me wandering off as a child?"

The bespectacled inmate shrugged. "Tabitha told me."

"Did you overhear us while you were eating lunch?"

"No."

"Good . . . ."

Clyde drove out of Piler Creek with a couple of boxed up pecan pies resting in his trunk, and two takeout coffees nestled in the cup holders—one black, the other a cappuccino. They'd gone to see Roy after their prolonged stop at the bakery, and left him with tears of joy over learning he could share his thoughts and feelings with Lee for the rest of his life.

Wyoming put an elastic band between her teeth and pulled her hair back with both hands. Holding the bushy pony tail in place with her left, she slipped the fingers of her right through the band, worked it over the blonde fluff until it reached her left index finger, and released it. "Well, Clyde, how does it feel to know Roy's no longer standing in your way with Blinda?"

He snickered. "If I didn't know better I'd say you were jealous, the way you said that."

"Far from it. She's just the type of woman you need."

"Any good looking woman who's not a mere floozy is the type of woman I need. I'm like you, never planning on tying the knot."

That pasted a confused look on her face that she instantly peeled away the moment she noticed him frowning over it.

"What's the matter?"

"Nothing," she replied unpersuasively. "I'm glad Roy's breaking up with her because he's absolutely right. It wouldn't be fair to give her false hopes that he might one day love her like he does Lee. Did you sleep with her last night?"

"No."

A short laugh indicated that surprised and pleased her. "Don't tell me she turned you down."

"Actually, with all the emotional turmoil and one too many beers, I just wasn't in the mood. Anyway, enough about Blinda, let's talk about Lee. So any time you want to visit her all you have to do is go to that motel lobby?"

"Right. Any day of the week except Sunday."

Lee had told Wyoming she didn't want him entering her world except on Fridays because of the rules that applied to her boyfriends. She'd have to officially break up with him to change his status as a suitor, and that would make it impossible for them to ever communicate again. "And she can't ever pull us into her world in a dream anymore, right?"

"Right. She only has the power to do that when it's time to deal with people like you know who, and don't you dare say that monster's name out loud."

He heaved a sigh. Lee's tragic situation had convinced them both she couldn't have had any motivation to mutilate

Robby except for the reason she'd given. "I'm so glad things didn't work out the way I'd planned when I met Lee on the internet. I wish there was some way we could get her and Roy together."

"Yeah . . . it's so sad we can't." She pulled her ponytail over her left shoulder and settled back against the seat. "Have you given any thought about how to approach Priscilla Booth if Liat and Ezra learn she's adopted?"

"No, but if they find out she was, I'll freak if she doesn't have the birthmark."

Wyoming picked up the cappuccino, lifted the lid, and took a sip. "Me too. It'd be too wild a coincidence since she looks so much like Lee."

"I wonder why Lee's boyfriends can only cross to her side on Fridays."

"For their safety . . ." she resealed the cup and stuck it back in the slot. "That's the only time the invisible portals at every entrance road to Turnaton can sense the man's presence and let him into her world without Lee having anything to do with it. The only other way in is through a sensor location like Hoyt brought me through. But if the man ever enters that way, he'll be trapped in her dimension for the rest of his life if he so much as kisses her any time afterwards, and there's nothing she, Hoyt, or Earl can do about it."

"Shit, that's the answer!" he gushed elatedly. "All she has to do is bring Roy across the barrier at that motel lobby and they've got it made."

Wyoming groaned and popped him on the shoulder. "Have you gone senile all of a sudden? If Lee ever sees Roy when they're both in the same dimension he'll go totally insane. You, on the other hand, could live happily ever after with her since she's not in love with you."

He'd forgotten that crappy fact. "Okay, let me make sure I've got this straight. If you or I go near any of those sensors,

Lee, Hoyt, and Earl will know it immediately, but we won't automatically enter their dimension."

"Right, one of them has to will us into it. They can only sense someone at those locations in Turnaton and Piler Creek who's been to their world before, and the sensors don't do them any good on Sundays. When they pull someone across at one, they have the ability to squeeze hours out of nanoseconds during the visit if they choose to, but only for up to half a second of our time. That's how Lee got me back before the clerk noticed I'd left."

That made his brain hurt and he laughingly told her so. "So you weren't sent back in time after all."

"Mm mm, but it sure seemed like it to me. We didn't go back in time after Larue jumped out the car either. When I told Lee about it she said the short while we were in Justified took such an infinitesimal amount of time in our world that no one on the highway could have seen us disappear. Time normally passes in her dimension at the same rate it does in ours, but us being with Larue when his presence caused the transformation, changed it while you and I were there—more drastically than Lee did during my visit—and it went back to normal after we automatically returned to the spot where Larue inadvertently prompted the occurrence. When she sent me back, her time immediately escalated forward to being in synch with ours."

He laughed. "That *really* screws with my noggin."

"Doesn't exactly do wonders for mine either." Wyoming retrieved her cup. "I asked Lee why God permitted them to have sex with normal humans, and you know what she said?"

"What?"

"God mercifully granted them that outlet because of the immeasurable length of their banishment." She cracked the lid, took a quick sip, and resealed it. "They're not allowed to approach anyone who's a virgin or married. Since that's as close as any of them can come to having a husband or wife,

God views the sexual relations as spousal—for the ex angel and the mortal—rather than fornication."

Jeb ambled into the bakery at a quarter to five, holding a Dr Pepper. Shayna gave him his usual chocolate éclair and admired his cute butt as he walked to the booth nearest the front door. Papa had only installed two for customers who wished to eat on the premises, in order to leave more room for displays to whet appetites and loosen pocket books. He and Mama were pleased with how quickly Priscilla was catching on. She'd handled several customers on her own without forgetting what they ordered, ringing up the wrong amount, or giving incorrect change. Papa took her to the kitchen a few minutes ago to show her how the ovens and pastry fryers worked.

They'd gotten to meet Clyde when he and Blondie Big Boobs returned to the front with her parents. Priscilla had giggled at the nickname she'd spontaneously given Wyoming Carter when Mama had taken them in back. She'd been disappointed to learn Clyde hadn't moved to Piler Creek after all, and lived way out west in Odessa.

The chimes announced a customer. She grinned at the redhead walking in. "Let me guess, one order of biscuit dough."

"And a box of oatmeal cookies please," the lady answered with a laugh. "Since you've gotten so familiar with me, may I ask your name?"

"Shayna Gold."

"Hi, Shayna. I'm Blinda Love."

"Nice to meet you, Missus Love."

"Oh I'm not married, and please call me Blinda."

⚬♥⚬

As the pretty Jewish girl went to a cooler for the biscuit dough, Blinda mused on Roy's phone call he'd made two hours ago, to say they needed to discuss their relationship.

"I know it's over," she'd said. "I knew it the moment Wyoming read Lee's message to you."

"I'm really sorry, Blinda."

"No, don't be. I'll be fine. It's you I'm worried about. I wish there was some way you could be with Lee."

"I appreciate that. You sure you're okay?"

"Yeah. Can we still be friends and not fall out of touch?"

"Of course. Would you like to go bowling with Matilda and me Wednesday night?"

They'd said goodbye after she accepted the invitation.

She glanced around while Shayna bagged her order, and recognized a boy sitting in one of the booths, eating a chocolate éclair. She'd seen him at the duck pond in Turnaton talking to a rough looking biker, rumored to be a drug dealer.

⚬♥⚬

Priscilla's jaw dropped when Ezra asked the question. Liat felt it should have been phrased more delicately than just blurting out "Were you adopted?"

"I can't believe Shayna told you that! I thought I could trust her!"

Ezra quickly shook his head. "She didn't tell me, Priscilla. That man I introduced to the two of you asked if you were."

"Clyde Burns?"

He nodded.

"Why?"

"He knows a woman who's trying to find her long lost daughter," Liat answered, figuring she'd best take it from here. "Clyde said you closely resemble her."

"So that's why he kept looking at me."

The disappointment on Priscilla's face came as no surprise. She and Shayna obviously found something about Clyde quite titillating. "Do you know who your biological mother is?"

"No," Priscilla sadly replied. "I was apparently abandoned. My parents adopted me from a state foster home."

"How old were you at the time?"

"They estimated my age to be six months. My parents chose the day the adoption was finalized as my birthday. Why didn't he ask me himself?"

"He felt it would have been inappropriate to ask such a personal question since you don't know him. Ezra and I assured him we'd inquire about it and let him know. There's one other thing he asked us to find out. Do you have a birthmark?"

An odd grin crossed Priscilla's face. "Have him call me and I'll let him know."

"So you do?" asked Ezra.

"I didn't say that. Maybe I do, maybe I don't, but if Clyde wants to know he'll have to ask me personally. My cell number is . . . ."

FIFTEEN

CLYDE DIDN'T HAVE a cell phone and never intended to get one. He didn't like Kindles or Nooks or any such devices invented for e-books either. Books weren't meant to be read on a screen, and mobile telephones were a pain in the ass, but like most people nowadays Wyoming had a smart phone. She'd given Liat her number and the baker called when they'd driven through San Angelo.

Priscilla Booth wouldn't tell anyone but him whether or not she had a birthmark, and had instructed Liat to pass on her cell number. He'd told Liat through Wyoming that he'd call Priscilla as soon as he got home. They were now fifteen miles west of Garden City, less than an hour from Odessa.

Shayna exhaled the pot she'd been holding in her lungs for at least five seconds. It felt blissful to be high again. Rarely had a weekend passed without her getting stoned since Jeb convinced her to smoke a joint with him last summer. That had been her first experience with drugs. Monday mornings she used her one-hitter to knock the edge off, and didn't mess with anything until Friday nights. Jeb had made her swear to the pact to keep from getting hooked—a code he'd lived by since picking up the habit in middle school. She'd begged him to stop when he confessed his secret vice not long after asking her to go steady, and when he'd refused, had sworn to break up with him if he ever dared try to do it in her presence. Mounting curiosity over what he found so appealing about marijuana prompted her to make an exception to her rule on a balmy Friday night last June, and she'd asked him to smoke up so she could observe. The smell alone had tempted her. Then her resolve was weakened further upon seeing how relaxed he'd become while beseeching her to share his second joint. She'd never, for even a second, regretted giving in.

They'd driven Priscilla home from the bakery and stopped for a burger before heading for their parking spot in Turnaton. Someone had plowed a path through a thick grove of evergreens near the golf course. There were a few places on either side where a car could weave between the tree trunks deep enough in the mini-forest to make them hard to spot from the dirt road.

She gazed at a lopsided opening amongst some branches, through which could be seen the hill the imaginary woman and her friends had climbed. Thinking about the hallucination stirred the memory of Blinda Love's peculiar question in the diner. *What* had *she meant about a woman living in an invisible town?*

❧

"I don't see why you won't just call her on my phone," Wyoming complained.

"Because every time I talk on one of those damn things the person on the other end keeps cutting out. We've got a lot to discuss if Priscilla has the birthmark, and I don't want to keep having to repeat myself."

Wyoming grinned. "I think you just don't want me to hear your end of the conversation, Casanova."

"Yeah, that's it," he retorted sarcastically. "Nothing I like more than seducing teenage girls over the phone. Life's too simple right now, so think I'll fuck things up by getting in trouble chasing jailbait."

"She's not jailbait, Clyde. Liat told me Priscilla recently turned eighteen."

"I didn't hear her say that."

"She passed that tidbit on when she called, thinking we might want to know. It's obvious Priscilla has ulterior motives so you'd better be careful. You give a girl that age an inch and she'll take a mile. I'm sure you noticed the way she and Shayna were looking at you."

He'd noticed all right, and his ego still glowed over it. Maybe Blinda hadn't been exaggerating about his so called charisma after all. "Well she won't be able to bluff. If she doesn't have a birthmark the conversation will end there. If she says she does I'll make her describe it to me. If she insists on doing it face to face, I'll say no and give her one last chance to tell me. If she still refuses, she'll be hearing a dial tone, and I'll ask Roy to take it from there."

"I don't recall hearing you describe the birthmark to him."

"I'll fill Roy in when I call him, if I wind up hanging up on Priscilla."

From what Larue could understand after pouring over all the legalese he could find on the subject, he didn't have a chance of getting a judge to revoke Mother's power of attorney over him. He'd been deemed mentally incompetent and only a psychiatrist offering proof he no longer suffered from his spells could request a hearing to have that label removed from his record. If Mother should die, her daughter would inherit control over him, so there was only one way to keep from spending the rest of his life at Callaway's.

Fake his death.

Clyde dropped Wyoming off at her apartment and she followed him home in her car, planning to leave after hearing his conversation with Priscilla. He microwaved two cups of instant coffee, left her in the living room holding the phone button down to be lifted on his signal, and went to his bedroom to call Priscilla Booth.

He dialed and a second later hollered, "Pick up, it's ringing!"

A click sounded in his ear as Wyoming lifted her finger. Two rings later Priscilla said hello.

"Hi, Priscilla, this is Clyde."

"I've been expecting your call." Her voice didn't carry the teenage excitement he'd expected.

"I know you have. Well, let's hear it. Do you have a birthmark?"

Silence.

"Priscilla, are you there?"

"Mm hmm."

"Well?"

"Yes, I have a birthmark."

"Describe it to me please."

"First tell me why the lady you think might be my mother abandoned her daughter."

He hadn't expected this. "Um, she didn't abandon her, she was forced to give her up for her daughter's sake. That's all I can say until you describe your birthmark."

"What sort of birthmark does her daughter have?"

"Uh-uh, you first."

Silence.

"Look, this is extremely complicated. Just describe your birthmark. If it matches I'll tell you everything I know."

"Okay, then how 'bout we do a little give and take. My birthmark isn't flesh colored. If I'm the girl you're looking for you'll know what color it is. If you're not willing to tell me that much, then you're not going to get anything else out of me."

"If I do, will you tell me the rest?"

"Mm hmm, unless you say the wrong color."

"If I say the wrong color then you're not the girl I'm looking for anyway. It's purple."

Silence.

"I'm waiting, Priscilla."

"I have a bright purple asymmetrical V on my inner left thigh just below my . . ." her voice trailed off.

"Vagina?"

"Mm hmm."

He made a victory fist. "I knew it had to be you! Your mother's name is Lee Milan, and you have a half brother."

Silence.

"Did you hear me?"

"I-I need a few minutes," she sobbed. *"I'll call you back in half an hour."*

"Okay, my number is—"

She hung up.

"Don't worry," said Wyoming from his living room phone. *"Her cell will have your number on it."*

"I can't let you past the gate without a security tag, sir."

Roy killed the engine and got out of his pickup. "Then have whoever's in charge come out here and talk to me."

The guard pulled out a cell phone.

He'd opened the shop and lined out his mechanics before driving to Callaway's Research Complex, stopping along the way to read a lengthy letter aloud in the parking lot of the Turnaton Arms Motel. After a syrupy introduction that he meant with all his heart, he continued with *I want to wish a happy Monday morning to the most beautiful woman I've ever seen!* and ended with *Goodbye for now, Lee. I'm off to Conroe to find out if our son is at that think tank like Clyde and Wyoming suspect. Yours forever, Roy.*

A nice two-seater go kart, driven by a teenage girl with acne, passed the inside of the gate. The wide lane apparently encircled the compound because she whizzed by again a while later—this time with a kid wearing thick glasses strapped into the seat beside her. She made another pass before a guy in a mock-military dress uniform, with a garish silver badge centered on his hat, crossed the road.

He'd been kept waiting twenty minutes.

The man stopped behind the gates and motioned for him to come closer.

"I'm Richard Allen, chief of security. What's your name?"

"Roy Milan."

"What brings you to Callaway's?"

"Larue Milan. He's my son and I'm here to see him."

A sympathetic smile erased the smugness on the guy's face. "I'm afraid you're looking for the wrong person, Mister Milan. Our Larue's father died when he was a baby."

"So there is a Larue Milan staying here?"

"Yes."

"Mind if I meet him?"

"No one without security clearance is allowed to enter the parameter, but we accept visitors on Saturdays from noon to eight. You can meet him then, providing you pass a background check. The guard will give you some paperwork to fill out if you're interested in obtaining a visitor's pass."

"Yeah, I'm interested."

"Just fill out the forms and you'll be notified of your status by phone in three or four days."

⟨⟩

"Blow my ever loving mind, Larue! Even Einstein couldn't crack such a complex equation in his head."

"Sure he could, Roger. He'd know to solve the fifteen parenthetical algebraic segments first, divide that solution by its cubic root, add that to the sum of the coefficients, and multiply the total by pi." He yawned and gazed out the window. Tabitha drove by in her go kart. "Of course pea brains like you could never learn how to do it without pencil and paper. Uh-oh, there's about to be a mishap."

"What do you mean?"

A string of cusswords filtered through the windowpanes.

"That. Tabitha just sideswiped a janitor's cart."

Roger snickered and started jotting down the methodology he'd been given.

Larue contemplated his next escape, necessary to enact his plan. If all went as calculated his name would be listed in the local obituaries—cause of death, homicide.

⟨⟩

They left the cafeteria and Jeb headed for wood shop. Shayna had American History first thing after lunch. Priscilla's dad had taken over the class as well as the track team after a stroke caused Coach Taylor's early retirement. She liked him okay, but he didn't have the old coach's sense of humor.

Having grown weary of big city life, Priscilla's parents had planned to move to a small town after she graduated from Hillcrest High School in Dallas. When they learned Piler Creek needed a replacement for Coach Taylor, her father applied for the job, intending to have his wife and daughter join him when the school year ended should he get it. An unusual situation at the nursing home altered the plan. Priscilla's mother had the perfect qualifications to replace the administrator, who'd been arrested for fraud. Such opportunities come few and far between in small towns, so Priscilla had agreed to graduate as a Piler Creek Pirate instead of a Hillcrest Panther.

Shayna settled into her desk with a smile, pleased she hadn't heard any gossip concerning the secret. She'd told Priscilla about seeing the imaginary people disappear on that hill outside Turnaton. Of course she hadn't mentioned what caused the illusion, saying instead, "I hope there's not something wrong with me, because I could have sworn they were real."

"Thanks, Roy, I'll pass on the good word." Wyoming slipped her cell phone into a hip pocket of her jeans and went to Clyde's office.

He looked up from a ledger. "What are you grinning about?"

"Larue's at Callaway's all right—Roy went there this morning. He applied for a visitor's pass and should be able to go see him Saturday."

"That's great . . .!" Clyde pushed away from his desk and whirled around in his chair, grinning at the ceiling.

"Well, I'd better get back to the counter, we're pretty busy."

"Need help?"

"No, but I'll holler if we do."

She rented out three bulldozers, two front end loaders, five backhoes, a crane, and a slew of portable generators before six o'clock finally arrived.

Soaking in her tub beneath a blanket of bubbles, Wyoming kept thinking about Clyde's statement: *I'm like you, never planning on tying the knot.* It bothered her then and it bugged her now. She had a valid reason for not wanting to marry and have children, but he didn't. The way his eyes lit up when he'd mentioned spoiling his nieces and nephews showed he obviously loved kids. He'd probably make a wonderful father, and god there were way too few in this wicked age.

Her dad left almost as much to be desired as her drunkard mother. He'd never had a problem with booze, but being an uneducated laborer in the oil patch, working sunup to sundown six days a week—a lot of times seven—had left him too tired to do anything when he came home but eat supper and doze in front of the TV during her childhood. Two weeks a year he'd been a joy to be around, then turned back into a grouchy ogre when each vacation ended. Clyde was fun loving, compassionate, energetic, and had a college degree. Not once had she heard him complain about how hard life was, like her father constantly did.

Priscilla had agreed to meet Larue after she'd finally

called back last night. Her half hour had turned out to be almost triple that. Oddly enough, she hadn't flirted with Clyde at all. Apparently she'd wanted to talk directly to him solely to find out all she could about her mother, despite having made goo-goo eyes at him at the bakery.

Stretched out on her bed naked, Blinda dialed and brought the phone to her ear.

"Hello?"

"Hi, Clyde."

"Blinda?"

"Mm hmm. Where are you?"

He laughed. *"At my house of course. You called me, remember."*

"No, silly, I mean what room."

"The living room."

"Guess where I am."

"Where?"

"In my bed, wearing nothing."

"Oh yeah?"

His seductive tone thrilled her. "Mm hmm. Why don't you do likewise."

"Oh you got it!"

"Good. Call you back in five minutes, you sexy thing."

He heaved a pleasured sigh and grabbed the receiver. "Well hello there, naked lady."

"What?!"

Oh shit . . . "Sorry, Priscilla, I thought you were someone else."

The call waiting beep sounded. "Hold on a second, okay?"

"Okay."

"Blinda?"

"Mm hmm." She said it slow and sultry.

"Listen, I'll have to call you back. We found Lee's daughter and she's on the other line."

"Really?"

"Yeah."

"Does Roy know?"

"Not unless Wyoming told him when he called her today to say he found out Larue's at Callaway's like we thought. Gotta go. Keep your clothes off and don't leave that bed!" He popped the button to bring Priscilla back. "Are you still there?"

"Yeah."

"Good. What's up?"

"I was so weirded out last night I forgot to ask who my father is."

"Lee didn't say but I'll find out for you."

"Thanks. Who did you think I was when I called, a girlfriend?"

"Uh, yeah. Let me apologize once more for that."

"You were going to have phone sex, weren't you."

He faked a laugh. "Nah, I was just popping off. We kid around like that when we call each other."

"I have phone sex a lot."

"Um . . . you do?"

"Nah, I was just popping off. See ya."

The doorbell rang before he could call Blinda back. He slipped on a pair of shorts and went to the living room. Wyoming was at the door. She raised her brows upon seeing his bare chest and apologized for waking him up.

"You didn't, I never turn in this early. I was . . . uh . . . never mind. Have a seat in the living room and I'll go put a shirt on."

He called Blinda and wanted to kill Wyoming when the hot redhead answered by saying, *"Wanna fuck?"*

"Dammit this just isn't my night, Blinda. You're not going to believe this but I just got crashed by company and have to go. Can I get a rain check for tomorrow night?"

An angry sigh filled his ear. *"We'll see . . . ."*

Clyde put on a t-shirt and went back to the living room. The tense look on her face and the stiff way she sat on his couch let him know Wyoming hadn't come over to discuss the situation with Lee. "What's up?"

She cleared her throat and asked if he had any liquor in the house.

"Yeah, that bottle of Jack you brought over Friday. You left your Mountain Dew too."

"Good." She went to the kitchen.

He stood there scratching his head for a minute, and decided to grab a beer. Popping the top off a Bud Light, he watched her pour a finger of whiskey in a tall glass before filling it to the brim with Mountain Dew. She was the only person he'd ever heard of that mixed the two. "What's got you so on edge this evening?"

"You . . ." she took a big gulp and lowered the glass.

Scanning the possibilities of what she meant by that, he settled on the most likely conclusion. "Ah, you think I should back off from Blinda, don't you."

"Yes, but that's not why I'm here."

"Oh-Kay. So why are you here?"

She took another big pull and puckered her lips while swallowing. "Curiosity for one thing. What made you so anti-marriage?"

"I don't have anything against marriage, it's just not what I'm looking for, that's all."

"Why?"

"Because I don't want to give up my freedom."

"Is that the only reason . . .?" she raised the glass again.

"Yep. Same with you, isn't it?"

"No."

He frowned. "Then why are you so against it?"

"Because of my upbringing." She set her drink on the cabinet and sighed. "My parents fought all the time. We're not talking mere arguing, Clyde, they *screamed* at each other in blind rage. Still do. They get so out of control it's a miracle none of their fights have ever turned physically violent. I can't tell you how many times they woke me up at night. I'd lay awake for hours until they finally exhausted themselves."

That really surprised him. Wyoming came off like the type of girl who'd been raised by Ward and June Cleaver. "I'm sorry to hear that, but you can't let your parents' squabbles dictate your views on marriage."

"Well they did and there's nothing I can do about it."

"You didn't have to drive all the way over here to ask me that. Why didn't you just call?"

"Because I've got another question to ask you, Clyde—a major one—and didn't want to do it over the phone."

SIXTEEN

"WOW, SO WHAT are you gonna do?" Shayna asked, the moment she closed her bedroom door.

"I'm not going to say anything to Mom and Dad until I meet him."

They'd just entered her room after Priscilla whispered a big secret on their way upstairs. Clyde Burns knew her natural mother and had also informed her of a half brother. "When do you get to meet your mother?"

Clyde wouldn't explain why, but said I can never go see her, and she can't come see me."

"Oh dear . . ." Shayna set down on her bed. "She must be in prison."

"Mm mm. I could visit her if that was the case." Priscilla grinned and sat next to her. "Before I came over I called him to find out who my father was. He doesn't know but said he'd ask Lee. He wasn't expecting me to call, and guess what he said when he picked up."

"What?"

"*Well hello there, naked lady.* He thought I was his girlfriend calling."

She giggled. "How embarrassing."

"Mm hmm. I played with his head a little, but immediately let him off the hook."

They'd moved to the living room. Wyoming sat on the couch with her drink, but he stood with arms folded, pondering her request. Her apartment lease would expire soon and she didn't want to sign a new one. "Do you really think you could stand living with me?"

"Unless there's another side of you I don't know about, I'm certain of it. I think we'd make great roommates, and I'd pay half the rent of course. I just love this house."

He snickered. "I'm not renting, I own it. My brother and I built this place from the ground up after I helped him build his. All I pay besides lights and water is property tax."

She gawked at him as if he'd just pulled his shirt apart to reveal the S beneath it. "So there *is* another side of you I didn't know about. That's awesome, Clyde."

"Thought I was just a number cruncher, didn't you. I put myself through college working as a carpenter. I learned a long time ago to keep quiet about being good with my hands because everybody *always* needs something repaired, and I don't like putting my tool belt on unless I absolutely have to. This is a three bedroom two-and-a-half bath. The spare bedrooms are full of junk, that's why I didn't show you around when you made supper for me. If you're willing to clean one of them out, do your share of household chores, split the grocery and utility bills, you're welcome to stay."

Her provocative lips stretched into an excited grin. "Whichever one has the half bath is the one I want."

"Makes sense. You can bathe in the hall bathroom. Now then, just where do you plan to store all my junk?"

She laughed. "If it's junk, why can't I just throw it away?"

"Because it's junk I wanna keep, that's why."

"Men don't know how to store stuff. I'll bet I can rearrange the other bedroom where it'll hold it all."

He shot her a cocky grin to show how crazy that notion was. "I'll call you a storage genius if you can pull that off. Speaking of pulling things off, I need to email Lee. Priscilla wants to know about her dad."

～✦～

Blinda had started out masturbating on her bed, but wound up in another room to finish. She'd been lying in the bathtub for several minutes with the drain open as warm water sprayed out of the faucet, delightfully massaging her slit. Images of Elvis shifted to Clyde and back again, almost as rapidly as a strobe light.

Suddenly both hunks froze in her thoughts. She grabbed her tits and arched her back as the hot orgasm began.

They stood above her naked, aiming their stiff cocks as they peed—their mingling hot piss, rather than water gushing from the spout, splashing against her clit. Sexily shouting obscenities, they begged her to climax, swearing it would make them come too.

"Oh yes, guys, I'm gonna do it! Ohhhhhhh . . . oh my god, oh my god . . . p-piss on me, piss on me, *PISS ON MEEEEE . . .!*"

Their urine turned to semen at the peak of her pleasure.

She pushed the drain knob with her big toe and let the tub fill as she savored the aftermath of an outrageously strong orgasm. She'd never even thought about golden showers before, much less find the idea erotic, so she was totally dumbfounded over the fantasy, and how ferociously it had thrilled her.

Eyes closed, she sighed, smiled, and muttered, "Oh, Roy . . . what *have* you created?"

～✦～

"You jerk . . ." Wyoming seated herself in front of Clyde's computer to peruse the email he'd obnoxiously refused to read aloud. Half an hour after emailing Lee, he'd checked to see if she'd replied, and she had.

He stood at the side of his desk, grinning over her irritation.

Hi Clyde,
First off, thank you so much for filling me in on my daughter!!! How fortuitous that my deciding to treat Wyoming to a piece of pecan pie led you straight to her! I can't help but think God must have put it in my heart to do that. Priscilla is a lovely name and I'm selfishly proud to hear she favors me. I'm REALLY looking forward to seeing her a week from next Sunday when Hoyt, Earl, and I cross over. Now on to her father.

His name is Vance Gore. He's six-three and has brown eyes. He was a trim, fit, handsome man with black hair when I knew him, but he's forty-nine now so those attributes have likely changed. I haven't sensed his presence from any of the sensors, nor have I seen him on my visits to the other side since I was forced to break up with him a week before releasing Priscilla. I apparently hurt him so badly he moved away from the area immediately after, so I have no idea where you'll find him.

He was a plumber by trade, and lived in a trailer park outside Piler Creek during our time together, which was very short as I got pregnant on his second visit. I've only had one other relationship that didn't last at least three years (by the way, I'm allowed only one boyfriend at a time in case I forgot to tell you).

That's all I know.

When you're finally able to talk to Larue all his memories will awaken as soon as you start explaining everything, and he'll be able to convince Priscilla that I was forced to give her up and am not purposely avoiding her now. The part of me that's in her will know he's telling the truth. I'm in the process of doing a self portrait where I'm conservatively dressed. I'll email a snapshot of it as soon as I finish so you can print out a copy for each of my children. Then they'll at least have a picture of their mother. It's heartbreaking I can't communicate with them directly. I am so very, very grateful to you, Clyde!!!!!

Always know that,

Lee

Shayna waited with bated breath to hear what Clyde had to say. He'd called a few minutes ago. Judging by Priscilla's vacillating expressions, the news about her father was apparently good and bad. Watching her pace back and forth, she noticed Priscilla's hips weren't perfectly round after all, but they certainly weren't square like a box. She'd trade butts with her if it meant acquiring those big shapely boobs as well.

How awful it must be not to know one's parents. She couldn't fathom being deprived of hers. Priscilla being unable to ever visit her mother or vice versa seemed very untenable if the woman was really alive as Clyde had said. She suspected he'd lied about that for Priscilla's sake. What else but death could make such an arrangement impossible?

Roy smiled while opening the shop. Blinda joined them last night and they'd had a great time at the bowling alley. As usual, Matilda scored above one-eighty, the highest he'd ever been able to reach. He'd come away with second place, barely edging out Blinda, who'd bowled a one-thirty-nine.

The awkwardness he'd anticipated upon seeing her again turned out to be a needless concern. She'd been as relaxed around him as if they'd broken up three years ago rather than only three days. When he'd called it a night at Matilda's apartment above the diner, Blinda hadn't tried to persuade him to change his mind. The two gals had been discussing hair products over coffee and cake. God only knew where the conversation would've gone from there, so he'd strategically bailed.

He raised the bay door and saw Hal getting out of his pickup. A light drizzle that had been falling for the last half hour turned to a downpour after he'd taken a few steps.

"Fuck!" the former cornerback yelled while running across the tarmac, exhibiting the same Deion Sanders speed he'd had in high school. Hal had suffered three severe concussions as a Piler Creek Pirate, otherwise he'd be a senior at some big name college by now, playing on a full scholarship and destined for the NFL. He flew into the bay and started shaking his arms to shed water from his sleeves. "Fuckin' serves me right."

"Why's that?"

"Jeb hit me up for cash twice to take Shayna to that new restaurant in Turnaton. Well, last night I decided to check it out myself and the fucking place hasn't opened yet. When I went to bust his chops for conning me, Mom said he was off somewhere with Tony Popp, and that she's been real worried about him. She thinks he's smoking weed."

He couldn't picture clean cut Jeb Turner and Tony Popp as potheads. "What makes her think they're doing that?"

"Nah, she wasn't worried about Tony. She found a pipe in Jeb's drawer. When she asked him about it, he said he'd just wanted to see what it was like and the tobacco made him sick, so he only did it that once. But later on she found a package of rolling papers. Jeb swore he'd never seen them before and one of his friends must have planted them as a joke. Lame, huh?"

"As a duck," Roy agreed. "So you think he used the money he bummed from you to buy marijuana?"

Hal nodded. "Or something worse. Mom said he came home Sunday night acting real weird, laughing about everything. Dad thought he was drunk and demanded to know who bought the booze for him. Jeb said he was just high on life. Anyway, I'll get the truth out of him or rip him apart trying."

"Oh boy . . ." Roy ran a hand over his face. "If he is messing with drugs and Shayna's involved, he'd better pray her parents never get wind of it. There won't be enough left of Jeb to bury after Ezra gets through with him, and Liat will pulverize his remains."

"Don't I know it. Well that valve job ain't gonna do itself. Guess I'd best get after it."

A Toyota pulled up. The passenger door opened and his other mechanic got out. George's wife drove off as he hurried inside.

"What's on the plate this morning, Roy?"

He grinned and pointed at his dad's fifty-seven Chevy, being restored for the third time. "What's the thing you hate the most."

George groaned. "Aw shit, I've gotta repack the wheel bearings on your old man's heap?"

"Only all four of them, and it's a classic, not a heap."

"That's for sure," Hal affirmed as he situated one of the Chevy's cylinder heads on a jig, preparing to drive out the old valve guides with an air chisel. "Say, how's everything going with Blinda?"

"We mutually decided to just be friends."

"Oh yeah? Then I guess you won't mind if I ask her out."

It didn't surprise him to hear that—Hal's eyes always lit up with lustful excitement every time Blinda dropped by the shop. "She's too old for you, hoss."

"How old is she?"

"Don't know, but you can bet your ass she didn't graduate high school too many years after your mother."

"But I like older women."

"Yeah, I know. Your last girlfriend was a whole year older than you. What happened there anyway?"

Hal made an acrid face as if he'd bitten into a lemon. "I got fed up with her bitching about everything. Nothing suits her. If that gal couldn't gripe she'd explode like a microwaved frog."

"She sure has a serious set of chili chongas though," sniggered George, raising the hydraulic lift until the Chevy's wheels were chest high.

"Yeah, she was a great lay too. That's the only reason I put up with her mouth for so long."

That caused a cold spike of misery to chill Roy's insides. He'd never be able to remember the thrills Lee must have given him. He went to his office so they wouldn't notice his foul mood and ask what brought it on.

∾⚬∾

Lee had occupied his thoughts all morning, drifted to the back of his mind during lunch while he'd visited with Matilda, and returned full force when he'd made a round trip to the Turnaton Arms Motel two hours ago. He couldn't wait to meet their son, and told her so as he finished writing his fifth love letter. She'd be reading the six pages with invisible eyes tomorrow.

His desk phone rang. A glance at the Caller ID showed the call came from Callaway's Research Complex.

"Hello?"

"Could I speak to Roy Milan please?"

"Speaking."

"Mister Milan, this is Richard Allen. I'm calling about your request for a visitor's pass. I regret to inform you that Larue's mother wouldn't approve it."

"You mean his foster mother," he said through gritted teeth. "What's her name?"

"Sorry, can't tell you—company policy. Have a good day."

Thursday afternoons were usually slow, but not this one. Wyoming had to ignore the cell phone vibrating against her right buttock, and let the call go to voicemail. Judy had a line of customers in front of her as well. The forty-year-old newlywed had returned from vacation Monday after spending the bulk of her two weeks honeymooning in Puerto Vallarta. Her last name had been changed for the third time, and Wyoming hoped she'd finally found the right guy. Being the first member of the upfront crew to quit snubbing her after learning she'd been given weekends off had automatically made Judy her favorite.

Wyoming pressed the buzzer, placed her customer's deposit in the cash drawer, and handed him an invoice designating which backhoe he'd been allotted. A gofer responding to her alert came through the back door, letting in the stench of diesel and exhaust fumes from outside. She pointed at him and said, "That guy over there will get you fixed up. Good luck on your project."

The next customer requested a jackhammer. Two more joined the end of her line by the time she got him taken care of. The cashiers were going to be pissed, but she wasn't going to let anyone take Thursday afternoons off anymore.

Clyde came out of his office. Seeing they were swamped,

he told Judy to take a break.

Fifteen minutes later Judy returned to the register and he relieved her.

Wyoming poured a cup of coffee, pulled out her cell, and set down at the computer desk. Her feet were aching from having to stand in one spot so long. She checked to see who'd vibrated her butt, and returned the call. Roy Milan answered on the third ring.

⚬⚬⚬

Blinda hadn't gotten the chance last night to ask Roy if Wyoming told him they'd found Lee's daughter. Matilda would likely have gotten curious and started asking questions. After he left they'd visited for quite a while. She'd hoped Matilda might mention her dead boyfriend, but the topic never came up. The guy must have really been something special to cause a teenage girl to say goodbye to love for the rest of her life, and she was dying to hear all about him.

She couldn't wait for tomorrow night to get here. Clyde would be picking her up at Midland International Airport, located only ten miles from Odessa. She'd decided not to have phone sex with him so he'd be all the more eager for the real thing over the weekend.

⚬⚬⚬

Tabitha had been sucking Richard Allen's dick for almost six years. He promised her a car when she turned eighteen. She knew he'd keep his word, because not only would he lose his job, but his freedom as well if the police were to learn he'd enticed a twelve-year-old to go down on him in exchange for a bicycle. No bribe could tempt her to let him ejaculate in her mouth, and he knew she'd report him if he ever dared to. When she'd started sprouting boobs he'd begged her to start blowing him topless so he could shoot on her chest instead of into a paper cup. Agreeing to that deal had netted her a nice leather jacket and a go kart.

She'd been wiping his jism off her tits when Larue's foster mom called, and hadn't finished buttoning her blouse when he'd phoned Roy Milan.

SEVENTEEN

WYOMING'S PLANS TO start moving his stuff out of the spare bedroom Friday evening got scrapped. She sat beside him on a Houston bound jet. From there they'd rent a car and drive to Piler Creek, located about ninety minutes from the airport. Turnaton, their destination, was closer to Houston, but Blinda said that particular route had miles of construction underway, and strongly advised against taking it. They'd be at Callaway's tomorrow, hanging around with Roy outside the think tank during visiting hours. If Larue ventured anywhere near the area he'd recognize them and they'd be able to talk to him through the wrought iron fence Roy described. After twenty-one years he most likely wouldn't place Roy, who certainly couldn't spot Larue, so they'd agreed to spend yet another weekend in southeast Texas.

Clyde couldn't help disliking Larue's foster mother even though he'd never met the lady. Refusing to let a stranger visit Larue he could understand, but if she'd really been acting in his best interest she'd have wanted to at least meet Roy herself and size him up since he went by Milan. It seemed pretty clear her actions were motivated by greed— she didn't want to risk Larue coming in contact with a blood relative. If she lost power of attorney she'd lose the goose that laid the golden egg. But she was destined to in the end, a DNA test guaranteed it. He hoped it wouldn't come to that for Roy's sake, because it required a lawyer to force the procedure, and no telling what it might cost to fight the legal hounds Callaway's could afford.

Roy passionately envied Clyde and Wyoming. They'd left half an hour ago to spend the night with Lee and meet up with him at the Turnaton Arms tomorrow morning. He'd be standing in the parking lot at nine-thirty so his sweetheart could read his Saturday letter before they arrived at ten. If Lee wasn't forbidden to reveal another location to her visitors, she'd be perusing all his future love sonnets at a sensor in Piler Creek.

The city limits sign read *Justified* just as Lee had assured it would in her email. Clyde steered the rental down the hill, across a level section of pavement, and coasted steeply downward, soon arriving at the first traffic light. He felt a little giddy as he turned left. Hands off though she was, he couldn't wait to see Lee again. Another left at the stop sign, and four blocks later they arrived at the blonde-brick house with evergreens lining the sidewalk.

Lee stood on the porch, smiling and waving. The instant he got out of the car Clyde knew this had been a big, *big* mistake.

Larue enacted the plan in his mind once more.

Callaway's would receive a ransom demand shortly after he escaped. He estimated they'd pay as high as a hundred

214 ARLEY OWENS, JR.

thousand dollars to get him back. The kidnapper's letter, pieced together from newspaper clippings, would read:

To whom it may concern:

I happened across a man whose mental state was in such disarray I felt compelled to take him into my home for his own protection. Imagine my surprise when I learned his condition was only temporary and he possesses an astounding intellect and amazing abilities that your scientists have been trying to duplicate for many years. I'm not greedy by nature but cannot pass up this unique opportunity to have my Good Samaritan-ship rewarded.

Larue Milan trusts me, and believes I will allow him to partake of my hospitality indefinitely. One hundred thousand dollars in unmarked bills of various denominations, all smaller than hundreds, will insure his safe return to you. Otherwise I'll offer him to a rather unsavory friend of mine with underworld contacts for that same amount. I'm sure he'll gladly pay me that sum as some foreign government is bound to reimburse him many times over my humble fee to acquire Larue once they receive proof of his talents, which can be easily displayed in a video.

This offer will expire at midnight three days after the post date. If by then I haven't received payment via the accompanying instructions, you'll never see Larue again.

They'd be instructed to drop the money into a dumpster at a location he'd decide on after making his escape. It wouldn't matter how many lawmen watched from afar, prepared to nab the kidnapper, for nobody would show up. They'd be forced to conclude something went wrong. Later on—at a site also yet to be determined—they'd find his blood on a piece of cloth, torn from the shirt he'd be wearing when last seen at Callaway's. They'd assume the kidnapper's underworld friend must have taken the prized guinea pig by force, and most likely killed the kidnapper while doing so. When the FBI and Interpol failed to uncover any clues to the whereabouts of Larue Milan, they'd eventually conclude whatever injury spilled his blood must have been fatal.

In order to change his appearance, he'd smash his nose with the side of a hammer and saturate the torn cloth by using it to wipe away the blood. With a shaved head and severely deviated septum, he'd survive as a pickpocket at first, memorizing the names and addresses of each victim in order to reimburse them before enjoying the dividends of shrewd investments made with their stolen cash.

Tabitha barged into his room and closed the door behind her. A cheesy smile on her face told him she knew something juicy that he didn't. "Okay, what are you dying to tell me?"

"Oh, nothing major, Larue—just one of the most important things you'll ever hear, that's all."

"What?"

She put her hands behind her back and started swaying side to side. "I know who your daddy is, I know who your daddy is."

"My father's dead."

"No he's no-ot, and I know who he is."

Shivers ran through his body: Tabitha wasn't joking. He bolted off the bed and grabbed her shoulders. "Who is he?"

"Roy Milan."

"How did you happen across this information?"

"Kiss me and I'll tell ya . . ." she puckered her lips and closed her eyes.

A whitehead at the corner of her mouth would have made him barf at the thought if he hadn't known she was teasing. "You've heard me mention that name lots of times, so how do I know you're not just making that up?"

Her eyes popped opened in synch with the pucker's disappearance. "Because I overheard Richard Allen talking to him over the phone yesterday. And I happen to know your foster mother wouldn't approve his visitor's pass so he could come see you tomorrow. Today I overheard a snippet from another conversation he was having with one of the guards, and that enabled me to put it all together. A guy tried to come see you Monday and claimed he was your father. It has to be Roy Milan, otherwise why would your foster mom refuse to okay his visit?"

He'd long suspected Roy Milan wasn't really his uncle, but what reasonable explanation could there be for the pretense if half his genetic code came from him? "Why would he and my mom want to keep me from knowing he sired me?"

She shrugged. "How should I know?"

Incest? That would explain it. Maybe Roy Milan really was his uncle after all, as well as his father. Or perhaps he and his mom were cousins.

It would have been very painful to disfigure his face—emotionally as well as physically—but he didn't have to worry about it anymore.

Learning his father was alive and looking for him, changed everything.

∽✢∾

Blinda wasn't home, so Clyde went for a walk, hoping to clear his head . . . .

∽✢∾

A fidgety expression had sprung to Clyde's face when

they'd gotten out of the car, and he'd asked Lee to send him to the other side. She'd taken him by the arm and granted his request is if knowing what troubled him. Wyoming stood on the porch gazing at her bewilderingly. "I don't get it. He was really looking forward to visiting with you, so I'm blown away. What's going on?"

Lee sighed and put her hands on her hips. "I hope he merely decided to stay at Blinda Love's house and wasn't motivated by something else that I'd rather not mention. You told me on your last visit that she was a beautiful redhead, remember?"

"Yes, but he'd already made plans to stay with her tomorrow night so I doubt that's the reason. Is that where you sent him?"

"Mm hmm. If I'd chosen to take him to another location you'd have seen me disappear with him and quickly reappear again. We can only send people to the other side from where we happen to be at the time. Those born in your world, that is. I couldn't have done that with Larue even if it hadn't been a Sunday when he came back. It requires the concentration of at least three of my kind to open the gateway to pass our offspring through.

"Since Clyde is still a potential suitor and drove that rented car here, it'll cause Justified to transform the same as it would if he walked beyond the city limits. When you leave tomorrow, just drive out of town and turn around. You'll be entering Turnaton. Once you do, no matter how often Clyde comes and goes it won't change to Justified again until next Friday. It'll be that way until I officially break up with him. I'm sure you'll find him at Blinda Love's house."

That reminded her of a mystery that had yet to be explained. "Speaking of that, the day after we met you, Clyde and I tried to go back to Leavenwood and Justified. But when we drove by the Leavenwood city limits sign we wound up in—"

"Piler Creek," Lee interrupted, "and when you left town it transformed back to Leavenwood. And the same thing happened when you reached Justified—you found yourselves in Turnaton after you topped the hill. That phenomenon will never happen to either of you again because your essence can only be extracted once. When a person is brought here in such a manner, he or she will experience the same thing the first time they visit Piler Creek or Turnaton, if they ever do. Let's go inside, I've got some fresh coffee waiting."

They went to the kitchen and she asked Lee if her supposition about the child killer was correct.

"Well, it's true Robby wasn't brought here in his sleep as you and Clyde were, but it all really happened. I told Clyde this is impossible to explain in a way you two could understand it. You really were in Robby's plane, and Clyde really did drive his car here. When we sent you back the mileage reversed to what it'd been before he left to come see me. However, the speedometer wouldn't have recorded a return trip if it hadn't changed, because it wasn't driven back to Odessa but sent there. In your world that period of hours went by in less than a second, so what else could you have thought upon waking rather than it was only a dream?"

That revelation almost made her faint, but she managed to compose herself.

"Are you all right, Wyoming?"

"Yeah . . . that just really shocked me that's all. What about the people Clyde interacted with along the way when he filled up his car, had lunch, and stopped for snacks? And what about our boss? In the dream or whatever it was, Thornton Kelly got pissed when I told him Clyde said he was sick. Yet he didn't remember anything about it when he came in bitching at him about your email. How do you explain that?"

Lee set a cup of coffee before her and sat down. "Once

again, it's impossible to in a way you'd understand. An extremely oversimplified explanation would be to say you were pulled into a possible future involving only the three of you and those you interacted with, that all disintegrated in everyone's memories except yours and Clyde's when that period of time was reeled back in to be replaced by what actually happened that Friday. The only events that remained of that possible future was Robby Gorgan's death and his crashed plane."

Clyde had walked a long way from Blinda's house and was ambling around a park with a big pond in the center of it. He couldn't stop lusting after Lee. It was as if he'd been given a love potion or had a spell cast on him, making him desire her like a drug addict craved a fix. His feelings for her had turned brotherly after learning how much she loved Roy, and he'd looked forward to visiting her as a friend, enjoying her beauty as harmlessly as if viewing a scenic landscape. But when he'd looked at her after getting out of the car, an abnormal hormonal surge prompted him to have her send him away—he'd have raped her on the porch in front of Wyoming if she hadn't. He'd never experienced such overpowering lust, and couldn't have controlled his actions any more than a horny dog could when a bitch came into heat.

No doubt he'd be sleeping in Blinda's bed tonight, but that didn't excite him, he only wanted Lee. Even if Wyoming were to throw herself at him right now it couldn't cool off the feverish heat of passion consuming him. The blood and gore splattered on Lee's naked body no longer prevented him from relishing the memory of her jutting breasts, lush pubic hair, and voluptuous ass. He wanted Lee Milan more than anything he'd ever longed for in his life.

He'd thought getting away from her would trip the breaker on this crazy lust circuit and cool things off, but it had only intensified his emotions, flooding him with regret over asking her to do it.

Think of Roy, he told himself, *that's what I've gotta do. He loves her, I only lust after her. He needs her, I only want her. He cherishes her, I only . . . shit, I've got to have her and that's all there is to it!*

⌘

Blinda hadn't gotten jealous when Clyde decided to spend the night at Lee Milan's, merely offended that he'd chosen to visit a friend instead of sleeping with her. Roy's dealings with Callaway's Research Complex had forced her to exchange her roundtrip ticket for another flight to leave next Friday. At least she'd have Clyde all to herself tomorrow after he came back from Conroe. Wyoming would again be staying at a motel, and they'd be leaving for Houston at noon Sunday to catch their return flight back to Odessa.

She'd driven to Piler Creek to hang out with Roy and Matilda for the evening. They'd been chatting over coffee in the diner for the last two hours, and Hal Turner, who'd fixed her car, joined them a few minutes ago.

Matilda excused herself to help one of her waitresses take care of a group of teenagers maneuvering into the circular booth. Hal waved at them. They all returned the gesture, and one of the boys came over, eyeing her all the way.

"Hey, Tony," said Hal, "how's it hangin'?"

"To the left like always," he returned with a grin before refocusing on her. "Um, ma'am, I overheard you say something last Saturday, and I'm curious what you meant by it. You said something about a lady living in an invisible town."

She glanced at Roy and saw the same *Oh shit!* look that must have been on her face.

Roy cleared his throat and grinned at the teen. "We were just joking around."

"Didn't sound like a joke to me."

"Well that's all it was, hoss."

Hal was frowning. "What's he talking about?"

"Aw, he just heard Blinda popping off last Friday, that's all."

"Yeah," she quickly added. "Like Roy said, we were just joking around."

The kid still looked skeptical, but returned to the booth.

Matilda came back after helping the waitress dole out banana splits and fountain drinks to the teenagers.

Her cell phone rang. She dug it out of her purse and frowned. The call came from a payphone in Turnaton. "Hello?"

"Blinda, it's Clyde. Where are you?"

She gasped. "I didn't know you could call from the . . . you know."

"I'm not in the invisible town. I had Lee send me to your house and am calling from a park about a mile down the road from there."

He was at the duck pond. Rapidly growing hot between the legs, she told him she'd be there in fifteen minutes, explained to Roy why she had to leave, and scurried out the door . . . .

Roy figured Clyde was in for a wild ride tonight. Blinda left the diner with the same fire in her eyes that'd blazed up when her lips parted to receive his first kiss—the intended goodnight smooch that hadn't ended until they'd reached the point of no return. She'd alleged that Clyde hadn't told her why he'd changed his mind about staying at Lee's. Her eagerness to hit the road made him think otherwise.

Hal seemed awfully disappointed she'd left.

Matilda took notice. "You're too young for her, Hal."

"Too young for who?"

"Blinda Love, that's who," she answered disapprovingly. "You've been drooling over her ever since you sat down. If you were in college like you should be, you wouldn't be stuck with the slim pickings of Piler Creek—you'd have a bevy of beauties your own age to choose from, instead of lusting after good looking older broads."

"The only reason I ever wanted to go to college was to wind up playing pro football . . ." Hal jabbed a finger against the side of his head. "This kept that from happening, so I've chosen to be a mechanic. I like working on cars, and you don't need a college education for that."

A harsh sigh flittered through Matilda's tired lips. "I wish I'd gone to college instead of taking over the diner when Daddy died. My mother talked me into it, and I shouldn't have let her."

Hal grinned. "You're lying out your ass, Matilda, you ran this place years before your daddy passed away. My mom told me all about how you pitched a walleyed fit to work here after you finished high school, and your parents finally gave in. Say, how's your mama getting along these days anyway?"

"Giving 'em hell at the nursing home like always," said Matilda, blushing over Hal calling her to the curb for embellishing her lecture. "My sister comes down to see her once in a great while, spends a couple of hours, then hightails it back to Longview, leaving me to listen to her bitch about her psoriasis and arthritic knees."

No matter how busy the diner got, Matilda always managed to squeeze in a quality visit with her eighty-year-old mother seven days a week. He'd never known anybody with Matilda's stamina. Roy doubted she'd ever allow anyone else to open or close the diner even if she lived to be a hundred, and if she did live that long, not a single day would be spent as a retiree. She took a break every evening, but never stayed away from the diner more than three hours when it was open.

Doing eighty-five until nearing the speed trap only strangers to the area were unaware of, Blinda heavy-footed the accelerator again once she got a mile past the highway patrol car lurking behind a billboard advertising potato chips. Beating her estimated time by three minutes, she parked at the duck pond and honked.

Her panties were soaked and she couldn't wait to get out of them.

Clyde got in the car, slammed the door, and said, "Take me to the Turnaton Arms Motel. I've gotta get back to Lee's house soon as possible . . . ."

The sandwich she'd eaten on the plane several hours ago had worn off. Wyoming mentioned being hungry, expecting to be offered some sort of snack. Instead, Lee grasped her arm and they were suddenly standing in the meat section of a supermarket.

"What would you like?"

She felt woozy and brought a hand to her forehead. "Please warn me in advance before you do anything like this again. Shocking surprises usually make me faint."

"Oh, I'm sorry." Lee gave her an apologetic hug and motioned for her to have a look around as if she was dealing with a customer. "This store has a great deli that includes a large variety of Mexican, Italian, and Chinese food, along with conventional fare. Hoyt raided it for the dinner I served Clyde when he first came to see me. I could take you to a restaurant if you prefer, but the only prepared food you'll find is whatever's offered from a buffet or on display. Anything else, we'd have to cook ourselves."

Two roasted chickens turning in a glass rotisserie caught her eye. She pointed at them. "Can we take one of those?"

"Sure, looks good to me too."

Lee soon had the chicken in a takeout box, placed a quart of potato salad on top, and handed it to her. She then bagged some hot butter rolls. Holding the sack with one hand, she lightly gripped her wrist with the other. "Are you ready?"

Wyoming nodded, and they were instantly back in the house. "Wow, I ought to make you take me on a shopping spree in a clothing store."

"I'd gladly do that, but your new wardrobe would disappear when you crossed to the other side." Lee's jovial expression suddenly faded. "Uh-oh, I'm sensing Clyde's presence at the motel. Excuse me, I'll have to contact Earl and Roy so they can see what he's up to."

Lee's concern worried her. "Why don't you go?"

"I don't dare." She closed her eyes and opened them a moment later. "Earl's on the scene."

The uninformative answer was disturbing, but she refused to dwell on the reason . . . it was too late to do anything about it.

"Just as I feared, he's begging to come back. Clyde can't come near me. I'll have Earl take him to Leavenwood before the clerk calls the police to have a madman removed from the premises. Earl will send him back at ten tomorrow morning and you can pick him up at the motel then."

That troubled her all the more. "Why can't he come near you?"

"Because things will only get worse . . ." a guilty look came over Lee, like a penitent in a confessional. "I knew I was very fond of Clyde, but didn't realize how badly I wanted to make love with him until he pulled up today. My yearning was so strong he sensed it, and knew immediately that if I didn't send him back he'd rape me if he had to. When my emotions entered him, they intensified everything he finds desirable about me. Until that sensation passes, he won't know any other woman on the planet's even alive. And if I were to see him in the lobby instead of just sensing his activities, nothing could keep me from pulling him into my world, because his emotions would inflame mine. Clyde will be normal again in a few hours unless he sees me. If he does, he'll never get over it."

EIGHTEEN

LIAT STARTED TO insert the ignition key, but her hand froze when she saw Clyde Burns inside the motel lobby. Thank God he hadn't seen her leave the room. Apparently talking to himself, he was turning round and round, looking upward with hands extended.

And then, he disappeared. *Just fucking disappeared!*

The key slipped from her fingers as she screamed.

Besieged with fear and astonishment, she stared at the empty spot where he'd been acting so curiously. She dared not ask the clerk if he'd seen it happen—the lobby's whole interior could be viewed from outside, and she was taking a big risk by not having left already. Peter, who always rented their room, would be coming out soon. He made his exits five minutes after her, as they dared not chance anyone seeing them together. Praying the creepy jitteriness that gave her gooseflesh wouldn't cause her to have an accident, she hastily retrieved the key, managed to get it into the slot despite her trembling fingers, started the engine, and turned the steering wheel with shaky hands she could barely control.

Clyde expected to be shocked when the transition occurred, but not like this. Earl appeared instead of the woman he had to have. "Take me to Lee."

"Can't do it, man. That lust you're feeling right now would own you if I did. I'm taking you to my place so you can cool off. Give me any shit about it and it'll be your last mistake."

Earl grabbed his arm and he found himself in an enormous living room furnished totally western. Portraits of Roy Rogers, Gene Autry, John Wayne, and James Arness hung beneath a six foot cedar two-by-ten with *Long Branch Saloon* burned into it. Beneath the paintings, all signed *Lee Milan,* sat a beautiful replica of the famous bar on Gunsmoke.

"The richest man in Piler Creek lives in this house on the other side," said Earl, grinning proudly, "but he doesn't have all this."

His passion for Lee faded a smidgen as he looked around. "What a great setup, man. Feels like I'm back in the eighteen hundreds."

Earl's smile turned wistful. "I loved living through that period. Had me an Indian squaw that cooked as good as she looked, and she waited on me hand and foot every Friday through Monday for thirty years. But the days of the old west were Hoyt's downfall. He reeled in a sexy cowgirl who wound up breaking his heart. That's when he swore off women, turned into a glutton, and developed such a foul mouth."

Blinda had been crying since Clyde got out of her car. She'd beaten the dashboard until her palms burned, and they now hung limply behind the top of the steering wheel. Every attempt to make him stay with her had failed, so she'd given in to his demand and was still there, feeling like an abject fool.

The Turnaton Arms didn't have reserved parking, lodgers had to leave their vehicles in a rectangular parking lot. From her vantage point she could see the entire front of the two-storey motel, as she'd parked in the back row instead of dropping Clyde off at the lobby, in order to try one last time to dissuade him from going back to Lee. A few minutes ago Shayna Gold's mother came out of a ground-floor room and glanced nervously around before hurrying to her car. She'd driven off, now a handsome man was peeking out the door, wearing the same cagey expression. They had to be having an affair, and it amazed her to see the guy couldn't be any older than forty.

When he stepped outside she quickly fished a tissue from her purse, blew her nose, and lowered the window. She honked to make him look her way, and waved for him to come over. Clyde refusing to stay hadn't cooled the heat in her loins—it only added a thirst for revenge to her burning desire for hot sex. The guy walking towards her had to be a good lover or the baker's wife wouldn't be screwing him on the side. Since he'd settled for an older woman tonight, she figured an invitation to pleasure her would be too tempting to pass up.

"What's wrong, ma'am?"

"I'm upset because my date bailed on me. I wonder if I could impose on you to have a drink with me. I really need someone to talk to."

A jumpy smile sprang to his worried face as he tried to appear sympathetic to her plight. "Uh, I'm sorry but I really have to go."

"Home to your wife?"

Worry turned to fear.

"I know the daughter of that woman you were with. If you're not a stupid man, you'll come home with me . . . ."

"We were cast to earth when civilization had fully taken root, many years after the flood," said Earl, holding a snifter of cognac. "The Almighty showed great patience with us by withholding chastisement when He created Adam. That's what caused our transgression. He knew our concern would only increase. It wasn't until He tricked Satan that we finally understood why He allowed the devil to tempt Eve so she could bring on the fall of man by seducing Adam to act contrary to God's will."

Clyde turned up the mug Earl had filled with tap beer, downed a big swallow, and set it on the bar. He pictured himself as a customer sitting in the Long Branch, listening to Doc Adams passing on some sage advice to Festus. However, he couldn't recall any episodes where the doctor shared his venerable wisdom on a topic such as this. "How did God trick Satan?"

"By allowing him to incite the mob so Pontius Pilate had no choice but to order the crucifixion. That was the coup de grâce for the fallen archangel and those who followed him in his rebellion. God cast all His wrath over the sins of mankind—past, present, and future—onto the Lamb of God, the only being worthy of such a sacrifice. Thus Christ bore the penalty for the sins of all humanity, and when He rose from the dead it proved God had accepted the sacrifice en toto, and His anger was appeased forever. God revealed his great love for man by that act, because it made every human being that's willing to repent, redeemable by faith in the propitiatory death of His only son.

"The devil knew God wouldn't condemn mankind, and had counted on using that as a legal loophole to keep himself from being cast to hell, as God isn't capable of acting unjustly. In so many words he planned to say, 'You can't punish me, because you didn't punish the human race, who rebelled against your will too.'

"But neither Satan, nor any of us, realized that God would indeed punish mankind for their sins. In God's eyes every sinner—from Adam to the last baby that will be born before Jesus returns—hung on that cross with Christ, and all their sins were atoned for by the purity of the blood of God's only begotten son.

"Every one of those demons showed they were incapable of true repentance. If there was any chance at all of Satan ever taking his eyes off himself in order to truly comprehend the glorious love and mercy of his creator, God would have spared him. Since God created all things and is omniscient, there's only one legitimate will—His. But the demon realm doesn't see it that way, and God knows they never will.

"Those like Lee, Hoyt, and I stumbled in our hearts, but never actually rebelled. God was extremely merciful by not allowing us to keep our first estates. We'd have begun to question His motives over other things, and eventually those doubts would have birthed rebellion in us. We lost our anointing like the fallen angels, but only temporarily. Seeing everything through human eyes gave us a radically different perspective, and we'll never doubt His infinite wisdom again."

It had been a rather dull night. Jeb only scored one joint and they'd smoked it an hour ago. Shayna found intercourse disappointing but Jeb loved it, since he got off every time. It had taken him a little longer to do so tonight. He'd almost lasted a minute, and ejaculated just as she'd begun to feel tingly.

She recognized Blinda Love's Ford in front of a pickup when they pulled to a stop at the last traffic light. Both vehicles turned right when the lights changed. "You'd better step on it, Jeb, it's nine twenty-five."

They'd left their love nest early in order to get two banana splits to go before the diner closed at ten. No one could beat Matilda Tyner's—she covered the ice cream with more crushed nuts than anyone else, and mingled pecan bits with the fractured peanuts.

"Look, I'm sorry," she told the weeping man standing in her driveway. "I don't know what came over me, I'm no blackmailer. Go home to your wife, I won't say anything."

He hurried to his pickup and sped away.

Blinda's conscience had forced her to let the poor guy off the hook, but her burning need still needed satisfying. She got back in the car and headed for Piler Creek. She'd caught Hal Turner undressing her with his eyes earlier. Hopefully the handsome young mechanic hadn't left the diner yet.

Jeb and Shayna walked in as the last customer was leaving. The look that sprang up on Hal's face made Roy cringe inside. He'd finally cornered his little brother.

Hal vacated his chair and pointed at the door. "Outside, boy! We gonna have ourselves a talk."

They disappeared down the sidewalk with Hal tugging

Jeb by the arm.

"What's got him riled?" mumbled Matilda.

Roy winked at her. "Brotherly concern. Hal will tell you if he wants you to know."

Shayna stood near the door, nervously rubbing her forearms together. Anxiety radiated from her like a boxer's wife listening to a heavyweight fight on the radio, with her husband matched against the champ.

Matilda asked if she wanted anything.

"Um, are we too late to get a banana split?"

"No, hon, I'll make you one."

"Two please."

He waved at her as Matilda walked off. "Come sit with me while you wait. Haven't gotten to visit with you in ages."

She gave him a twitchy smile and sat down. "Hal seems really pissed."

"Yeah . . . you have any idea why?"

"No, I was hoping you could tell me."

"Maybe he's worried about his brother." He sipped some coffee while reading Shayna's face. "Do you know of anything Jeb might be into that would cause Hal to worry about him?"

A light shake of her head was unconvincing.

"Seems he borrowed some money from Hal, claiming he wanted it so he could take you to a new restaurant in Turnaton. Trouble is, it hasn't opened yet. You wouldn't happen to know what he really spent that money on, would you?"

"Mm mm . . ." Shayna looked off into space and started drumming her fingers on the table.

"Man, sure hope he's not doing anything stupid like smoking dope."

Her shocked façade left little doubt she was smoking it too. A teardrop trickled down her cheek. She swatted it like a fly and fretfully rubbed it off. Lying didn't come easy for

Shayna, but he knew that's all she'd do if he questioned her in detail.

By the time Matilda brought the banana splits, Jeb returned holding a hand over his left eye. The other glistened with tears. Hal's angry countenance told the whole story, removing all doubt.

Matilda grabbed her waist. "What the hell's going on, Hal?"

Jeb shot Hal a panicked look with his uncovered eyeball.

"My kid brother and I just came to an understanding, that's all."

"Why'd you hit him?"

"To let him know I mean business." Hal glared at Shayna. "I figure you know it too, girl. Right?"

She gave him an anemic nod and brushed another tear away.

"Okay, this stays here this time. If you two renege on the promise Jeb made me, I'll know. That happens? Mom, Dad, Ezra, and Liat are gonna hear *all* about it. Savvy?"

Both teens nodded.

Hal hissed an angry breath and said, "Roy, I'm gonna give these two a break and not embarrass them in front of Matilda, but I want you to fill her in. If either of you see Jeb or Shayna acting odd in any way, let me know and I'll get to the bottom of it pronto. Jeb, you and Shayna grab your treats and come with me. Your butts are mine tonight. Put it on my tab, Matilda."

Jeb finally lowered his hand and picked up the banana splits.

Blinda came through the door. She stared at Jeb's shiner while saying hello to Shayna, who gave her a nervous "Hi" in return. "Well, Roy, Clyde changed his mind again."

That confused the hell out of him. He figured those two would be tearing up her bed by now.

Hal's livid expression softened as a polite smile surfaced.

"Blinda, this is my brother Jeb."

"Nice to meet you, Jeb. What happened to your eye?"

"Long story," said Hal. "We were just leaving."

Blinda's face dropped. Apparently she'd intended to blow off the steam she'd built up for Clyde on Hal. Those kids definitely needed a good talking to, but Roy figured it might be better coming from him. "Tell you what, Hal, why don't you stick around and keep the ladies company. I'd like to tell Jeb and Shayna about what happened to my cousin."

Hal agreed and Blinda cheered right up.

Peter called twenty minutes ago and compounded her dismay over Clyde's disappearance. Liat had been in a stupor since. A woman had seen them leave the motel room and said she knew Shayna. She'd threatened to expose them if he didn't follow her home. He'd done so, only to have her tell him to go on, and that she'd keep her mouth shut. Peter worried she wouldn't.

If the lady had no proof it would be her word against theirs. Shayna would believe her mother and drop the matter, but once Ezra heard the allegation he'd demand a confrontation with the accuser—not from suspicion, but to insist she stop defaming his wife. If he were to learn the man's identity, he'd know the woman wasn't lying, having been aware of Peter's inordinate fondness that infamous summer he'd worked for them. And no telling how many times he'd caught her gazing at Peter. He'd never said anything, but only a blind man could have failed to at least occasionally notice her admiring glances.

She summoned her strength and called Peter's cell phone.

"Hello?"

235 MILES TO JUSTIFIED 235

"Can you talk?"

"*Yeah, I'm at a bar trying to settle my nerves.*"

"Does she know your name?"

"*I don't think so, I sure didn't tell her. She didn't mention yours either, but she obviously knows what you look like.*"

"Hmm . . . can you recall her address?"

"*No, but I know the way to her house so I can get it.*"

"Are you at a bar in Conroe or Turnaton?"

"*Turnaton.*"

"Good, do that. You can find out her name on your smart phone by providing that information, can't you?"

"*Yeah.*"

"Good. Ezra won't be home from temple for at least an hour. If you find out before then, call me. If not I'll call you some time tomorrow . . . ."

Two banana splits sat on his kitchen table untouched. Shayna and Jeb were gazing at them to keep from facing him.

Roy stood in front of his cabinet with arms folded. "My cousin Don was an honor student like the two of you, and was president of the student council at a big high school in Houston. Everybody expected him to be a huge success but he started messing with dope, and guess where he is now—in prison serving a life sentence. You see, his habit got so expensive he had to start dealing drugs to support it.

"Don started out smoking grass, but wound up on heroin. He turned three people on in his living room, giving them a sample of what was supposed to be some real quality shit he'd just scored, but guess what—it hadn't been cut. Don didn't know that of course, or he'd have never shot those kids up. Well, it killed all three of them, and what was once a very promising life is being wasted behind bars."

They were both eyeing him now.

"I know you think you can take it or leave it, but you can't—dope will take you in the end. I'm guessing you guys started messing with marijuana first, and like ol' Don, figured you'd do a little harmless experimenting with other stuff, thinking it'll never go beyond purely recreational use. Am I in the ball park?"

Jeb nodded and Shayna covered her shame-stricken face.

"Look what's already happened. You've resorted to conning your brother for cash, Jeb. Where's it gonna go from there, stealing from him? Let me take you step by step through my cousin Don's life . . . ."

♫

When Matilda called it a night an hour ago, Blinda had invited Hal to her place for a nightcap, and they were sipping tequila screwdrivers in her living room. He possessed an alluring confidence, slouching in an armchair with his feet crossed on the ottoman. He'd taken Matilda aside to discuss something before they left the diner. She hadn't been able to hear what he said, but it had sure put a look of concern on Matilda's face. The matter was clearly confidential, so she'd kept her nose out of it.

"How long have you been working for Roy?" she asked from the sofa.

"Eight years. I started working Saturdays when I was a freshman, and have been with him full time since I finished high school four years ago. It's the only job I've ever had."

That made him no older than twenty-two, unless he'd flunked a grade or two, but the gap in their ages didn't bother her in the least. They weren't contemplating marriage, and might never get together again after tonight. His sexual talents were all that concerned her at the moment. That, and to get even with Clyde. "I suppose you know I didn't ask you here merely to have drinks."

He gave her a sexy smile. "I was sure hoping not . . . ."

Shayna couldn't stop crying. She'd always respected Roy, and to have him know this shameful truth about her was unbearable. Jeb wept too, for the same reason. They'd been total fools and should have known it, but it had taken this to expose that horrid fact. "R-Roy, you missed your calling. You should have been a preacher. Never have I felt so repentant."

"Amen," sobbed Jeb.

Roy cast her an admonitory frown. "That better not be soft-soap coming out of your mouth, Shayna—it better mean you're not going to mess with drugs anymore."

"Oh it does!" she assured. "Jeb and I thought if we only got high on weekends we could never get hooked. When you said your cousin started out as just a weekend warrior too, it terrified me."

"How long have you been getting high?"

"Since last summer."

"What about you, Jeb?"

He looked down at the melted ice cream sitting before him. "Since middle school. I deserve a lot more than this black eye from Hal. If he hadn't kicked my ass no telling how bad this would have gotten. Hell, I corrupted my own girlfriend. Shayna begged me to stop when I told her I was blowing weed, but eventually I talked her into trying it instead."

"And it was love at first toke," she shamefully reported. "Then I corrupted Jeb because I wanted to try hallucinogens. Who knows when I'd have been tempted to see what intravenous drugs felt like."

"Or me," said Jeb. "Thank God it never got that out of hand."

"Please don't tell our parents, Roy. Jeb and I swear it'll never happen again."

She shrank inside as he stared at her without speaking— his narrowed eyes warning louder than words that she'd have to face her worst fear should that vow ever be broken. An eternity seemed to pass before he finally voiced it.

⊙⊱✿⊰⊙

Peter had gotten the woman's name and she planned to go see her tomorrow. Such a volatile matter dared not be handled over the phone. Liat lay beside her sleeping husband, trying to come up with a suitable lie to explain what Blinda Love saw. What she'd seen happen to Clyde keep interfering with her thought processes, for it defied any explanation save one: most unbelievable, yet now uncannily plausible.

Years ago, while she was still breast feeding Shayna and Joseph had yet to graduate high school, Ezra contracted two carpenters, an electrician, and a plumber to build a sauna house by the swimming pool. The plumber had to be replaced because he'd shown up drunk one morning, claiming a town just like Turnaton existed in a separate realm, invisible to human eyes, and he'd been drinking all night because a woman who lived there had broken up with him.

"I can't handle living here anymore," he'd said. "Just

dropped by to let you know I quit."

Ezra, patience soul that he is, had implored him not to, humorously adding, "All women live in a different realm. Go home and sober up. You'll forget all about this nonsense when you wake up in the morning."

The grief-stricken plumber had rejoined with, "This ain't the booze talking, Ezra. Sorry to leave you high and dry like this, but I'll be in a different state this time tomorrow."

NINETEEN

EARL LATCHED ONTO his arm and in a flash they were standing in an alley behind the Turnaton Arms Motel. "Hopefully no one will see you appear back here. No telling who all saw you vanish last night, but there's nothing we can do about that."

The next instant Clyde was alone. He walked towards the closest end of the long structure and came around the front to find Roy parked near the lobby. Wyoming drove up and scooted to the passenger side of the rental car.

Roy got out of his pickup and hollered, "Why don't you guys ride with me and save the extra mileage?"

"That fancy truck of yours looks like a gas hog," he responded with a grin. "My deal allows unlimited miles, so you should ride with us instead."

Blinda had set her alarm to wake Hal at seven so he could get to work on time. She'd gone back to sleep and finally woke up a little before ten. A rubber lay in her bedroom waste basket, but last night had been a flop. Not a syllable left his mouth when she'd given him head—he'd only moaned and sighed—and hadn't even done that much during intercourse. She'd soon figured out he'd been concentrating to keep from coming prematurely. His movements had been slow-paced and practically robotic, very disappointing. In the beginning her fantasies had again alternated between Elvis and Clyde, but guilt over using the young mechanic overpowered them, so she'd faked an orgasm to force Hal to ejaculate. Claiming to be too tired for another bout, she'd pretended to go to sleep, lying awake for a long time afterwards with eyes closed, thinking about Clyde.

The doorbell rang. She yawned while slipping on her robe, and went to answer it, surprised to find Roy standing there.

"Hey, Blinda."

"Hi . . ." she glanced beyond him and saw Clyde behind the wheel of an unfamiliar car parked at the curb in front of Roy's pickup. It momentarily confused her, then she recalled he'd flown to Houston instead of driving from Odessa. Seeing Wyoming on the passenger side made her stomach tighten with jealousy. "Thought you'd be on your way to Conroe by now."

"I am. Just wanted to let you know I'm leaving my pickup here. You don't mind, do you?"

She shook her head and yawned again. "So you're riding with Clyde and Wyoming?"

"Yeah. Don't know when I'll be back, but it'll be sometime today."

"Best of luck with Larue."

"Thanks, I'll need it . . . ."

The doorbell rang again before she finished her first cup of coffee. She looked through the peephole and saw Shayna's mom standing there. *Oh no, the poor woman must be worried out of her mind!*

"I'm so sorry about what happened last night," she blurted immediately after opening the door.

The adulteress gave her a tranquil smile. "No need to be. I came here to explain everything. May I come in?"

"Sure." She led her to the kitchen. "Would you like some coffee?"

"Please . . ." the unexpected guest casually made herself

comfortable at the table as if they'd been friends for years. "Since you only know me as Shayna's mother, let me introduce myself. My name is Liat Gold. I recognize you of course, and want you to know my husband and I appreciate your business. His name is Ezra, by the way."

"Nice to meet you. I'm Blinda Love." She filled a cup for Liat and topped off her own.

"It's a pleasure to make your acquaintance as well. What you saw last night at the motel isn't what it appears. I promised the gentleman I wouldn't mention his name when I told him I was coming to see you. I hope what I'll be telling him about this impromptu visit will settle the poor dear's nerves. For simplicity's sake, let's refer to him as Bob."

Blinda held up her right hand as if swearing to an oath. "Before you say another word, let me do some explaining of my own. There's this guy I really like who wound up at my house last night without a car. Instead of staying with me, he made me take him to that motel so he could be with another woman.

"I'd gotten extremely aroused before I learned he wouldn't be sleeping with me, and he hurt me so badly I wanted revenge. Hell it could have been any decent looking guy, I didn't care—all I wanted was to get even and get off. I was sitting in my car bawling when you left that room, and when Bob came out I saw a perfect opportunity for vengeance, so I threatened blackmail to get him to follow me home. By the time we got to my house I'd come to my senses and told him to go on, promising I wouldn't tell anyone what I saw. And I won't. If you still feel the need to explain, go ahead, but I swear no one will ever hear anything from me about you two being in the same motel room."

Liat took a sip of coffee and smiled. "Thank you for being so considerate. From the sound of things it would seem you're better off without that guy."

She sighed. "I'm making him sound like a heel, but he's

not. He met the woman before we crossed paths, and they're just friends. He didn't stay with her at the motel last night, that's just where she arranged to pick him up. He's from West Texas and had initially planned to spend last night at her house and come see me today. For some reason he decided to stay with me instead. I was unaware of that and had gone to Piler Creek. He called me on my cell phone and by the time I got to Turnaton he'd changed his mind and I couldn't talk him out of going back to his original plan."

"Your guy lives in West Texas?"

"Mm hmm, Odessa."

Liat's eyes flared with an astonished gape. "Oy, is his name Clyde Burns by chance?"

Now she was the one gawking incredulously. "You know Clyde?"

"We met last Sunday at the bakery."

"Then you must have met Wyoming Carter too."

"I did indeed, lovely thing. Since you were still at the motel when Bob left, did you see Clyde go into the motel lobby?"

"Yes."

"Did you notice anything unusual happen after he did?"

Her brows shot up. "No. By then I'd started crying and was pounding the hell out of my dashboard, but I know what you must have seen—Clyde vanish."

Liat nodded. "It was the most frightening thing I've ever witnessed. Can you tell me what happened?"

"You wouldn't believe me—you'd think I was crazy—but you don't have to worry about Clyde. He's all right."

"No, I must know. Why did he disappear?"

It dawned on her the harrowing experience with the vanishing car would still be torturing her if she didn't know about Lee Milan and her phantom world. Liat needed to hear the truth, even if she wouldn't believe it. "The woman he went to stay with lives in a separate dimension patterned after Turnaton and Piler Creek. That lobby is a portal, and she pulled him into it."

A big grin spread across Liat's face—not a patronizing smirk, but an appreciative smile. "So that plumber was telling the truth after all."

"Plumber?"

"Yes. He spoke of a woman who lived in a town where Turnaton is, only hers was in a different realm. He moved away because she broke up with him."

"When was this?"

"Long ago. Shayna was only four months old."

She told Liat about the car appearing, how she'd met Roy because of the wreck, and everything she knew about Lee Milan.

"And that's the woman Clyde went to see last night?"

"Yes. He was like a man possessed."

"I wonder if he's still there."

"No, he's on his way to Conroe with Roy and Wyoming." She explained why, adding that Lee also had a daughter by another man and had asked Clyde to find her, having only a birthmark to go on. "He succeeded, but I don't know anything about her other than that."

"I do," said Liat. "This is an unbelievable coincidence. She's a friend of Shayna's. Clyde saw her at the bakery and quizzed Ezra and me about her because she heavily favors her mother. He asked for our assistance, afraid he'd upset the girl because she didn't know him. After he left we asked her if she had a birthmark but she would only tell Clyde. She must not have given him permission to let us know. I'm sure he would have told us otherwise. My heart breaks for Roy, poor guy."

⨏⨏

Roy sat behind Wyoming in the rental car while Clyde chauffeured them to Conroe. Neither had uttered a word since leaving Turnaton half an hour ago. "Why are you guys so quiet this morning?"

"Just tired," said Wyoming.

"What'd you do, stayed up late visiting with my sweetie?"

"Mm hmm."

He chuckled. "You better not have tried to hit on her, Clyde. Blinda told me you changed your mind about staying with Lee, then decided to go back."

"I wound up spending the night at Earl's house instead."

"How come?"

Clyde and Wyoming exchanged concerned glances.

"What's wrong?"

Wyoming cut her eyes to him. "He can't ever see Lee in person again."

"Why?"

"You'd be upset if we told you the reason." She turned her head, leaving him frowning at the back of her blonde mane.

Anxiety blasted through him in hot, nerve-pounding waves. "Tell me anyway."

"Please leave this alone, Roy," Wyoming urged, still facing the windshield. "It would hurt your feelings."

That doubled his angst. "I don't care, one of you better tell me before I come unglued."

Clyde edgily adjusted his grip on the steering wheel. "Tell him, Wyoming. It'll hurt less coming from you."

"He doesn't need to hear it from anybody," she insisted.

"Yes I do, goddammit, tell me!"

Wyoming vented a harsh sigh, gave him a quick glance as if to assess his state of mind, then quickly turned forward again. "Lee will never love anyone but you . . . but that doesn't keep her from being lonely for a man. I think you can understand she likes Clyde or she wouldn't have invited him to spend the weekend with her after they met on the internet. When she saw him yesterday, it abnormally aroused her. That somehow overwhelmed Clyde with passion. He thought it would go away once she sent him to the other side, so he asked her to do so."

"But it didn't," Clyde stated jadedly. "I tried to fend off the urge to have her bring me back, but couldn't. I made Blinda take me to the motel and begged Lee to come get me. Earl showed up instead, took me to his house, and explained what I was going through. A few hours later I finally cooled off, but if I ever see her again that lust will never go away. And if Lee sees me, instead of just sensing my presence at any of the sensors, it'll stir her up so bad she won't be able to resist pulling me into her world."

Pain and anger whirled inside him like an F5 tornado. Being burned at the stake couldn't hurt any worse than the inferno of jealousy blazing in his gut. "Lee doesn't really love me then—she couldn't possibly."

Clyde shot him an irate frown and turned his attention back to the road. "Hold off on that shit, man. You know you really love *her,* but did that keep you from lusting for Blinda? No."

Wyoming shifted around to face him. "I warned you it would hurt your feelings."

"Not as much as it pisses me off."

"Lee would feel the same if the tables were turned, wouldn't she," Clyde reprimanded.

"Yeah, I suppose so, but that doesn't make me feel any better about it."

"Look, the important thing is we managed to avert the disaster, and I'm not ever going back there, so you don't have a thing to worry about."

"Until loneliness causes her to lure another man to her world," he fired back, "and she gets the same kind of hots for him."

"You needn't worry about that," said Wyoming. "Lee

figured out what happened. She'd never met a potential suitor while carrying out an execution order before, and had to send us back before she could even hold hands with Clyde. Her natural curiosity about what being intimate with him would be like got supercharged because she was so emotional over reading your letters. That accidentally set the stage for this odd set of circumstances. It'll never happen again no matter how many boyfriends she goes through from now on."

His letters being the catalyst gave him a deep sense of relief, but it hurt like hell to hear she was curious about what screwing Clyde would be like. He reminded himself he'd been just as guilty over Blinda, as Clyde had pointed out. Not only that, his curiosity had been satisfied. "So she doesn't have to worry about going as ape-shit as the guy lusting after her, like what almost happened with Clyde?"

"That's right," Wyoming assured, enforcing it with a smile that soon faded as she turned thoughtful. "You have to bear in mind Clyde is very special to her because of that favor he did concerning you—and is still attempting to accomplish with Larue, not to mention finding her daughter as she asked. No matter how much any other man wants Lee, it won't increase her interest in him because she's in love with you, and she'll never feel as close to anyone else as she does Clyde because they won't be able to help her like he did. She told me you'd have been her last lover ever if it wasn't for the unbearable loneliness.

"Imagine what it's like being stuck in her world, having only Hoyt and Earl to talk to. And it must have become a living hell for her after she couldn't see you on the weekends anymore. That's especially true now that she's locked in this conundrum. Lee can't lure another man there until she either breaks up with Clyde or he dies. But she has to officially end it in person, which she doesn't dare do. The moment they see each other they'll make love on the spot because of the lust that'll engulf them. When Earl pulled him into that world at the motel, it set up a different scenario. From now on if Clyde touches Lee in any intimate form—even a peck on the cheek—he won't be able to leave her dimension. So she's stuck with this miserable situation until the day he draws his last breath."

That not only killed his anger, it made him feel selfish. He had Matilda for an outlet, but Lee would have to satisfy herself for the next thirty to forty years if Clyde lived a normal lifespan.

Liat liked Blinda Love. Being an excellent judge of character, she felt she could trust her as well. Nonetheless it wouldn't be wise not to defuse the matter with the lie she'd so carefully devised. "Bob, as we agreed to call the man you saw last night, is a gentile who converted to Judaism some years ago. His wife, a fiery Southern Baptist, would leave him if she were ever to find out. So we meet in secret after sundown every Friday, which is when the Jewish Sabbath begins, and worship together—using a taped message to guide us through it. A rabbi friend of mine records his ceremonies and allows me to borrow the DVD containing the previous week's message. And there you have it. For Bob's sake, I hope you'll keep the promise you made not to tell anyone."

"Oh I will," Blinda pledged with a broad smile. "Tell him he doesn't have a thing to worry about."

She appeared to believe her, so not only had the bomb been dismantled, the explanation of Clyde's disappearance had enlightened her to the existence of an invisible world, proving that plumber hadn't been crazy. And she'd made a new friend to boot.

All was well with the world she lived in, but learning the inhabitants of the other were condemned angels waiting for the return of Jesus Christ severely distressed her, as it defied her faith. She wanted to visit this Lee Milan because it appeared Messiah had indeed come to earth over two thousand years ago as Christianity claimed. Perhaps she could explain why most of the Jews of that day didn't believe it.

Larue harnessed himself in the passenger seat of Tabitha's go kart, and she took off. Neither of them had people awaiting them in the visitor's center like the kid from Dallas. Mother seldom came to Callaway's except to pick him up the weekends he got to go home. His so called sister never visited him. Thinking about her stirred a buried memory that he couldn't dial up.

Tabitha drove around the compound several times, then they went to the game room. He set down at one of the computers and started a chess match, selecting the highest level of competition.

Papa had bought her a used car when she got her license. Shayna had wanted a new one but he'd said, "No, sweetheart, you'll have to wait like your brothers did." The wait would end in a few weeks when she'd be presented a brand new set of wheels as her graduation present.

Her cell phone rang just as she started the engine.

"Hello, Priscilla."

"Hey. Thought I'd invite myself over if you don't have any plans."

"I was about to head for Turnaton. Jeb's playing golf with Tony Popp, and I'm going to join them for lunch."

"Mind if I tag along?"

"Not at all . . . ."

She felt ever so grateful to Hal and Roy. The craving to get high made its presence known, but she'd refused to give into temptation, and had flushed her hashish down the toilet. Jeb made her swear to a new pact when they left Roy's house last night. They swore to each other never to indulge in anything stronger than wine or beer for the rest of their lives. Hard liquor of any sort they deemed as taboo as drugs.

A wonderful life lay ahead for the two of them and they dared not jeopardize it like Roy's cousin Don had done. They planned to attend college at Texas A&M and major in computer science. Two years after they got married, they'd start their family. When their first baby turned one they'd go for number two, and stop there. She hoped pregnancy would increase her bust size, but feared it would only be a temporary enhancement if it did. Mama said such increases rarely remained long after milk production ceased. Her older two sisters-in-law had finished giving birth before she'd gone to kindergarten, and the youngest had been busty to begin with, so she'd yet to witness the phenomenon.

Priscilla was standing at the curb when she arrived at the Booth's house.

Taking Roy's advice, Clyde pulled to the side of the road

about fifty yards from the western edge of Callaway's Research Complex. Roy had seen a girl repeatedly circle the wrought iron boundary in a go kart, and they hoped she'd be at it again today so they could flag her down. Roy would then tell her he was Larue's father and ask her to bring him to the fence. They hiked to a section of it perpendicular to the gates' location, and waited.

"Tony Popp's pretty cute, isn't he," said Priscilla.
"Yes, but not as cute as Jeb."
"How long have you known Tony?"
"Since fifth grade. That's when he moved here."
"And Jeb?"
"All my life."
"Where did Tony live before?"
"Merkel."
"Is that in Texas?"
"Mm hmm. It's a small town near Abilene." She tossed Priscilla a grin. "You sure seem curious about Tony all of a sudden. Do I detect a possible crush?"
Priscilla giggled. "Possibly."

Bored with spider solitaire, Tabitha asked Larue if he'd like to take another spin around the compound.
"If you'll let me drive," he answered simultaneously with the screen announcing he'd checkmated the computer.
"You know you can't drive, Larue. One of your spells

might come over you."

"I promise not to go fast. You can grab the steering wheel if I lose coherency."

"Sorry, too risky."

He narrowed his eyes with a testy squint. "How come you won't say who bought that go kart for you?"

"You already know the answer to that stupid question."

"That particular go kart retails for close to two thousand dollars. That's a lot of money to spend on a kid you're not close to."

She crossed her arms beneath her breasts. "Who says he's not close to me?"

"He?" Larue stated suspiciously. "How do you know it's a he?"

"I don't, but it's the logical assumption since we're talking a go kart. A woman would have bought me something feminine."

"I know you're lying, Tabitha. Why are you being so secretive about who gave it to you?"

How in the world am I going to explain my car when I get it? she thought with a panic.

"Well?"

"Look, all I know is someone from the store dropped it off at the gate, and told the security guard it was a gift for Tabitha Gershwin, and the donor wished to remain anonymous."

Larue got off the stool and gazed down at her skeptically. "Horse hockey, as Colonel Potter would say. Somebody here at Callaway's owed you a big favor and you chose that go kart as the payoff. Who was it, and what did you do to get it?"

"You can ask Richard Allen. That's exactly what happened."

A sarcastic laugh reinforced the disbelief in his eyes. "I'm aware it was really left at the gate, but that was merely arranged to keep everybody in the dark about who bought it."

"Think what you want, Larue. I'm going for a drive. Are you coming or not?"

"Yeah. I could use some fresh air to take away the smell of this bullshit you're laying on me."

⚬⚬⚬

Larue knew he was riding in the go-go, but couldn't recall the name of the girl beside him, holding the thing that guided it.

"You're having one of your spells, aren't you. Boy am I glad I didn't let you drive."

"Hey, Larue!" he heard a man shout. "It's me, Clyde Burns."

"You know him, Larue?" the girl asked.

"No can . . . think . . . h-have to . . . wait."

The go-go stopped.

"Hi there, my name's Clyde Burns and I'm a friend of Larue's."

"And I'm his father," spoke another man. "Larue, look at me. I'm your dad."

"Sorry, mister, but he can't comprehend much of anything right now."

"We know about his problem," said another girl. "How long has he been out of it?"

"It just started. I'm Tabitha Gershwin. You there, who claims to be his father, what's your name?"

"Roy Milan."

"Where do you live?"

"Piler Creek."

"No s-say!" he screamed while covering his ears.

"What's wrong, Larue?" the go-go girl asked.

"N-No say . . . hurt L-Larue."

"Don't say what, Piler Creek?"

He nodded as fast as he could, feeling very frightened.

"Tabitha, my name's Wyoming Carter, I'm a friend of Larue's too. His foster mom won't allow Roy to visit his son. Could you please tell us who and where she is so we can reason with her?"

TWENTY

CLYDA HAD NOTICED a lot of Roy in Larue, but couldn't detect any of Lee's features. His hair and eyes were the same color as Roy's, both a lighter shade of brown than Lee's. Larue's mindless state hadn't relented by the time they left Callaway's after Tabitha Gershwin informed them his foster mother was Clarisse Ferrell and she lived in Brenham. He checked the speedometer when they arrived. They'd traveled seventy-three miles from the think tank.

An overweight woman, on her knees digging in a flowerbed, craned her neck and looked behind her when he stopped at the curb. She had one of those stern unattractive faces that didn't give age away—she could have been as young as thirty or old as fifty. He got out of the rental and started up the walk. Wyoming stayed in the car with Roy. They'd decided it would be better if Larue's foster mom didn't know her golden goose's father had come along until the ice got broke.

The lady dropped a hand spade into a bag of potting soil, rose to her feet, and brushed off her knees. "Can I help you?"

"Hi, are you Clarisse Ferrell?"

"No, I'm her daughter Ethel, she's in the house. Who are you?"

"A friend of Larue's."

"You work at Callaway's?"

"No, I'm from Odessa. My name's Clyde Burns."

The front door opened and out stepped a slender woman, whose appearance surprised him. He'd expected Clarisse Ferrell to look like a lowlife taker, one of those people that felt the world owed them a living. Instead, she gave off the ambiance of someone who'd worked hard all her life, earning every red cent she'd ever made.

"Hi there, I'd like to talk to you about Larue."

"He's Clyde Burns, Mother," said Ethel knowingly.

"Ah, so you're the one that picked him up when he was wandering down the highway."

"Yes, ma'am. I guess Larue told you about me then."

She nodded and looked at the rental. "Who's that with you?"

"Just a couple of friends."

"Larue doesn't like Callaway's. That's what you came to tell me, isn't it?"

"Um, no. I came to tell you I found his father. That's him sitting in the back."

Instead of the hostile reaction he anticipated, she calmly said, "I don't know where you got that notion, but Larue's natural mother told him his daddy was dead."

"Larue's mom had her reasons for lying to him about that. That man over there is Roy Milan, and a DNA test will confirm he's Larue's father."

Her daughter looked worried, but Clarisse nonchalantly waved for Wyoming and Roy to join them. "I see we've got a lot to talk about. We might as well all be comfortable—it's hot out here."

A few minutes later they were sitting in her living room drinking iced tea. Roy asked Clarisse to tell him how she'd wound up as Larue's foster mom.

She took a sip from her glass and smiled. "According to the man who called me from Callaway's to see if I minded you visiting Larue, you've lived in Piler Creek all your life, so you're bound to be familiar with that big grassy hill near the Turnaton golf course."

Roy nodded.

"I was camped out there with my scout troop—I lived in Conroe at the time and one of my girls who'd moved there from Turnaton said it would be an ideal spot. Anyway, this darling little boy, naked as a jaybird, was aimlessly walking around with a weird glassy look in his eyes. I covered him with one of my extra scout shirts and had my girls search for his family, thinking he was a retarded kid who'd wandered away from his folks' campsite, and had unwittingly taken off his clothes.

"The girls couldn't find who he belonged to, so we kept him with us. The next morning he was sharp as a tack, said he was Larue Milan from Justified, and claimed he'd never suffered such a strange mental lapse before. To this day he believes Justified is a real town, and nobody can convince him otherwise." The smile faded. "Why haven't you been looking for him long before now, Mister Milan?"

"It's Roy, and the reason's hard to explain."

"Hard to believe actually," Wyoming chimed in, "but there's no doubt Roy's Larue's father."

Thin, colorless lips spreading into a mocking smirk, Clarisse said, "Larue told you Callaway's pays me for the right to study him, didn't he."

"Mm hmm."

"How interesting. Tell me something, Miss Carter, did either of you know Mister Milan before you picked up Larue?"

"We met him the day before as a matter of fact."

"I see." She took another drink and reacquired the patronizing leer. "What arrangements have the three of you made to divvy up the money from Callaway's—a third each, half for Larue's alleged father and a quarter for yourselves, or some different percentage?"

"This isn't about money!" belted Roy, eyes blazing with insult. "I want him out of that place because he hates being there. I'm his dad and I can prove it. Whether we go to court over this is up to you, but my son's going to be liberated."

Seeing things were getting out of hand, Clyde aimed his

friendliest smile at Clarisse, who was having an angry staring match with Roy. "We don't want to cause you any inconvenience—I'm sure you want the best for Larue as much as we do. Larue didn't say why he hates Callaway's. Would you mind enlightening me?"

His charm hadn't done a thing, but the question made her unlock eyes with Roy and focus on him. "Larue doesn't like being analyzed, but what he really hates is having to stay at the complex. Weekdays he's in the hands of two scientists and has to spend the first three Saturdays of every month in communal activities with the other inmates, as he calls them, before visiting hours. They're all geniuses and the administrators force them to rub elbows so they won't feel so much like freaks of nature. Being with like-minded people is designed to keep their morale high.

"None of them are anywhere near as intelligent as Larue though. He doesn't have a peer, so it doesn't help him at all. Sundays are the only days they have to themselves, but they can't leave the complex. They get to spend the last weekend of every month and thirty days each summer at home. The only other times they get to leave are Thanksgiving, Christmas, and Easter. The scientists in charge of him have told me Larue's intellectual gifts are greater than any mathematician's in recorded history. He'd be wasting those gifts hanging around here, but no one can make him understand that."

The woman's tone and expression reeked with sympathy for her foster son. Here was an assiduous soul by all appearances, who seemed to think Larue being at Callaway's served him best. His initial opinion of her had been wrong, it seemed. "How many days are they allowed for those holidays?"

"Only one for each. I pick him up in the morning and have to take him back before ten that night." She cut her eyes to Roy. "If you're really Larue's father, then you must know where his mother is."

Roy froze, so he jumped in. "Could I persuade you to ride back to Turnaton with us?"

"Why?"

"So you can meet Lee Milan. If you're willing, it'll settle everything."

Wyoming waved for his attention. "We'd have to clear that with Lee first, Clyde. You're not *think*-ing." The nervous grin she wore warned him he'd just fucked up.

Clarisse's work-worn features contorted with indignance. "Do I look like a fool? If she lived in Turnaton the authorities would have found her twenty-one years ago. You think I don't know you've got an imposter willing to pose as Larue's mother? Go ahead, take me to court, you don't scare me. You don't have a clue how important Larue is to the higher ups at Callaway's. Mister Milan won't just be fighting me, he'll be taking on a multi-million dollar conglomerate. Now that's all I have to say on the matter, and I want you all out of my house right now."

Oh cursed fate, why did he have to go bonkers at such a critical time? Tabitha said she'd seen his father with Clyde and Wyoming while he'd been trapped in la-la land. She'd walked him to his room, where he'd finally snapped out of it ten minutes ago.

"Stop pouting, Larue, you should be happy. Roy Milan will get you out of here before long. I'm going to miss you badly. I hope you'll come visit me after he does."

"Do you know where he lives?"

"No." A funny look rose on Tabitha's face when she said it. "I want you to call Clyde or Wyoming for me Monday, they should be back in Odessa by then. I'll pay you back." Callaway's didn't allow the inmates to have cell phones, and toll calls were deducted from their weekly allowance of ten dollars for children, twenty for teens, fifty for those eighteen or older. "They'll know where Roy Milan lives, then you can call him and set up a time for him to meet me at the same spot where you talked to him today."

The dodgy expression on her pimply veneer grew stronger.

"What are you hiding from me, Tabitha?"

"Nothing."

"Are you sure?"

"Mm hmm."

He knew she was lying.

Tabitha had no intention of calling Clyde Burns or Wyoming Carter for the same reason she hadn't informed Larue his father lived in Piler Creek. She'd be losing him soon enough and certainly wasn't going to hasten the process. Callaway's would never be the same without him.

She'd known him since her intelligence had gotten her noticed in a Houston orphanage at the age of eight. The research complex had been designed for mentally gifted children with unique capabilities. Most left the center at twenty with a master's degree in whatever field they'd been schooled in, but Larue was so special scientists studied him instead of teaching the amazing braniac. Clarisse Ferrell was the only parent Callaway's paid—all the others were thrilled to have a child in this special institution with admittance requirements no amount of tuition could satisfy.

The only thing she dreaded more than him leaving was

her own departure. She considered Callaway's Research Complex home, and Larue her favorite brother.

❧

"That's Liat Gold's car," said Roy when they got to Blinda's house. "Wonder what she's doing here?"

Clyde parked behind it and killed the engine. "Guess we're about to find out."

Blinda stepped out on the porch with Liat, who was apparently leaving. Last night only Lee mattered, but now the hot redhead captivated him again, making his gonads prickle with expectation. He looked forward to being alone with her when Wyoming left for the motel. Hopefully Roy wouldn't hang around long.

"I didn't know you two were friends," Roy hollered with a grin as they made their way up the walk.

Liat smiled back. "We weren't until today. We've been having the most interesting conversation about Justified, Leavenwood, and Lee Milan."

Roy and Wyoming gawked at her stupidly. He could only do the same.

"Close your mouths," she laughed, "you might catch a fly. A confidential matter we were discussing inadvertently opened the door. Years ago a plumber Ezra hired spoke of a woman who lived in an invisible town. He moved out of state without finishing the job because she broke up with him. I happened to mention it and that started the ball rolling."

"How many years ago?" Wyoming eagerly asked.

"Shayna was just a baby."

That had to be Priscilla's father, thought Clyde. "Is his name Vance Gore?"

"I never knew his name. Blinda told me you found Lee

Milan's daughter, so I presume it's Priscilla and she wouldn't permit you to tell anyone."

He nodded. "Priscilla wants to keep it to herself for the time being."

"I won't let on that I know then. Are you suspecting that plumber is her father?"

"Yeah. Lee said he was a tall, handsome man with brown eyes and black hair. He'd be forty-nine now."

"It could be him then. He told Ezra he was leaving Texas immediately, but didn't say where he was going. I overheard the conversation, and he spoke like he didn't have a particular destination in mind. I doubt Ezra will remember his name, and it was so long ago he wouldn't have it in his financial records. He destroys his bank statements and ledgers when they're no longer needed for the IRS."

Even if Ezra could recall the name it wouldn't matter, since the plumber didn't say where he was going, and could have moved countless times since. Vance Gore could be anywhere. It would be up to Priscilla to find him, and he doubted she ever would.

Liat cleared her throat and said, "I've been informed you're not going home until tomorrow. Are you planning to visit Lee Milan before you do, and if so, may I please accompany you?"

"Uh, no I won't be going to see her, but I'll ask her if Wyoming can take you. I'll have to do it by email." He'd noticed a nice computer setup in Blinda's den while checking to see if the room looked like Lee's.

They all went inside, he fired off a message to Lee, and got her reply about twenty minutes later. Afraid she might mention Roy, he'd asked him to wait in the kitchen so he wouldn't overhear anything and possibly put her in jeopardy. Wyoming, Blinda, and Liat stood nearby as he read the email aloud.

Hi Clyde,

Hoyt, Earl, and I have been enjoying the baked goods of Gold's Bakery in Leavenwood since it opened in Piler Creek years ago. How pleased I would be to meet Liat Gold. We've seen her and her husband many times on our visits to the other side. I won't be able to sense her presence since she's never been in my world before, so tell Wyoming to go behind the motel lobby with her, and once satisfied no one's looking, hold her hand and wave the free one, and I'll bring them through the portal. WHATEVER YOU DO, DO NOT COME WITH THEM!

I so regret not ever being able to see you again!!!

Lee

Liat phoned Ezra, told him she wouldn't be there to fix his supper, and that Roy would explain why he'd have to fend for himself. Roy took off for Piler Creek, and Wyoming left with Liat. Staring through Blinda's peephole, the second the rental started down the road Clyde turned and said, "Take your clothes off, woman!"

Blinda shot him a lusty smile. "Say it to me dirty, Clyde— *real* nasty!"

His rod responded right away to that. It wouldn't let him down tonight. "Ah, you like dirty talk, huh? Well get your fucking clothes off before I rip them off your beautiful body. I wanna pleasure my horny eyes awhile before ramming my dick into your cunt."

"Nastier!" she cried while unbuttoning her blouse. "Use the F word—call me a bitch, a whore, a slut."

"Okay, you beautiful whore, you hot fucking bitch—" he pulled his pants down to his knees "—get those big titties and your hot pussy uncovered and get to sucking on this, slut." Throbbing with anticipation, his blood-gorged shaft awaited her pretty mouth.

"Oh yes, El—er Clyde—that's it! Eeeeeeeeew, I'm so hot for you, baby! Keep telling me to suck it while I'm doing it!"

♋

Shayna had never seen Tony Popp feeling awkward about anything, but something about Priscilla really made him nervous. She suspected he fancied her, since he kept hanging around. They'd eaten lunch at Dairy Queen, cruised around Turnaton in Jeb's four-door Mazda, and were now parked at the duck pond with all the windows rolled down. She and Tony had left their cars there after the golf match ended hours ago.

Tony sat behind Jeb, with Priscilla sitting closer to the middle of the back seat than the door. She kept leaning forward when speaking to her or Jeb, ostensibly so she could look at them while doing so. Shayna applauded the slick maneuver—Tony couldn't help but notice her big boobs in profile each time she did it.

"Wanna hear a knock-knock joke, Tony?"

"Sure," he timidly answered Priscilla.

"Okay, you start."

"Knock-knock."

"Who's there?"

Jeb and she laughed immediately, but Tony didn't catch on until Priscilla said, "Gotcha. Made that one up myself."

"Really?" said Tony, grinning with embarrassment.

"Nah, that joke's been around longer than I have. Shayna tells me you used to live in Merkel."

He nodded.

"Did you like living there?"

"Uh . . . yeah, it was okay."

Priscilla's presence had never intimidated Tony before, but then he'd never been around her without the rest of the gang. Their fearless leader was acting like a shy nerd. She'd definitely razz him about it, but not here and now. It'd become clear Priscilla had set her cap for him and didn't need any distractions. Poor Tony hadn't made that connection yet.

❦

No wonder that plumber was so heartbroken, Liat thought the second she saw Lee Milan. The woman was gorgeous, and she greatly coveted her agelessness.

❦

Ezra had invited him to stay for supper. They'd eaten beef pastrami sandwiches and were still in the kitchen, sipping coffee.

"All right, Roy, let me in on the joke. What is my crafty wife really up to?"

"I'm not pulling your leg, she's in Justified. She mentioned a plumber telling you about it a long time ago—it's that invisible town where the lady lives who dumped him."

The big Jew's thick eyebrows zoomed towards each other, causing a deep crevice to form from the upper bridge of his nose to the middle of his forehead. "Oy vey . . . and you really had an affair with that woman who lives there?"

"Yeah. Clyde figures that plumber is the father of the daughter Lee had years after she bore my son Larue. Liat didn't know his name. Do you remember it?"

Ezra numbly shook his head.

CRƏৎৠ

Wyoming giggled at Liat's shocked expression. Lee had taken them each by the hand and they were standing in the Leavenwood Gold's Bakery.

"This is identical to ours!"

"Yes, Liat," said Lee, also grinning. "Hoyt has three favorites—your cinnamon rolls, toll house cookies, and German chocolate cake. Mine is your pecan pies. Earl doesn't have much of a sweet tooth, but occasionally enjoys your glazed doughnuts."

Liat put her hands on her waist and sighed. "Oy, Ezra would turn inside out if he knew our goods were being consumed for free."

"Tell him we appreciate it."

"How can you take merchandise without affecting the inventory in Piler Creek and Turnaton?"

"That's just the way things work here. What would you like for dinner . . .?"

TWENTY ONE

LIAT FELT LIKE Alice in Wonderland. Lee stole their dinner from a supermarket deli, zapped the three of them to a liquor store, swiped a bottle of Jack Daniels, and transported them to her kitchen in the blink of an eye. She and Wyoming were holding all the items, as Lee had to grasp their arms to make each instantaneous trip.

After dinner she took them to a jewelry store, and they were like three greedy little girls, going through rings, necklaces, bracelets, earrings, brooches, and pendants. Then it was off to a dress shop, each of them gaudily adorned with diamonds, rubies, emeralds, and pearls. They took turns modeling for each other in formal gowns and sexy evening dresses, having a great time doing it. When they finally tired of that, they put their own clothing back on for comfort's sake, and returned to Lee's house.

"I've never had a woman friend," said Lee, rather sadly, though smiling. "Now I've got two, and realize what I've been missing all these years. I never got to know any of Earl's or Hoyt's lovers because they were all jealous of me. Hoyt swore off women in eighteen eighty-seven, and no one's caught Earl's eye since his last girlfriend passed away years ago, so Wyoming was the first woman I've gotten to talk to in decades. I hope you two will stay up with me most of the night. I'll return you from my backyard tomorrow before dawn so no one will see you appear. I won't be able to after sunrise, since tomorrow's a Sunday. Blinda can drive Clyde to the motel to get the rental car."

"I'll stay as long as you want," Liat assured. "I told Roy to let my husband know I might not be coming home until tomorrow."

"Me too," agreed Wyoming. "But won't you be taking a terrible risk of accidentally seeing Clyde if you send us back from your place?"

"Not at all, there aren't any sensors near Blinda Love's house. I can send you back from anywhere in my world, but I can only bring you into it at a sensor location. The only time we can see the other side is when we open the gateway to it, like we did with Larue. Except for our visits there of course. I have no idea who may be hanging around the portals in Turnaton or Piler Creek unless it's someone who's been to Justified or Leavenwood before."

Wyoming donned a devious grin. "Speaking of Piler Creek, if you'll tell me where the sensors are, I know a guy who'd be most interested to know their locations, if you know what I mean."

Lee named several, then said, "You both need to be very selective as to who you take into your confidence about the existence of this world. No more than five non-lovers can be brought here in a generation, and this one won't end until the gynecologist that did my tubal ligation passes away. He was the first during this time span, and you two make it three. Robby Gorgan doesn't count because he was brought her for execution. We won't be able to prove you're not crazy except to two people.

"Earl and Hoyt can alert Larue to their presence during our visits to the other side. For example, they could pick up a book and wave it about. They can even do the same with a person of his choosing—but only one, and only if he asks them to. We can't do that with anyone who wasn't born in our world—it's forbidden, and the penalty's unbearable. Since we can't be seen or heard, we can only seek a lover through a written message that can't even hint at what we are, unless said lover somehow already knows about us."

"What's the penalty?" Liat asked.

"I'd rather not say."

"Please, I must know."

Lee closed her eyes and solemnly uttered, "Disobedience to any of the restrictions placed upon us would be a flagrant act of rebellion, mocking the second chance to resume our first estates God mercifully allowed us. The violator would instantly become a demon, destined to suffer eternal damnation like Satan and his minions at the end of time."

⌘

Lying on his side against Blinda's back, left forearm draped over her breasts, blissfully spent penis nestled along the crack of her firm ass, Clyde savored a glorious victory over last week's failure.

"You're uncanny, Clyde," she muttered, lazily. "You seemed to know exactly when I wanted you to speed up or slow down. I love the shape of your dick."

That hurled his already inflamed ego to the top of the flagpole. "It likes you too."

"I had my doubts about that all week."

"Understandable." He gave each tit a light squeeze, and rested his hand on the right one, cupping it.

"I've never came three times before, Clyde."

"You really brought the beast out in me."

A light giggle left her lips. "I did, didn't I. Do you think I'm perverted?"

"Nah . . . just hotter than hell, that's all."

"Maybe we're both perverts."

He chuckled. "Well if we are, so be it."

"Can I say something about Roy without hurting your feelings?"

"Sure." He gritted his teeth, certain the overly inflated balloon of his self-esteem was about to get popped by a verbal needle.

"We only had sex once, but he unwittingly changed me—brought something to life I didn't know was lurking inside, and I came twice. Before then, I'd never had an orgasm from intercourse alone. I fantasized about Elvis the whole time, and it was the most thrilling thing I'd ever experienced. I almost called you Elvis during foreplay, but after you started making love to me, I couldn't think of anything but how good it felt."

Her butt valley got narrower as his shaft swelled.

They'd all had a couple of drinks and were feeling pretty mellow. Wyoming listened attentively as Lee responded to a question posed by Liat concerning the resurrection of Christ: she wanted to know why the Jews didn't believe it really happened.

"The Jews weren't the only ones that didn't believe, Liat. Very few of the Samaritans and Roman soldiers around Jerusalem at the time did either. But all the disciples closest to Jesus *were* Jewish, and even they wouldn't have believed if He hadn't appeared to them. Most of them suffered a martyr's death, and their willingness to die rather than renounce the resurrection was God's way of offering proof to the world that Christ rose from the dead, without catering to carnal awareness—for the just shall live by faith, not merely by what they perceive with their physical senses. Abel had faith, Cain didn't. Peter had faith, Judas didn't. One Jew has faith, another doesn't, and it's that way through all the races of man. Faith is simply taking God at His word no matter how contradictory the circumstances might appear. Satan wants people to believe God doesn't exist. Failing in that, he does his best to convince them God's either a liar, or is totally indifferent to the plight of mankind. Unfortunately, he's enjoying much success with both tactics in this day and time."

Blinda had let the phone keep ringing as another round of bells dinged in her head. She'd came twice more, raising the ratio of orgasms to five for her, only two for Clyde. It seemed unfair, but she certainly wouldn't trade. She switched the lamp on to check the ID and saw Hal Turner on the screen . . . .

"Hello?"

"Hi, it's Blinda. What's up?"

"Sorry to call so late, but I stayed at the shop till eight and just got out of the tub. I'm overhauling the engine on Roy's daddy's car and wanna surprise the old guy by having it ready by Monday. I'll be wrapping it up tomorrow. Anyway, mind if I come over?"

She didn't want to hurt Hal but couldn't think of a tactful way to let him know he'd only been a one night stand—and a very disappointing one at that. "Listen, I hate to tell you this but I was angry with my boyfriend last night. I used you and I'm sorry."

"Roy told me you guys broke up."

"I wasn't referring to Roy."

"Oh . . . a past boyfriend, huh?"

"Something like that."

"Ah, feel kinda stupid."

"Don't. You're a nice guy and I hope you won't hate me."

"No, don't worry about it." A nervous laugh followed. *"If you ever need to use me again just holler."*

"I won't. Bye, Hal."

Clyde sat up and covered his midsection with a pillow. "Something I should know?"

She yanked it away and started caressing his balls. "You really pissed me off last night, so I got even with Roy's handsome mechanic. It was a mistake . . . one I'll never make again."

"So we're going steady now?" he asked, tongue in cheek.

"Don't make light of my feelings, Clyde."

"Your feelings . . .?" he raised his brows. "Watch that noise, I'm not a one woman man."

She sandwiched the base of his now flaccid penis between her thumb and fingers, and started wobbling it back and forth. "Believe it or not I'm glad to hear that."

"Why?"

"So you'll keep sleeping with me after Wyoming finally comes on to you."

His dick started rising. It hurt to know the possibility of screwing Wyoming was the reason, rather than her hand.

"I'll never be more than a friend to her."

"But you'd like to be more than that, right?"

"Yeah, to be honest."

"Well it's only a matter of time before you will be. I've watched her change since meeting you two. She seems more enthralled with you each time I see her, and a little more jealous of me."

They'd gotten through security and were waiting to board their plane. Clyde had been studying Wyoming and didn't notice anything different about the way she acted around him. Blinda was merely viewing the situation with jealous eyes, he concluded. She'd be flying down next Friday to spend the weekend. The way she talked, she'd be happy to do that just about every week. That worked out perfect for him. The hot redhead was the best lay he'd ever had, and to have her as a lover without any trappings of a courtship, with practically no maintenance, was an unbelievable stroke of good fortune. Things were rolling his way in spades, he couldn't allow a roommate to muck it up.

Liat went to the office and poured herself a cup of coffee. She needed a rest before being stuck up front until closing when Shayna and Priscilla left. Lee had sent her and Wyoming back to the real world at half past three this morning. She'd dropped Wyoming off at the Turnaton Arms on her way home, gone to bed as soon as she got there, and had lain awake for an hour before finally winding down enough to fall asleep.

Last night had been an incredibly exhilarating experience, but one she could only tell Ezra about. Shayna would never be able to keep it to herself, so she couldn't be told—they'd become the laughing stock of Piler Creek.

The bakery opened at six a.m. every weekday. They worked the morning shift, Terry and Jean closed—except for Wednesdays, when they alternated so the gentiles could attend their church's midweek evening service. Ezra went to work two hours before the bakery opened, in order to prepare an adequate supply of fresh bagels, doughnuts, and popular pastries for their many early-bird customers to breakfast on. She usually arrived a half hour before opening.

Sundays the bakery didn't open until eight, but she hadn't gotten out of bed until seven-thirty. She'd rushed to work and a steady stream of customers had kept her at the register.

Clyde and Wyoming had dropped by on their way home, and she'd gone in back with them, as Shayna and Priscilla had just arrived. Inexplicably, despite having heard Roy's testimony as well, Ezra didn't believe another dimension existed, offered no explanation as to how they could all be mistaken, and had refused to discuss it any further. She'd retired to the office when Clyde and Wyoming left two hours ago.

The door opened and Ezra walked in. "I didn't want them to know."

She frowned. "Didn't want who to know what?"

"Clyde and Wyoming to know I believe you. Roy had already persuaded me, but I'm very unsettled because of the religious implications, and didn't want to discuss it in their presence. But that's not what I want to talk to you about. I need to tell you something that will be very hard for me to say. Hearing about Roy's strange situation with the woman he loves, got me to wondering if perhaps I made a serious error in judgment long ago. I've been stewing on it all day and am unable to resist the notion that if I dare voice it, a change will occur, enabling me to rectify the situation. Remember how upset I was when Shayna started dating Jeb?"

Where are you going with this, Ezra? She didn't voice her thought because of the pensive look on his face. She wanted to hear it and feared he'd clam up if his train of thought got sidetracked. Something obviously weighed heavy on him, and he needed to get it off his chest. "Yes, and I well remember finally making you accept the situation by pointing out she'd wind up an old maid if you didn't let her go out with a gentile since there aren't any Jewish boys her age around here."

He looked to the ceiling and sighed. "That didn't upset me a fraction as much as discovering my wife was making love with one."

All energy gushed from her body with a gasp that vacuumed her lungs. She gaped at him open-mouthed, too shocked for tears to come at the moment. *All mighty God, please let me die right now!*

The prayer went unanswered.

Ezra silently tormented her with his soul-stirring eyes that had captured her heart at first sight in a New York synagogue. He just stood there gazing at her, saying nothing.

"How long have you known?" she timidly inquired with a quaking voice that sounded alien to her ears.

"Since it started. I overheard you telling Peter you were in love with me but would make love with him that one time. Before leaving as you'd thought, I realized I'd forgotten my hat and as I started for the back to get it, I heard you speaking. I quickly snuck away, went home, and cried. The pain was so severe I couldn't bear the thought of sex—I saw it as my enemy and thus, became impotent. I wanted to spare you the misery of knowing that I knew. That was the error in judgment I spoke of."

Tears gushed from her eyes. Her sobs were so violent she had to cough for air. Nothing could be worse than this—the man she worshipped knowing she'd been unfaithful. If only he'd scream, or even beat her, the misery might be bearable, but putting her welfare before his own, flooded her with such intense self-loathing she couldn't go on without him knowing the whole truth—the awful shame engulfing her would drive her to suicide if she didn't. When her diaphragm finally stopped convulsing and she could almost breath normally, she forced herself to look at him. "I-I didn't stop at just that one time, Ezra."

"I know."

"I've been meeting Peter at a motel each time I delivered

Edna her cake."

"I know."

"H-How?"

"Does it really matter?"

She could only nod—words wouldn't come she was bawling so hard.

"David Beckermann's niece Mary worked as a clerk at one of the motels in Turnaton. One Friday Peter rented a room. He didn't remember her from school but she recognized him. A short while after he left the lobby, she happened to be looking in the direction of that room and saw you go inside it. She told David about it, and he fabricated a clever cover story to convince her it wasn't what she thought, but he knew better and told me. Him being a rabbi, Mary naturally believed him. I pleaded with him not to tell anyone else and he swore to me he wouldn't. From what I surmised, Peter alternates between the four motels in Turnaton because three Fridays later he rented a room there again, and once more she saw you enter it a few minutes after him. This was over ten years ago. Luckily the job bored Mary and she quit after seeing the two of you the second time. If she should ever ask you, Peter met you those two times to help him plan a surprise birthday party for his wife, with you supplying a cake especially designed for her. He chose to do it at that motel in Turnaton because neither of you lived there, so there'd be little risk of anyone seeing the two of you together."

"E-Ezra," she finally managed, "can you ever forgive me?"

"I forgave you right off, dear. How else could I have stayed with you?"

"It'll never happen again, I swear!"

"Don't make promises you can't keep, Liat," he somberly replied, his tone still sympathetic rather than angry.

"May God strike me deaf and blind if I don't. Oh, darling, it kills me to know I'm responsible for your impotence—it just *kills* me."

He set down and again stared at her unblinkingly, the hurt on his face compounding her guilt a thousand fold. "I will now ask the question that has plagued me for twenty years. What did I lack in bed that made you turn to Peter?"

"Nothing," she answered honestly. "I was foolishly enthralled that such a handsome young man professed to have fallen in love with me when I was about to turn forty— which was driving me crazy at the time as you'll recall. I really thought that if I gave in that one time it would rid me of the temptation, and I'd clear my conscience by confessing it to you years down the road, when you could be assured it would never happen again. Oy, did I learn a bitter lesson. Giving in to temptation only makes it grow stronger."

Ezra exhaled a bleak sigh. "Perhaps it wouldn't have if I'd been able to continue taking care of your needs."

His sympathy made her hurt all the worse. "Damn you, Ezra, stop being so understanding, you're killing me! You may be right, but we'll never know. Either way, I'm going to call Peter this instant and tell him we're through."

A glorious feeling of renewal rose within her as she picked up the phone, but it got stifled when Ezra took it away from her and cradled it. "This is not the time to do that, dear. Shayna or Priscilla might decide to call someone, and how would you explain what they might possibly overhear?"

Before she could say he was right, Ezra sealed her lips with a passionate kiss.

Shayna left the bakery at five with Priscilla. Mama had the oddest smile on her face when she'd come up front to relieve them.

"I think your parents must have knocked off a piece."

"Priscilla, that's disgusting!"

"Well something sure put a lilt in your mother's step. The woman was glowing."

"Yeah . . . I noticed that to."

"Why else would the door be locked?"

"It sometimes does that on its own." The paper towel roll had gotten pretty thin so she'd tried to go in back to get a new one. Not being a big deal, she hadn't bothered knocking to have one of her parents unlock the door.

They strolled down the street to the diner, and found Jeb and Tony waiting for them at the counter. Matilda wouldn't let just two kids hog the booth. She waved for them to come over and slid into it, leaving Priscilla to see where Tony would sit in order to park next to him.

The guy was still unbelievably shy around her.

Roy saw what Clyde meant with only a glance at Priscilla Booth. Even if he hadn't seen her walking into the diner with Shayna, he'd have known that had to be her, she looked so much like Lee. It was a shame the beautiful teen had sworn Clyde to secrecy—he'd love to talk to her. Hopefully he'd be able to soon. He planned to find a lawyer in the morning and start the wheels turning to liberate his son.

On the very baking table where her first adulterous act had killed Ezra's libido, it had been reborn. Liat felt like a new bride again. He'd been wonderful—as filled with passion as on their wedding night, and just as stiff. He'd made her come hard, blissfully wonderfully hard, like he'd never failed to do before her foolish lust had wrecked their sex life. She'd called Peter the moment Shayna and Priscilla left. He'd bawled vehemently, and begged her to reconsider, threatening to kill himself if she didn't, but she'd firmly stood her ground. Hearing he had nothing to fear from Blinda Love failed to console him in the least.

She'd heard Shayna or Priscilla try to open the door while Ezra was making love to her. They must have wondered why it'd been locked, but who cared. Now she could have a heart to heart with her daughter, apologize again for slapping her, and declare that *yes,* her parents did still have sex. She giggled at the thought of saying, "Well, Shayna, why the hell do you think we locked the door?"

Ezra pinched her butt as she rang up an order of apple fritters.

The moment they were alone she turned and kissed him.

He grabbed her beasts and reluctantly withdrew when the chimes announced another customer.

She couldn't wait to crawl in bed with him tonight.

They'd driven to Midland International in his Malibu. Now they were back in it heading for Odessa. "Wyoming, I've given it a lot of thought and I've decided against letting you move in with me."

"Why?!" she gasped.

He didn't have to look to see the shock on her face—he could feel it from the sound of her voice. "Look, last night I closed the deal with Blinda. Most weekends she'll be flying down to stay with me. It'd be too awkward having a roommate. Sorry."

Wyoming started bawling. He cut his eyes to her and couldn't believe the painful grimace she wore. "Hell it's not the end of the world. Just find another roommate and rent a house."

"It wouldn't be the same."

"Why?"

"Because you wouldn't be there, you stupid prick!"

Radically taken aback, he didn't know what to say. He tried to come up with a tactful way of telling her she'd be more than welcome if she'd put out, but couldn't think of one. Then he got to wondering if Blinda could be right about Wyoming after all. Was it only a matter of time before she'd come on to him? The thought aroused him until he recalled her saying she found something about his house soothing. *Shit, Wyoming sees me as a fucking father figure!*

TWENTY TWO

WYOMING SET AN empty glass on the coffee table and reached for her cell phone. She needed to get away from Clyde—her feelings were out of control. During their visit with Lee, Liat had mentioned her son Joseph managed a store Ezra owned called Hats & Boots. Plans were in place to build a much bigger one in Turnaton for Joseph to run, and Ezra was looking for the right person to take over in Piler Creek. Certain she could handle the job, she hoped her management experience at Kelly's Rentals would convince him to give her the chance to prove it. Clyde had dropped her off half an hour ago, and she'd been sorting it all out while sipping a tall, stiff drink.

Liat answered with a chipper hello.

The commissary pot roast tasted unusually good so Larue went back for seconds. He'd endured an extremely boring Wednesday morning session with J.T. and dreaded having to spend the afternoon with Paul. Tabitha claimed she hadn't been able to get hold of Clyde or Wyoming. He couldn't believe she expected him to swallow such bullshit. Little did she know he'd talked her nine-year-old friend from Dallas into calling Clyde before breakfast by offering him five dollars. The kid came through for him, and he'd given him another five to keep quiet about it.

Tabitha showed up late for lunch. Something about her

seemed different, it took him a second to figure out why. Her forehead—that had looked almost as rough as sandpaper since she'd gotten acne at puberty—was practically smooth, but that wasn't the only change: she'd lost five pounds and fourteen-point-one ounces as well.

"Have you gone on a diet?"

"No, do I look like I have?"

"You've lost some weight is why I asked."

She grinned and took bite of ungarnished mashed potatoes.

"Why didn't you put any brown gravy on those?"

"Lost the taste for any type of gravy."

Potatoes and gravy, especially French fries smothered with cream gravy, had been her favorite food since he'd known her. "If you'll leave two ounces of that roast on your plate it'll translate to a five ounce loss in weight since you're eating your potatoes plain. Your metabolism has sped up slightly."

"Oh really?" she said through a big smile. "Then pull it off for me, Larue. I can't calculate exact measures by sight like you."

He pinched off the exact amount, leaving three-point-six-three ounces on her plate, and popped it in his mouth.

Roy's bank account was eight hundred dollars lighter. The lawyer claimed he needed the bulk of it to pay for his and Larue's DNA tests. Whatever the total tab wound up being didn't matter—he'd mortgage his recently paid off house if he had to. He'd gotten a phone call from Clyde after opening the shop. A boy from Callaway's contacted him at Larue's request and Clyde, rightfully so, had told the kid to assure Larue his daddy would be at Callaway's at one o'clock this Saturday, waiting for him outside the fence.

Thanks to Wyoming he'd read his last three letters to Lee in Piler Creek, choosing the stadium parking lot for today's recitation. He figured using a different sensor location each time would make him less conspicuous. Liat dropped by the shop yesterday and they'd discussed her visit with Lee, after which she'd passed on some interesting news. Wyoming would be taking over the existing Hats & Boots when Ezra got the new one opened at Turnaton. She'd start training under Joseph Monday after next.

The oldest two Gold boys were doctors, with a clinic in Houston. Joseph left college with a marketing degree and convinced Ezra to invest in his idea of selling unique western wear, aimed at covering every body part from the soles of customers' feet to the tops of their heads, including every conceivable form of undergarment. Joseph's advertising skills brought in people from as far away as San Antonio and Lafayette, Louisiana. All the merchants benefited from the out-of-towners who came to Piler Creek for baked goods or cowboy attire, and his auto-repair shop was no exception.

Even though it would undoubtedly be successful, Ezra wouldn't hear of opening another bakery. A staunch perfectionist, he refused to allow anything with the Gold brand on it to escape his close inspection. Hats & Boots sold the fruits of others' labors, so he'd okayed that expansion when Joseph approached him with the idea.

He'd asked to speak to her in his office but she'd coldly refused, so Wyoming still didn't know about the kid calling him from Callaway's. Clyde couldn't tell her in front of the cashiers—they might start asking questions. She'd been a bitch to him the last three days, and he guessed changing his mind about letting her move in had brought their friendship to a screeching halt. Monday morning she'd given Thornton her two weeks notice. If he hadn't overheard, he'd still be clueless about her moving to Piler Creek. Her new job sounded like a step up all right, but he knew she wanted to leave Kelly's Rentals because of him.

Five o'clock finally arrived and he went home without bothering to tell her bye.

Settled in front of his computer with a cold beer, he checked his emails and saw one from Lee.

Hi Clyde,

I'm being ever so selfish but I beg you to come to me—I can't bear the thought of going without sex for such a long time. Don't worry about waiting till Friday, leave as soon as you can and I'll pull you into my world at the Turnaton Arms.

You'll be stuck with me for the rest of your life but I promise you won't regret a single minute of it. Think of how wonderful it'll be to know your woman will never age and will still fervently desire you even when you turn into an old man.

I know you must be worried about leaving your friends and loved ones behind, and concerned for their grief of having you disappear from their lives, but I'll make it up to you and I promise you won't regret it.

Please come to me now, PLEASE!!!!!!!!!

Passionately awaiting your arrival,

Lee

Lust as overpowering as what besieged him last Friday surging through him, he booked a one-way flight to Houston. He'd be flying out of Midland International Airport at midnight.

◦✸◦

"You got us instead of Lee for your own good, motherfucker, now quit bitching about it."

Clyde yanked the cigar from Hoyt's mouth, grabbed him by the collar, and got right in his flabby face. "Call me that one more time and I'm gonna stomp your fat ass!"

"Easy, killer," said Earl, pulling his hands off Hoyt. "That's just how he talks, don't take it personal."

"Where is she?"

"I knocked her out with chloroform. Now listen, if she tries to get you to come back again all you're gonna get for your trouble is the same shit Hoyt and I are giving you now. Lee sees you as the closest thing she can have to Roy, and she's so hot-blooded anyway the combination overrode her common sense. I know she's beautiful and I know how much you want her, but you can't let her ruin your life, Clyde. You don't want to be stuck here with us, it'll drive you crazy. You're human all the way, man—you need the highs and lows of your world, the static existence you'll find here will grow old real fast, and even your lust for Lee won't enable you to bear it."

"Bullshit," he said defiantly, "as long as I'm with her I'll be in heaven."

Earl shook his head. "You feel that way now but it won't last. You'll be climbing the walls begging to go back before a year passes, and we won't be able to accommodate you. Never seeing any of your family and friends will start to eat at you like a cancer, and eventually you'll begin to view Lee as a mindless robot programmed to want to fuck you around the clock.

"Have someone read her emails before you do from now on. If she even hints at having you come here, don't read it or you'll get the same hots you're feeling right now. Seeing her words is what transfers the lust—hearing someone else read them will only tempt you normally, and you'll know better than to give into it. I'm sending you back, and you'll leave the motel immediately if you know what's good for you."

Head spinning, Clyde looked at the clerk, who asked if he'd like a room. "Um, no I uh . . . I changed my mind about staying here."

He headed back to Houston in the rental car he'd planned to leave abandoned at the Turnaton Arms Motel. Instead of enjoying a life of ease in a lustful paradise, he had the pleasure of being stuck with two useless plane fares and a rental car fee because of Lee's impulsiveness. If he couldn't catch a flight home in time to make it to work—which would cost him a night's sleep—he'd also be paying for a motel room and a long distance phone call to let Thornton know he wouldn't be coming in. Messing with Lee was getting expensive, not to mention exhausting.

Clyde came to work looking like ten miles of bad road. Ignoring him as she'd been doing since Monday, Wyoming poured herself a cup of coffee and went out back to sip it.

One of the mechanics wolf-whistled. She rewarded his crass appreciation of her appearance by giving him the finger. Thornton stepped outside before he could retaliate, told her good morning, and started his Thursday morning inspection.

Blinda's plane landed on time at eight-oh-five p.m. Clyde got half hard the moment he spotted her amongst the disembarking passengers. It was Friday and he'd have the hot redhead all to himself until Sunday evening.

Liat enjoyed a piece of cake with Edna and headed for Blinda Love's house. She'd decided to kill the time Ezra would be at the synagogue by visiting with her new friend. Her hubby used to refuse to make love on Shabbat eve, but she'd warned him this morning that rule would no longer be tolerated. He'd laughed and started fondling her breasts.

"I'm serious, Ezra," she'd stated firmly.

"I know you are. This will be my last attendance. I'll be informing David of it after going through the motions one last time for his sake. Before I formally convert to Christianity I'll be spending every Sabbath hence learning about Yeshua. God only knows at the moment where I shall obtain such information, but it won't be from some denominational preacher I assure you. I'll be home no later than a quarter after eleven, so be prepared."

She'd grabbed the back of his hands and pressed them hard against her chest. "I'll be waiting in our bed with legs spread, my darling."

Blinda wasn't home so she drove back to Piler Creek, feeling joyful in spirit and righteously amorous in body as she looked forward to making love with her husband. Her only thoughts of Peter were sadness that he mourned their parting. She wouldn't miss him at all. Lust couldn't hold a candle to true love, and that's all she'd ever felt for him. She'd turned her cell phone off so as not to hear him call, which he was bound to do, and probably already had several times this evening.

"Are you serious?"

"Absolutely," Blinda sighed out.

Clyde got up and started pacing around naked. Blinda was likewise, frowning at him from his bed. He'd been thrilled she'd let him leave the lights on, few women permitted that, but he'd never pissed on one before. She wanted him to do just that, aiming his stream at her clitoris. "Look, I pride myself on being totally open minded about sex, but I'm not going that far. Besides, I don't want to get my bed wet."

She laughed. "We won't be doing it here. I'll be laying in your bathtub getting myself off on the running water, and when I say the word I want you to pee on me while I come."

"Where did you get such a kinky idea? It wasn't Roy, was it?"

"Mm mm. I was so horny when I called you to have phone sex that when you weren't able to do it, I got in my tub and used the faucet stream for relief. Just before I came, I pictured you and Elvis standing above me peeing on my clit, urging me to climax, and promising it would make you get off too. Oh, Clyde, it was so wonderful. Please do it for me. You've made me come twice already tonight, and this will be like dessert after the main course. Please?"

Wyoming couldn't understand the problem. She'd copied

the address from Clyde's forward and pasted it on the address bar, so it should have shot through cyberspace directly to Lee. Instead, a notice of delivery failure fired right back to her each time she hit *Send.* She'd wanted to tell Lee about moving to Piler Creek and that she hoped to visit her regularly.

It felt weird not being with Clyde tonight. They'd been together every Friday night since Lee had drawn them into her world for the execution of that awful child killer. No doubt he was with Blinda right now, probably in his bed. She didn't know how he'd gotten to her exactly, only that he had in the most serious way. Her younger sister was a fifties junkie, especially the music, and one of the tunes she liked the most, *Why Do Fools Fall In Love,* stubbornly kept playing in her head, adding to her depression.

She'd guarded her heart carefully since officially swearing off marriage—never intending to give it away—but somehow Clyde had stolen it.

That fucking Jew had no right to keep him from his woman. With Ezra out of the picture, Liat would soon come back to him . . . for good. Peter parked the stolen motorcycle in the rear of the synagogue, pulled off his ski mask, and lit a cigarette. One more car had to leave before he could take down his rival and the rabbi, who also had to be killed so it would look like the work of a militant anti-Semitic. It shouldn't take long for the vehicle to depart because he knew from Liat that only Ezra hung around with the rabbi after the service ended. Several people could have ridden to the synagogue in it, so he couldn't run the risk of getting overpowered, as the revolver only held six rounds.

To establish an alibi, he'd parked directly in front of the lobby of the Turnaton Arms Motel, rented a room, and waved at the clerk before stepping inside. Five minutes later he'd snuck away on foot. Liat didn't know he always bought a bag of marijuana every Friday before meeting her. His dealer, a Mexican biker, conducted business at a park in Turnaton with a large pond. Late last night he'd hidden a heavy twelve-foot chain in some dense shrubbery there. He'd met the guy at his usual time and left him lying at the bottom of the pond with three bullets in his back, and the chain wrapped around his corpse to keep it from floating to the top. After he took care of Ezra, he'd ride back to Turnaton the long way, the route he'd taken to Piler Creek, and leave the Mexican's motorcycle at the park with the keys in the ignition.

Clenching the cigarette with his teeth, he pulled out a forty-four magnum, filled the three empty chambers, clicked the cylinder back into firing position, reattached the silencer he'd ordered from an internet gun site when it'd become clear Liat wouldn't come back to him as long as Ezra was alive, and waited—impatiently.

Shayna thanked Papa with a kiss on the cheek for letting her spend the night with Priscilla, and told Rabbi Beckermann goodnight. Mama hadn't gotten back from delivering Edna's cake, and she wasn't allowed to stay overnight with a friend without their permission. She'd called Mama's cell phone several times earlier but had only gotten her voicemail, so she'd driven to the synagogue to get Papa's okay. Priscilla had ridden with her.

They drove off and headed for the diner to meet up with

Jeb and Tony.

David Beckermann grabbed his old friend by the shoulders and gaped at him disbelievingly. "Ezra, what devil has put such foolishness into your heart to make you believe this nonsense?"

"No devil," he wearily replied, "it was an angel who spoke to my wife. Rabbi, you wouldn't believe me if I tried to explain it all to you. Yeshua really did rise from the dead on the third day and that can only mean Messiah has two advents, and the first one was fulfilled at that time. I'll be spending every Sabbath hence researching the truth surrounding Christia—"

Ezra's forehead exploded—blood and brain splattered across David's face. Before he could comprehend what was happening, a sharp pain rifled through his chest, followed quickly by another.

TWENTY THREE

LIAT AWAITED HER husband in their bed, which once again served as a love nest rather than merely a soft place to sleep. Rabbi Beckermann must be trying to convince him not to convert to Christianity, she assumed, for he was ten minutes late. Shayna would be coming home at midnight, so if he didn't get here soon they'd have to subdue the sounds of their lovemaking. She decided to call her and extend her Friday night curfew to one o'clock.

A thrill ran up her spine when Shayna said Ezra had given her permission to spend the night with Priscilla. She hurried down the stairs and stretched out on the couch like a nude model. Her hubby was in for a delightful surprise when he opened the front door.

Clyde wondered what kind of tiger he had by the tail. Blinda was apparently a nymphomaniac. He'd refused to pee on her, so she'd demanded he screw her again before she went insane. She'd begged for it once more since, and he'd exhausted himself giving in to her lustful pleas. The weekend he'd so looked forward to was turning into a nightmare. He'd boned her three times in one evening, and still had to get through Saturday and most of Sunday. On top of dreading that, her insistence on him spouting obscene phrases had gotten old fast, and he felt used. He also felt ashamed for using her. Guilt riddled his conscience and he couldn't shake it off.

Shit, I'm no different than she is, he thought, taking a good hard look at himself and hating what he saw. *We both see a member of the opposite sex as mere bodies to use for our own pleasure.*

His brother had told him he'd get tired of bachelorhood eventually and settle down. He'd laughed at the notion, but now couldn't help wondering what married people shared that he'd never experienced. Having never felt guilty over sex before, and not once pondering what marriage had to offer, as he found himself doing now, he feared his brother might be right.

"I can't imagine not being married, Clyde," the words came back to him verbatim, rudely. "A man's got to have a soul mate to be whole."

Could that be true? Was he missing something special in life by going through it without a wife? He quietly slipped out of bed to keep from waking Blinda, and tiptoed to the living room to call his brother.

"Hello?"

"Hey, bro, it's Clyde. Hope I didn't wake you up."

"Nah, me and the old lady always stay up late watching TV on Friday nights. What's on your feeble mind?"

"A question."

"Well ask it."

"Why do you think a man has to have a soul mate to be whole?"

A round of laughter flew into his ear. *"Uh-oh, you fooled around and fell in love with somebody, didn't you."*

"No, nothing like that. Just wondering, that's all."

"Yeah? Want me to tell you why you're wondering?"

"Sure. Go ahead, smartass."

"You're thirty-nine and it's finally dawning on you, you don't have a damn thing to lose. All you've got to show for your life is material things, nothing that can't be replaced.

Everything you own except your house could get stolen, and a fire or tornado could even take that away. When a man finds the right woman he discovers something magical that's irreplaceable—and he sees that magic manifest before his very eyes in his kids. That's what life's really about, bro. Sex takes on a whole new meaning with your soul mate, and when you finally settle down with yours, you'll wonder how you ever made it without her."

"Um, how will I know when I find her?"

"You already know, butthead, or you wouldn't be asking me about a soul mate."

He scratched the back of his neck and heaved a sigh. "Well I don't."

"Yes you do. Can't wait to meet her."

His brows rose as Wyoming sprang to the front of his mind.

"Clyde, are you still there?"

"Yeah, thanks for the pep talk. I'll let you go."

Liat called the synagogue and no one answered, so she thought Ezra must be on his way home. When thirty minutes passed without his arrival, she got dressed and drove down there to see what was keeping him so long.

He pushed the doorbell and geared up to force his way into her apartment before she could slam the door in his face.

Wyoming finally opened it after two more rings—wearing a bathrobe and an angry scowl. "What do you want, Clyde?"

"To talk to you."

"At one o'clock in the morning?"

"Sorry, but it can't wait."

She peered over his shoulder. "Where's Blinda? Thought she was going to spend the weekend with you."

"Left her at my house crying because I told her we couldn't see each other anymore. Woke her up to do it as a matter of fact. I booked her a room at a motel and called a cab to take her there. If she can't change her return flight from Sunday to Saturday, I'll be paying for another night because she's not welcome in my house anymore. The only woman I want to stay there is you. I think you must see me as a some sort of father figure but—"

"The hell I do, get your ass in here before we wake the neighbors." She grabbed his arm, yanked him inside, ordered him to sit on the couch, and plopped down beside him—all swelled up like a blow fish. "Finish what you were going to say after that father figure shit."

He took a deep breath, trying to calm his racing heart. It didn't work. This uncharted territory he found himself in made him nervous as hell. "Blinda made me do a lot of thinking tonight . . . um, I'm not exactly sure how to put this."

"Try," she said insistently, her angry eyes commanding him to continue.

"I never thought this would happen to me, I really didn't. I'm tired of being a noncommittal playboy—feel pretty shitty about it, to tell you the truth. I think I must be ready to settle down. I know I'm a lot older than you, and you could do a lot better than me, and don't want to get married to anybody anyway, but I want you to think about . . . ."

"Think about what? Spit it out, Clyde."

"Um, being my wife, because I think I love you."

The strange look that jumped on her face made her appear insulted yet thrilled at the same time. "You think you love me . . . you *think* you love me. You only *think* you love me?!"

"Uh, I'm pretty sure I do, yeah."

She turned cold as ice and got off the couch. "I tried to email Lee earlier and it wouldn't send. Do you have any idea why?"

"Don't try to change the subject, Wyoming, this is too important. Since you don't see me as a father figure then you must think you love me too, or you wouldn't have gotten so bummed out over me changing my mind about letting you live at my house."

"Humph! Did it ever occur to you I might think of you as a brother?"

"Nope, and I can tell by the way you're stalling you don't." He tried to recall exactly what his brother said. "I'm thirty-nine, and what have I got to show for it? Nothing that can't burn up or get stolen. I think you're the right woman for me, and together we'll have something magical that'll never pass. And we'll see that magic in our kids."

Her hands flew to her waist. "Our kids?!"

"Mm hmm."

"Our kids," she mumbled, a stupefied gape frozen on her face.

"Yep. Our little rug rats."

She leered at him as if he'd lost his mind, then suddenly started crying.

"Oh boy. You don't want kids, huh?"

"Kids don't have a fucking thing to do with it, Clyde—I've explained how I feel about marriage."

"Yeah, well I told you how I felt about it too, but my attitude has changed. I think yours has too but you won't admit it."

"No!" she tearfully shouted. "I'll admit I fell for you, Clyde—don't know exactly when or even why it happened—but I can't marry you."

He got up and gave her a quick kiss on the lips. "You're just scared, and believe me so am I. I want you to think about something for a minute. You don't want to get married because of your parents' bickering, but they must really love each other or they wouldn't have stayed together all these years. I don't like to fight and you don't like to fight, so there's nothing to worry about. Maybe your mom and dad get some sort of kick from their arguments, but you and I don't need that."

Her eyes tearfully searched his. He saw hope in them, along with doubt trying to dispel that hope.

"Trust me, Wyoming—trust me in spite of your fear. I'll never intentionally hurt you, and I'm trusting that you'll never hurt me, just to be cruel. You already love your house. That's right I said *your* house. Call Ezra tomorrow and tell him you can't take the position because you're going to marry me. You don't have to work anymore unless you want to, but if you do, I'm sure we can persuade Thornton to keep you on."

A deep sob rocketed out of her mouth and she pushed him away. "I'm so fucking scared I don't know what to do! You're making me want to go through with it, Clyde, but what if it's a mistake?"

He kissed her again and held her tight. "There are no guarantees in life, Wyoming—I'm taking just as big a chance on you as you are on me. But look how happy Ezra and Liat are, and they've been hitched for almost half a century. What do you say, will you marry me?"

ᴄᴍᴠ

The coroner had given Mama a strong sedative and Shayna feared she might have to take one as well to keep from losing her mind. Mama's hair had turned completely white—not gray like the locks on her temples that she refused to dye, but the color of snow. Someone shot Papa and Rabbi Beckermann. Joseph had called her to say she needed to get home immediately, and wouldn't say why except that Mama needed her. She'd been up with Priscilla well after midnight, putting a puzzle together when the call came. Poor Mama had gone to the synagogue to see why Papa was staying so late and found him dead, lying beside the rabbi, who hadn't survived his wounds either.

Shayna wanted to die herself, she hurt so badly.

Blinda managed to get her return flight switched from seven-forty p.m. Sunday to five-thirty a.m. Saturday, and would be landing in a few minutes. Staring out the window at the Houston skyline, she kept trying to figure out what she'd done to turn Clyde against her. He'd woke her up and told her to get dressed because a cab was on its way to take her to a motel. The only explanation he'd given while heading out the door was he'd made a mistake in inviting her down, and they'd be going their separate ways from that point on.

They seemed to be such kindred spirits sexually, the change in his attitude completely baffled her. She'd never witnessed such a radical shift in a man's behavior since putting up with her ex-husband's for the last time. Maybe all men were assholes by nature, but she couldn't live without having one take care of her erotic needs.

An idea popped into her head: the ultimate sexual fantasy

that carried with it a guarantee of sensual gratification and no chance of being jilted. She still had the looks for it, and oh did she have the appetite. *I'd probably be a big draw for at least five years,* she thought excitedly.

Wyoming rose at eleven, made coffee, and called her mother. After they spoke, the dams of her emotional reservoirs burst the moment she hung up, and she didn't stop crying until all the pain and regret of her childhood had flooded away. She collected herself, and phoned Clyde.

"Hello?"

"I'll marry you."

"Great! What changed your mind?"

"Had a heart to heart with my mom, something I should have done a long time ago. I asked why she stayed married to Dad when they fought so much. Here's what she said: 'I love your father but I've *never* liked him.' Then why did you marry him, I asked. She said, 'Because he's got something I need—something no other man has. Don't ask me what because I can't tell you, I just know it's there.' Well, Mister Burns, you've got something I need. Don't ask me what, because just like my mother, I can't tell you. Now I wish I hadn't made you go home last night."

"Don't be, I'm glad you did. The first time we make love will be on our wedding night."

She giggled. "Then we'd better get hitched soon, stud."

"You know it. Do you want a wedding or can we just get the license?"

"Let's get the license Monday. I'm sure Thornton will give us the afternoon off when I tell him I'll stay on if he'll do it. Judy's off this Monday and I'll get her for a witness. You find the other one."

"My brother will be overjoyed to do it, and to hell with an afternoon off—I'm telling Thornton we need the whole week off for our honeymoon."

Lee hadn't gotten a love letter today. He'd been so nervous and excited about this meeting he'd driven to Conroe yesterday afternoon, discovering when he checked into a motel that he'd left his cell phone at home. Before leaving Piler Creek he'd stopped at the stadium and held out a note to inform her of his plans. Roy choked back a sob when his handsome son walked up to the fence. Larue looked different in his right mind. He could see a lot of himself in the young man, but felt those traits were a marked improvement of his own. "Larue, I'm your father. My name is—"

"Roy Milan," finished Larue with a tearful smile. "It's fantastic to see you again after all these years. Why did you and Mom pretend you were my uncle?"

Lee had told Clyde that all of Larue's memories of the world she lived in would come back once he heard some of them, so he started from the beginning.

Before long Larue's hands were pressed against his cheeks, and a look of awe was frozen on his face.

It made Roy think of Jack Benny's familiar pose. He relayed all he knew and added, "Your sister lives in Piler Creek. Lee passed her through the gateway at six months, so it doesn't change into Leavenwood because of her."

A reminiscent smile had replaced shocking surprise, and Larue's hands had migrated to his waist. "It's all very clear to me now—all the details of that world, and the repercussions if children aren't sent away before reaching the age of ten months. Should I call you Roy or Dad?"

His eyes turned misty. He had to blink several times to clear his vision. "I hope you'll call me Dad. I hired a lawyer and he's going to get our DNA tested. The results will get you out of here."

Larue donned a pained expression. "I hope you haven't spent a lot of money already because that'll be a waste of time."

"Why's that?"

"Your DNA won't show up in my blood in this world, only Mom's."

Peter planned to wait three weeks before calling Liat. That should give her enough time to grieve for Ezra and allow her womanly needs to start fully manifesting again. She had a stronger sex drive than his thirty-five year old wife. The kid's burgers were ready. He took them off the grill and laid two steaks on the hot grid. His nostrils were filled with the flavorful smell of searing beef. Nothing said family like a Saturday afternoon barbecue. He'd miss scenes like this after the divorce, but the joy of having Liat as his bride would take away any remorse. Once she accepted his proposal, he'd let his wife know their marriage had come to an end.

The shocking news had knocked him into a surreal daze.

Clyde sat staring at the phone he'd cradled a few minutes ago after Wyoming called him. Ezra had been murdered in cold blood, along with his rabbi. Liat was under heavy sedation and Shayna—who'd spoken to Wyoming when she'd phoned to inform the Gold's she wouldn't be available to take over the store in Piler Creek after all—said the whole family feared for her sanity. She'd discovered the bodies and had been found wailing and running in circles when the rabbi's wife came to the synagogue to see why he hadn't come home. Liat hadn't spoken a single intelligible word to anyone, not even her kids.

The phone rang and the ID said *William Milan.*

"Hello?"

"Clyde, it's Roy. Got bad news. I spent the afternoon talking to Larue and all his memories and knowledge of Lee's world came back to him like she told you they would. He said my DNA won't show up in his blood in our dimension, only Lee's."

That snapped him out of his lethargy. "Aw shit, you're kidding me!"

"No. I asked Larue if he could be mistaken about that but there's not a doubt in his mind. I want you to email Lee and let her know so she can holler back. Maybe she knows some other way to prove I'm his father."

He seriously doubted she would but didn't say so. "Is your first name William?"

"Yeah, William Roy. Why?"

"Saw it on the ID. Anyway, I'll email Lee right now and call you when I get her reply . . . ."

Roy hung up with Clyde and went to the diner for supper.

When he got there he found most of the customers jabbering about who could have committed some murder. Matilda came over to take his order, and he asked what was going on.

She bitterly smacked her lips and sighed. "Somebody gunned down Ezra Gold and David Beckermann at the synagogue last night."

He rushed to his pickup, sped to the Gold's house, and grabbed Shayna when she opened the door—squeezing her to him while kissing the top of her head. "I just heard, darlin', I'm so sorry . . . ."

✦

Lee's reply came at seven-thirty. Clyde settled at his desk and forced down the last of a ham and cheese sandwich. Ezra's murder had taken away his appetite. All at once he remembered Earl's warning to have somebody else read her emails first, and bailed from the chair. Wyoming had come over an hour ago, so he told her to do it.

"Did you ask her why my emails to her wouldn't send?" she said while taking the chair.

He nodded. Wyoming didn't know about his midweek flight to Houston that Lee's email had forced him to take, but didn't ask why he'd asked her to read this one.

"Hi Clyde," she read. "First off, please accept my apology for my weakness last Wednesday." Wyoming frowned at him. "What does she mean by that?"

"Um, I'll tell you later. Go on."

"About your question concerning Wyoming being unable to email me. I don't know the reason, but none of my friends on the site where we met can email me either, so I assume only you can. I can't email anybody other than you. That email to your boss was the only one I've successfully sent to anyone besides you. I can't send him any more either. His address automatically appeared on the address bar when I was instructed at the courthouse to email him to convince you and Wyoming that you hadn't merely dreamed about coming here. Told you it was impossible to explain. We weren't able to access the internet at all in our world until a few months before I sent you that friend request.

"I am *so* excited to hear Roy and Larue have met at last on the other side, but very saddened by the fact Larue's right—Roy's DNA won't show up in his blood there. Tomorrow we'll get to visit your world from noon until seven p.m. Earl and Hoyt will be searching for all they can find on Larue at Callaway's Research Complex. Maybe they'll stumble onto something that will help the cause. I'll be in Piler Creek hoping to find Priscilla. I can't ask you to tell Roy this, Clyde, but it would be a very good idea if he wasn't in Piler Creek during that time frame. That way I could search for Priscilla freely without fear of accidentally spotting him and driving him out of his mind.

"Please offer my sincerest condolences to Liat for the loss of her husband, and thank you for telling me about it, so very sad that it is. We wouldn't have known about Ezra's murder until the local weekly paper appeared in the newsstands in our world, unless overhearing someone mention it tomorrow after we cross over.

"Now for more sad news. I can't think of any way to prove Roy is Larue's father. Neither can Earl or Hoyt. I do have a suggestion though. See if you can persuade the head honchos at Callaway's to let him go home to his foster mother every weekend instead of just once a month as you told me. Maybe that would make things more tolerable for him. He obviously can't live with Priscilla's adopted parents anyway, even if they were willing to take him in. I can at least breathe a sigh of relief of knowing he's now keenly aware of the dangers of ever entering Turnaton or Piler Creek, so that's a huge weight off my shoulders. I've nearly finished my self portrait for my kids, and will email you the picture the moment it's done. Thanks again for everything, Clyde. Lee."

Wyoming got up and took a sip of the drink she'd made after eating supper. "Okay, what happened last Wednesday? I knew you'd had a late night because it showed when you came to work Thursday."

He blew out a sigh and laid it all out.

"My god, no wonder you looked so fried. The next time I visit Lee I'm going to give Earl and Hoyt a big kiss for saving my life. It would have killed me if you'd gotten stuck over there. Now I've got another question for you, lover boy. Why didn't you tell Lee we're getting married?"

"Didn't think about it I was so bummed over Ezra and learning a DNA test wouldn't solve the problem with Larue. I'll do it right now."

She waved him off. "Don't worry about it. You need to call Roy and tell him to stay out of Piler Creek from noon to seven tomorrow. Do you still want to get married Monday or put it off for awhile because of Ezra?"

"Putting it off won't bring Ezra back, but we can spend our honeymoon near Piler Creek at whatever lake resort is nearest, and attend his funeral."

"Yeah, I like that idea, Clyde. After you call Roy let's find out which resort will be the first place we make love . . . ."

A ballpoint pen, floating in midair, kept flipping back and forth as if being manipulated by an invisible hand. Larue grinned, once he got over the initial shock. He knew it couldn't be his mother or he'd already be insane, so it had to be Earl or Hoyt. This was a visitation Sunday for the three condemned angels. He'd calculated all of them upon recalling his mother telling him they were paying a visit to the other side when he was a one-year-old. That was the first time she'd visited the real world after having him. He'd never gotten to go with her, but had to wait at a park in Justified until she got back. She'd limited her visits to a half hour because of him. "Okay, you've got my attention."

Seemingly on its on, the door opened, and he followed the pen out of his room. It led him to a men's room where a stack of papers floated in the air. He chuckled and said, "If it's Hoyt with the pen then drop it and pick it up. Otherwise I know it's Earl, and Hoyt's holding the papers."

The pen started making large circles.

"Got it. Earl's the pen and Hoyt's the papers."

Hoyt extended them, obviously wanting him to read the handwritten message. He took the stack and found only the front page had been written for him.

Hello Larue,

We know your memory's been restored, congratulations! It's Earl, writing on behalf of Hoyt and myself. We found these documents in the chief administrator's office. What you're holding in your hands is a copy of each. Get these to your father, Clyde Burns, or Wyoming Carter as soon as possible.

Good to see you in a healthy state! You were at death's door when I toted you to the hill. As you no doubt remember, we have to bail from here at seven, until then we'll be enjoying your company. Go on about your day as if we weren't here.

He wiped away a tear. Since the moment his memories returned, he'd been missing those guys almost as much as his mom. "There's a friend I want to play a trick on, her name's Tabitha. I'm going to pretend I've acquired magic powers, and each time I slap at the air I want one of you to tap whatever body part I say I'm magically slapping. Do it lightly, though. Come on, I'll stash these papers under my bed and we'll go see her . . . ."

∽✺⌒

Larue walked into the game room with a rascally smirk on his face. She stopped playing asteroids and got off the stool. "What are you looking so mischievous about, Larue?"

"Nothing, Tabitha. I'd like to show you something though. Wanna come to my room and see it?"

"Sure." She followed him to his room.

"I found a cool trick in a book about magic. Watch this. I'm going to pat your back without touching it."

She felt his hand on her back but all he'd done was pat the air. "Wow! How'd you do that?"

"Like I said, magic. I'll now tap the top of your head."

His hand moved up and down in front of his chest but she felt it hit her head. "Holy shit, Larue!"

"Cool trick, huh?"

"I'll say! How'd you do that?!"

A sly grin crawled across his face. "Tell me who bought that go kart for you and what you did to get it, and I'll tell you. Otherwise forget it."

Larue wouldn't tell anyone, but she didn't want him to think her a slut. He'd know if she made something up because she'd never been able to fool him about the go kart being an anonymous present. Her pimples really grossed him out so she'd never given any thought to approaching him like a boyfriend, cool as that would be. Thinking of him as her favorite brother had kept her from ever attempting it. But several days ago her skin had started clearing up of its own accord. She'd caught him noticing it, and temptation had begun to take hold. This setting provided a golden opportunity.

"I'm waiting, Tabitha."

"Uh, Larue, I know a pretty cool trick myself, one I'm sure you'll like. How about I show it to you, and if you like it as much as I think you will, you show me how to do your trick?"

"And if I don't like it?"

"Oh I'm pretty confident you'll love it." She got down on her knees in front of him, and quickly unzipped his pants.

"What are you doing?!"

"You'll see." She heard the door open and turned in a panic to find she'd only imagined it. Nobody ever came into Larue's room on Saturday but her, and she feared he'd stop her if she broke the momentum by taking the time to lock it, so she returned to the joyful task at hand. "To do this trick, I'll require your penis. Now just relax and let me show you how this works."

He'd never felt anything like it. Early and Hoyt had crept out of the room—at least one them had—and it had alarmed Tabitha, but she'd quickly resumed her *trick,* pulling his penis out and clamping her mouth on it. She could keep doing this nonstop for the rest of her life as far as he was concerned. Pleasure he'd never known existed held him spellbound.

Sex had been off limits to him in his own mind, so he'd never given much thought to it. Fellatio, cunnilingus, intercourse, masturbation—he knew of them all technically, but not experientially. Mere a priori knowledge of such things held no bearing to the empirical, at least concerning fellatio. His invisible friends must have known what was coming and felt compelled to give him privacy, he reckoned. He guessed Tabitha either thought she'd only imagined the door creeping open, or upon seeing no one had come inside, felt safe proceeding.

His intellect didn't lend itself to lust, but Tabitha had changed his thought processes on the matter forever—acute awareness of that swelled up from within his innermost being. He'd been missing out on one of life's most unique, and perhaps it's most joyous pleasures. Not sure of what his part should be in this sexual exercise, he merely stood there sighing, feeling so good he never wanted it to end. Tabitha seem to love it too.

Without stopping her sublime sucking action, she unbuttoned her blouse, removed it, and her brassiere. His hands zoomed to her breasts of their own accord. The wondrous way they felt made him ejaculate.

Tabitha moaned and moved her head faster until there was nothing left for his ejaculatory ducts to empty. Then she stood up and took off her shoes, jeans, and panties.

He groaned. Her pubic hair overwhelmingly enthralled him.

"This is the first time I've swallowed, Larue, so consider yourself privileged." She crossed the room and locked the door. "I've never made love before, so this will be a first for both of us. I'd like to kiss you, but I know my face grosses you out."

Her excess weight had dwindled to eight pounds and four-point-two ounces. Without the clothes she didn't look chubby at all, only excruciatingly beautiful. "No, just your pimples, and you don't have any right now. Rinse your mouth out first, and be aware that I know nothing about the proper procedure for kissing a girl."

She giggled. "You're so cute. Be right back. Take off your clothes and get in bed."

TWENTY FOUR

HE'D CAUSED TABITHA to feel pain at first, then she'd started moaning with immense pleasure. While maneuvering his penis in and out of her vaginal canal, he'd soon deduced what stimulated her most effectively, and had calculated the precise pressure to apply, along with proper rapidity of movement, to produce the most gratifying sensations for her. It surprised him to find he greatly enjoyed kissing her. That, too, had been rather simple to evaluate, and he'd brought her to the first orgasm with the appropriate lip and tongue application, even though her clitoris was designed to trigger such a response, rather than her oral faculties. She'd had several of them since, and this time when she climaxed he relaxed the computed amount of willpower to keep from ejaculating, and pulled out of her to release his semen onto her stomach, thus avoiding the possibility of impregnation.

"You're every girl's dream come true," Tabitha said breathlessly. "How could you be so incredible your very first time, Larue?"

He explained the procedure.

"Wow! Guess I'm spoiled for life. How will I get by without you when you leave?"

"I won't be able to leave after all."

She frowned at him. "But you told me you spoke with Roy

Milan yesterday. He is your natural father, isn't he?"

"Yeah."

"Well all you have to do is take a DNA test. It'll prove Roy's your dad and that'll break Clarisse's legal guardianship over you."

He got up and started putting his clothes on. "Tabitha, I'm going to tell you about me—everything, from the very beginning. Because of the magic trick, hopefully you'll believe me. That was no trick. Two invisible men from Leavenwood—an invisible town that stands right where Piler Creek does in our dimension—were tapping and patting you in response to my command. They can only enter our world seven times a year on a Sunday, and though they can manipulate physical things in our dimension from noon to seven on such days, they can't make themselves be seen or heard. I was born in their world and my mother is an angel, condemned to live in human form until the second coming of Christ . . . ."

They were smooching on his couch, careful to keep their hands in the safety zone so they wouldn't go too far. The phone interrupted them.

"Hello?" said Clyde.

"Hello. This is Tabitha Gershwin, we met at Callaway's Research Complex if you'll recall."

"Yeah, I remember you, Tabitha. What can I do for you this evening?"

"A little while ago Larue told me all about Lee Milan, Earl, Hoyt, Justified, and Leavenwood. Larue explained the problem of proving Roy's his father—that his DNA can't be detected in Larue's blood by human technology. I couldn't

find Roy's number so I called you. I'll turn eighteen next month and that means I'll be a legal adult. Could you find out if Larue can marry me without Clarisse's permission, and if it will break her legal hold over him if he can?"

He raised his brows and scratched between them. "Does Larue want to marry you?"

"Oh yes. We've fallen in love."

"Am I to assume you'll get him out of there if you can marry him and it releases him from Clarisse's guardianship?"

"Yes, but we'll have to wait until after I've gotten my degree here, because I want to finish my education at Callaway's. It's very prestigious and practically guarantees a very high-salaried position. I'll be making our living for us because of Larue's condition."

"Um, could I speak to him?"

"You could, but all his phone conversations are monitored. We can only call from a central area that's closely supervised, and the supervisors have all been instructed to eavesdrop on Larue because of his escapes. I promise he's in full agreement with all I've told you."

"Okay, I'll try to find out. How do I get in touch with you, just call Callaway's and ask for you or what?"

"Don't worry about that. I'll call you this same time next Sunday."

"Could you make that Monday? I'll be returning from my honeymoon next Sunday."

"Oh really? Congratulations!"

"Thanks."

"Okay. I'll call you a week from tomorrow."

"I've got a better idea. Call Roy instead. His number is . . . ."

CR&

Larue scanned the documents Hoyt had given him, and found among them the legal stipulation and capacity assessment copied by Callaway's from Mother's papers. Written therein was a bald face lie that he was mentally incapacitated to such a degree that at no time could he make a rational decision on financial, medical, or legal matters that would serve his best interest. That should have read the reverse—*most of the time* only he knew what served his best interest.

Tabitha came back and explained she'd called Clyde because there weren't any listings for Roy Milan at Piler Creek. "Clyde's going to find out for us and pass the information to your dad. He gave me his number."

"Good. Inform security you're clearing Roy Milan as a visitor, then call him and tell him to be here Saturday. I have some documents for you to pass on to him . . . ."

Clyde rented a one bedroom cabin on Lake Conroe that had internet capabilities. He'd be carrying his laptop in order to communicate with Lee and keep her abreast about Larue. He booked it for Tuesday through Saturday, since they were driving down and wouldn't get there until after Midnight. Thornton got pissed that he hadn't been given notice in advance, but cooled off when he learned Wyoming wanted to continue managing the store.

They got the marriage license at nine, purchased their rings immediately afterwards, tied the knot at eleven, and hit the road at two p.m.

"Psssst, in here."

Tabitha turned to see Richard Allen holding open a storeroom door. He used it when he wanted a blowjob on weekday mornings. Security guards came and went from his office during that time.

"I'm not doing that anymore, Richard."

"Like hell!" he hissed in whisper. "If you wanna keep that go kart you'll get your butt in there now."

"Oh, I'm keeping the go kart," she whispered back, "but you're off the hook on buying me a car. If you hassle me about it in any way I'll report you."

His face dropped. "Aw, come on, please?"

"No, and that's final." She walked off. No one but Larue would ever receive that pleasure from her again.

Richard had coaxed her into going down on him the first time by asking if she'd ever seen a grown man's wee-wee.

"No," she'd answered.

"You plan to get married some day, don't you?"

"Mm hmm."

"Well, the more you know about your husband's, the more he'll love you. I can show you what he'll really like and you'll be an expert at it when you marry him. I'll buy you a bicycle if you'll let me teach you."

In a way she felt grateful to Richard. If he hadn't taught her how to give head, she probably wouldn't be engaged to Larue.

Roy didn't open the shop, and wouldn't until Thursday, the day after Ezra's funeral. The moment he'd seen Liat—hair turned white, eyes blank and hardly recognizable—he knew she'd have to be institutionalized. He'd asked the sheriff, a close friend since childhood, to show him the crime scene photographs. Ezra's upper face had been blown away by a hollow point forty-four magnum bullet that entered the back of his head and exited the front. The gruesome sight had driven Liat out of her mind. She wouldn't respond to anyone, not even Shayna, who had to hand feed her. When food entered her mouth, instinct caused her to chew and swallow, but she did so seemingly unaware of taste or texture. Shayna had to be very careful when giving her coffee because Liat swallowed any beverage the same mechanical way—cold, tepid, or hot.

It was Monday afternoon and she hadn't spoken a word since Friday night.

He'd spent yesterday at Blinda's house, getting away from Piler Creek as a cautionary measure as advised to by Clyde. He hoped Lee had gotten to see Priscilla. Blinda had fed him lunch and afterwards blew his mind by saying she was changing vocations. She now aspired to be a porn star. The tragic news about Ezra and what his death had done to Liat had really shaken her up, but not nearly as much as her new occupational goal rattled him.

"Why would you want do such a crazy thing?" he'd asked.

"I think I'd be great at," she'd answered.

"No doubt about that but—"

"Roy, don't worry about me, I know what I'm doing. I'll be using a stage name and no one in my family would be caught dead watching porno, so none of them will ever know. I've already contacted a producer in Los Angeles through the internet. He told me to send him some nude pictures, and said if I have the face and body for it, he'd arrange an audition. He doesn't want any self-taken snapshots, so would you mind taking them for me?"

She'd gotten mad at him for refusing, but had let him stay for supper anyway, after which he'd gone home to find a message on his answering machine from Tabitha Gershwin.

He'd called his lawyer first thing that morning and learned that as long as Larue was deemed mentally incompetent, he couldn't marry anybody without the written consent of his legal guardian. Hopefully the documents Larue planned to pass on to him through Tabitha would contain something his lawyer could use to have that guardianship annulled. Having his attorney cancel the DNA tests meant he'd be reimbursed two thirds of the initial fee, but he'd told him to hang on to it because he hoped to apply it to the cost of a further legal chore.

By the time they reached Brownwood, desire had compelled them to consummate their marriage in a motel room and complete their journey tomorrow.

Wyoming's body was everything he'd imagined and more. He'd never seen breasts like hers. They were so perfectly symmetrical and flawless he'd have thought they were a mannequin's if seeing them in a photograph. The nipples came to a sharp point, indistinguishable from the areoles, and were such a light shade of pink they barely contrasted with the creamy smoothness of the large mounds.

Also naked, he stood before her with arms outstretched, holding her hands while feasting his eyes.

Wyoming was blushing. She'd wanted to crawl under the covers immediately after he'd insisted she disrobe before him and allow him to drink in her bare womanliness.

"Are you just gonna stare at me all night, Clyde?"

He grinned and glanced down at his erection. "Well, as you can see, I'm really enjoying it."

"You're not hurting my eyes either."

"I love you, Missus Burns."

"And I love you, Mister Burns. Don't you think it's about time we showed each other how much?"

He picked her up, carried her to the bed, and began showing her.

Shayna was sitting between Jeb and Priscilla. Each held one of her hands. Her brothers, sisters-in-law, nieces, and nephews were weeping. Mama sat in the midst of them with dry eyes, totally unaware of the proceedings. Practically the whole town had shown up for Papa's funeral, being held in the high school auditorium because of the anticipated large crowd. Shayna couldn't cry any more. Longing for vengeance overpowered all other emotions. She wanted whoever did this to Papa to pay for it with their life. The monster had not only killed him and Rabbi Beckermann, but had stolen Mama's sanity as well.

She'd spoken with the sheriff and learned all he knew. He wouldn't give her the name, but said someone had called him after the murders became public knowledge to report having seen a man wearing a ski mask drive a motorcycle away from the alley behind the synagogue last Friday night. The Turnaton police found a body wrapped in chains in the duck pond. They discovered the man had been shot three times, and the bullets matched those that killed Papa and the rabbi. They'd drug the pond after finding blood on the ground not far from a motorcycle that hadn't been moved the whole weekend. Both belonged to the dead man. Jeb knew who he was because he'd been his drug connection.

The sheriff surmised that the killer had shot the drug dealer in order to use his motorcycle to keep his own vehicle from being noticed in Piler Creek. After completing his bloody deed, he'd returned the motorcycle and made his escape. Motorcycle tracks in the alley behind the synagogue, and a cigarette butt—the same brand as several found near the motorcycle at the duck pond—were his only clues besides the bullets and chain. No clear motive, and so little evidence, made this a very difficult crime to solve, the sheriff had informed her. It appeared to be the work of a Jew hater, who'd apparently murdered the Mexican biker for the sole purpose of using his motorcycle. Since he hadn't merely stolen someone else's, he must have been acquainted with his victim.

TWENTY FIVE

CLYDE HAD ONLY attended one funeral in his life, his grandfather's. This one had two corpses—one dead and sealed in a casket, the other breathing and sitting with her family, completely unaware of the surroundings. He'd thought someone's hair turning white over extreme fright or shock was a myth, but Liat's snow-white mane proved otherwise. It amazed him how quickly things could change. That pretty Jewish lady and her robust husband had the world by the tail only a week ago. Now he was dead and she'd lost her mind because of it.

The rabbi in charge of the proceeding invited everyone to the cemetery for the graveside service. He took Wyoming by the hand and escorted her outside.

Priscilla came over and said hello.

"Hi," Wyoming reciprocated. "How's Shayna holding up?"

"About as well as can be expected. I'm surprised to see the two of you here."

He explained why they'd been able to attend.

"Congratulations. How sad to interrupt your honeymoon with a funeral, but I know Shayna really appreciates it. Are you guys going to the cemetery?"

"No, we're on our way back to Lake Conroe."

"I'm not going to the cemetery either, I have a phobia about graveyards. Can we visit for awhile before you go? I'd like to hear more about my mother and Larue . . . ."

ᝏᝏ

Roy kissed Liat and Shayna on the cheek as he passed by the front row at the close of the graveside ceremony, shook hands with the three Gold boys, and headed for the diner.

He found Clyde and Wyoming sitting with Priscilla when he walked in. Clyde waved him over and introduced him to her.

"It's a real pleasure to meet you," he told the pretty girl. "You sure take after your mother."

Her eyes flashed. "You know her?"

"Yeah. I'm Larue's father."

"Really?!"

"Um, yeah," said Clyde a little nervously. "Priscilla, do you know if Liat happened to mention visiting a town called Justified to Shayna?"

She shrugged. "Shayna hasn't said anything to me about it if she did. Why?"

"Well, I hope she did—then you won't have such a hard time understanding why you can't go see your mother. But I figure Liat probably didn't, because I'm pretty sure Shayna would have told you about it."

Priscilla pulled out her cell phone and laid it on the table. "I'll call her in fifteen minutes and find out. The graveside funeral should be over by then."

"Go ahead and do it now," said Roy, "I came from there. Ask if Liat told her about going to see Lee Milan."

She phoned Shayna and learned Liat hadn't said anything about visiting Lee.

Clyde sighed and folded his arms across his chest. "When you meet Larue, and hopefully that'll be sooner than later, he'll explain everything. You'd never believe us if we were to tell you. Liat could verify it, but unfortunately—"

"She can't because of what happened," finished Priscilla. "Why are you being so mysterious about this, Clyde? If you know what town my mother lives in, why can't I go see her?"

"You'll just have to trust me. There's something inside you that will know Larue's telling the truth. We can't trigger that in you, only your brother can."

Roy put a hand on her shoulder and smiled. "You can meet him Saturday if you'll come with me to Conroe . . . ."

◌⟊⟊◌

Larue came into the visiting area, but ignored him and didn't stay long. Tabitha had the documents neatly wrapped in a towel. Roy accepted her gift, went to his pickup, handed it to Priscilla, and returned. The visitor's pass clipped to his shirt pocket gave him the right to come and go, but he wanted to get the papers out of Callaway's quickly as possible in case any of the security guards got curious and insisted on inspecting what appeared to be a package encased in terrycloth rather than wrapping paper.

Tabitha put her lips to his ear and whispered, "Larue wanted to see you but didn't want to draw any attention to the two of us. I'm dying to get to know my soon to be father-in-law."

"Looking forward to it too," he quietly replied. "Get Larue and go to the spot where we met. You're about to meet your future sister-in-law."

◌⟊⟊◌

Larue started crying the moment he saw Priscilla. He got out of the go kart and hurried to the fence. The reaction caused a lump to rise in Roy's throat.

Priscilla's eyes dampened as well. "Hi, Larue."

"Hello . . . you look so much like our mother it's mind boggling."

"You resemble your dad."

"I know," Larue proudly agreed.

Roy had to look away to keep from bawling himself—he'd give anything if Lee could be here. Clyde and Wyoming were supposed to be. They were either running late or had changed their minds, which he found hard to believe. The emotional wave rolled away, and he turned his attention back to the siblings.

Priscilla reached through the fence and lovingly caressed her brother's face. "I'm told only you can make me understand why we can't go see our mother, so please fill me in."

Each sentence seemed to shock her more than the last, but it was clear she believed every word. She wrapped her fingers around two wrought iron bars, leaned her forehead against a horizontal brace—above which the fence rods extended another two feet—and cried unashamedly. At length she looked up at Larue, who'd gotten it out of his system, and said, "How have you dealt with knowing you're half angel?"

Larue pried her hands from the fence and held them. "I didn't recall that until recently, when Roy passed on the information Clyde Burns told him. It made all my memories of our mother's world return. Before that happened, all I remembered was she claimed to have once been an angel, and I thought she was delusional in thinking that. But we're not really half angel, Priscilla. When our mother was cast to earth she became pseudo-human, and that's what our other half is made of. I just can't believe how much you look like her."

Tabitha came over and introduced herself.

Clyde pulled up behind Roy's pickup and winked at Wyoming. "Just in the nick of time."

They were late due to stopping at a print shop. Lee had emailed her finished portrait. He'd printed out two copies from his laptop. Wyoming took his arm and they walked to the fence where Roy stood beside Priscilla, conversing with Tabitha and Larue on the other side.

Wyoming handed Lee's children her picture. Larue and Priscilla stared at their copies as if gazing upon a priceless treasure.

"She's so beautiful," sobbed Priscilla, tears streaming down her cheeks.

Larue showed his to Tabitha and her brows rose. "Wow, Priscilla, you look just like her."

The siblings hugged each other through the fence. When their embrace ended, Larue turned to Roy. "I know how to solve everything, and I owe it all to Tabitha. Mother, that is Clarisse Ferrell, is a good woman who's got a weakness—the greedy streak concerning her house. She can't afford one like it on her own.

"I'll make the chief administrator an offer I know he'll accept. In return for Callaway's paying off her house, I'll cooperate with the scientists for the rest of my life, but as an employee rather than a guinea pig. They'll pay me a salary so Tabitha and I can afford our own house, and my hours will be the same as the scientists'. I'll go home at five every weekday and be off every weekend. Tabitha knows exactly how to take care of me when I suffer a mental lapse, so there's no danger of them losing me by my wandering off, which is why they won't let me go anywhere except Mother's. I'm sure Mother will release me from her guardianship and power of attorney under those circumstances.

"If not, then get Priscilla and me in front of a judge with this picture and you. He'll see the resemblance between Priscilla and Mom, and you and me. Mine and Priscilla's DNA will look exactly the same, which is impossible in human terms, and the judge will have to conclude Lee Milan is either a remarkably different type of woman, or an alien from another planet whose genetic code is so overpowering the DNA of the sires of her children can't be detected. If that fails, your lawyer can play hardball with something I found in the documents—a gross exaggeration of my mental lapses. But none of this will be necessary, I'm certain of it. Tabitha is my life saver."

TWENTY SIX

"COULD I SPEAK to Liat, please?" he'd called the house phone anonymously because she wouldn't answer her cell. Shayna had picked up, he assumed.

"Who's calling?"

"An old friend."

"I'm terribly sorry but she can't speak to you or understand anything you say. The death of her husband caused her to have a nervous breakdown."

The shock made him drop the phone. He picked it up, and sobbed out, "Is this Shayna?"

"No, I'm Liat's caretaker."

"Why isn't she in a hospital receiving treatment?"

"I'm afraid she's beyond that. She'll never be in her right mind again."

Peter hung up the phone without saying goodbye, and carried out the promise he'd made to himself if Liat refused to come back to him. Suicide note complete, he put the pistol to his head and fired.

Shayna had learned from Priscilla that she hadn't been hallucinating when she'd seen those people going up the hill. More shocking still, the man the African American had carried on his back was Priscilla's brother Larue. Clyde and Wyoming had paid her a visit before driving back to Odessa from their honeymoon, and through conversing with them, she'd deduced that she and Jeb hadn't been hearing things at the front door that Friday night he'd been eating her. It must have been Wyoming and her boyfriend ringing the doorbell and pounding on the door.

Wyoming conjectured that because she and her boyfriend had been pulled into that invisible world by Priscilla's mother without their knowledge, something must have temporarily tampered with the barrier just long enough for Jeb and her to hear them. She'd promised to speak to Lee Milan about it and see if she could explain it.

As shocking as all the revelations had been, none stunned her more than learning Mama had visited that invisible world only six days before Papa got killed. Her brothers hired a fulltime housekeeper to watch over her at home, so she wouldn't have to live the rest of her life in an asylum. The psychiatrist said her sanity could possibly return, but cautioned it seemed unlikely.

Shayna knew in her heart it never would, but kept hoping anyway. If only Mama hadn't been the one to find him dead and see him in such a horrific condition, her deep love for Papa wouldn't have driven her over the edge, and she'd have found the strength to carry on.

A man who lived in Conroe had confessed to the slayings in a suicide note before using the same gun he'd shot Papa with to kill himself—neglecting to mention the motive for the murders, or why he'd chosen to take his own life. He'd gone to high school in Piler Creek, and her brothers said he'd worked for Papa the summer he graduated. That was the only time there'd been any interaction between them, and they'd gotten along fine.

He'd left for college that fall and his family moved to Houston. The sheriff couldn't find anyone who'd seen him in Piler Creek after that. Rabbi Beckermann's wife said as far as she knew her husband had never even spoken with him, much less anger him in any way. The killer had left behind a wife and three kids. His widow couldn't enlighten the police at all, claiming the whole deadly affair baffled her as much as them. Unless he'd told someone else his reasons and they came forward, no one would ever know why he shot Papa.

She sat beside Wyoming with Jeb on her left in a small auditorium at a place called Callaway's Research Complex. Tony, now going steady with Priscilla, occupied the chair on the other side of Jeb. Roy had just given the bride away and Clyde, as best man, handed Larue the ring. Priscilla stood beside the pretty girl with a slightly blemished face that would become her sister-in-law in the next few minutes.

Priscilla's adoptive parents sat beside Larue's foster mother and her daughter. Matilda Tyner, who'd accompanied Roy, and Blinda Love were the only others she knew in attendance. The rest were either Callaway employees or students. Blinda would be buying her biscuit dough from Terry and Jean from now on. They'd taken full charge of the bakery after an equitable business arrangement had been worked out with Joseph, and now closed on Sundays instead of Saturdays.

Larue looked ecstatically happy. Tall and handsome, she could see a lot of his father in him. Larue's foster mom had rented his tuxedo, refusing to permit him to dress casual as he'd wanted. She'd also purchased Tabitha's elegant wedding dress.

Shayna felt a tear trickle down her cheek as he kissed his new bride. How sad it was that Mama couldn't help her plan her wedding, and Papa wouldn't be able to walk her down the aisle to give her away to Jeb.

⸂⸃

Standing behind the Turnaton Arms Motel holding Shayna's hand, who in turn held Liat's, Wyoming waved as a signal for Lee to bring them through the portal. The idea originated with Larue during his wedding reception upon hearing about what happened to Shayna's mother. Clyde passed it on to Lee from a computer at Callaway's and she'd responded with, "It can't hurt, so why not take a chance?"

Larue theorized the flash of light would shock Liat, then seeing Lee would stir the memory of having been drawn into that dimension before, forcing her psyche to leave the recesses of her brain where it had sought refuge to keep from facing reality.

Lee appeared, and Liat's blank face suddenly convulsed with sorrow.

"Ezra! Oh, Ezra!" she cried while dropping to her knees and covering her face with trembling hands.

Shayna started crying. "Mama, you're back—oh thank God!"

Following Larue's instructions passed on through Clyde, Lee immediately returned them to the real world.

Larue had been confident of initial success, but warned there was a ninety-nine-point-nine percent probability Liat wouldn't retain her sanity unless Lee sent them back as soon as possible, due to the vast amount of pent up grief her mind could no longer shield her from once she regained coherency. That had to be released in her own world, and once she got through the process, a prolonged stay in Lee's would no longer pose a threat.

Liat wrapped her arms around Shayna's legs and held fast, as if clutching a life preserver in a stormy sea. Mournfully wailing her dead husband's name as she continued to weep, Liat responded when Shayna cried, "Look at me, Mama, so I know you're all right!"

"Oh, Shayna, you've lost your father!"

"I know," she sobbed, "but I've got you back!"

Wyoming helped Shayna put her weeping mother in Jeb Turner's car so he could take them home. She then got in the rental and drove back to Callaway's Research Center, where Clyde waited with Larue and Tabitha, his bride of four hours. Jeb and Shayna had driven to Piler Creek from Callaway's to get Liat and meet her at the motel.

Lee Milan would have to live without a man's touch for as long as Clyde lived, but at least she had Liat and Shayna to keep her company on a regular basis. Now that Shayna had crossed over, Lee could sense her presence any time she neared a portal. Wyoming planned to visit on occasion, but Odessa being so far away made it impossible for her to do so very often. Shayna would be a great comfort to Lee because she could keep her updated on her children, being Priscilla's best friend.

TWENTY SEVEN

THE PORN WORLD would have to get by without her. Blinda had found the perfect lover—an incredibly virile man who completely accepted and even encouraged her kinky sexual proclivities. Tall and muscular, he could summon an erection at will, had uncanny staying powers, a very long tongue that he really knew how to use, and was indefatigable. When they weren't in his bed, he romanced her with champagne dinners, long walks in the moonlight, and fascinating tales of bygone days.

At first it had been purely a physical thing on her end—especially since he wasn't particularly handsome—but somewhere along the way she'd fallen in love with him. Now she knew why no one could replace Lee Milan in Roy's heart. True love blew everything else away, and once it came there was no denying it.

She'd never wanted kids but that too had changed. Despite her age, she yearned to bear his child, and would gladly marry him if she could. Not only was that prohibited, she could only go see him on Fridays, and had to leave before sundown on Mondays.

The night of Larue's wedding she'd found a note lying on her pillow that read:

Hello Blinda, my name is Earl. I know you're aware of Justified and Leavenwood, myself, Hoyt, and Lee, so I'll cut to the chase. We got to visit the other side today, and Hoyt and I were at Larue's wedding. I rode back to Turnaton with you, sitting next to you in your car. I spent the rest of my allotted time in your house, watching you. I promise you a

real good time if you'll drive to Piler Creek after you get off
work next Friday.
　When you get there you'll see Leavenwood on the city
limits sign. Just drive on into town and pull into the open
bay of Roy's Automotive, and you'll find me there waiting
for you. I'm black, so if cross racial romance is out of the
question, don't bother coming.
　Hope to see you Friday!
　Earl

Having never dated a black man, or ever desired to, she'd wadded up the note and thrown it away. Then, realizing she'd most likely have to screw one on camera at some point after she broke into the porn field, she figured it might be wise to experience it at least once beforehand, so she'd know what to expect.

His amazing physique had caught her eye right away, but his rather wide nose and heavy lips put her off. Then, he'd started talking.

"I can tell by that look on your face you've never been with a black man before, and you're having second thoughts about coming. Go ahead and leave if you want to, but I promise you'll be missing the best sex any man can give you. I've got over two thousand years of experience, and I know what women want. More importantly, I know what a woman needs along with that erotic fulfillment—tender words, romantic gestures, a loving heart, sensitivity to her feelings, and a listening ear.

"I'd never seen you before, and when you walked in and sat down at Larue's wedding, you stirred something up in me that hasn't been aroused in many years. I never approach a woman unless I'm sure I desire her enough to do right by her all the way. I want to be your man for the rest of your life, Blinda. It's not just your beauty that turns me on, I'm drawn to your inner being as well, and I can help you in a way you don't realize you need at the moment. Your spirit is starving, though you don't know it. You have a head belief in Christ, but He needs to be in your heart, where at the moment only lust dwells. Let me turn that sin-tainted lust to untarnished desire. I can't officially take you as a wife, but I can sure love and teach you like one. When those like me take a lover, The Almighty sanctions that relationship as if it's a marriage. That means you won't be guilty of fornication when you sleep with me—you'll be as blameless as if I was your husband."

He'd then taken her by the arm and she'd totally freaked to find herself standing in a luxurious bedroom alone. A moment later he'd appeared, totally nude, and said, "Here I stand naked before you, Blinda, with nothing to hide. Please take me as your faithful loving man."

Gaping at his splendid erect penis, without uttering a word she'd shed her clothes and laid down on the bed.

The thrills he'd given her had been unimaginable, and she'd spent the next three days in heaven. When he made her leave, she'd thought the next Friday would never arrive, and had given up the silly notion of being a porn star. The following weekend hadn't passed before the thought of living without him became unbearable, and slowly she'd begun to feel the need to get right with the Lord. Earl had assured her a full awakening would eventually come, and bring life to her dead spirit once it did.

She lay in his arms, wonderfully sated, yet troubled. "Earl, what am I going to do when I get old and you quit finding me desirable?"

He touched her face and sighed. "If I only loved you for your looks you'd have a right to worry, my love. I told you I never approach a woman unless I'm prepared to give her my all. Lee's only been in love once, with Roy Milan. Me, I've never been with a woman I wasn't in love with. Lee fell in love with Roy when he was a young man of twenty-five. He's in his fifties now, but her love for him hasn't changed, and she'll still feel the same if he lives to be a hundred. That's the way true love is. It never dies. I took one look at those apple-green eyes of yours and fell in love with the woman behind them. I'll admit I then noticed your hot body, but that was, is, and always will be secondary to the Blinda who dwells within it. I'm yours for life."

✂✿✒

When Tabitha finally confessed how she'd gotten the go kart, Larue told J.T. Glade about Richard Allen, and made her testify against him in court. She hadn't wanted to until he'd pointed out Richard would likely approach some other young girl the same way. It turned out he had—a thirteen-year-old who lived near him in Conroe. Two more girls came forward and he got convicted.

The chief administrator had agreed to Larue's proposed arrangement, but instead of having to buy a house, a very nice one was being built for them behind Callaway's, and they'd be moving in upon its completion. She couldn't wait. Meanwhile they were still living at the compound in Larue's quarters, which he no longer viewed as a jail cell.

They'd been married two months and Larue had only suffered a few mental lapses. He speculated that having sex on a regular basis so benefited his metabolism that the spells should decrease even more as time went on. She disagreed. Their love for each other was responsible—she knew it in her heart.

✂✿✒

Liat laid a bouquet of flowers on Ezra's grave, told him how much she missed him, and strolled across the cemetery to a small statue of two cherubs playing harps. Hoyt appeared, took her arm, and transported her to Lee's house.

Her dear friend had their biweekly afternoon tea and pecan pie waiting. Though they lived in two separate worlds, they had much in common, living in widowhood bereft of their men. Lee was to Roy what Ezra was to her—a departed soul mate, never to be seen again in this life. Lee could hear Roy, and Ezra could hear her, but neither of them could answer back. Ezra's desire to learn the truth about Yeshua surely must have granted him salvation, since he'd definitely intended to convert as she'd done.

She now understood Ezra's lack of desire for sex during her adulterous years. Losing him had taken hers completely away. The hatred she felt for Peter couldn't be put into words. For him to be so stupid as to think he could get her back by killing Ezra sickeningly amazed her. If he hadn't killed himself she'd have gladly done the job for him. It was sinful to have such thoughts, but only God could take them from her. She trusted He would in time.

Clyde couldn't believe how much married life agreed with him. His brother had been right: a man wasn't whole without his soul mate, and in about seven months the other prediction would be verified—the magic he felt with Wyoming manifesting before his eyes. A doctor had confirmed she was pregnant. She'd given his house a much needed woman's touch right away, and somehow did manage to move all his junk in the spare bedroom with the half bath into the other one, so she could turn it into a nursery. His siblings swore vengeance, all three planned to spoil his kid rotten to get even.

He liked every member of Wyoming's family, especially her parents, and had witnessed a few of their knock-down drag-out spats. That, he could live without, but it hadn't changed his opinion. Her dad was from the old oilfield—the new one being as much a contrast as flag football to tackle—and guarded his tender side for fear of looking like a sissy, but it sometimes slipped out anyway. The dude had a heart of gold, as did his mother-in-law, who'd taken an instant shine to him. She liked her booze but it didn't like her. Wyoming saw her parents as white trash. He'd chastised her for calling them that, and explained his stand.

"Your mom *is* an alcoholic, I agree with you there, but she's a grand old gal just the same, and I love her dearly. She and your dad get off on arguing—don't ask me why, but they do. I think it's cathartic for them, because I sure see love in their eyes when the squabble's over.

"Take away their fights and your mom's drinking, and what have you got? Two hard working people with salty character, who call a spade a spade and won't tolerate hypocrisy. They don't want to live in a nicer house because they're happy right where they are in that double-wide mobile home. Why? Because it holds the memories of you and your siblings as kids. They know what's really important and don't give a damn about what isn't. Yeah, they're chain smokers, big deal. Some of the greatest men and women this world has ever known were too—and a lot of them weren't exactly teetotalers either. I admire your mom and dad for not worrying about keeping up with the Joneses. What you call white trash, I call two solid people who what you see is what you get, and I feel privileged to call them my in-laws."

She'd started bawling and said, "I've never looked at it that way. You're my rock, Clyde, thank you so much."

My Rock had become her nickname for him during their

honeymoon. It stemmed from her feeling safe, secure, and protected in his presence. He'd felt a little insulted when she'd confessed that'd been what initially attracted her, and not once had she ever mentioned his so called charisma.

TWENTY EIGHT

LARUE BADE PAUL and J.T. a good evening, walked through the gates, circled halfway around the compound, and crossed the recently poured concrete path that led to his new house. Callaway's had footed the entire bill, including the furniture, and deeded the handsome four bedroom structure to him. Mother and Ethel had helped Tabitha decorate it.

Priscilla and Shayna would be arriving in a couple of hours, along with their boyfriends, to spend the weekend. All four were enrolled at Texas A&M. Priscilla and Shayna were roommates.

He liked Shayna, Tony Popp, and Jeb Turner—Tabitha did too—but he *loved* his sister, and treasured every moment he got to spend with her. She had a very unique sense of humor and enjoyed shocking him. He'd met her adopted parents at his wedding, and saw them a second time when Tabitha had driven him to College Station in their new car so he could give Priscilla her graduation presents: a chess set and some jigsaw puzzles. Tabitha had been in attendance when she'd gotten her high school diploma. The Booths still didn't know the truth about their mother or the world she lived in, and Priscilla wanted to keep it that way. Her adopted brother would remain in the dark about it too. Larue had laughed when Priscilla told him the guy had given her the nickname Box Butt.

"Mind if I call you that?" he'd asked.

"Try it, and see how long you live, Bubba."

"Bubba?"

"Yeah, that's my pet name for you, Larue."

"Well I need a pet name for you too, so why can't I call you Box Butt like your brother?"

She'd hugged him and said, "He is my brother, but you're my Bubba—my blood brother. How about calling me Sissy?"

"No, I need to come up with one of my own."

Tonight would be the first time she'd hear the name he'd decided on: *Little Lee.*

Reaching the porch, he turned towards Callaway's Research Complex and inhaled a breath through his nose, enjoying the late autumn smells provided by the woods. He'd hated that place for two decades, but now that it served as his livelihood rather than a comfortable prison, he felt proud to be a part of it.

TWENTY NINE

WYOMING GOT THE registers filled, and poured herself a cup of coffee. It was quite a challenge pulling the bank bag from the floor safe these days due to Clyde Junior, now a week overdue. She'd had mixed emotions about getting pregnant as a newlywed, figuring on having Clyde all to herself for at least a year before starting a family. He'd insisted on trying to have a baby right away and had been ecstatic initially, yet the larger her uterus had grown, the more nervous he'd gotten. Meanwhile she'd come to grips with it and looked forward to motherhood. Her parents constantly reassured him he was going to be a wonderful dad, but fear of the unknown had Clyde tied in knots.

"What do I know about raising a kid?" he'd asked when she'd neared the end of her first trimester.

"As much as I do, Clyde."

"You're a woman. Maternal instinct will guide you, but what if I fuck up?"

"You won't. Quit worrying about it, you'll be a great father."

"But what if I'm not?"

"You will be."

She'd wearily given the same answers to those questions at least two dozen times afterwards. She knew he'd be all right once the baby came, but meanwhile he was driving her crazy. He'd been a nervous wreck since the due date passed, and had gotten worse each day since.

He was in his office, sent there at her command so she could enjoy a few minutes of peace and quiet before Judy arrived.

So far Lee hadn't given in to temptation again, but to be safe she still read all her emails before Clyde. The last one had contained the answer to a question they'd both been pondering—how often those three ex-angels had to execute a criminal. Through all the years they'd been bound to earth only sixty men and three women had been brought to justice by them. Lee didn't anticipate many others, if any, before the second coming, which she, Hoyt, and Earl felt couldn't lie very far ahead.

Blinda Love didn't pose a threat to her anymore. She'd fallen in love with Earl, according to Lee. Clyde had snickered at the news and said, "Earl must have a real perverted streak."

They'd learned through Lee that she belonged to a rank of angels midway between the lowest and highest. Each of the roughly ten thousand cast to earth were given a physique commensurate to the degree of doubt about God's wisdom that lurked within—the greater the doubt, the less attractive the appearance. Their race had been chosen for them arbitrarily and all were represented. Earl could just as easily have been given the body of a Chinaman or Eskimo instead of taking on the form of an African American. The ex-angels could only communicate with those in their particular geographical location, so Lee didn't know how many children had been spawned by her kind, only that the same rules and limitations applied to all of them. Earl and Hoyt were both apparently sterile. Lee suspected, but didn't know for sure, that all the males of her kind were.

The leaders were forced to live without neighbors, while all the others of a gathering were bound to the town nearest them. Before modern civilization they'd all lived in tents that didn't have a replica on the other side, and subsisted on wildlife and whatever grew in their particular area. In those days a special tent housed the equipment Lee, the leader of her group, now used in the courthouse.

They'd all been bound where God knew towns and large cities would eventually be built. Lee could live anywhere she wanted, so long as it lay within the city limits of Justified, which happened to be the name of every leader's town because of executing exceptionally evil criminals whose deaths were *justified.* Earl and Hoyt were likewise limited in their town, and couldn't reside in the same house. The name Leavenwood was a combination of Leaven, representing sin in Biblical symbolism, and Wood: the last part of *Wormwood,* symbolic of bitterness.

There were much nicer homes in Justified, but Lee didn't want to leave her current one because that's where she'd happened to be living when she met Roy. Earl lived in the biggest house in Leavenwood, while Hoyt never stayed at the same place for long.

Thornton came in, said good morning, and went out back to check on the mechanics. Not long after he left Judy showed up, along with the first customer of the day.

Wyoming grimaced and backed away from the cash register. "Tell Clyde to get out here."

Judy did so and he came running.

"What's wrong?!"

"My water broke. Take me to the hospital."

"Can you believe that guy?" Judy giggled.

Her *Rock* lay sprawled out on the floor behind the counter.

Clyde had fainted.